# The buzz on
# ((FREQUENCIES)):

### From the critics:

"A cult hit." –*The Seattle Times*

"In the tradition of *1984, Brave New World,* and *Fahrenheit 451,* ((FREQUENCIES)) is a meditation on the place of the individual in a society increasingly equipped to infringe."
–*Seattle Weekly*

"Brilliant... The concepts contained within this novel are vast and complex. ((FREQUENCIES)) buzzes of a new world order." –*The Daily*

"Ortega's first novel portrays a 21st-century society on the verge of breakdown or transfiguration. Combining straightforward storytelling with experimental prose, this eccentric tale of conspiracy and cosmology belongs in large sf collections." –*Library Journal*

"Technologized." –*Publishers Weekly*

### From fellow authors:

"((FREQUENCIES)) is excellent. The characters are right there and real...and the concept is quite prophetically freeky." –Jody Aliesan, author of *Desire* and *Loving In Time of War*

"Two pages in, I was interested. Ten pages, and I was captivated. This book's got it all. Thrills, spills, chases, explosions, fights, sex, conspiracies, gadgets... I heartily recommend ((FREQUENCIES))." –Christine Morgan, author of *Black Roses* and the *MageLore* trilogy

"Full of invention and creativity...you won't want it to end." –Christopher J. Jarmick, author of *The Glass Cocoon*

## From the readers:

"An amazing work of art. It glides easily into the higher ranks of all the books I've read to date...an awakening." –E. Bangs, Seattle, WA

"Thoughtful, fast-paced, charming and insightful. The ideas/context/world which Ortega envisions are both believable and magical." –S. Southey, New York City, NY

"In a word, fantastic. Quite possibly this book could be said to be the left-brain equivalent to *The Illuminatus Trilogy*." –G. Licina, Seattle, WA

"A book for our generation." –M. Donald, Lebanon, MO

"((FREQUENCIES)) has a philosophy that challenges me. The romance dances. The chapter intro's are brilliant. Ashley Huxton is easily one of the best characters I have EVER met in print." –J. Johnson, Seattle, WA

"Profound...HIP...totally cool!"
–V. Ellison, San Francisco, CA

"This book has put into words what many people are feeling about the future right now." –J. Levy, Rome, Italy

"No hold barred... A page-turner that does not compromise." –F. Browne, Oakland, CA

"Extremely entertaining...I literally could not put it down until the very end. ((FREQUENCIES)) is dead on target as a great example of the genre." –M. Walker, Seattle, WA

# "What's that buzzing sound?"™

((Are you a freeker?))

OMEGA POINT
PRODUCTIONS

# ((FREQUENCIES))

## Ω ∞ Δ α

# JOSHUA ORTEGA

# ((FREQUENCIES))
An Omega Point Productions™ book

First printing, trade paperback ((alpha version)), October 2001

PRINTING HISTORY
Limited-edition trade paperback ((beta version)), August 1999

ISBN 0-9671120-2-8

ΩΩΩΩΩΩΩΩΩΩΩΩΩΩΩΩΩΩ
Omega Point Productions™
PO Box 85690
Seattle, WA  98145-1690
Phone: (206) 729-6509
FAX: (630) 214-6115
info@omegapp.com
www.omegapp.com
ΩΩΩΩΩΩΩΩΩΩΩΩΩΩΩΩΩΩ

PRINTED IN THE UNITED STATES OF AMERICA BY:
MORRIS PUBLISHING    KEARNEY, NE

9 8 7 6 5 4 3 2

*To everyone and everything that helped me get to this Ω point.*

*Thank you.*

# ACKNOWLEDGEMENTS

I would especially like to thank the following individuals for their
contributions to the book:

Alexis Coronetz, for the love, encouragement, friendship, and advice,
and for being an all-around beautiful soul.

Jeffrey Morris, Sunny Knight, and Mark Stromberg, for generously
volunteering their time and energy to help me smooth out the tale's
rough edges.

Jessica Panetto, for being there at the project's $\alpha$ point, and for all of
the wonderful suggestions, support, editing, and advice along the
way.

Cynthia Lair of Moon Smile Press™, for her extremely helpful advice
on publishing and the book industry in general.

Sue Aho, for doing such an amazing and incredible job in bringing my
logo designs to perfection.

John Borszcz, for shooting down the trouble when the going got tough.

PKD, for exploring the bounds of reality and sharing them as stories.

And my mother, Sharon, and my father, David, for all of the
guidance, wisdom, overstanding, and love.

. •.

## NOTE FROM THE AUTHOR

There is a glossary found within the appendix of this book. Please refer to it when you are unable to find the word or term you are looking for in your dictionary.
It should be there (along with lots of other interesting things).


Now, on to the show...

*"We are all one.*
*A living, incorporate frequency emission.*
*A single electromagnetic wavelength called life."*

*–Dr. Adrian Wellor*

# Ω

# Chapter 1
## ((Law and Order))

*"It was as if an infinite number of frequencies had converged at one single point in space and time, their combined vibrations forming a seemingly coherent structure out of an apparently random disarray. Order out of chaos...*

The red lighting of the surrounding garage projected onto Marc McCready's face like a dull, unfocused laser sight. He eased back into the soft Gelaform™ cushioning of the driver's seat, placed his left thumb upon the dashboard scanner, and apathetically spoke his current password.

"Whatever."

The uniview screen mounted in the car's central console glowed to life, quickly resonating into the Ordosoft™ logo–the Greek letter alpha melded with the "r" in the word "Ordosoft™." The corporation's symbol then morphed into a cartoonish image of Marilyn Monroe in a white dress.

"Biochip scan and password/voicewave confirmation completed," she said in the digitally sampled voice of her famous likeness. "Good morning, Agent McCready."

"Yeah, we'll see," McCready said with a yawn. He placed his tongue behind the bridge of his teeth and sucked in a few times, tasting the bitter aftertaste that the instant latté had left in his mouth. "Voice-rec on."

The shapely toon batted her lashes and smiled. "Voice recognition activated."

McCready rubbed his face with the palm of his left hand, attempting to wipe away the drowsiness that he had been feeling all morning.

The attempt failed. He wasn't surprised.

"Patch me through to HQ," he said.

"Connecting to Freemon Headquarters–Seattle division." The cartoon morphed into an image of the department's logo–a circle around the iconic face of a spotted owl, its pitch black eyes staring out at the viewer. "Secure satellink confirmed. One moment, please."

"N.J., deactivate vocal confirmation," McCready said, his gaze remaining fixed upon the owl's accusatory eyes. "You don't need to tell me everything you're doing."

"That's unusual, Marc," breathed Marilyn's voice, "you normally prefer vocal confirmation."

"Well, sweetheart," McCready said to the car, "I guess things change, don't they?"

The Freemon logo transformed into the head and shoulders of fellow agent Erik Takura. He was seated in front of the uniview screen at his desk, the usual cheshire grin stretched wide across his face. "McCready," he said with a subtle laugh, "you supposed to be up yet, slick? I don't think your face is quite ready to show itself to the world today."

"And yours *is*?" McCready asked, as he looked over Takura's appearance.

Multiple piercings on his ears, eyebrows, nose, and lower lip. Raven black hair to his shoulders, the ends dyed pumpkin orange. Implanted green eyes the shape of a cat's.

"Always," Takura replied, his grin widening to reveal his perfectly straight, immaculately white rows of teeth. "What's goin' down?"

"You're the one with the satellink in his head, you tell me." McCready shifted in his seat, molding the Gelaform™ to the contours of his back. "Any freeker activity I should check out before I come down there?"

"I'll take a look," Takura said.

McCready could always tell when Takura went online. The slight twitch of his head, the momentary droop at the corners of his mouth, a dilation of his feline pupils...then Takura was back to normal. Or, McCready thought, at least as normal as someone with a microprocessor and a modem in his brain *could* be.

"Okay," Takura said as he mentally surfed the data waves,

"accessing freereads...scanning for freekers, crossreferencing location... Wetwyre™ in Kirkland has some activity, but Ignacio's already responded..."

Ignacio was on a case. Now McCready had something to look forward to. Even if his day turned out to be as shitty as his morning, at least he could count on a twisted tale from Ignacio.

"...Boeing®, no," Takura continued, thumbing a gold lip ring, "Microsoft®, no... Okay, wait–here we go. I think I got one for you. Farmaceutical Solutions™ in Redmond... An employee there...Lee Samuels... Doesn't look like he's voicing his thoughts yet...but there are a lot of employees around him if he decides to get chatty..." Takura nodded. "Yeah, this one's worth checking out. I'm sending the GPS coordinates to Marilyn."

A falter in the grin, pupils constricting, and a jerk of the head, Takura was offline.

McCready stared at him, wondering what it would be like to experience cyberspace that intimately, to immerse yourself within the digital matrix just by thinking the thought. No external cables, no screens, no gogs or contacts...all of it occurring within the confines of your cybernetically augmented mind. What would that be like?

"What?" Takura asked, noticing McCready's pause.

Nothing, McCready thought. But the feeling expressed itself anyway. "I don't think I could ever do what you do, Tak. Have all that shit installed in my head."

Takura's grin became a full-blown smile. "That's because you're a relic, McCready! Look at you. You got a car named after a twentieth-century movie star, you pack a weapon with bullets, you have *the* most archaic piece of bionic hardware on the entire squad... Face it, slick," he said with a shrug of the shoulders, "you're just not ready for the future yet."

McCready glanced down at his forearm, then back to the uniview screen. "Fuck you, borg-boy," he said with an uneasy snicker. "I'm as ready as anyone."

"Hey, don't convince *me*," Takura said. "Convince yourself. I'll see you when you get here." Takura's image morphed into the owl logo, then the Marilyn toon.

McCready pulled the black leather glove from off of his right hand, revealing the mechanical prosthesis beneath. He wiggled his five artificial digits, each of their motions producing a barely audible whirring sound.

"Archaic, huh?" McCready grumbled.

Well, he had to admit, it sure wasn't state of the art. He could've chosen the model with near-perfect neurological stimulators and a grafted, gengineered skin. Or the luxury option–having a clone grown from his DNA, storing it in cryo, then harvesting the parts as needed. An arm here, a liver there...

But both of these possibilities required some type of direct brain stimulation, either through implants or neurochemical injections–and McCready didn't want anything or anyone fucking around with his head. It was bad enough already that everyone in the technologized nations had freereads grafted onto their skulls. Anything else only added insult to injury.

"Marc," Norma Jeane said, "the necessary coordinates have been programmed into my global positioning system. I'm ready to engage the frequency emissions violator when you are."

"Right." McCready pulled the glove back over his bionic hand, then flexed it into a fist a few times to make sure the fit was tight. "Time to get to work."

"Manual or automatic?"

"Manual, Norma Jeane. I'm definitely feeling manual today." He cracked a few of his knuckles. "Hope you weren't in the mood to drive yourself."

"Considering that I wasn't programmed with moods," the Chevy® stated, as the cartoon Marilyn pulled a chair out of thin air and seated herself, "I don't think that will be a problem."

"Well, alright then, everybody's happy. N.J.," McCready said, "pop the roof."

The garage roof parted open. Shafts of sunlight cut through the dull red glow. McCready winced.

He reached into the inside pocket of his trenchcoat, pulled out his Obsidians™ sunglasses, placed them onto his face. Just like the commercial–immediate glare reduction, with no color or vision loss. He relaxed his eyes. Perfect.

Wrapping his left hand around the soft rubber grip of the steering wheel, McCready said, "Let's fly."

The car activated its GS systems as the Marilyn toon, now dressed in aviator pants and a leather helmet, climbed into the cockpit of a biplane and fired up its propellers.

McCready reached down with his right hand and grasped a lever which resembled an RPM throttle on an old military fighter jet. He looked up at the sky through the Plexiglas® section of the vehicle's roof, saw no airborne traffic overhead, and smoothly pulled the lever backwards.

The Chevy® Polaris™ lifted silently off the ground, up through the sunlit opening. As McCready emerged from the garage adjoined to his Bellevue residence, he panned his head from side to side, taking in a 180 degree view of his environs. The unusually sunny March day allowed for a crystalline view of the surrounding area.

To the east were the iridescent, mirrored, and gleaming contemporary skyscrapers of Bellevue's corporate district, set against the backdrop of the snow-capped mountains of the Cascades and the glimmering waters of Lake Sammamish. To the south, Mount Rainier perched upon the horizon like an angry god, its partially exploded top serving as divine testament to the quake of 2022. Hovering majestically in the heavens above Lake Washington to the southwest, was the sky-city of Mercer Island, while across the lake and to the west, downtown Seattle's formidable–though somewhat antiquated–skyline juxtaposed itself in an awkwardly beautiful way with the Olympic mountain range behind it.

McCready watched a green Lexus® fly by in front of him, checked the holographic rear-view screen, spun the steering wheel to the left, and faced the car in a northeasterly direction that would put him in line with Redmond. "Music, N.J.," he said.

Norma Jeane hopped out of the biplane and dashed behind it. "Do you have a particular selection that you would like to hear?" She slinkily walked out into view, now attired in a red evening dress.

"Nope." He popped a caffeinated peppermint into his mouth and began to suck on it, thankful to be rid of the latté's lingering aftertaste. "Why don't you surprise me."

The cartoon danced a few steps sampled directly from *Gentlemen Prefer Blondes*, as the opening drum beat of Maxwell's "Gravity: Pushing to Pull" started to pulse through the stereo speakers.

"Nice choice," McCready said, running his fingers through his spiky, uncombed hair. "Let's get this show on the road." The bass dropped, keyboards blended, and McCready pressed down firmly on the acceleration pedal.

The car shot forward, a midnight black bat out of hell.


As he reached the outskirts of Redmond, McCready reduced his speed to 90 m.p.h., descended from the law enforcement/emergency vehicle altitude, and said, "N.J., flip the map on."

The dancing Marilyn morphed into a highly detailed, three-dimensional grid of the surrounding civic area. The Farmaceutical Solutions™ building was highlighted with a glowing red outline, while McCready's position was represented by a tiny, precisely rendered icon of the Polaris™.

"That close already..." he said as he eyed the map. "N.J., go ahead and take over."

The grid reverted back to Norma Jeane, now seated inside of a red '57 Chevy®, one hand on the steering wheel and the other adjusting the rear-view mirror. "We will be arriving at Farmaceutical Solutions™ in a few moments," she said with a confident smile. "Please relax and enjoy the ride."

McCready released his hands from the controls, clasped his fingers together, and stretched his arms out in front of him. As usual, last night's sleep had been a little rough. McCready's entire body was stiff and sore. He felt like a cadaver experiencing rigor mortis. Or something twisted like that. He scrunched his shoulders up to his neck, let out a long and drawn out yawn, and looked ahead at downtown Redmond.

While not quite as large and sprawling as Bellevue's downtown, Redmond's structures were every bit as impressive and modern as those of its southern neighbor. The look and feel of the landscaping, though...that was an entirely different story. Whereas Bellevue had a few city parks and the occasional tree here and there, Redmond was virtually overflowing with vegetation. Gardens, parks, and arboretums were everywhere. Its streets were lined with tall firs, cedars, and spruce, its rooftops covered with small trees and shrubs. Climbing vines grew off buildings, overpasses, streetlights...you name it. The place was a tree-hugging, city-dwelling liberals' wet dream.

And that was exactly how Ordosoft's™ founding father, W.A. Huxton, had planned it. He'd gradually redesigned the city since his company's flagship campus was built there in the 1980's, transforming an ordinary suburban area into this outlandish synthesis of high technology and fertile flora.

What was that Huxton soundbyte they always used to show? McCready asked himself. Something about the two being the same... "Science and nature are ultimately the same phenomena–pure information at work." Yeah, that was it. He used to say that line to justify all of his personal visions and conquests. "Used to say" because Huxton didn't say much of anything anymore. Not publicly, at least. He now lived an isolated life in a mysterious Tibetan Shangri-La,

6

having turned over control of Ordosoft™–arguably the world's most powerful corporation–to his son, Mason, roughly twenty years ago.

"I've received clearance from security," N.J. said, extending four rubber tires from the bottom of the car. "Please prepare for touchdown."

As the Polaris™ settled onto the roof of the Farmaceutical Solutions™ building, McCready pulled a pack of Kamel® Kloves™ from his trench's front pocket. He shook a single cigarette out of the red package and placed it between his lips. "Open door, N.J.," he said. "Driver's side."

McCready stepped out of the car, onto the roof's smooth concrete floor. Immediately, he noticed a strange smell in the air...almost electric. Ozone? He turned his head towards the sky. Maybe they're doing some molecular modifications today. Shouldn't be filtering down here, though. Whatever. McCready flicked open his silver Zippo® and brought the flame to the Kamel's® tip. He took two deep pulls from the clobacco cigarette, and exhaled the pungent smoke over the hood of his car.

"Alright, N.J.," McCready said, activating the Obsidians'™ cameras with the touch of a small sensor, "start sending my visuals to HQ's databanks. I'll be using the wristcom to keep in contact. Close door and activate security systems." McCready walked away from the Polaris™, dropping the Zippo® back into his pocket as he looked around for the elevator entrance to the building.

Aside from the stained-concrete landing zone, the surface of the roof was either covered with a brown-and-white marbled tile or sunken, dirt-filled planters containing your usual corporate mix of weather resistant/aesthetically pleasing vegetation. A few wooden picnic tables were also scattered about the area, presumably for the employees to use during their lunchbreak. Cute, McCready thought. A little playground for the company's kids, 'cause mom and pop CEO loves their little workers *sooo* much. This place was indicative of the reason he never moved to Redmond–too much bullshit. A corporation didn't give a cloned whore's ass about its employees, so why pretend otherwise? Whatever turns you on, he figured.

McCready walked to the opposite end of the roof and found the elevator entrance near a 10-foot pine. Passing the tree, he took a long pull from his cigarette, blew the sweet, spicy smoke through his nostrils, and touched a button on the elevator's control panel.

"May I help you?" asked a nasally male voice from a speaker set into the panel.

7

Of course, McCready thought, or I wouldn't have pressed the fuckin' button. Procedure and formality–you had to love 'em. "Agent Marc McCready," he said, staring into the minicamera above the speaker, "I'm here to investigate a possible frequency emissions violation."

"You're a Freemon?" the voice asked with an eager curiosity.

"Right." McCready extinguished his Kamel® in a bowl of sand set atop a cedar-framed garbage can.

"I bet that's an *exciting* job, isn't it?"

"No, not really–you have to spend too much of your time answering idiotic questions from bored employees."

Silence from the other end of the speaker.

Then the voice said, "Please place your thumb over the scanner for biochip confirmation." Any trace of excitement was now completely gone.

McCready put his left thumb on the panel's scanner. A flash of red laser light, and the elevator doors began to open.

"Your identity has been confirmed, Agent McCready. Please enter. And have a nice day."

"Yeah, right," McCready said, walking into the elevator's latté brown interior.

The doors closed behind him, and the generic female voice of the elevator's computer asked, "Which floor would you like?"

"Corpo and security," he said.

"Thank you."

The elevator started its descent. McCready read the big black letters written across the inside of the doors:

## FARMACEUTICAL SOLUTIONS™

Below it, in smaller print, their current slogan:

### MAKING YOU BETTER.™

The saying was a little trite, but it had a certain amount of truth to it. A few years back, after his mother was diagnosed with liver disease, she had received a life-saving transfusion of a blood protein, serum albumin, which had been created through the company's founding enterprise, bovine pharming–a process in which cloned female cows were gengineered to produce pharmaceutical drugs through their milk. The drugs could then be extracted from the lactic fluids, and transferred to the human recipient. From moo to you, he joked to himself.

The elevator came to a stop. "Thirteenth floor. Corporate police and security." The doors parted open, revealing two large figures dressed in black suits and ties. "Have a nice day."

"You must be my escorts," McCready said. He pulled out his badge and showed it to the two corpos. "Agent Marc McCready, Freemon."

The blonde, crew cut, nearly albino member of the pair took the walletlike badge from McCready's hand and opened it. A holographic Freemon logo projected out from a tiny laser lens into the air above the badge. She raised it before her face and tilted the ID back and forth, carefully examining all angles of the three-dimensional owl logo. For a moment, McCready wondered if the muscular blonde was actually verifying the hologram, or if she was simply enjoying its artistic qualities. Then he got a good look at her eyes. Unnaturally pallid, like bleached sapphire. Definitely implants. They must have been designed to look for all of the hidden stuff, all the codes and data that were locked deep within the matrices of the hologram in order to differentiate it from a simpler, less detailed counterfeit.

"Keep door open," McCready said aloud, knowing that the elevator would automatically shut on his ass otherwise.

The blonde nodded her head a few times as she finished examining the hologram, briefly looked up at McCready, then handed the closed badge over to her bearded cohort.

The black-bearded man, who had a much darker skin tone and a bit more fat mass than the blonde, stoically gazed at McCready as he took the badge from her hand. A data port was embedded in the side of his shiny bald head, and a thin cable stretched from the center of the implant down to a silvery device encased around his right index finger. He reopened the ID, raised his metal-tipped finger to the lower section of the badge, and ran his digit across the various bar codes. A tiny laser flashed at the end of the silver fingertip, adding a temporary reddish hue to the black zebra-stripes.

"ID vital info matches the biochip scan done on the roof," the corpo said in a low voice. "He's who he says he is." He handed the badge back to McCready with a friendly nod, then unplugged the microthin cord from the side of his head.

"So where can I find an employee named Lee Samuels?" McCready asked.

"We'll take you to him," the bald man said. "By the way, I'm

9

Seth. She's Nikki," he said, gesturing towards the blonde, whose icy
blue eyes were coldly fixed upon McCready's face. "But she don't say ·
much, so don't be expectin' to have no conversation with her."

"Don't worry," McCready said, meeting Nikki's glacial stare,
"I won't be." The two massive corpos stepped into the elevator car,
downsizing it from a full-size to a compact. McCready was glad he
wasn't claustrophobic.

"Sixteenth floor," requested Seth. The elevator's doors closed
and the car began to move again. Seth looked down at McCready
without tilting his head, instead shifting only his eyes. "So Lee
Samuels is freekin' out, hm?"

"Yup," McCready said.

"That's bugged–dude's usually real quiet."

"That's how it is sometimes–the ones you'd least expect."
McCready touched a tiny sensor on the left side of his Obsidians™,
activating the biochip/FE scanner hidden in the bridge of the
sunglasses. A translucent, pyramid-shaped hologram displayed itself
onto the Obsidians'™ lenses. "Just goes to show you can't always tell a
person's thoughts from their demeanor alone." The rotating pyramid
was located on the right side of his field of vision, its holographic
qualities causing it to appear as if it were actually being projected out
into the real space in front of him. "Sometimes you gotta look a little
deeper."

"Sixteenth floor," the elevator said, coming to a rest. "Training and development."

McCready stepped through the parting metal doors, into the
bright fluorescent lighting of the cubicle-infested 16th floor. No
NatraLites™? he asked himself. This company could sure as hell
afford them, so why weren't they using them? Granted, this was the
floor where they trained their new employees, but still...

McCready didn't like fluorescents. In fact, he hated them.
The way they coruscated on the periphery of your vision, lingering
there like epileptic ghosts until you paid conscious attention to them.
Then once you *did* pay attention to them, the little bastards would
temporarily go back to whatever hell it was that spawned them,
only to return the minute your focus was diverted. Fucking annoying,
the way they did that–let alone the fact that information could be
transmitted through them.

"Samuels is just up this way," Seth said.

As he moved into McCready's line of sight, the Obsidians'™
scanner started to transmit information to the lenses' displays. Below

the rotating pyramid, in the same holographic manner, the corpo's name and social security number were displayed: Seth Jordan Samson, #082-773-3504. The pyramid itself now exhibited a greenish-yellow hue, indicating that Seth's thoughts were active yet ordinary, parking him right into the acceptable range for normal human thinking.

McCready looked over at Nikki, assuming that she was going to trail right behind Seth, but the tall blonde was still standing there. The scanner transmitted the new data: Natasha Nikita Fedorova, #235-686-1612. The yellowish-orange color of the pyramid showed that her thoughts were very active, but still well within the legal limits. And even if Nikki did think outside of the limits, she seemed like the type who wouldn't be much of a threat since she didn't appear to share her thoughts with anyone else.

With her hand, Nikki motioned McCready to follow Seth, her gaze as frigid as ever.

"Alright, lady," McCready said. "If you insist." He tailed Seth down the hallway, Nikki fell into place directly behind him, and they moved deeper into the 16th floor's interior. McCready briefly looked back at his albino shadow, then peered into a few of the employee's cubicles.

All were basically the same, barring some occasional, minor differences. The employees would sit in their Gelaform™ chairs with the rollers at the base, while working, training, or teleconferencing on the uniview screens in front of them. The minor differences were found in the content, arrangement, and neatness of personal items found on the employee's desk, and the slight variations displayed upon the Obsidians'™ frequency emissions scanner. In fact, the variations in their frees were almost *too* slight. Nearly every employee was in the green alpha range, whereas with most corporate trainees there were fluctuations up into the beta and gamma ranges. So far, Seth and Nikki were the only people in the building who were even close to those ranges–and they didn't even work on this floor. Interesting, McCready thought. He looked up at the fluorescents.

"You hear that?" Seth asked.

"What?" McCready said, snapping out of his previous train of thought.

"Sounds like yellin' or somethin' from up ahead."

"It's Lee Samuels," Nikki said, in a voice much softer than her appearance would indicate. "He's making some very odd statements..." She turned one of her cybernetic ears towards the sound.

"And being quite loud about it."

"Shit," McCready said, matching Seth's quickened pace. "He must be vocally freaking out." He followed the corpo around a few corners and bends, and within seconds, they had reached Lee Samuels' cubicle.

A crowd of employees were gathered near the compartment's entrance, partially blocking McCready's view of the freeker. "What's that buzzing sound?" Lee Samuels called out. "It won't stop! What's that buzzing sound?"

"Please go back to your cubicles," Seth announced to the curious coworkers. "The situation is being dealt with. Please go back to your work."

"Do you hear it?" Samuels asked. "The buzzing–it's everywhere. All of you, just stop what you're doing for a moment and *listen*. You'll hear it. It's always there. It never stops."

As the employees followed Seth's commands and returned to their workstations, McCready quickly scanned over them. A few had now reached the yellow beta frequency, but there still wasn't a single person in the gamma region. Confrontation with a vocal freeker usually had more of a stimulating effect than this... McCready detached a small white-noise generator off of his utility belt, then placed the spherical apparatus at the cubicle's entrance to prevent any unnecessary sounds from leaving the area.

"All these electronic devices buzzing constantly!" The intensity in Samuels' voice was increasing. "It's the hive–they keep sending messages to us through their goddamn buzzing devices!"

McCready finally got a good line of sight at Samuels, though at this point, he didn't really need the Obsidians™ to tell him whether or not the employee was freeking out. Still, there was the official confirmation on the display: orangish-red at the base, ascending into deep, blood red at the eye of the pyramid.

A full-blown freeker reading.

An omega.

"They're controlling our minds with their technology!" Samuels shouted, frenetically shaking his outstretched hands in a pleading manner. "Electric pheromones! Our thoughts are not our own!"

"Look, Samuels," McCready said calmly, pulling out a black and gray device which resembled a small remote control, "I'm gonna give you one chance to calm down, shut up, and relax. Do you understand me?"

12

# ((FREQUENCIES))

"Don't you see?!" Samuels grabbed his head in frustration. "The electric pheromones have made us mindless drones! We're just stupid little insects following the hive mother's bidding! We don't even know we're being controlled!"

McCready raised both his voice and the device at the slender man. "Samuels, I'm dead serious–shut the fuck up, or I'm *shutting* you up." He lightly pressed a button, causing a bright red dot to appear upon the freeker's forehead.

"The queen bee keeps transmitting the electric pheromones and we just keep on following them without ever questioning why. Why? Why not ask why? *I* know why."

Seth looked over at McCready. "He ain't listening to you, man. All he's hearin' is that pheromone shit he keeps talkin' about."

"But what I don't know–the one thing I can't figure out..." Samuels paused, his face shellacked with desperation. "Who's the queen? Who...is...the goddamn *queen*?!?"

McCready firmly pressed the button, emitting an invisible, concentrated electromagnetic pulse that shot straight to the red homing-dot. Lee Samuels immediately lost consciousness and began falling forward to the floor. His knees barely touched ground before his lightly freckled face smashed into the marbled tile with a sickening thud.

There was silence for a few seconds.

"Shit," Seth said, squinting his eyes and rubbing his beard. "That must'a hurt." He looked at McCready, head slightly cocked. "You hit 'im with a disruptor?"

"Yup," McCready said.

Seth moved a few steps forward and peered over the freeker's prostrate form. "But it looks like he's in a coma or somethin'."

"He is. We're not issued the typical disruptors–the ones that simply affect motor coordination." McCready kneeled down beside Samuels' head, noticing a thick stream of blood trickling out from somewhere on the employee's blank face. "Ours affect the synapses in the reticular formation of the brain, inducing a temporary coma."

"Damn," Seth said. "You guys don't play around."

"Nope." With his gloved right hand, McCready grabbed a fistful of Samuels' red hair, and slowly pulled his head up from the cool tile. An oozing, sticky sound was barely audible as the large laceration underneath his cheekbone separated from the blood beneath it. McCready looked up at Seth and Nikki. "Either of you got a cauterizer? Mine's busted."

Nikki stepped forward, reached into a vest pocket, and pulled out the requested item. She scanned the penlike laser a few times over the open wound and soldered it shut.

"Thanks," McCready said, as he carefully laid Samuels' head back onto the tile. "I wasn't *about* to drag his bleeding ass into my car." He removed a tiny metallic/ceramic disc from the side of his utility belt, lifted Samuels' body up slightly, and placed the GS disc underneath the freeker's abdomen. Samuels rose up about one meter off the ground, and hovered there motionless.

"So now what happens to him?" asked Seth, nodding his head in the direction of the floating body.

McCready stood up from his crouched position and lifted Samuels' blue overcoat from the back of his chair. "Well, first he goes back with me to the Hill for processing. Then from there," he said, using the overcoat to wipe some blood off of his boots, "it's up to the judges. Maybe reprogramming in a rehabilitation center if him or his relatives have the money to afford it."

"And if they don't?"

"Then he'll probably end up in a workcamp," McCready said, wiping the final crimson smear from his soles. "Unless they think his crime was serious enough–then they might use his body for medical purposes. Or convert it into raw industrial material in a micronizer. It's hard to tell." He threw the bloodied overcoat onto the floor, covering the excess human liquid which had spilled from Samuels' face. "Whatever the case, I doubt you'll be seeing him again."

McCready pressed a button on the side of his wristcom, prompting the cartoon Marilyn to appear upon the miniature screen. "N.J., contact HQ and let 'em know I've handled the freeker situation here. A basic, routine I&D–nothing out of the ordinary."

Seth plugged a mini microphone into his head and began to inform his superiors about the incident.

"Will that be all, Marc?" N.J. asked, as she picked up the receiver of an old-fashioned telephone.

"Actually," he remembered, looking up at the fluorescent lights, "do one more thing for me. Access our database and tell me how many freeker incidents have occurred at Farmaceutical Solutions™ this year."

Nikki curiously looked at McCready, her blonde brows frowning down as her eyelids squinted around her icy orbs.

"Including this one," Norma Jeane said, replacing the receiver onto the hook, "four."

"And it's only March. That's what I thought." McCready clutched Lee Samuels' loose sweater and walked towards the cubicle's exit, easily dragging the weightless man behind him. Glancing back at Seth, who was still talking into his mini-mike, McCready stopped and said, "Hey, Seth."

"Hold on," Seth said into the microphone, "the Freemon's talkin' to me." He looked at McCready. "Yeah?"

"Tell your bosses to ease up a little on the subliminals." McCready pointed up at the fluorescents.

"What do you mean?" Seth asked, looking up towards the lights.

"The fluorescents," McCready said. "Just like in the super-markets, they're being used here to transmit information—except it's not price changes that are being transmitted, and it sure as hell isn't digital price tags that are receiving it."

Seth looked a little puzzled. Or tried to. "What is it then?"

Underneath the Obsidians™, McCready's eyes glanced at the mike. More than likely, Seth's superiors were hearing what he was saying firsthand—and they probably weren't smiling. Oh well, McCready thought. Fuck 'em. I've got jurisdiction in this matter.

"What it *is*," McCready assuredly stated, "is that the subs coming through the fluorescents are restricting the employees' thoughts too much. As a corporation, you guys have the legal right to use subliminal suggestion techniques, *provided* they don't interfere with any of the articles of the Frequency Emissions Act. And right now, by constantly keeping your employees in the alpha range...you're causing them to randomly freek out." He paused for a moment to gauge Seth's reaction. On the FE display, Seth's reading was now a pure orange color—McCready had touched a nerve. "And that's a direct violation of the act. In other words, what you're doing here is illegal."

Seth slowly nodded his head, an indication that he was receiving some kind of instructions or orders from his superiors via radio implant. "Thanks for bringing this matter to our attention, Agent McCready. We'll make sure this doesn't happen again."

Yeah, McCready thought, you'll make sure you aren't *caught* again. You and the overseers are only gonna abide by the law until you devise a less obvious method for limiting your slaves' cognitive freedom. Then you'll use your fancy new mind trick, regardless of whether it's legal or not, 'cause you're a corporation and you can get away with whatever the fuck you want. "I'm sure you will,"

McCready said, smiling the most plastic smile he possibly could.

Seth nodded a few more times. "You think it's the alpha transmissions that are causing the problem?"

The question was so ridiculous, McCready had to let out a sarcastic laugh. *Like you don't already know*, he thought. *You're just trying to play stupid to make your guilty corporate ass look more innocent. Okay, whatever. You want me to play along and humor you? Fine.* "Human minds are like balloons," McCready said, his vocal tone revealing his annoyance, "right? And their thoughts are like the air that fills these balloons. If you don't let them release a little bit of air from time to time–which is what they're doing when they think outside the alpha range–then they're going to burst." He held his hand up, made a fist, then quickly flared his fingers out. "Pop." He pointed at Seth and Nikki. "Then *you've* got an omega on your hands," pointing the same finger at himself, "*my* annoying ass has got to respond to a situation that could have been avoided," he nodded down at Samuels, "and some poor bastard like *him* has gotta go to the workcamps or the fuckin' micronizer."

McCready shook his head with frustration as he knelt down and picked up the white-noise generator from off the ground. He stood up, reattached the generator to his belt, and walked away from the two corpos, towing the reticularly challenged body of Lee Samuels behind him. "Just be a little more careful in the future, alright?" McCready said without turning back.

Neither Seth or Nikki said anything in response.

As he walked past the infinite rows of homogeneous cubicles, observing the subliminally induced employees going about their busy work, McCready couldn't help but think of a honeycomb.

# Chapter 2
# ((A Butterfly Dreaming))

*...or so it would seem.*
*For, while this structure was indeed built with the stuff of coherency and order, it evolved into a creation which was chaotic and unpredictable in its nature, constantly shifting and changing depending on the perspective with which it was viewed, and thus experienced. When seen with hope, joy, and blessedness, the structure could be quite wondrous and beautiful...*

Refracted rays of brilliant sunlight shone down through the domed glass ceiling, their lustrous energy reflecting off the tiny beads of sweat sprinkled across the face of Ashley Huxton. Her eyes closed in concentration, head tilted up towards the warm solar radiance, hands raised high into the air above, Ashley gracefully held her arabesque with the momentary pause in the triballet's song.

As the music began to play again, she fluidly moved across the polished wood floor of her dance studio, performing a series of light, quick steps which gave the impression that she was gliding, weightlessly, upon the air.

The sounds coming through the studio's speakers were a combination of African drums, including the bongos, hourglass, and congas, coupled with samples drawn from Tchaikovsky's *Swan Lake* and *Sleeping Beauty* ballets. Ashley had played the drums herself, meshed them together on her 88-track, then layered the Tchaikovsky loops over the percussion, creating a form of song which the media had dubbed "triballet," or tribal ballet. She didn't really care much for the term, however–it seemed contrived and unnecessary, like so many of the assorted labels and titles which the media immediately branded upon any new idea or artform. To her, it was simply music. That's all.

Gaining momentum from the lithe, fleet footwork of her previous move, Ashley sprang high into the air, kicked one leg out from her body in a swift, scissorlike motion, and nimbly landed with both feet together. Without pausing, she did a succession of small bouncing steps, interlacing them with the eloquent motions of her arms and the occasional circling of her legs. Her fluid movements matched the music perfectly, as both expressions were not confined to the rigid standards of traditional ballet, but rather, were a celebration of freedom, flow, and spontaneity.

As an hourglass drum raised an octave in a manner resembling a human voice, a sample from the fairy dances in Act III of *Swan Lake* looped over and over, producing a beautifully hypnotic melody. Ashley performed a final aerial circle with her left leg, quickly brought it in towards her knee, and smoothly pirouetted on the point of her right toe. After a series of eight continuous revolutions, she slowly leaned forward on her right leg, then gently extended her left leg backwards until it was in line with her torso. As she elegantly held the pose, the Tchaikovsky loops subtly faded away, leaving only the sounds of soft drumming behind.

Ashley took a deep, life-affirming breath, then calmly righted herself from the arabesque position. She looked up at the bright sun above, closed her eyes, and let the warm waves of celestial energy wash into her being. "Thank you," she whispered, her lips shaping into an appreciative smile. Taking one more slow, strong breath, she turned her face from the sun, and opened her eyes to the dance studio surrounding her.

Everything was still there...the holographic paintings hanging upon the rounded, rainforest green walls, the ballet barre which curved around the entire circular room, the hardwood floors beneath her feet... Funny, she thought, for a moment I wasn't even sure if I was *in* the studio anymore. And maybe I wasn't...and maybe I'm not now. Who knows? I could be the butterfly dreaming it's a person who dreams of being a butterfly...

Smiling at the notion, Ashley walked over to the curved wooden bar where her olive brown towel was hanging. She dabbed the cotton cloth lightly upon her face, brushed it along the length of her glistening arms and legs, then delicately moved it across her black tank-topped leotard.

Slinging the towel over her shoulder, she exited the studio through an oval door and entered a tall, cylindrical hallway. An impromptu show of chaotic animation began to play upon the passage's ceiling and walls, its colorful fractal imagery moving flawlessly in sync with her motion. Ashley walked the length of the cylinder, chromatic spirals and vibrant whorls swirling about her, then stepped down from the hallway when she had reached the sunken living room.

The overall shape and design of the room, which she referred to as her "playroom," was similar to that of the studio–cylindrical walls going up into a rounded ceiling–only much greater in size, with a tintable plexiglass dome rather than actual glass. While she liked the look and refractive qualities of glass better, the Plexiglas® was much more likely to hold together in the event of an earthquake–so she opted to put the crystal in the studio and the plastic in the play-room. That way, she figured, if an earthquake hit, she wouldn't die in the playroom sitting in front of the uniview screen or something silly like that. And if it happened while she was in the studio? C'est la vie. At least she would die dancing and happy...

Directly across from her, opposite the studio passage, was a huge curved bookcase filled with an eclectic array of titles which she had collected over the years. She had ancient books that were hundreds of years old, some classics and some obscure; books from the 20th century, up until the period in the 21st century when environmental concerns and cheap, portable univiews made paper reading material obsolete; censored books that didn't officially exist in the Library of Congress' records, the ones that weren't contained in, and couldn't be accessed through, any of the uniview's public channels.

The collection was quite impressive, an exclusive luxury al-lowed to her because she was a Huxton...a luxury which few others could enjoy. And she hated that fact. Well, not hate, actually. Did the world really need any more hate? She didn't think so, and there-fore tried not to use or feel the word. Words created reality, after all... So, she disliked that fact. Why weren't resources more spread around? Why should she be able to have something that others couldn't? And most of all, why could she think these thoughts while others might be blacklisted or investigated for doing the exact same thing? It was all wrong, she knew that much for sure. But did it have to be this way? And if it didn't, then how could it change? Ashley clasped her hands together, closed her eyes, and sent out a silent prayer to Gaia for guidance. It was time to visit her soon.

Stretching out her arms, she walked over to a fluffy beanbag chair and sat down on top of it. As her body began to sink into the pliant piece of furniture, she wandered her eyes around the room.

Many of the objects in the playroom, just like in much of her house, were colored a shade of brown or green—from the ottomans, couches, and terra cotta planters situated atop the plush, carpeted floor, to the myriad ornaments, artwork, and hanging plants which adorned the circular walls. She had always associated these colors with life and earthiness, two qualities which she sadly found missing in so many of the people and places around her. There was so much despair and apathy in the city, as if the inhabitant's emotions, their very souls, had been stolen by... She tried to think of the perfect word... By logical demons...that was close...*techno*logical demons...better... Technodevils. That was it.

Technodevils—the entities who controlled and directed this cold, ordered, and unfeeling world which she was born into. But wouldn't that definition include Ordosoft™? And her father, brother, and grandfather? Goddess, she thought, her face turning to a frown, how depressing. Most of my immediate family could be ostensibly characterized as purveyors of lifeless living.

Lost in her thoughts, Ashley was slightly startled when one of her cats jumped on to her lap. Surprise quickly gave way to affection, and she began to stroke her hand along the silky, tortoise-shell fur of the feline's back. "Hey there, Mau-Mau, how are you?" she asked. "So where's your buddies? Where's Sekhet and Bubastis? They not playing with you today?"

The cat meowed loudly.

Ashley laughed. "No? That's okay, though," she said, rubbing the top of the kitty's head, "I'll play with you." The hooting of a spotted owl suddenly sounded over the playroom's speakers. "Actually, Mau, I guess I'll have to finish playing with you *after* I take this call." She tenderly placed the cat onto the carpet, and walked over to an intricate tapestry hanging from a brass cylinder mounted to the wall. Mau-Mau immediately trotted along after Ashley, rubbing against her smooth, bare legs when she had reached her.

Ashley pressed a button on the wall, and the large tapestry rolled up into the cylindrical housing, revealing behind it a thin uniview wallscreen. It had always bothered her, the thought that someone could jack into your set at any time and just *watch* you, so she used the tapestry to cover the camera installed in the uniview. How or why people ever agreed to the notion of letting a camera into their homes, she could never really understand. *Now* it made sense—everybody was used to it and the society was dependent on it—it was just "the way it is." But when televisions, phones, and computers were still separate devices, why did they choose to have all three combined into the ultimate Big Brother device? What made it so important to them? She hoped it was something more than just the "C" word. It had to be something more than that. When she had the chance to speak with her grandfather in Tibet later this week, she would definitely have to remember to ask him. After all, Gonpo certainly would have some enlightening insights into the subject, considering he was one of the main forces backing the uniview's creation.

She pushed another button, this one located near the base of the curved screen, and manually activated the voice recognition. Like the cameras, the auto voice-rec wasn't one of her favorite features either, since the microphone was always turned on, waiting for someone to activate it. Therefore, she had the manual button installed so she could turn the mike *completely* off when she wanted to. "Uniview on," she said. The Ordosoft™ logo appeared briefly upon the screen, then morphed into a photograph of lush, moss-draped temperate rainforest. "Who's the incoming call from?"

An AT & T® logo superimposed itself over the rainforest photo, then was replaced by the words, "Adam M. Huxton." Big bro, she thought. This should be interesting. "Put the call through."

The rainforest transformed into an image of her older brother, seated in an expensive wicker chair on his outdoor patio, a bottled Cognihance™ smartdrink in his hand. "Hello, Ashley," he said.

"Hello, Adam," she replied, crossing her arms. "And to what do I owe this pleasure?"

Adam adjusted his Ordosoft™ print tie and looked up at the sunny sky above. "It's a lovely day, isn't it?"

She smiled. "Yes, it's a gorgeous day, Adam...but that's not what you're calling me about, is it?"

He smiled back, nodded, and took a sip of the neon orange liquid. "It's true, Ash." Adam paused for a moment, then leaned forward in the chair, his moussed brown locks staying perfectly in place. "I'm calling about mother," he said. "She hasn't been doing too well lately."

"*Which* mother are you referring to? The clone or the real one?"

Adam's forehead furrowed with unpleasant surprise. "Our

21

only mother, Ashley, that's who. The living one. And you," he said, pointing a condemnatory finger at her, "should begin to treat her that way. Your attitude is *very* likely part of the reason she's not feeling well."

"*My* attitude?" Ashley's face flushed red. "How can you say that? What about you and dad's attitude, huh? You *both* knew I wanted to let mom die a peaceful death–and you didn't give a shit about my opinion! You went right ahead and stuck her in cryo or bio-stasis or whatever the hell it is, and *completely* ignored what I had to say!" She lightly bit her lip, shook her head, and looked away from the screen. "Then, as if that wasn't bad enough...you cloned her." She looked back at the screen with furious eyes. "*You fucking cloned my mother*!" She let out an exasperated laugh. "And you talk about *my* attitude? Well, fuck you, Adam!" she yelled, throwing the cotton towel at the uniview screen. "Fuck you and dad both!"

"There's no need for the hostility, Ash!" Adam shouted back. He sat up in his chair, breathed in, and closed his eyes, his thick black lashes making him look almost angelic. Almost. "Let's calm down," he said, lowering his voice. "I understand what you're saying."

"Do you?!"

"Yes, I realize it wasn't exactly fair to you, an–"

"That's an understatement."

"Okay, yes, that's true–but please, let me finish what I was about to say."

Ashley bent down to pick up the towel, and noticed a tense look on Mau-Mau's face. "I'm sorry, girl," she said, caressing the fe-line's head. "Sorry for sending that energy your way. It's okay now." She picked up the damp towel and stood up to face the uniview once more. "Go ahead."

"Ashley, I realize that this whole situation hasn't been fair to you. Father and I had hoped you'd eventually see our point of view, but... I'm beginning to doubt that that's ever going to hap-pen. And..." He paused momentarily. "I apologize, Ash. I mean that. I apologize that we hurt you. I assure you that wasn't our intention. We simply did what we felt was the right thing to do for the family. Neither of us could bear to lose mother, so we did everything in our power to save her."

"But mom was supposed to die, Adam. It was her time. That's just part of the natural cycle of life–we're *supposed to die*. It's not a bad thing. And she was okay with it...she was ready–but you two weren't, and that was selfish. That was wrong. You should have let life take its course."

Adam glanced down at the patio's floor, and said, "But life isn't quite what it used to be, is it, Ash?"

"I guess not," she said. "It used to be something sacred."

A Post-It® reminder popped up on the uniview screen, the yellow graphic covering her brother's image and temporarily muting out his voice.

"Oh no, I forgot!" Ashley said, as the reminder faded away.

"What?" Adam asked in a concerned tone. "What is it?"

"I have a meeting with Professor Brennan at the UW today! How did I forget?" she asked herself. "Adam, I'm sorry, but I have to get moving!"

"I understand, Ash, but... The reason I called in the first place–I was wondering if you could do me a favor."

"What's that?"

"Would you please come to the skyland this afternoon? If not for...mother, then would you at least do it for me?"

"It's really that important to you?"

He nodded. "It is."

"Then I'll be there, Adam," she said. "Okay?"

Adam smiled. "Thanks, Ash."

"You're welcome. Uniview off." She deactivated the voice-rec, then bent over and kissed the top of Mau-Mau's head. "I gotta go, Mau. Watch the house for me, okay?"

Ashley rushed into the downstairs bathroom, which, like every other room in the house save for the bedroom, was circular in design. She slipped out of her ballet shoes, peeled off her Nanopôr™ leotard, opened the etched glass shower door and turned on the water pressure full blast. Hopping between the two shower-heads' flowing streams, she quickly rinsed her hair and washed her body, then swiftly dried herself off. With a towel wrapped around her body, she darted out of the bathroom, through the playroom, up one of the spiral stairwells, into her pyramid-shaped bedroom. Two cats, one pitch black, the other dark brown, sat atop her spacious waterbed. Both meowed at the sight of her.

"Sorry, guys," Ashley said, sliding into some loose silk pants, "I love you, but I can't give you any attention right now!" She threw on a matching khaki blouse, snatched a nearby sweater, rushed back down the stairs, through the playroom, finally reaching the sunlit vestibule which led to the front door. She took a short, terse breath and exhaled. Then she slipped into a pair of suede slides, walked down the ivy-covered passageway, and stepped onto the lush garden path which led to her car.

As she passed through the diverse menagerie of plants and trees, she looked down at her thin gold watch. The 24-karat band consisted of eight interlocking infinity symbols, while its round face contained an Anasazi-like spiral which rested underneath the wavy, hieroglyphic hands. Still have about twenty minutes, she thought. Not bad, considering I almost *completely* forgot about the meeting.

Reaching her forest green Lexus®, Ashley placed her right thumb upon the door's scanner lock. It verified her identity, she opened the front door, then seated herself into the padded leather driver's seat. She shifted a little to try to get comfortable, but wasn't very successful. The seat was almost a little *too* soft and cushy–not quite what she would have chosen had she picked out the car herself. But, she wasn't the one who picked it out–her father had. She just wanted something simple, but he insisted on getting her *some* type of luxury car for her 25th birthday, and wouldn't take no for an answer. At least he didn't get her a Rolls®, though. And he did pick out a good color. Poor me, she laughed to herself. Poor little rich girl, her car was too nice for her! Like that was really some kind of problem. She had it easy, and she knew it. Not that her economic status didn't present its own set of problems, but life could definitely be a whole lot worse–and she was grateful for the fact that it wasn't. Truly.

Ashley placed her thumb on the ignition scanner, the Ordo-soft™ logo made its usual, ubiquitous showing, then upon the screen appeared a green infinity symbol, set against a brown, barklike background.

"Hello, Ashley," said the car, in a voice composed entirely from the sounds of various flutes. "Would you like to fly, or would you prefer me to?"

"I'll do the flying," Ashley said. "I'm gonna need to go a little faster than your programming allows." She grasped the black, helicopter-like control stick, and slid her forefinger around the green accelerator trigger. Pulling the stick backwards, she raised the car into the air, high above the forested eight-acre estate.

"Would you like some music to accompany your journey?" the flute-voice asked, its infinity symbol pulsing in rhythmic harmony with its speech.

"Sure, that sounds good." She pulled the accelerator and the vehicle moved forward. "Something that's relaxing–but not *too* slow."

"Very well." The car began to scat a jazzy, up-tempo tune.

# ((FREQUENCIES))

Singing along with the Infinity–which is exactly what she called the creation, feeling that it was already bad enough that a wonderfully illogical concept like infinity had been named in the first place, and not wanting to add to the problem any further by naming it once again–she aimed the Lexus® GS 800™ to the northwest, and increased her finger's pressure upon the trigger.


Minutes later, the mountains surrounding her Issaquah estate were visible on the horizon behind her. She was speeding over one of West Bellevue's gated communities, en route to the university, when she noticed a black Polaris™–definitely belonging to some type of law enforcement agency–hovering in the air above a residence. She quickly reduced her speed to the legal limit, realizing that she was going to be *really* late if she got pulled over.

Better to take it easy and be only a few minutes late–she was sure Professor Brennan would wait. After all, he *was* the one who suggested the meeting, even though it was she who first approached him with the inquiries into the origins of the freeread technology. She recalled their unie conversation last week, and the way his typically uninterested face was lit up with excitement...almost like he couldn't wait to talk to her about the subject. Yeah, she assured herself, he'd wait.

Leaving Bellevue, Ashley continued on towards the Westside, across the waters of Lake Washington. Different types of watercraft, from hydroplanes to hovercrafts to houseboats, littered the lake's sun-streaked surface, appearing to her like little hi-tech bath toys. As other GS vehicles passed by in the air around her, she began to approach the 520 floating bridge. The double-decker freeway, which hovered about twenty feet above the water's surface via GS technology, contained five lanes of traffic going each way on both of its tiered levels. Passing over the bridge and looking down at the gridlocked, gravity-bound vehicles below, her mind was instantly filled with thoughts of wealth and privilege. She couldn't help it–transportation was such an obvious visual example of inequality. In fact, it was so simple and striking to her, that she had even written her honors thesis on the topic while she was at the university.

In the paper, she'd pointed out that the wealthy upper class were literally on top of society, flying around in their expensive GS crafts, high above the congested traffic below them, while the underprivileged lower class owned no vehicles of their own, and were forced to rely on the crowded, city-supported transportation such as the monorails and autobuses. The middle class majority were right in between, owning their own vehicles, but still bound by the laws of gravity. It was an incredibly simplistic notion–ridiculously, even–and that's why she liked it so much. For her, truth existed in the simple, rather than the complex, aspects of life.

Reaching the water's end, Ashley arrived at her point of destination–the University of Washington. She passed over the lakefront location of Husky Stadium, then dropped her altitude as she reached the main campus. After finding a parking space in one of the upper-level garages near the dorms, she extended the rubber landing nubs from the bottom of the Lexus®, and gently set the car down.

As she walked away from the GS 800™, a smooth, silvery sphere, slightly larger in size than a human fist, flew over from another area of the garage. It stopped in front of Ashley, hovered there for a moment, then extended from its base a thumb-sized scanner. "Please pay before leaving," it said in a robotic voice which reminded her of old science-fiction movies. "Digital cash or credit?"

"DC's," she said, placing her right thumb on the scanner.

"Thank you. Have a nice day," it said, then immediately flew off towards another incoming car.

Ashley walked over to the parking garage's elevator and waved her hand over the "down" arrow. The elevator chimed as the car reached her floor, and the nicked metal doors parted open. Inside was a young man of Middle-Eastern descent, most definitely a student, judging from the big, yellow "U of W" logo inconspicuously plastered across his purple sweatshirt. He was wearing a pair of Sony® uniview goggles which were connected by a thin cable to some type of CPU hidden inside of his backpack. A giant grin appeared upon his face at the sight of Ashley.

"*Hey* there," he said.

"Hey," she replied with a smile, as she stepped into the elevator. She went to touch the "ground floor" button but stopped when she saw that it had already been selected. A uniview screen was on each side of the elevator, all showing the exact same program.

"You a student?" he asked, touching the peach fuzz above his upper lip.

Ashley nodded, as the elevator doors closed with a clunky sound. "Aren't we all?" The car started its descent.

He began to nod back, stopped briefly with a look of puzzlement, then finished nodding his head "yes." "So, uh, what's your major?"

"Oh, life and living...that sort of thing." The screens were currently touting the merits of the university's cybernetics labs. Images of people and machines and people-machines kept flashing back and forth.

"Biology, huh? That's chill. Mine's kinda similar–bioinformatics. It's been my focus since elementary. You know about it?"

She asked, "The study of how information theory and its technologies are applied to the fields of genetic analysis and biotechnology?"

"Uh..." He laughed. "Yeah."

She smiled. "I've heard of it."

The car came to a stop, and the doors opened up. Ashley stepped out of the elevator, onto the paved path in front of her.

"Where are you walking to?" he asked, following her out of the elevator, kittenlike.

"To the library–Suzallo." She continued down the path, past the dorms and the National Guard building. "I'm meeting with a former professor of mine."

He increased his pace, now walking right beside her. "I'm going that way also–my next class is in Kane. Mind if I walk with you?"

"No," she said, "that's fine."

As they approached the quad area, the university's old, orange and red brick buildings began to appear. She caught a hint of springtime blossoms in the air.

"By the way," he said, extending his hand, "I'm Sherif."

She shook his hand. "Nice to meet you, Sherif. I'm Ashley."

Reaching the quad, she took in a deep breath and smiled. The Japanese cherry blossoms that filled the area were in full bloom, and the brisk breeze was carrying both the snowlike petals, and their delectable scent, magically through the air. The grass, the brick pathways, nearly everything on the ground around them was covered with the thousands of petals whose majestic ride upon the wind had finally come to an end.

"It's absolutely enchanting, isn't it?" Ashley said.

"What is? The blossoms?"

"The blossoms," she said, turning her head towards the sky, "the sun, the breeze...everything."

He shrugged his shoulders. "I guess so. This is my second year, so I've gotten kind of used to it all." He looked around at the trees as they continued walking. "What's really chill is how they're

27

arranged. Did you know the trees are planted in the shape of a 'W?' Y'know, for 'Washington?'"

Ashley nodded with a heartfelt laugh, Sherif's fondness for the trees' arrangement striking a poignantly humorous chord within her. The truth often made her laugh, and his words and outlook were a telling example of the way style and trivia had supplanted substance and significance in America and the rest of this brave, new world order.

"What?" he asked. "Did I say something funny?"

"No, Sherif," she said reassuringly, "you didn't. Our culture did."

Two seagulls shrieked in unison as they flew by overhead, and he asked, "What do you mean?"

Though it was likely Sherif had some type of academic clearance to think about and discuss the subject, Ashley wasn't sure what his restrictions were, and didn't want to risk the possibility of freeking him out. If someone discussed freeky thoughts without the proper clearance, it could cause them to be negatively databased, investigated, or worse, arrested. Because of her status, *she* didn't have to worry about those kinds of things, but she was always careful to realize that not everyone was so fortunate.

"Oh, nothing. So," Ashley said, changing the subject, "I take it you're wearing the gogs for academic purposes?" She smiled. "Or are they simply a fashion statement?"

Sherif laughed. "No, they're not a fashion statement. I'm just studying some chem notes right now. I've got a test later today." They reached the end of the quad, and were now stepping onto the smooth crimson bricks which covered Red Square. "I don't know what I'd do without them–I save so much time being able to walk around and study all at once. The convenience is great."

Oh no, she thought. He said the "C" word.

Convenience–possibly the most harmful concept Western civilization ever created. How many trees had been cut down, how many cultures displaced, how much of the Earth had been raped in the name of "convenience" she couldn't even imagine. Well, actually, she *could*, but she didn't want to. She liked being aware of evil things and knowing where they were to be found, but didn't necessarily want to visit them any more than she had to.

"Just make sure you know where you're going, Sherif."

"I do, don't worry," he said. "Once you get used to them, you can see right past the text and graphics."

28

# ((FREQUENCIES))

He seemed oblivious to the possibility of her statement having more than one meaning. Which, she figured, was probably a good thing, since she was trying not to freek him out...but, at the same time, she always wanted to spark at least a little bit of questioning in each person whom she encountered.

"Especially when you shrink the screen or make it translucent," he added. "Though the eyemouse doesn't respond as well when you do that."

As they entered Red Square, she looked to her left, towards the ornately carved facade of Suzallo Library, in search of Professor Brennan. Since the human traffic passing through the Square was relatively light, she was able to pick him out of the crowd with ease. Brennan was wearing his regular gray wool overcoat with the matching black- and gray-speckled hat. He held on to a thin silver cane with one hand, while the other was holding a small handheld uniview.

Ashley looked back at Sherif. "I've gotta go now, Sherif, but it's been nice talking to you. Good luck on your exam."

"Thanks." His gaze shifted downwards. "And thanks for walking with me, too."

"Thanks for walking with *me*," she replied. "You're a nice person to share time with."

"So are you," he said with a slightly nervous laugh, starting to backpedal away. "I'll see you around."

She smiled. "Sure." As he turned away from her, towards Kane Hall, she said, "Sherif."

He swung around. "Yeah?"

"One more thing."

"What?"

"The trees will always be more beautiful than the way they're arranged."

"I know," Sherif said. "Matter over method, right?" He smiled, turned, and headed to the hall with a spring in his step.

Ashley smiled too. Maybe he wasn't so oblivious to what she was saying—maybe he was just testing *her* out. Live another day, learn another lesson, she laughed to herself, as she began to walk in Brennan's direction.

The professor's back was turned to her, but when she had nearly reached him, he suddenly turned around and looked up from his uniview screen. "Boo," he said in a quiet tone.

A bit surprised, she asked, "You felt me coming?"

Without saying a word, he turned the uniview towards her.

Upon the screen was a live-feed image of herself.

"Oh, I see," Ashley said, "you cheated. You just patched into the university's camera network. I thought you had sensed my presence or something."

"I did," he replied. "This technology is simply an extension of my eyes, is it not?" He turned the uniview back to himself.

"It is, but it isn't." Ashley looked at him looking at the screen looking at her. "So how long have you been spying on me, professor?"

"Since the parking garage," he said, walking away from the library towards Drumheller Fountain. He touched his cane to the ground occasionally, but it was there more out of habit than for anything else. His bionics ensured that he could walk like a man half his age. "You're late."

"I know," she said. "I'm sorry about that. I had a really nice long workout today, and then my brother called and-"

"No need to explain, dear," he said. "I was a little late myself. We're currently working out the final details of the aeonomics curriculum, and I had a few tasks to complete before I could come down to Suzallo." They walked down the gray concrete steps which led to the fountain. "Immortality's going to pose some interesting economic dilemmas, Ashley."

"I can imagine."

"Yes," he said. "I'm sure you can." Reaching the rim of the giant fountain, which was spouting water about fifteen feet into the air, he turned the uniview off, then placed it inside of his pocket. "But enough of that subject." He looked at Ashley. "You must be wondering why I was so eager to meet with you."

Light mist from the fountain's spray blew coolly onto her face. "I am," she said.

"Come." He motioned to one of the weathered stone benches. "Let's sit down." Ashley walked over to the bench, and they both took a seat. Brennan pulled a lighter and pipe from his inner coat pocket. "Do you mind?"

"No, it's fine. Go ahead." She wasn't just being nice, that was the truth. Since Brennan was an immortalist *and* they were behind the gates, she knew that he would be smoking a non-addictive, non-carcinogenic strain of tobacco. Plus, she didn't mind because pipes just smelled a whole lot better than cigarettes.

"Thank you." Brennan flicked the angled flame of his pipe lighter, raised the fire to the bowl, and gently took a few tokes. Savoring the flavor of the chocolatey-smelling tobacco, he looked off into the distance, and said, "You may or may not know this, Ashley, but my wife and I were recently divorced–after having been married for over seventy years."

"I...I didn't know that, professor. I'm so sorry to hear that..." Ashley shook her head slowly, trying to imagine what it would be like to be with the same person for that long. "All that time spent together...wow."

"Wow, indeed," he said. "It makes one suddenly quite intimate with loneliness, wanting nothing more than to go jump off the proverbial cliff." Brennan smiled musingly. "But, one soon realizes–if they're fortunate enough–that everything happens for a purpose. My wife leaving me, and the resulting loneliness, has caused me to introspect more than I ever have before–and I have learned a great deal about myself in the process." He paused for a moment. "As a man gets older, Ashley, he begins to see the things that were not so apparent to him when he was younger–things that were hidden from his view because of his brashness or arrogance. These things can cause him to look back on past deeds and see them in a new light–to see that, if given the chance to do it all over again, he might do them a bit differently than he did before...that he may have made some mistakes." He blew out some tobacco, little smoke distress signals rising from his mouth. "I've recently seen those things, and realized those mistakes."

Ashley looked him in the eye with empathetic compassion. She'd been there before. "Then you don't need to have any regrets, professor. If you're fortunate enough to become aware of your mistake, and you grow from it–really, truly learn from it–then you've turned something negative into something positive. You don't need to have regrets if you've learned the life lesson the mistake taught you."

He nodded. "Yes, this would be true if it only involved myself. But, unfortunately, this mistake had repercussions *far* beyond my own personal sphere of existence...which is why I have regrets." His eyes squinted slightly. She wasn't sure if it was from the breeze blowing some smoke into his eyes or if it was from the memories. "And regrets can only be alleviated by somehow trying to make amends."

He's not just talking about his marriage anymore, she realized. Was this going to be some sort of giant confession? That certainly wasn't what she was expecting when Brennan had asked her to meet with him. Ashley was all at once curious, apprehensive, and fascinated by the possibilities of what he might say next. She said not a word, and patiently waited for him to continue.

"Ashley," he said, "I've known your grandfather and your

family for a long time, but when you came to the university, I finally had the chance to get to know *you*. And I'm very glad that I've had that opportunity. You were, and always will be, one of my favorite students–one of the few who came into my classes and actually taught *me* a thing or two, rather than always agreeing with everything I had to say. You were always questioning everything, even if that meant sacrificing a grade to voice your opinion." He smoothed his white beard with the palm of his hand. "You're truly a unique individual, my dear. You're experimental, innovative, and willing to think outside of the accepted boundaries–a true scientist, in the best sense of the word."

"Thank you," she said, feeling very flattered by his remarks. "Coming from you that means a lot."

"You're welcome," he said. "But it's not a compliment, it's the truth. Look at you now–you're not even enrolled at the university, yet you're still conducting your own research. That's impressive."

Ashley smiled. "Thanks."

Brennan nodded, then took a few more draws from the pipe. "I see more than just a scientist in you, though, Ashley–above all else, I see hope. I see an honest, genuine caring for other people and other creatures, and a willingness and desire to make this world a better place. Those are rare qualities to find these days, as I'm sure you already know...hell, those were rare qualities in the past–I know that I lacked them when I was younger. I was a great scientist, but I was selfish, and had no compassion for other beings. Essentially, I had no respect for life." Looking down at the pipe, he extinguished the burnt tobacco by pressing his thumb into the bowl. "And this caused me to make some very, *very* short-sighted decisions...and now I must make amends." He looked up from the ashes and said, "When you called me last week, and asked me about the origins of the freeread technology, I realized at that moment that–if there is such thing as a God–this was God's way of allowing me to make up for my past transgressions."

That explained the look of excitement–no, better make that revelation–on his face last week...but that still left the question of "why." "How do you mean...?" she asked.

"I mean that, through you, I can ensure that one man's vision and hopes do not die in secrecy with me. I can keep them alive by revealing to you the truth." He surveyed the area in an almost cautious manner, and said, "You see, Ashley, the man who created the freeread technology never intended it to be used in the manner that it is now."

A bit confused, she asked, "You're referring to yourself, right?

I mean, you are the one who developed the technology, aren't you?"

"Yes, I *developed* it, but I did not create it–someone else did."

"But in the uniview records you're credited with its creation..." Ashley contemplated the implications of his statement. "So," she said, a rush of adrenalin passing through her body along with the full realization, "you're basically saying that all of the records regarding the technology's origins have been fabricated–that it's all a lie."

Brennan closed his eyes and nodded slowly. "That's what I'm saying. Essentially, all I did was steal the creator's idea..." Shame appeared upon his countenance. "And then I applied it in a way that absolutely and utterly degraded his ideals."

He stopped for a moment, letting out a small cough. "Before I go any further, I want to make sure that I'm not forcing any of this knowledge upon you, or making you an unwitting participant in its disclosure. I want to be completely sure that you know what you're doing, because the truth–once known–can never be forgotten. It stays with you always, whether you want it to or not. That is, of course, unless you choose to have those areas of the brain which are tied into that specific memory removed or inhibited..." He smiled. "But I think you see my point. Would you like me to continue, or...?"

"After a setup like that? Are you kidding?" Ashley laughed at the notion of turning back now, just when her research was beginning to yield the kinds of unexpected results that she had been hoping for. "Of course I want you to continue!"

"Well then," he said with a redemptive, hopeful gleam in his eyes, "let me tell you the story of Dr. Adrian Wellor."

# Chapter 3
# ((Westside Stories))

*...when viewed with indifference, dispassion, and apathy,*
*it often became dull and tedious, while a gaze filled with anger,*
*despair, and disrespect was sure to cause the structure to become quite*
*horrible and wretched."*

Morris Ignacio looked into the eyes of the three Freemon surrounding him, just to make sure their attention hadn't wavered.

Takura's cat eyes were eager, ready to pounce on the next word. Jung Ran looked at him intently, her dark brown irises alight with anticipation. Essence's iridescent, pupil-less orbs showed avid interest. He clearly had their attention–so he decided to wait a few more seconds before he continued. Just to build up the suspense.

"Damn, Morris," Essence said, "you just gonna sit there and stare at us or are you gonna finish the fuckin' story? Shit," she said with a small laugh and a smile, "we ain't got all day!" Essence didn't smile often, but when she did it was gorgeous–rich, full, chocolate brown lips parting to reveal ivory white teeth and tight pink gums. He carefully studied her mouth for a moment and imagined what it would feel like to have it wrapped around him.

Ignacio smiled at Essence and took a slow, drawn-out sip of coffee from his black ceramic Starbucks® mug. Over the brim of the cup, he looked around the headquarters' interior, briefly watching the other Freemon as they went about their various tasks and duties. Currently, the large building was bustling with the activity and clamor of well over twenty agents.

"So the freeker pulls his dick out..." Takura said. "C'mon, Mo, what happens next? Did you nap him?"

"He won't even finish a story without stopping and watching the way people react to it," Jung said. "You think he's going to hit the freeker with a disruptor before he can watch a little more?"

Ignacio laughed at Jung's comment–incisive as usual. "Es verdad, Jung, es verdad." He took another sip of coffee, then set the mug down on the desk beside him. "Bueno," he said, "so the guy unzips his pants, unfurls his flag, grabs a tight hold of it, and starts shakin' it around like it was a puppy who had just pissed on his brand new coat–you know, fuckin' it up with an attitude!" He shook his head and laughed, the vision still fresh in his mind. "Then, he starts screamin' down at it, real loud–'You were meant for reproduction but all you are is a sterilized piece of shit! All you're good for is fucking whores and coming when the sexsims tell you to! You can't even make one single goddamn baby!'" Ignacio looked back up at the others. "The employees around him are literally freekin' out, you know? Blud's normal one minute, the next he's flashin' his pito at 'em! And then, he keeps on goin' with his schtick–'You can't even get it up sometimes! What good is the credit you got if you can't even do what you're made to do, hunh?!'"

"Imagine what your wife must be feeling," came a familiar, raspy voice from behind Ignacio.

He was wondering when he was going to show his unkempt face this morning. Smiling, Ignacio looked up from his pelvic area and turned towards the voice. McCready was wearing his usual hunter-green trenchcoat, the usual khaki pants, and of course, the usual Obsidians™. He reeked of clobacco–still smoking the usual Kamels®. "Hola, huedo," Ignacio said. "¿Qué pasa?"

"What's up?" McCready asked. "Apparently not you from what I just heard." He seated himself on Essence's Gelaform™ chair.

Essence looked at McCready, her perfectly sculpted, ebony face turning to a scowl. "Fool, I didn't say you could sit in my chair."

"Cuidado, patrón," he said to McCready, "I see a storm blowing your way." The warning was for McCready's own good. Ignacio knew Essence's temper could flare up quicker than a plasma torch–and then burn you worse. She had the harshest, toughest persona of just about any of the Freemon, undoubtedly due to the fact that she was one of the few who had been recruited directly from the workcamps. She'd personally seen shit that most people only saw edited on the uniview, or at most, had simmed in VR. She'd seen the *real* thing, and it showed. And maybe that was why Ignacio found her so attractive. So intriguing. She knew things he didn't.

"Well, too bad," McCready said to Essence. "You're sitting in mine."

"So?" Essence asked.

McCready touched the side of his face, rubbing some of his light black stubble. "So I'm sitting in yours–now kick my ass or deal with it."

Essence raised her left hand toward McCready, then pointed at him with her index finger. She gave him a look both playful and malicious, as the bronze chain connecting her pierced ear and nose glinted under the NatraLites™. "Don't tempt me, McCready," she said. "I just might." And that was no lie. She could–and would–do it. With just a point of the finger and a thought, she could nap his ass instantly, since her disruptors were implanted in her hand and tied into her nervous system.

"Forget about it, Ess!" Takura said. "I want to hear how the story ends *before* I have to get back to work!"

"Yeah, the man's trying to hear a story, alright?" McCready said with a wry grin. "Show some respect."

"Shit..." Essence brushed her hand into the air towards McCready as if she was trying to get rid of a bad smell. "Lucky I don't knock you in your grill."

Ignacio laughed hard. McCready was always pushing Essence's buttons in the wrong way. "You tired of living, McCready?" he asked. "You play with fire, boy..."

"You get burned," McCready said. "I know." He pulled out a device resembling a laser cauterizer and pointed it towards Essence. "Which is why I always carry an extinguisher." He shot a small burst of chilled nitrogen gas from the device's tip.

Essence quickly moved back from the cold burst, then leaned forward and threw a swift jab at McCready.

McCready raised his right arm in time to deflect the blow, Essence's implanted brass knuckles clanging hard on the metal alloy of his bionic limb. Ignacio could tell the punch was thrown more to mess with McCready than to actually knock him out. If she had truly intended to hurt him, he'd already be sprawled out on the ground, bloodied and unconscious.

Sensing that Essence wasn't going to throw another jab, McCready relaxed his arm a little bit. "Alright, so what *is* the story at hand?" he asked, still cautiously eyeing Essence. "Fill me in."

"Naw, man," Takura said, "you don't get a recap–you already wasted enough time! I'm ready to hear the rest of the damn story!"

"Briefly," Jung said to McCready, picking up a navel orange from off of her desk, "Ignacio responded to a freeker reading over at Opticon™ in Kirkland." She looked down at the bar code and Sunkist® logo gengineered into the skin of the orange, then started to peel it. "A guy was freeking out about sterilizing himself for DC credits, and then..."

"He whipped out his tunnel rat and started playing drill sergeant with it," McCready said. "I get it. Thanks for the update, Jung." He looked up at Ignacio and extended his hand. "Please continue with your sordid tale, amigo. You have my complete and undivided attention."

"Gracias." Ignacio reached down to his groin, grabbing the air in front of it like an imaginary cock. "So now the freeker's so angry and worked up, he's not just shakin' his pito anymore, it's more like he's strangling it–trying to choke it to death for all the shit he thinks it's responsible for. And he's bein' hella loud now, so I start reaching down to my belt to grab my disruptor. As I'm doing this, he's still yellin' down at it and starts saying, 'You worthless shit, you can't reproduce, but there's still one thing you're good for, isn't there?! You can still piss, can't you?!' Y no mento," Ignacio said with a hearty laugh, "vato starts pissin' on his desk, his uniview, the employees around him–everything."

Laughter from the other four Freemon.

"Hold up," Takura said with a grin, biting into a green spirulina Power Bar®. "Everything would include *you*, wouldn't it?"

"It would have," Ignacio said, "if I hadn't been keeping the recommended spatial distance between an agent and a conscious freeker. But I was–so that put me *outside* his urinary range."

"Alright," Takura laughed. "Go on."

"So," Ignacio continued, "vato manages to sprinkle on a few other employees before I can get a good bead on him. Holding in my laughter–'cause I'm tellin' you, I wanted to just start bustin' up–I nap him and he drops to the ground, his pito still hangin' out the front of his pants like it was playin' fucking peek-a-boo. Now at this point, I'm ready to slap a GS disc on him and be up out of there, but then one of the people that got pissed on starts freekin' out also. She starts talkin' about, 'If they can hear us *all* the time, then why do we even bother to speak? What's the point, when everything you say is heard by someone, somewhere? I've designed laser microphones that can

37

hear through windows, walls, buildings...' She looked right at me then, her white cashmere top all stained with yellow piss, and calmly says, 'We've even designed ones that can hear you from outer space. Did you know that somebody, or some*thing*, is listening to us right now? And they're documenting everything? Did you know that?'"

Ignacio paused, mimicking her numb stare. "So now I'm figuring I'm probably gonna have to nap her, too, 'cause the other freeker's thoughts have already infected her. But then, before I get a chance to even think my next thought, this *other* blud, who also got pissed on, starts goin' off on what *she* was talkin' about. 'And I've worked on lasers mounted into satellites that can lock on to an earthly target and destroy it instantly. At the speed of light. That means you're never safe. Anywhere. You can be hit with a laser at any time if they decide they want you dead. The optical eyes in the skies—they see everything.'"

"So what'd you do?" asked Takura.

Ignacio waited a long second, and said, "Since they weren't freakin' out real bad and they weren't yellin' or screaming, I decided I'd go easy on 'em. I put away my disruptor..." He picked up his coffee and took a sip. "And that was pretty much it–I walked over to both of 'em, placed a white-noise generator around their necks, then called the corpos over to take 'em to their in-house holding cells for disinfection."

"Waitaminute," Essence said. "What did you do with the pisser?"

"The usual," Ignacio replied. "Isolated him, detained him, brought him here for processing, then sent him off to the judges for sentencing."

"No, no," Essence said, shaking her head to match her words. "I know the procedure–I mean what did you do with dude's dick?"

"Yeah, slick," Erik said, laughing, "did you just leave it hanging out while you dragged him to your car, or did you put it back in his pants for him?"

"You fuckers are all depraved," McCready sneered.

"Meaning you're not?" Jung asked.

"I didn't say that," McCready replied. "I just said that you all were."

Pointing at himself, Ignacio looked at Takura with disbelief. "You think *I* was gonna touch his dick?" He fervently shook his head. "No. ¡No quiero un pito en mi mano! I told the corpos he was company property and it was their jurisdiction to make sure *their* property could be removed from the premises in a less objectionable manner."

"What a load of crap!" laughed Jung. "Did it work?"

"Sí–luckily they were both rookie corpos who were afraid to cause a stir by contradicting a Freemon. So one of 'em slapped on a pair of rubber gloves, and tucked junior back into bed. Then I carted him away." Ignacio smiled. "End of story."

"Man," Takura said, "you always get the crazy cases, Mo. You must be, like, a magnet for weirdness or some shit."

"He is," Jung said, noticing the director of their division walking towards them. "And a magnet for Moore."

"Freemon Ignacio," boomed the deep, bass-heavy voice of Harold Moore, "so nice of you to detail the accounts of your day to your fellow Freemon with so much energy and enthusiasm." The director paused, the dark brown skin on his forehead wrinkling into disapproval. "If only you could channel that same verve into isolating your frequency emissions violators *before* they have a chance to spread their memetic infection to others." Broad-shouldered, standing six feet four inches tall, the director was an intimidating physical presence. "Need I remind you of your memetics training?"

"No, sir," Ignacio said. "I remember." One of the most basic rules of the Freemon memetics curriculum was: In a situation where there is an imminent threat that a freeker could spread an infectious meme, isolate first and ask questions later. Ignacio knew he'd fucked up. He had broken a rule, and Moore stuck to rules like a Rasta to reefer–religiously. "I apologize, sir," he respectfully said. "I'll make sure it doesn't happen again."

Moore nodded. "See that you do, Ignacio. It's essential that a veteran Freemon like yourself set a proper example by following procedure correctly." He stoically stared at Ignacio, then at the four other agents surrounding him. Turning his Medusa-like gaze back at Ignacio, Moore said, "You're one of the oldest–and best–agents we have, Ignacio, but if you break the rules...you're gonna break yourself. Understand?"

"Sí." The director was going easy on him right now, and Ignacio knew it. He could have been docked credit, suspended, or worst case scenario, demoted–but Moore had chosen to do none of those things. Ignacio was lucky getting off with only a verbal grilling, though in actuality, it wasn't luck that had gotten him off the hook, it was history. He'd known Moore for well over twenty years, dating all the way back to their original FBI training. Moore thought of him as a friend, and Ignacio was glad that still counted for something.

"Now," Moore said, "on to more pressing matters. The city police are currently responding to a disturbance taking place in the Rainier Valley. Multiple freeread violations have already occurred there, and the likelihood of an outbreak is high if we don't isolate the infected individuals quickly. Ignacio," he said, adjusting a cufflink on his black suit, "I want you, McCready, Kwon, and Sommers to respond to the situation. Takura, I want you to notify the police that we're sending some agents over to assist them, then continue to monitor the situation online. This will be a joint federal/local operation, and even though you do have jurisdiction in these matters, please be respectful of SPD's methods and procedures–work with them and they'll work with you. Now, get your butts over there ASAP." He started to walk away towards his office, then turned around to face them once again. "And Ignacio..."

"¿Sí?"

"Try to prevent the omegas from pissing on the alphas, OK?" Moore nodded, showed the slightest hint of a smirk, and resumed his walk to the office.

Laughter from the other four Freemon.

"Yeah, yeah..." Ignacio said, picking up his black leather jacket. "Well, don't just sit there," he said to his fellow agents. "You heard the man–let's get movin'! ¡Vámonos!"


Ignacio and McCready flew out of the Beacon Hill headquarters' garage, Sommers and Kwon following right behind them in a similar, standard-issue Polaris™.

He had decided it would be a good idea to split Essence and Marc up, so he'd assigned her to fly with Jung. Ignacio would have volunteered himself to go with Essence, but he didn't want to be in the same car with her right now–too much temptation. And he'd been giving in to temptation a lot lately.

They began to head south on automatic towards the Rainier Valley, as some 20th-century funk song played on McCready's stereo. "All o' my purple life," came the singer's synthesized voice through the speakers.

"You ever listen to anything *new*, McCready?" Ignacio asked.

"Nah, not really," McCready said, reaching into the back seat to retrieve something. "Everything put out now's just a bunch of watered-down crap. You listen to the uniview and everybody sounds like fuckin' androids on barbiturates." He returned from his back seat

40

quest with a bright plastic snack bag. "Back in the day, people still actually sang with some feeling."

"There's still some good shit bein' made today." Ignacio took a sip of Coke® as he watched the cartoon Marilyn, currently dressed in blue jeans and a tie-top, dance to the music on the uniview. "You just gotta look for it."

"Yeah, well, I guess I'm not looking then." McCready tossed a few of the small, reddish-orange snacks into his mouth and noisily munched on them.

Ignacio glanced over at McCready's food. "Those any good?"

McCready handed him the bag. "I wouldn't call 'em 'good.' More like 'not bad.'"

Ignacio ate a few, made a sour face, then looked at the front of the bag. "'Tiny Tamales™?' This shit does *not* taste like tamales. Tastes more like dog food." He gave the bag back to McCready.

"What do you expect, man? It's dog food for people–that's what all these little packaged snack foods are. Kibbles N' Bits®, Tiny Tamales™–same shit, different species."

"If they're just dog food, patrón, then why does everyone keep eating 'em?" Ignacio loved asking McCready questions like this. Guaranteed entertainment.

"Because everyone's too fuckin' stupid not to," he said. "We buy what we're sold, when we're told." A look appeared upon McCready's face–the same look which always appeared when he spoke about society–best described as a combination of frustration, disgust, and disappointment. "Man, we've been trained so well... There's no creature on the whole fuckin' Earth that's better trained than us. People put dogs to shame when it comes to obedience."

"Marc," Ignacio said with a laugh, "it's a good thing you're a Freemon."

"Why's that? 'Cause of my thoughts?"

"Sí."

"Wouldn't matter–I'd just keep the thoughts to myself. They don't give a fuck what you think as long as you keep quiet."

"But you wouldn't be keepin' quiet," Ignacio said. "That's not your nature. You'd be freekin' out in regular society–talkin' away like there was no tomorrow–trust me. I'd have already had to come for your ass by now." He laughed. "Actually, it'd probably be Essence who came for you."

"Fuck that," McCready said. "I'd rather chew on razor wire." He pulled out a toothpick and placed it between his lips. "Hey, speaking of Essence–what's up with the way you look at her?"

"What do you mean?" Ignacio asked, feigning ignorance.

"'What do I mean?' You know what I mean. The way you act towards her, the way you treat her–you know."

"She *is* fine," Ignacio confessed, realizing there was no point in lying to McCready. If he could trust anyone with his secrets, it was Marc. For one thing, he'd known him for over four years, ever since McCready transferred from the SPD to the Freemon, and had found him to be a solid and reliable individual. Second, McCready tended not to let other people get too close to him–whether they were Freemon or not–and therefore didn't really have anyone to gossip *to*. Third, and most important, McCready had revealed to him so many of his fringe beliefs that, as his superior, Ignacio could utterly wreck his career and life at any time if he decided to do so. He ran two fingers lightly over his mustache, and said, "Somethin' about her that just turns me on, patrón. Her harshness, combined with that body and face..."

Ignacio imagined himself, his Levi's® and boxers pulled down to his knees, sitting at the edge of a bed covered with velvety, purple sheets, Essence standing there before him in her tight black bodysuit. He looked up and down the mental figure, examining everything from her curly black hair to her large, firm breasts; from her thick, rounded hips, all the way down to her muscular thighs and calves. He especially found himself drawn towards her nipple ring–the round, brass metal piercing through the taut, shiny plastic fabric of her bodysuit, penetrating all the way, deep, into the soft warm flesh beneath. Ignacio wanted his lips around her nipple, to tongue the cold metal in his mouth. In his mind, he leaned his head forward, towards her pierced breast, just as she reached out and grabbed a firm hold of his exposed erection. He opened his mouth, her hand began to slowly move up and down him, he closed his eyes and–

"Damn," Ignacio said, snapping out of his daydream and noticing the steady, throbbing pressure rising underneath his boxers. "Tell me you wouldn't love to rip off that bodysuit and just start...mmmm. Tell me you wouldn't."

"Alright," McCready said. "I wouldn't love to rip off that bodysuit and just start 'mmmming' her."

"Bullshit," Ignacio said.

"Trueshit, man–she freaks me out. She's a fake–iridescent eyes, a face scanned straight from Victoria's Secret®, tits that defy gravity..."

"And this is *bad* to you?"

"Yeah, man, it's fuckin' creepy. You ever seen the mug shots of her from before the plastic surgeries and augmentations? Was she even female?" McCready asked with a laugh. "I'm sorry, but there's no fuckin' way I could have sex with anybody who changed themselves that much."

"What are you, a maricón? What does it matter what she used to look like? Look at what she looks like now!"

"I don't care, man–it just doesn't seem right."

Ignacio laughed. Sometimes McCready was so old-fashioned, he made compact discs seem cutting edge. "'Right?' Where did you come up with that idea? Nobody gives a shit what's 'right' any-more–we're in 21st-century America, patrón! This ain't no holy land! Don't fool yourself." He laughed again. "I'm tellin' you, boy–forget that moral bullshit. It'll just tie you down and make you weak."

"Maybe, maybe not," McCready said. As the music continued to play, synthesized flutes mixing with heavy bass, he added, "Don't take this the wrong way, man, but...honestly, I think Irena is a hundred times more attractive than Essence. I mean, your wife is truly a beautiful woman, not some high-strung, half-human, laboratory concoction from the workcamps."

Ignacio felt anger rise up within him, and he questioned why this was happening. Was it because McCready was criticizing Essence? Because he found his wife attractive? Or was it because McCready's comments brought to light the obvious fact that Ignacio was always trying to hide from himself–that he didn't really care for his wife like he used to? It was a combination of all of them, and Ignacio didn't like it. Through incensed eyes, he looked over at his fellow agent and said, "Watch yourself, Marc."

McCready, staring straight ahead at the holographic billboards covering the city's skyline, noticed neither the look in Ignacio's eyes nor the tone in his voice. "You got a loving wife, two great kids..." he said unmindfully. "A true family. That's a rare thing, man. I don't see how you could think of that Frankenstein chick when you got-"

That was not what Ignacio wanted to hear. Not with the thought of nipple rings and plastic fabric still parading throughout his mind. "¡Callate!" he shouted, slamming his fist down hard onto the vehicle's dashboard. "I told you to watch it, McCready!"

McCready put up his hands, palms facing out towards Ignacio. "Whoa, Morris," he laughed in a surprised and uncomfortable tone, "ease up, man! Damn. I didn't mean anything by that. I just..." He shook his head and looked away from Ignacio. "...I just think you have a lot to be thankful for," he said, more to himself than to Ignacio. "That's all."

McCready was speaking truthfully–Ignacio *did* have a lot to be thankful for–but there was always two sides to every story. Someone had once told him that nothing is wholly true, but everything is partly true. Ignacio could relate to that right now. It was true that he should be thankful for Irena and the kids–and he was grateful for them. Family, stability, and comfort were what most people strived all of their lives to attain. But, at the same time, Ignacio was so goddamn *sick* of comfortability. He was sick of coming home, night after night, to the same woman, the same sex, the same house, the same uniview programs...the same life. And this was why he found himself inventing excuses to stay out late after work; why he found himself outside the gates more and more, indulging in everything from alcohol to whores; why he found himself fantasizing about Essence, and every other female who turned him on, so much. He wanted the life he and Irena had together, but he also wanted more excitement. More intrigue. He wanted both.

"Marc," the car said, "we are nearing the coordinates that Agent Moore sent to me. Would you like me to land in an appropriate area, or would you prefer to take manual control?"

"Manual, N.J.," McCready said with irritation. "I want to survey the area before I set us down." He was obviously pissed off, and, as Ignacio's temper cooled down, he realized that McCready had every right to be. Ignacio knew that he shouldn't have exploded on him like that. But he had, and he couldn't change the fact now. He'd have to make it up to him later.

"Enlarge rear-view screen 15 percent," McCready said, bringing the car down from its emergency vehicle altitude, "zoom in 20 percent, and show only the feeds coming from the bottom cameras–that should give us a good idea of what's going on down there."

The scene below came into focus, as Led Zeppelin's "Kashmir" started to play on the stereo.

"¿Qué...?" Ignacio asked.

There were numerous SPD vehicles–ranging from the typical sky-blue patrol cars and Hummers®, to the specialized SWAT tanks and helicopters–surrounding and barricading an area about the size of three large city blocks. Inside the area was a crowd of at least a hundred citizens, presumably residents of the housing complexes found within, angrily marching around with some type of simple weapon in their hands. They were holding everything from kitchen knives, baseball bats, and glass bottles, to basic home-security devices such as pepper sprays and stun guns. As yet, the people were only yelling at the police and not attacking. The occasional object was being thrown, but the police paid no attention to it, easily deflecting the projectiles with their large riot shields. It appeared neither side was escalating the conflict. Yet.

What the hell was going on here? Ignacio asked himself. This was what Moore had referred to as a "disturbance?" Shoot, this was more like a full-blown riot. The director wasn't known to down-play a situation–which meant the scene had most likely intensified since Moore was informed about it. Ignacio looked over at McCready. "What do you think?"

"Definitely some kind of riot," he said, stopping the Polaris'™ descent as he examined the screen. "But bigger than anything I've ever seen. When I was with the department, we occasionally had to deal with crowds and protests and what not, but I don't remember anything this big in size or intensity happening. Just look at the police response," he said, putting the tip of his finger into the holographic screen. "They don't bring out those SWAT tanks unless something big's goin' down." He breathed a heavy sigh. "Fuck, this is gonna get ugly."

Ignacio wanted more information before he engaged a situation of this magnitude. It was important to isolate freekers as quick as possible, but in a case like this, where infection was already widespread and the area was secure, the rules changed a bit. "Let's give a call down there and find out what's goin' on," he said. "Any idea who'd be running the police op?"

McCready nodded. "Should be Maggioli. N.J., is there a Louie Maggioli in the area?"

The cartoon Marilyn gave him a big "thumbs-up." "Biochip data shows a Louis Bruno Maggioli currently in the general vicinity."

"Alright, good," McCready said. "Patch me through to his wristcom."

A few moments passed, then the slightly chubby, heavily pockmarked face of Louis Maggioli appeared on the uniview screen. "McCready," he said in a gravelly voice, taking a fat cigar from out of his mouth, "long time no see. I take it this ain't no personal call."

"'Fraid not, Louie," McCready said. "Strictly Freemon business. What's goin' on down there?"

"A riot," Maggioli said with an obnoxious laugh. "What the fuck else does it look like? Them sunglasses too dark to see through?"

McCready smiled. "I appreciate the display of witty humor, Luno, but would you mind tellin' me what the riot is all about? We've got multiple freeker readings down there and we're gonna need to do some isolations–quick."

"Well, quit your yappin' then and get your ass down here. I don't have time to talk to a wristcom all day." Maggioli took a puff from his cigar, then blew the smoke towards the screen. "I got me a ruckus to attend to." He severed the connection, his face morphing into the cartoon Marilyn.

"Ey, patrón," Ignacio said, lightly tapping McCready's shoulder with the back of his hand, "that where you get your personality from?"

"From ol' Luno? I sure as hell hope not."

"Luno?"

"You know, like 'luna,' the moon–but with an 'o,' so I don't offend his strong masculine identity."

"You call 'im Luno 'cause of the craters on his face?" Ignacio laughed. "That's cold, blud, that's cold."

"Yeah, but what's really cold is that he thinks I'm just combining his first and middle name together, so he never really minds · when I call him that. In fact, other people on the force even started callin' him Luno while I was there." McCready laughed. "They thought it was a fuckin' term of endearment or something."

Ignacio's wristcom began to vibrate. Still laughing, he touched a button on the side of the device.

"What's the situation?" Jung asked. "Are we going down there, or are we waiting till the dust settles?"

"We're gonna go down and get a debriefing from the head of the police op, Jung," Ignacio said, trying to sound a bit more serious than he felt. "Then we'll go from there. Just follow us."

"Will do," Jung replied.

"Luno," Ignacio said, letting out a few final laughs as he turned off the miniature screen. "That's cold as a pole, patrón."

McCready smirked. "N.J., lock on to Maggioli's location and land us nearby."

The Polaris™ flew towards the requested destination, as the Marilyn toon seated herself inside of a '57 Chevy®. Ignacio smiled, partly at the cartoon and partly because of the cartoon's owner. "Marc," he said, placing his hand on the younger Freemon's shoulder, "lo siento mucho–I'm sorry."

"No problemo," McCready said with a laugh. "It's cool, man, I'm used to it–I piss everybody off. Why should it be any different with you?"

"Because it *is* different with me, Marc. Tú es mi compañero de armas–mi hermano. ¿Comprendes?" Ignacio smiled, affectionately shaking McCready's shoulder. "Let me make it up to you–come over to my house tonight and have dinner with mi familia."

"It's okay, Mo, really," he said. "There's nothing to make up. Besides, Hungry Man® will be hella disappointed if I don't eat his compartmentalized dinner tonight."

"I'll say one last word to you about the subject, then I'll drop it." Ignacio paused. "Molé."

"*Chicken* molé?"

"Sí."

"*Irena's* chicken molé?"

"Sí."

"What time's dinner?"

Ignacio let out a loud, bellowing laugh as the Polaris™ settled onto the ground, right next to a GS patrol car. Jung and Essence landed directly behind them.

As Ignacio and McCready got out of the car, the scene–aided now by the sounds and not just the sights–assumed the insane aura that was to be expected in a situation like this. There was yelling and screaming from both sides of the barricade, various types of police sirens and chirps, the crashing sounds of glass breaking and objects being thrown. Add to this the sights of multiple flashing lights and the sheer number of cops, police vehicles, and citizens in the area, and–for an extremely ordered society–the scene could be aptly described as a shot of raw, black-tar anarchy straight into the city's bloodstream.

Essence and Jung stepped out of their car, surveying the situation as they joined Ignacio and McCready.

"¿Es muy loco, no?" Ignacio asked, spreading his arms out to the surrounding scene.

"It's definitely that," said Jung.

Essence looked around through her swirling, rainbow eyes. "Reminds me of the workcamps," she said. "Except tamer."

"Let's go check it out," McCready said, firing up a cigarette as he moved towards the SPD blockade. "Louie should be right in the area."

As they neared the barricade's perimeter, Louis Maggioli walked over to greet them, two cops in full riot gear flanking his sides. "Well, well, well," he said, stogie in hand, "there he is–the big Free*man*, Marc McCready. Such an honor to see you again in person." He laughed that obnoxious laugh again. Ignacio had known this character barely ten minutes and he already wanted to smack him upside his head.

"Everybody," McCready said, "this is Louie Maggioli–he's runnin' the police op today." A helicopter passed overhead, its thin blades barely making a sound. "I'm sure you'll enjoy his classy personality–hell, he's the guy who put the 'ass' in class."

"Still got that smart mouth, huh, McCready?" Maggioli took a few draws from his Don Diego®. "It still get you in trouble like it used to?" He laughed. "I bet it does."

Ignacio was sick of hearing him talk. "I'm Freemon Ignacio," he announced, pulling out his badge. "And I'm in charge here. Let's skip the unnecessary commentary– just give us the facts about what's going on." He touched the side of his wristcom, activating the tiny microphone housed within it, as well as the microcamera and b/free scanner installed in his contact lenses. He looked over at Essence, and the ultrathin lenses automatically scanned her: Essence Freesia Sommers, #285-947-3213. Pure orange on the pyramid.

Essence nodded, indicating that the microcameras inside of her eyes were also sending a live feed to the Freemon databanks. Two live-feed records were always preferable to one.

"You want the facts, huh?" Maggioli looked Ignacio up and down, slowly nodding his smooth, bald head. "Okay, Freeman, here's what we know. Yesterday, in front of these same housing complexes, a few of our officers had an altercation with some punks who were conducting an illegal, non-commercial gathering."

"And what was the nature of this gathering?" Ignacio asked, as his scanner transmitted its data to the lenses' displays: Louis Bruno Maggioli, #027-892-9212. Yellowish-orange. Ignacio figured he'd get a reading like this from Maggioli–typically alpha-beta, sometimes crossing into the lower gamma range when confronted with unusual conditions or freekers, but rarely, if ever, thinking deeply about himself, the current situation, or his place within it–and that was exactly how it was supposed to be. If Maggioli had been in the omega range right now, he'd be in the wrong line of work.

"There were about ten of 'em," Maggioli said, "all teenagers, sittin' in a circle and playin' their jungle drums real loud–thinkin' they were little Tarzans and Shaka Zulus an' shit. You know how all the kids are into that tribal crap." He held one finger up. "Hold on, I got a call."

"Luno," came the female voice through his wristcom, "we're all ready over here–area's secure and all live feeds from the street-cams have been temporarily disabled. Just give us the signal when you're ready for us to engage."

They still called him Luno, Ignacio thought. He glanced over at McCready with a smile. McCready gave him a sly smirk back.

"Not too long now, Mortara–stay ready." Loosening his collar, Maggioli looked back up at Ignacio. "Where was I?"

"The kids and the drums," replied Ignacio.

"Oh yeah," said Maggioli. "So the officers tell the kids to disperse, the kids talk some smack back at the officers, one thing leads to another...and the officers end up bustin' a few of the punks' heads in the process of arrestin' 'em. Only problem is, they get a little *too* excited, and kill three of 'em."

Ignacio cocked an eyebrow. "You mean they killed these kids in front of the whole neighborhood?"

"Right."

"Please tell me they had the intelligence to use their laser pistols."

Maggioli shook his head. "They used fists and steel whips–it was messy."

Ignacio stared at Maggioli with disbelief. These were basic rules of *all* law enforcement agencies that the officers had gone against. Simple rules: In public, always use weapons that can strike from a distance–the more subtle the attack, the less likely it will be to evoke an emotional response in anyone viewing the incident. Always try to avoid the use of lethal force, especially in front of civilians–if lethal force is deemed necessary, it should always occur out of sight, away from the public's eye. If the public use of lethal force cannot be avoided, always use a laser or microwave pistol to execute the task, preferably a single shot to the heart–thus ensuring a quick, clean, and efficient kill, since lasers destroy and cauterize all at once and microwave damage is only visible on the target's insides. Simple rules–so why hadn't they been followed?

"What the hell were they thinking?" Ignacio asked.

"Hey, bein' a cop ain't easy, Freeman," Maggioli said. "They must'a just snapped that day, I don't know. But I *do* know that all four officers are on suspension right now until further review.

Anyhow, just about a half hour ago, a bunch of these kids' family comes out in front of the complexes and they start shoutin' at everyone who's passin' by and causin' a ruckus. They didn't do nothin' like this yesterday, but suddenly today they're mad as hell and they ain't gonna take it any more. So somebody calls the cops, but by the time the patrol car gets down here, the crowd that *was* only family has grown now to nearly a hundred people. The officers on the scene immediately-"

Maggioli stopped mid-sentence, as a bottle came flying out from inside the barricade and crashed nearby, sending shards of green glass everywhere. "That's it," he said. "I can't wait any longer to secure this area. The update's gonna have to wait. Mortara..." he said into his wristcom, carefully looking over the scene. "Commence engagement."

As soon as Maggioli spoke the word, laser strobes mounted on the SWAT tanks and helicopters pulsed intense bursts of light into the eyes of the angry mob, immediately blinding them by damaging their retinas. As the people confusedly staggered around, the police hit them with concentrated blasts of sound, completely taking away their hearing and inducing an even stronger sense of vertigo and bewilderment than they were experiencing before.

The cops in riot gear adjusted their thick black body armor—especially making sure their visored helmets were thoroughly secure, since that was their main protection against the strobes and sonics—then rushed into the barricade and surrounded the crowd on all sides. Ignacio estimated there were about forty riot cops, all wielding electrified batons and dense plastic shields capable of shooting large bursts of pepper spray and immobilizing foam from their centers. After forming a tight circle around the disoriented mob, the police closed in.

The citizens never had a chance—they were like unthinking atoms caught inside a fusion reactor. The cops huddled them together into one big nucleus with their shields, then released all of the crowd's energy by shocking them with their batons. It was all over in well under a minute. All that remained of the mob was a pile of comatose bodies—male and female, black and white, young and old—each of them with blank and confused stares etched into their unconscious faces.

And from here it was only going to get worse. Since they were low income, they would be processed and sentenced quickly, many before they even had a chance to awake from the baton's shock. For most of them, that sentence would be termination in a micronizer, where their biomass would be converted into energy and raw materials. A select few, maybe ten or twenty, would be detained for questioning about the incident, then placed in a workcamp where they would more than likely spend the rest of their lives doing who knows what. Each camp made people do different things–or did different things to people. If even one citizen made it back home from today's incident, Ignacio knew it would be a miracle.

As the strobes discontinued their flashing and the cops put away their batons, Maggioli said, "Nice job, Mortara–real nice. Now cart the sleepers into the paddy wagons and tell everyone to get ready for a sweep of the complexes. We gotta see what we got left in there." Maggioli turned off his wristcom and looked over at Ignacio. "Just another day on the Westside, right?" he laughed. It wasn't even obnoxious anymore, it was detestable. "I imagine you guys'll be accompanying us on the sweep, so you can-"

Ignacio held up his hand. "Shh," he said, feeling a vibration on his wrist. "Call's coming in." He touched his wristcom.

"Ignacio, everything chill over there?" Takura asked. "I was watching the streetcams, but then a bunch of commercials came on."

"Está bien," Ignacio said. "The cops took care of the situation. We're just about to sweep the housing complexes and the surrounding area, then we'll know a little more."

"Let me know when you do," Takura said. "Moore wants to know...well, more, when you get the chance. Also, we just got a call from Mercer Island requesting assistance from a Freemon. Moore specifically stated that you, Jung, and Essence are to stay there at the scene, and he wants McCready to head over to the skyland." Takura paused. "Man, that must have been crazy over there. I got more than a hundred freeker readings before they were flatlined. Something weird's going on."

"Sí, es muy extraño," Ignacio agreed, staring at the sheer number of unconscious bodies being taken into the paddy wagons. "Is that all, Tak?"

"At least for now," he said. "Just contact me with the updates–you know the frequency. I'm ghost." Takura's image faded from the small screen.

Ignacio looked at McCready. "Guess you're headin' out of here, patrón." The contacts' scanners read McCready's data: Marcus Christopher McCready, #153-034-0916. Omega red, as usual.

"That's fine with me," he said, taking a pull from what

remained of his cigarette. "I don't really have any desire to be here."

Maggioli laughed. "What, you feelin' sick? Can't stomach police work no more?"

"Nah, pig," McCready said, "just sick of the stench coming from you and your filthy pen." He flicked his cigarette at Maggioli, turned around without seeing whether or not it hit him, and walked away towards his car. "See you tonight, Ignacio," he said loudly over the din.

"Fuckin' idiot," Maggioli muttered, brushing the ash marks off his coat. He looked at the remaining Freemon. "You guys ready to go sweepin'?"

Ignacio checked his wristcom to confirm that his surveillance devices were still recording. "Sí," he said, "let's go. You can finish your story about what happened earlier as we walk."

"Oh yeah, right," Maggioli said, as they entered the barricaded area. "One question, though," he said, moving out of the way of an armored officer who was dragging a limp body in each hand. "What part of the story we at?"

## Δ

:

# α

## Chapter 4
## ((Virtue and Reality))

*"Within most frequential structures, there existed entities who
desired to play the very strings which the structure itself was
composed of, in order that they might conduct the harmonic melody
which the frequencies instinctively vibrated in tune with. In essence,
these beings sought to bend and shape the fundamental frequencies
into a creation of their own design, thus allowing them to control the
way that they, and all others around them, would perceive and
experience this ephemeral, eternal structure which came to be known
as 'reality.'*

The day could not have been more perfect.

The sun was shining brightly, not a cloud in the sky. The
ambient temperature was warm, the air moist yet refreshing, carrying
upon it the lovely scents of springtime blossoms. The gray jays sounded
their cheerful songs from the branches of the giant evergreens
covering the surface of Mount Si, as squirrels and chipmunks eagerly
scurried about in search of their next meal.

He stood in front of the trunk of a large Douglas fir, examining
an interestingly shaped burl which was growing out from it. As he ran
the tips of his fingers along the wooden outgrowth's many curves and
grooves, he took a generous bite from a plump, juicy apple, and softly
crushed the piece of crisp fruit between his molars. The ambrosial
taste of the apple was so sweet, so succulent, he continued to take more
bites, and soon he had reduced the formerly round and red fruit into an
off-white, cylindrical core.

"Don't ruin your appetite, love," his wife said from behind him. "That's already your second piece of fruit." She gently laughed, and lovingly placed her hand upon his shoulder. "We haven't even had the salads and sandwiches yet."

"Oh, I'm still hungry, dear, don't worry," he replied. "I wouldn't dream of ruining my appetite today." He placed his hand upon hers, and turned around to face her.

"Well, I'm quite pleased to hear that. I would hate to think that my hours of toil and labor should be spoiled by some young upstart who grew herself from a tree!" She nudged him, and smiled that same, fantastic smile which won him over so many years ago.

He ran his fingers through her long, auburn hair, and looked deeply into her dark brown eyes. She was everything to him–his life, his world, his hopes, his dreams–and he never, ever wanted to lose her. He tried to say something to express this to her, but, finding himself so overwhelmed with emotion, no words came forth from his lips. A lone, single tear escaped from his right eye, attempting to communicate what his tongue could not.

"What?" she asked with concern, carefully wiping the tear from his cheek. "Are you all right? What is it?"

Her questions only hastened to bring forth more tears, as his mind thought of all the many answers. He embraced her tightly, buried his face into the safe, warm space between her neck and shoulder, and released the flood of emotions which had been rising within him throughout the day.

She kissed the side of his head, and nestled her cheek against him. "It's all right, love. Everything's all right," she said softly, massaging the back of his neck. "I'm here, the children are here...everything's fine."

He wept until he could weep no more, until his caged and pent emotions had completely liberated themselves. He breathed in deeply, shaking a little as he did so, and pressed his wet face against hers. "I love you so much, Dominique–so much more than you can ever know. I'm sorry if I haven't always expressed my-"

She put her fingers to his lips. "Shhhh...no apologies, love. I know that you love me. You're telling me now, right now, and that's all that really matters. You're seizing the moment," she said, delicately wiping the moisture from beneath his eyes. "And the moment is all that we ever truly have, isn't it?"

"I suppose you're right," he said. Taking another deep breath, he laughed, "As usual."

# ((FREQUENCIES))

Dominique hugged him, her loving embrace as comforting as the womb from which he came. "I love you, Mason Huxton," she said. "And I always will. Don't ever forget that." She slowly released her embrace. "No matter what the future might bring."

"I won't forget," Mason vowed. "Ever. I promise." He took her hand, rubbed his finger lightly upon her diamond wedding ring, and smiled. "Should we go see what the children are up to?"

She nodded, and they walked together toward the open clearing which they had chosen for their picnic site. Reaching the red-and-white checkered blanket, Mason looked around for the children. They were nowhere to be found. Slightly puzzled, he looked over at Dominique and said, "Now where could they have gone?"

"They must be around here somewhere," she replied.

"Adam?" he called out. "Ashley?"

"I'm over here," came his daughter's voice from the direction of a few large rocks.

Mason looked toward the voice's origin, but saw nothing. "Where?" he asked.

"Over *here*, silly!" Ashley said, poking her lightly freckled face out from behind one of the rocks. She smiled, revealing the cute little empty space where her last baby tooth had been, then moved back behind the rock again.

"What do you suppose she's up to?" Mason asked his wife.

"With Ashley," she said with a laugh, "only she knows."

"Ash?" he said loudly, enough so that his daughter could hear his voice. "What are you doing over there?"

"Watchin' bugs!" she replied.

Mason smiled. That was his daughter, all right–always exploring something, and curious about everything. "What kind of bugs?" he asked.

"Just *bugs*, daddy!" Ashley said. "It doesn't matter what they're called! They'll still be what they are!"

Mason laughed. She was such an odd child, yet still he loved her so. "It matters if they're called 'bees,' dear!"

"They're *not* bees, dad!"

"Okay, that's good then," Mason said. He and Dominique sat down on the picnic blanket. "Ash," he called out again, "where's your brother at?"

"Somewhere!"

Mason turned to his wife, a look of humorous disbelief upon his face. "Dominique, I think we've created a little monster."

55

"Well, at least she's an adorable little monster, Mason," Dominique smiled, as she began to remove the food and drink from the wicker picnic basket.

"Yes, this is true. Though, sometimes-" Mason paused for a moment. "Wait," he said, hearing something in the distance, "I think that's Adam's voice."

"Father," excitedly shouted his son from somewhere beyond the trees. "Father!"

"We're over here, Adam!" Mason shouted back. "Just follow my voice!"

Seconds later, Adam came bounding out through the trees as fast as he possibly could, carrying some sort of object in his small hands. "Look what I found!"

"What is it?" asked Mason.

"I found it in the woods!" Adam said. "Look!" He held up a cubic object about the size of an orange.

Mason stood up, and took the cube from Adam's hands. Its primary color was green, but it was speckled with hundreds of tiny black dots. Upon closer inspection, Mason noticed that each black dot was actually the Greek letter alpha. There was also an extremely thin fissure running around the outside center of the cube. Curious, he thought. The letter alpha...it reminded him of...what? He suddenly felt like he was forgetting something very important. "I wonder what it is?" he asked.

"Twist it, father," answered Adam. "Then you'll know."

Mason gave Adam an inquisitive look, then glanced back down at the cube again. Why did the cube seem so familiar? He turned to Dominique.

"Go ahead," she said. "Give it a try."

Grasping the cube firmly with both hands, Mason started to twist it. When he had applied the correct amount of pressure, the cube clicked into a new position, and light briefly glowed out from the fissure. He looked at Adam. "Like that?"

Adam nodded, adjusting his navy blue baseball cap. His body then rippled, as if it were made of liquid, and morphed from the child of ten he was then into the full-grown man he was now. "Hello, father," the adult Adam said. "I hope this doesn't come as a shock to you–but you have a meeting with me in ten minutes."

"No, it's...it's fine, son," Mason said as he began to remember. "It's quite all right." He looked over at Dominique, who was carefully removing the plastic wrap from a platter of sandwiches, paying absolutely no mind to Adam's transformation.

"I tried my best to ease you out of the experience," Adam said. "Did I do a good job, or was it too drastic?"

"You did well, Adam," he said, feeling a little sad as the full realization washed over him. "You did well..." Mason had programmed an alarm of sorts into his dreamworld, to ensure that he wouldn't "oversleep," and stay in his virtual experience too long. With the advanced technology his father had given him, it was possible to lose oneself for hours, even days, if there wasn't some kind of alarm feature built into the program. "I remember everything now," he said.

Mason had created the reality so that when he gazed upon the alphas on the cube, it would trigger the program to deactivate some of the selective memory inhibitors which allowed him to fully immerse himself into his virtual world. He had found from experience that it was best not to deactivate all of the SMI's at once, for this could induce a migraine headache so strong as to make one nauseous to the point of vomiting. Therefore, the twisting of the cube was programmed to be the action that would unlock all of the remaining SMI's, thus allowing full memory to return to him without the adverse side effects. The cube twist also triggered the reminder that he had a meeting with Adam—and what better way to remind himself of a meeting with his son, than to have his son's virtual counterpart refresh his memory for him? Now, all Mason had to do was turn the program off.

He took one last look around the area, said a silent goodbye, and twisted the cube a final time. It glowed at its fissure once again, but this time the light completely engulfed the cube, causing it to dematerialize in his very hands. Adam and Dominique—and of course Ashley, though she was still playing somewhere behind the rocks and wasn't currently visible—then disappeared in a manner similar to the cube, the light which they had been composed of glimmeringly dissipating into the atmosphere around them. The strangest part came next—reentry into realtime.

The rocks, the trees, the ground, the sky, and everything else around him suddenly started to fold in upon itself, as if he were watching a time-lapse movie of a flower blooming—except in reverse. As the flower of the virtual reality began to close, and sky and earth became one, the realtime reality began to assert itself. Beyond the flower, which was closing in around him like he was its pistil and stamen, Mason could see the details of his office coming into view.

The polished oak desk in front of him, the black leather chairs sitting atop the large oriental rug, the books and devices lining the ceiling-high shelves, and all of the other office particulars quickly came into focus, as the previous reality continued collapsing inward until it became the size of a pin prick. The tiny virtual omega point hovered briefly before Mason's eyes...and then it was gone. He no longer had the perception that he was standing, but rather, was now fully aware that he was sitting down in the executive chair behind his desk.

Mason was back in realtime.

He reached forward and picked up the green, alpha-covered cube from his desk, gave it a twist, and deactivated the tiny electromagnets which attached the flexible, meshed neural net to his head. The thin technorganic tendrils sucked themselves back into their housing, and he removed the headpiece. He stretched out his arms, yawned, and rubbed his face.

As his fingertips touched his eyes, he was surprised to find them moist and sticky. He realized that he must have been crying not only within the virtual world, but also in actuality. Reaching into the inside pocket of his suit, he pulled out a cloth handkerchief, wiped the drying tears, then stood up from his leather chair and walked over to one of the many tinted windows set into the walls of his large office. As he approached the darkened pane of glass, a photoemissive cell sensed his presence, and automatically lightened the window's tint.

Mason gazed out at the giant, sprawling Ordosoft™ campus before him, and marvelled at the magnificent combination of natural wonders and man-made structures contained therein. From his 33rd story window, he could see it all so clearly: miniature forests, grand museums, fountains, streams, houses, ponds, zoos, offices, arcades, grocery stores, restaurants–the Redmond campus was a city unto itself. It was sheer brilliance the way that his father had created the company's headquarters, making it so much more than simply a place to work–it was a place to experience. People came from all over the world to see the campus' sights, and workers everywhere longed to become part of the company's force. His father was true genius, a visionary of the highest degree–and Mason could think of no greater honor than to have the privilege of being his son, and continuing his father's legacy.

"Mr. Huxton," came his secretary's voice through the desktop intercom, "Adam is here to see you."

Mason walked to the intercom and placed his finger upon a small sensor. "Thank you, Isadora. Please send him in." He circled around the desk, seated himself in the executive chair, and touched a button at the tip of the armrest, deactivating the office door's security systems. He picked up the headpiece and cube from off the desk, opened a drawer, and discreetly placed them into it.

The large double doors, comprised of a nanotech synthesis of mahogany and titanium, swung open as Adam approached them. "Hello, father," he said. "How are things today?" The doors automatically shut behind him, making nary a sound.

"Things are as usual, son," Mason replied, leaning back into the chair and placing his hands together at the fingertips. "In order."

Adam sat down in one of the black leather chairs across from Mason's desk. Each chair had been placed about as far from the desk as was possible, though not so far as to make it hard to hear or be heard. "I take it then you've already spoken to Intel® about the proposed changes in their neural nets?" he asked.

"Yes, I told them that we approved of any minor alterations that would enhance efficiency, so long as those changes did nothing to diminish our access and control over those same networks."

"Sounds good," Adam said. "What about Hitachi®?"

"I thought that the color, resolution, and depth perception on their new line of holoviews was absolutely magnificent. I informed them that they would have full and complete endorsement from Ordosoft™."

"Well, I'm sure they were pleased to hear that. And how did it go with the White House?"

Mason confidently nodded, forming his fingers into a pyramidal shape. "I spoke with the President just about an hour ago, and she assured me that the new rounds of anti-trust hearings will be over with before they begin. She apologized, but said that it was still important for the government to give the appearance that they did not approve of monopolies."

"It still seems ridiculous to me," Adam said, pulling out a Food For Thought® smartbar. "For god's sake, father, we've owned the world's operating systems for over fifty years. You'd think by now the government would just give us an official endorsement and be done with the whole tired charade."

"You would think, wouldn't you?" Mason opened a small cabinet built into his desk, grasped an old, slightly dusty bottle from the opening , and placed it in front of him. On top of the bottle was an elaborate pump mechanism, designed especially to preserve the precious vintage within. "But, even with a society as civilized as ours, pretensions are still necessary in order for the shepherds to keep the sheep in their pastures." He reached down again, returning this time with two glasses, both of them wide and curved at the bottom, forming into a smaller opening at the top. "Can I interest you in a glass of Nieport®–1912?"

"Now what would be the use of eating these," he said, pointing to his concentrated food bar, "if I were to consume *that*?" He laughed. "I'm trying to enhance my mind, not cloud it."

"Very well then." Mason poured himself a small glass of the aged port. Raising his cup to the NatraLites™ above, he watched the light refract and sparkle inside of the rich, ruby liquid.

"Father, that alcohol will be the death of you, I swear. They say that every drink you have decreases your life expectancy by-"

"Oh, shush," Mason said with a laugh. "Let a man indulge his vices in peace." He brought the glass to his nose and breathed in the fruity aroma. Splendid. He then moved the glass to his lips and took a slow, delicate sip, making sure to savor the sweet nectar before . he swallowed. "Perfect. Now, off the business and on to the personal... Did you speak with Ashley today?"

Adam finished chewing, then answered, "Yes, I did."

"And...?"

"And she said that she would come by Xanadeux later today."

Mason raised his eyebrows. "She agreed–just like that?"

"Well, no. She yelled at me a bit, then gave me a small lecture in biological fundamentalism–you know, typical Ashley stuff."

"Oh yes," he said. "I know." Random instances of Ashley's odd behavior flashed through Mason's mind. In elementary, when she convinced the other children to ask "why" every time the teacher said something, regardless of whether or not the instructor wanted a response; refusing to live in the most prestigious sorority house in U-Village and instead choosing to live in the dormitories; the time in precollege when she suddenly decided that she would drop out for a while, just to "see what it was like."

"It's funny," Mason said, "I always tell myself that it's just a phase she's going through–that she'll grow out of it eventually." He moved his hand in small circular motions, swirling the port inside the glass. "Adam, I've been saying that for over *twenty* years now. "

"Well, I still say you should have given her *some* form of

neurochemical therapy when she started to exhibit the attention-deficit behavior. It might have cured her right then and there."

"And it might have destroyed her creativity and ingenuity," Mason replied. "The whole point of ADD therapy is to make the unusual child conform to the current definitions of normality–to make them more like the others." He took a sip of the swirling alcohol. "I don't want my children to be like the others, Adam. I want you to be unique, and I want you to be free enough to have the ability to innovate–even if that means risking the possibility that one of my children might be so free as to never see my point of view. Better to risk that than to risk having a typical child. After all, a typical, normal alpha-beta could not even *begin* to comprehend what it means to run a company such as Ordosoft™. If Ashley should ever decide to become an integral part of the company, then she will need her ability to think beyond the boundaries of those around her... She will need to be different."

"Well," Adam laughed, "she's certainly achieved that distinction with flying colors, hasn't she?"

"Indeed." Mason poured himself a little more port, and asked, "Do you think she's actually going to come by the skyland today?"

"That's what she said to me."

Mason nodded. "Good," he said. "And thank you, son, for doing that. I can't emphasize how very important it is that Ashley shows at least *some* type of support for your mother." He paused, thinking about Dominique. "She's having such a difficult time right now..."

"Which, I assure you, father, is only natural. I mean, just imagine her position–you're awakened from a genetic accelerator only to be told that you're someone who you barely have the faintest glimpses of ever being. That takes some time to accept." He took a bite of his smartbar. "It's unfortunate, but...until consciousness uploading is perfected, cloning will always be hard on the clones."

"Please don't say that word, Adam–you know I don't care for it." He set his glass down. "Your mother has been 'reborn,' not 'cloned.'"

"Yes, sorry, father," Adam said. "I forgot. I apologize."

"If your mother *thinks* she's only a clone, then that's all she'll ever *be*. However, if she can see herself as being reborn, she can become who she was once again." Mason stared at Adam. "And that's what we all want, isn't it, son?"

"Of course," Adam said, guiltily looking down at the carpet. "Nothing could make me happier. I...I want mother back just as much as you do." He wrapped the unfinished smartbar, and placed it into his pocket. He looked up at Mason again. "And how is she today? Any better than yesterday?"

"She's not quite as...introverted as she was yesterday, but she's still acting rather strange. As I was getting dressed this morning, she just sat there in bed, mumbling to herself in an almost conversational way."

"That doesn't sound good."

"No, it doesn't. I'm having Sofia stay with her until I return." Mason paused, looking over at the darkened windows to his right. From his current distance, the tint caused everything outside to appear a depressing shade of gray. "I don't know what's happened, Adam. I knew that your mother's rebirth would present its difficulties, but...I never expected it to be like this."

"Neither did I," he said. "But things will get better, father. They always do." Adam's wristcom beeped, and he briefly glanced down at it. "I'm sure Ashley's visit today will only improve mother's condition."

"That's what I'm hoping, son." Mason rubbed his thumb along the contours of the port glass, and asked, "Did Ashley happen to mention to you what time she would be coming by Xanadeux?"

Adam shook his head. "She just said that she would be coming by at some point today."

"Then I should probably go there now. I'd like to make sure to be there when she arrives." He took a final sip of port and stood up. "Care to join me?"

"Unfortunately," Adam said, straightening out his slacks, "I won't be able to come by until later. I have a lunch appointment to keep."

"Business?" Mason asked, walking out from behind his desk.

"No," Adam said with a smile, "most definitely pleasure. Though I wouldn't mind getting down to business with her."

"Someone I've met?"

"No, I just met her the other day–tall, blonde, curvy," he said, rounding his hands around his breastbone. "She's positively magnetic."

Mason shook his head and smiled at Adam's comments. His son revelled in the playboy role *far* more than he ever did. "What about intelligent, thoughtful, interesting...those kinds of qualities?"

"Actually," Adam said, "I hadn't gotten that far yet." He smiled again, and walked over to Mason. "Take it easy today, okay?"

He placed his hand upon his father's shoulder. "Promise me you won't strain yourself?"

Mason put his hand on top of his son's, and nodded in agreement. "I suppose I should say the same for you, shouldn't I?"

"Was that a joke?" Adam laughed, as he walked away toward the door. "Be careful, father, or you might find yourself developing a sense of humor–and where would Ordosoft™ be without your 'ruthless businessman' image?" The doors opened for him as he approached. "Take care," he said. "I'll see you at Xanadeux."

Watching Adam leave his office, Mason felt a smile creep up at the corners of his mouth–a smile of pride. Unlike Ashley, Adam had turned out exactly how Mason had wanted him to be: responsible, logical, intelligent, and disciplined. Well, he consoled himself, at least Ashley was intelligent.

As the doors closed behind his son, Mason walked to the wood-panelled wall behind his desk, and waved his hand over the sensor. A large portion of the soundproof panelling drew back, accordion-like, revealing behind it a huge uniview screen.

His face illuminated by the green glow of the Ordosoft™ logo, Mason said, "Voice-rec on. Connect me to Burke."

"Connecting," said the uniview's soothing female voice.

A few seconds passed, then the chiseled visage of his chauffeur materialized upon the screen. "What can I do for you, sir?" he asked, tipping his hat toward Mason.

"Meet me on the roof."

"Right away, sir."

"Voice-rec off," Mason said, closing the wood panels. He picked up his Oxford® coat from the back of his chair, reached into the inside pocket, and pulled out a small remote control. Putting on the coat, he pointed the device up to the ceiling and pressed a button. A large, silver, circular shape on the ceiling began to open up like a camera shutter, albeit at a much slower speed. When the shutterlike pieces had fully retracted, a disc–barely smaller than the opening itself–started to descend from the ceiling, directly in line with both the circular hole above, and the circular design on the oriental rug below. The disc continued its descent until it was exactly one inch above the rug, then hovered there motionless. Where the shutters had previously been, there was now an open passage leading up to a green-lit room.

Mason touched the intercom. "Isadora, should you need to contact me, I'll be at Xanadeux." He walked over to the glowing disc and

63

stepped on top of it. After pressing another button on the remote, the disc elevated him up through the opening in the ceiling. Once fully inside the upper room, Mason headed toward the exit. The small, green-hued room was very simple and plain, and contained within it only emergency-related items: an extinguisher, a laser pistol, a GS backpack, and a few other select objects. It served as his personal access to the roof, and not much else.

As Mason reached the exit, the door slid open quickly with a slight hissing sound, allowing beams of sunlight to flood into the room. Mason raised his hand in front of his eyes until he had adjusted to the light, then stepped out onto the building's verdant, gardened roof. The door immediately hissed shut behind him.

From his location in the exact center of the roof, he walked over to the northwest corner of the building where a small redwood was growing. Just as he reached both the tree and the edge of the building, an exceptionally long, black Rolls-Royce® limousine rose up from below and stopped directly in front of him. The rear doors opened, and a wide, telescoping walkway extended out toward Mason.

The tinted driver's side window rolled down. "Sir," Burke said, "your carriage awaits."

Mason nodded, stepped onto the walkway, and seated himself inside the back seat's plush, dark green interior.

"Where to, sir?" asked Burke through the intercom.

"Xanadeux," Mason replied, taking off his coat and putting his feet on an ottoman.

"Right away," Burke said. The limo ascended into the skies above, and flew south toward Mercer Island.

"Voice-rec on," Mason said. "Connect me to Xanadeux master bedroom." A 2-D, holographic screen projected out from the limo's ceiling.

The alpha logo appeared, then morphed into the image of Mason's butler, Marcel. His face was very close to the camera, causing his features to become somewhat warped and distorted. He looked distressed. "Sir," Marcel said, "am I ever so glad you called."

"What is it, Marcel? What's the matter?"

"It's your wife, sir."

In the background, Mason heard what sounded like a scream. He tried to look beyond Marcel to see what was happening, but the butler's face was blocking most of the picture. "What's going on there? Is she all right?"

"She's in no physical danger, sir, but her mental state is currently...shall we say...quite precarious." He looked back at something, then turned around to face the camera again. "Perhaps you should see for yourself." Marcel moved away from the camera, allowing Mason to see the full details of the scene. On the white chiffon bed, Sofia was sitting beside his wife, attempting to calm her down by rubbing her back in a motherly fashion.

"Don't touch me!" shouted Dominique in a shrill, unnerving tone. "I don't even know who me is!"

Sofia looked toward the camera, her normally assured composure shaken and frayed. "She won't calm down, sir. I'm trying my best." She turned to Dominique again. "Dom, it's all right. Look," pointing out toward the screen, "there's Mason. It's okay. Look."

"Everything's all right, dear," Mason said, hoping his words would have some sort of calming effect. "I'm on my way right now."

Dominique looked at the camera and began to sob. "I'm sorry, Mason...I'm so sorry."

"It's fine, it's fine," Mason reassured her. "Don't worry, Dominique. We'll work it all out. Everything will be fine."

She placed her head in her hands and sobbed even harder. "Oh god, who am I?" she asked without looking up. "Everyone's telling me who I am and I don't even remember myself...I'm so sorry..."

Mason put his hand over his mouth, and felt a lump rise in his throat. "Dominique..."

"Who am I?!" she suddenly screamed. Sofia moved to comfort her, but Dominique started to wildly slap at her. "Get away! All of you, get away!" She faced the camera again, her eyes blazed with a madness that he had never before seen in her. "Why did you do this?! Why am I here?" She began to pull the sheets from the bed and toss the pillows about. "WHY AM I HERE?!"

"Marcel!" Mason shouted. "Make sure she doesn't harm herself!"

Marcel moved to the edge of the bed to help Sofia control Dominique. "Sir," he said, looking back at the camera as a pillow ricocheted off of his head, "please hurry."

"Intercom on," Mason said, in a tone much louder than was necessary to activate the system. "Burke, get to Xanadeux as fast as possible–now!"

"Yes, sir!" Burke replied.

The limo immediately increased its speed, and Mason was momentarily thrown back against the seat. "Intercom off," he said, watching Sofia and Marcel desperately try to restrain Dominique.

"WHY AM I?!" his wife shouted over and over, as she kicked and screamed in a manner which reminded him of some wild animal from a Discovery Channel® program. "WHY AM I?!"

Yes, why? Mason asked himself. Why are you like this? Why are you suddenly freeking out, when you were fine just...

Another thought came rushing into his mind–a possibility that he hadn't considered, but one that suddenly made everything fit together.

"Command: split screen and turn volume off from Xanadeux site," Mason said. The holographic screen bisected itself, the bedroom scene shrinking in size and moving to the right, an Ordosoft™ logo appearing on the left. He pulled out his handkerchief and patted away the perspiration which had formed at the top of his head. He carefully brushed his hair back with his hand, then ran his fingers lightly across his eyebrows.

Confident that his face was projecting an air of assurance and control, Mason cleared his throat, adjusted his tie, and said, "Connect me to Freemon headquarters."

α

# Ω

## Chapter 5
## ((Island in the Sky))

*But, as in everything, there was always balance, and surely as there were those who sought to rule and control, there were those who endeavored to undermine and subvert. There could be no light without day, no life without death, no yin without yang, and thus the harnessing of the fundamental frequencies was a tenuous enterprise at best. To seek total control of reality was like grasping water–one moment it was there, the next it was gone."*

"*The* Mason Huxton?" McCready asked, not sure if he had heard him correctly.

"*That* Mason Huxton," affirmed Takura.

Cruising over the waters of Lake Washington, the Rainier Valley fading quickly into the distance behind him, McCready glanced ahead at the approaching skyland, then looked back down at the uniview. On the screen was a wooded environment which looked like it had been drawn entirely in black-and-white line art. There was a careful attention to detail, and everything in the scene was meticulously depicted. In the foreground, a very large cat, with equally large claws, sat perched upon the branches of one of the colorless trees.

"Did he say what for?" McCready asked.

"No," the animated cat replied, his tail slinkily moving around, "he didn't give any specifics."

Rather than using a uniview, Takura was mentally projecting out through cyberspace via the satellink hookup in his brain. He was presenting as his usual avatar, the cheshire cat from *Alice's Adventures in Wonderland*. Not the purple one from Disney's® *Alice in Wonderland*, as Takura was wont to remind McCready, but the original black-and-white one from the old book drawings.

"All I know is that Huxton personally contacted Moore," Takura said, resting his feline chin upon his paw, "asked him to send a single Freemon over, and requested that we keep the entire incident as quiet as possible. Me, you, and Moore are the only ones who know about it." He licked the back of his paw, then added, "And we're supposed to keep it that way. Moore doesn't want us speaking to anyone else about the situation."

"What about Ignacio? He's okay, right?"

"Not even him. The info's supposed to stay with us only–at least until further notice."

McCready rolled his eyes. "Man, that's bullshit, Tak–we always talk about our cases. What the hell am I supposed to tell him? That it's too 'top-secret' for him to know?"

"No, don't make it sound interesting, that'll just make him *more* curious. Try to make it sound as boring and mundane as possible."

"Like...?"

The cheshire cat shrugged its shoulders. "Be creative," he said. "Use your imagination."

"I don't have one–they're illegal." McCready felt the car raise its altitude, and he looked up from the screen. Mercer Island was now directly in front of him.

Even though McCready saw it every day on the skyline, the entire structure still tripped him out–it was so unreal, especially up this close. A nanotech city of giant mansions, rolling hills, and bountiful forests set atop a huge, jagged and craggy, earthen base–all of it miraculously hovering in the air through a godlike manipulation of the Earth's geomagnetic field. It was like something out of a bad science-fiction movie–the ones that ask you to suspend a little *too* much disbelief–except for the fact that it was real.

Takura's mouth widened into a grin, revealing the rows of sharp teeth lining his jaws. "You love to make things easy, don't you?" Starting at the tip, his tail began to slowly fade away. "Just tell him that you had to go isolate a butler who was freeking out about his servitude. It was very boring, and all he kept talking about was how he couldn't stand to refer to his employer as 'master' anymore." The tail had completely faded, and now his body was disappearing as well. "There. That wasn't so hard, was it?"

"Nope, not at all." The car raised its altitude even further as he passed over the southern tip of Mercer Island. On the rear-view screen, McCready caught a glimpse of the forest-enclaved fusion reactor which powered the entire skyland. "Alright then," he said, "'the butler' story it is. I'll update you on how the real story pans out when it's finished."

"Perfect." All that remained of the cheshire cat was the huge toothed grin. "You know the frequency," he said. "I'm ghost." The smile dissipated like the rest of him had, and the Wonderland domain morphed into the cartoon Marilyn dancing away in front of a Wurlitzer® juke box.

The music volume returned to its previous, louder level. The Beatles' "Revolution" was the current selection—one of McCready's favorites. He mumbled along with the tune, in a monotone voice that sharply contrasted the inspired vocals.

As the scenery unfolded before him, McCready saw a Dodge® Trilobyte™ crossing his path in the distance. He'd seen footage of them on the uniview, but he had yet to see one in person. McCready touched a sensor on the side of his sunglasses and made a few circling motions with his fingertip, activating the Obsidians'™ binocular mode. He could now see the features of the vehicle as clearly as if it were sitting on the top of his hood.

The Trilobyte™ was unlike any other vehicle on the market. Shaped like its namesake, it was a magnetically propelled GS craft, available in one specific trademarked shade—Fossil Brown™. There was a lot of fuss at first about the Trilobyte's™ magnetic propulsion having a disrupting effect on nearby computers, but apparently the engineers had found a way to prevent that from happening. Or at least that was what they were currently saying, McCready thought. Technology always had this morbidly funny way of immersing itself completely into your life *before* revealing the aspects of itself that would utterly fuck-up you and everything else around it.

"Marc," the car said, "I've been instructed by Xanadeux to relinquish control of my operating system. For security reasons, it would prefer to land the vehicle itself."

Rich people, he laughed to himself—the most paranoid fuckers on Earth. Guess they had to be, since they were always having to protect all that shit they didn't really need.

"How should I respond to it?" Marilyn asked, pulling out an old-fashioned microphone and tape recorder.

"Tell them, 'Sure, if that will in any way make your day a

safer one. Safety is our number one priority at the FBI.'"

Marilyn hit the "stop" button on the tape recorder and set down her microphone.

McCready knew his sarcasm would be lost on the artificial intelligence that was Xanadeux, but still, the temptation was too much to resist. A few moments later, a large canopied bed appeared on the screen. The nightgown-attired Marilyn crawled into it and fell quickly asleep, little animated "z-z-z's" rising from her head.

Xanadeux was now in control.

The car's acceleration increased, and within seconds, McCready was able to see the enormous, alpha-shaped Xanadeux estate. The entire perimeter of the area, which comprised the "lines" in the alpha letter, was an extremely dense forest of plants, trees, and shrubs indigenous to Washington state. There was no visible wall around the property other than the forest itself, but he had heard it was protected by a powerful, invisible electromagnetic field–which, undoubtedly, was used not only for security purposes, but also to keep Xanadeux oh-so very aesthetically pleasing to the viewer.

Inside of the forested perimeter, which was equivalent to the open space within the alpha character, everything was layered in concentric rings. First there was the ring of typical rich people things, like ridiculously bright, green golf courses (he counted at least three), clay tennis courts, and big grass fields which he assumed were used for polo or rugby, though he wasn't really sure and didn't really care either way. Next there was an equally typical, but much larger, garden ring which featured plants from probably every corner of the goddamn globe. And then...then it diverted a bit from what would typically be called "typical."

The garden gave way to a giant hill–which was of course placed perfectly in the center of the skyland so everyone could see it–and upon this hill sat the biggest fucking mansion that McCready had ever seen in his life. It was obscene, but he had to admit it was also incredible. The place was more like a castle than a mansion, really–composed of ancient-looking, lichen-covered stone, complete with a surrounding moat and drawbridge, turrets which reminded him of the rook pieces on a chessboard, and tall, pointed spires which looked like they would be very effective at impaling someone. Courtyards, swimming holes, and even little cottages dotted the inside of the sprawling structure. The castle was as unreal as the skyland itself.

"Good afternoon, Agent McCready," an androgynous voice

announced over the car's speakers. "Welcome to Xanadeux." The sleeping toon morphed into a bodiless head floating in some type of formless, green dimension. The head was almost human, but not quite–more like an android that had been purposefully designed not to look *too* much like a person. It had slightly curved, glowing slits for its eyes and mouth, no nose, skin which resembled rubber more than flesh, and a small alpha placed directly in the center of its forehead like a third eye. "I will now be flying your vehicle into the main courtyard's parking area," it said. "Enjoy the ride."

The castle drawbridge started to lower itself via its thick iron chains, just as Xanadeux brought the Chevy® down to the entryway's level. As the car neared closer and closer to the castle, McCready began to wonder if he was going to collide with the underside of the still-opening bridge...but he quickly realized Xanadeux had synchronized everything to perfection. Just as the planked wooden drawbridge reached the other side of the moat, the Polaris™ smoothly passed over it–with maybe an inch to spare–and flew through the opening.

The entry into the castle had looked a lot more dangerous than it probably was. Since Xanadeux was controlling both the drawbridge and the car, and probably every other mechanized or computerized system on the estate, it was less than a simple task for it to make the entrance into the castle an exciting one–and Mason Huxton obviously wanted his visitors to experience some form of excitement when they came to Xanadeux, or the whole place wouldn't be the giant playground that it was.

As the Polaris™ zipped through the castle's arboreal, open-aired courtyard, Xanadeux took it on the path of most resistance, constantly darting the vehicle back and forth between the numerous tall trees which filled the area. At first, McCready found himself more annoyed than excited with the AI's ostentatious displays of its capabilities, but when a few of the trees actually moved *themselves* out of the car's way, he found himself experiencing an emotion which was definitely akin to excitement–if not exhilaration. Looking back to see if the trees were still moving, he remembered being nine years old, on a trip to Disneyland® with his parents, when he gazed down at the bright city lights on the Peter Pan ride, trying to see if there were little people running around the mini-metropolis. He couldn't remember if there were any miniature people down there, and not wanting to remember any more about that year or his father, he diverted his train of thought back to the present. Xanadeux could even control the *trees*? he asked himself. What the hell didn't it control?

The car abruptly decelerated as it emerged through the freaky forest, passing by a few small cottages which reminded him of gingerbread houses. In front of these Candyland® cottages, there were several people, all dressed in simple, peasantlike clothing, toiling away in their gardens with shovels, rakes, hoes, and spades. It was hard to tell whether they were male or female, since their backs were turned towards him and they all wore shawls on their heads.

Xanadeux glided the Polaris™ near one of the garden toilers, reducing the car's speed to a crawl. The shawled individual dug deep into the moist earth with a metal spade, then reached down into the softened soil, and sensually ran both hands through it. Assuming the person was so immersed in their labor that they hadn't taken notice of his car, McCready was a little surprised when the garden toiler suddenly turned to face him. Then he was *really* surprised when he saw that the face hidden underneath the shawl was the same, almost-human countenance of Xanadeux's uniview avatar. The android stared at him for a moment, its curved mouth especially looking like a smile at that instant, then turned back around and continued with its work. The village of android gardeners, McCready thought, as the car resumed its movement. A bad horror movie in the making. He shook his head. Rich people...

Exiting the android village, McCready came to a giant, circus-like canopy. As the Polaris™ neared it, two large flaps peeled open to allow entry.

"We have now reached the main parking area," Xanadeux said, as they entered the canopy's interior. "I believe you'll appreciate what's inside, Agent McCready."

The andy wasn't bullshitting.

McCready's jaw literally dropped. He worshipped the 1900's in general, and had a devout fondness for its cars in particular, and this canopied, vehicular shrine contained more 20th century automobiles than he had ever seen in his heathen life. Even on the uniview he hadn't seen so many antiques in one place. In just one quick sweep of the area, he saw a Model T®, a Mustang®, a Prowler®, two Corvettes®–including a Stingray®–an Impala®, a Viper®, an Aston-Martin®, and various other makes and models that he didn't even know the names of. Suddenly Huxton's extravagance didn't seem so bad anymore... McCready was eager to get out of the car and explore.

Xanadeux flew the Polaris™ to an empty parking space, gently landed the car, and opened the driver's side door. "Enjoy your stay," it said in its asexual voice.

"Yeah, I think I will." McCready's words were immediately confirmed as he stepped out of the car and spotted, on the other side of the Jaguar® he was parked next to, a pristine, cherry-red '57 Chevy®. He quickly moved around the rear of the Jag™ to get a closer look at the heavenly creation. When he reached it, he simply stood there and stared in religious awe. The sharklike fins, the pointed taillights, the shiny chrome bumper–it was amazing. He reached his hand forward to touch the sacred machine.

"Please don't touch the vehicles," said the voice of Xanadeux from behind him.

McCready retracted his hand. "Oh yeah, right," he said without averting his eyes from the Chevy®. "Sure."

The Xanadeux android walked up beside McCready. "It's beautiful, isn't it?"

McCready glanced over at the android. Same face as the others, but this one was dressed in a dark green security uniform, packing a laser pistol, a napper, and a few other devices. "That car's more than beautiful," McCready said. "That car's the bomb."

"I'm assuming that's a figure of speech and not a warning or a threat?" Xanadeux asked.

"That's right, Xanny. 'The bomb' means it's dope, fresh, phat, chill, nasty, hunny..." McCready looked at Xanadeux with a subtle smile. "Hella cool. But no one really uses that saying anymore–not after all the terrorism at the turn of the century." McCready pulled out a cigarette and lighter.

"There is no smoking allowed within Xanadeux," the android brusquely stated.

McCready nodded, putting his smoking equipment back into his pockets. "I even heard that at one point during the early 2000's," he said, still eyeing the Chevy® up and down like a voluptuous goddess, "just saying the word 'bomb' would get you a direct visit from the FBI or the DCC–especially once they installed the word-rec technology on everybody's phone lines."

"I see," Xanadeux said in an unimpressed tone. "Thank you for the colloquial information, Agent McCready, but we should now be getting to the main house so that you can meet with Mr. Huxton." The android began to walk towards the big top's exit. "Follow me."

McCready trailed after Xanadeux, taking a final look back at the Chevy® before he left. "Maybe Huxton'll let me take it for a spin, eh?"

The android's only response was a small, curt laugh.

There were several other Xanadeuxs–these ones dressed like chauffeurs–busily cleaning, waxing, and detailing the antique vehicles near the tent's exit. The androids paid no attention to them as they walked by, completely engrossed in their task at hand. It was hard for McCready to imagine how Xanadeux could coordinate every android and thing on the estate all at once, but then again, it was hard for him sometimes to even imagine the concept of AI at all–computers that could think like humans...but in a way that was exponentially faster and infinitely more efficient. Weird shit, McCready thought. He wondered how much longer it would be before all of the AI's got together one day and decided they really didn't need those annoying, fleshy humans anymore.

They headed north from the canopied parking area, towards a set of wide stone steps which led up to the palatial mansion ahead. "Whoa," McCready caught himself saying as he gazed up at the stately structure.

Its overall shape reminded him a little of the White House, except Huxton's pad, with its venerable look of antiquity and regality, put the Oval Office to absolute shame. Whereas the White House looked like a phony movie prop for a useless figurehead President–which, McCready realized, was all that it really was–the main house of Xanadeux actually *looked* like the place where a powerful President would live. No, he corrected himself, this place looked more like the palace where the *King* of America would reside–which, he quickly realized, it basically was.

The mansion's tall wooden doors opened up as they approached. They were greeted by an older man with grayish hair dressed in a butler's uniform. "Good day, Agent McCready," he said with a small nod, in an accent which had traces of both French and English, "I'm Mr. Huxton's butler, Marcel." He looked over at the security android. "That will be all, Xanadeux. Thank you."

"You're welcome," the android said.

Marcel turned to McCready. "Please come in, sir."

McCready entered into a large entrance hall with very high ceilings. A good distance ahead of him was a curved staircase which rounded up into the banistered outer rim of the upper level. An older woman briefly looked down at him from over the railing, then disappeared out of sight. Above the railing, directly in the center of the ceiling, was a huge candle-lit chandelier which hung about sixteen feet off the ground. To his right was a room filled with all kinds of antique musical instruments, and to his left was a monstrously large space which looked like it would be used as some type of banquet hall for the fancy shindigs he assumed rich people always threw. McCready was surprised to find that the exterior stone of the mansion was nowhere to be found within. Instead, polished wood of assorted types decorated not only the walls, but also the ceilings, the floors, the stairs, the doors, and most everything else in view. Guess a Prozac® gray, cold stone interior wouldn't exactly feel very homey, would it? he asked himself.

McCready looked back at the butler, touching the sides of his Obsidians™. "So what am I here for, anyway?"

Jean Marcel Meraux, #318-74-8331, said, "Mr. Huxton will be down momentarily, sir, and he will inform you of the situation himself." His FE reading was yellowish-orange–active, but nothing serious. Too bad, McCready thought, remembering Takura's story idea–no butlers freeking out about their servitude. That would have been funny, but it wouldn't have made much sense. Huxton was keeping this thing under wraps for a reason–and it had to be about more than just a freeking butler.

"In fact," Marcel said, glancing up at the stairwell, "here he comes now."

"Hello, Agent McCready," Mason Huxton said as he walked down the stairs. "I hope that you found your ride into Xanadeux an enjoyable one." Huxton stood about six feet, medium build, and was dressed in a black, extremely expensive-looking suit. He had carefully styled, dark brown hair, looked about the same age as McCready, and moved with a confident assurance that showed he was well aware of the fact that he was one of the richest men in the world.

"I'll admit," he said, walking across the red carpet pathway, "I was impressed."

Mason William Huxton, #694-63-6494, smiled and said, "Good." Reaching the base of the stairs, he extended his hand towards McCready. "I would be greatly disappointed if someone were to find it dull or uninteresting." The pyramid was orangish-red.

"I think it's safe to say you've insured yourself against that possibility." McCready shook Huxton's hand, making sure not to exert too much pressure. His bionics, though antiquated, could easily crush bones if he wasn't paying attention.

"And one can never have too much insurance, can they?" Huxton asked. "I don't think so–and that's why you're here. Now, come with me upstairs and I'll acquaint you with the situation." He ascended the stairs and McCready followed. "I assume you've been informed by Agent Moore that everything we discuss today is strictly confidential?"

"Yup."

"And your sunglasses–they're not recording, are they?"

Interesting, McCready thought. He knows my cameras are in my glasses, even though every other Freemon at our branch has theirs in their contacts or implants. Huxton certainly does his research. "Nope," McCready said, "not unless you want them to."

"I don't," Huxton said.

They reached the top of the stairs, curved to the right with the banister, and walked straight ahead towards a partially opened door at the end of a long hallway.

"Until I find out more about what's going on," Huxton said, "I want absolutely no information leaking out–especially the specifics." Reaching the door at the end of the hall, Huxton stopped, placed his hand upon the wooden doorknob, and turned to face McCready. "It is of the utmost importance that Huxton family matters be kept personal and private," he said in a tone that was more hushed than before. "There are simply too many individuals out there who would love nothing more than to unearth some...'dirt' on us, so to speak."

Huxton pushed the door open, revealing a bedroom of typical Xanadeux proportions–gigantic. It was decorated in soft tones of white, rose, and lavender, with chiffon and lacy things draped all over the place. McCready could smell some type of powder or perfume in the air–something flowery, maybe jasmine or lily. In the center of the room was a king–no, it was way bigger than a king–more like a god-sized canopied bed upon which two women were seated next to each other. The older of the two was the same woman who had looked at McCready over the banister. It appeared she was consoling the younger woman. He scanned over both of them. Sofia Amity Grant, #364-93-5176. Pure orange. Dominique Evangeline Sanscrainte-Huxton, #808-42-0202. Bluish-green, with scintillating oscillations indicative of a cloned mind. McCready studied her frees a little longer, just to make sure he was reading them correctly. He was–she was definitely a clone.

McCready had heard that she'd been ill for the last few months, but this meant that the illness had to have been a *lot* more serious than it was reported to be. He had never heard anything in the media–or even within the bureau–about Huxton's wife being cloned. Not even rumors. Huxton wasn't kidding when he said he liked to keep his family matters private.

"Dom," Huxton said softly to his wife, "this is Mr. McCready, the specialist that I told you would be coming by today."

She didn't respond to his words, but kept staring down at the bed sheets. The older woman continued to gently run her fingers through Dominique's hair.

"He's going to do a few readings on you," Huxton said, glancing over at McCready with a nod, "and see if he can find out more about what it is that you're feeling. I'm going to the study to make a quick call, and then I'll be right back. Okay?" Again, no response. Huxton stared at her for a moment, waited, then looked back up at McCready. "I'll be just around the corner," he said. "Please come join me when you're through." He walked over to his wife, gave her a small kiss on her forehead, and left the room.

McCready turned back towards the two women. The older one looked up at him with tired eyes. There were a few scratches underneath her cheekbone. "Uh...hi," he said. "I'm Marc."

Sofia nodded a few times, turned her head, and gazed out a nearby window.

Why had Huxton just thrown him out here like this? he wondered. Why hadn't he been debriefed? He wished he knew more, because right now he felt incredibly intrusive and unwanted. McCready looked back at Dominique, who still appeared very spacey and distant. The FE pyramid was now a deep purple. Delta? She obviously wasn't in deep sleep–her eyes were wide open. And she was just in the low alpha range a second ago. She started to mumble something, and then the pyramid grew brighter–quickly through blue and green, holding momentarily at yellow, then shooting straight past orange up to red. Dominique began to shake violently, her expression turned to one of anger, and her eyes became eerily intense.

Sofia stood up, and took a fearful step back from her.

"I'm not even really me–I'm just a clone," Dominique said. "I'm just a copy of someone else. If that's all I am, then who am I?" She looked at McCready, clenching her teeth together like she was in pain. "Who am I?!" Her shaking then stopped, her reading shot down to theta blue, and her eyes lost their intensity.

"It won't stop," Sofia said under her breath, covering her mouth. "Lord, it won't stop."

Now McCready at least had the answer to the question of "what am I here for?" He asked Sofia, "How long has this been going on?"

77

"Since yesterday afternoon," she said. "It's horrible...she was never like this before." She began to cry. "I'm sorry," she said, wiping her long, gray hair away from her tearing eyes, "but it's so hard to see her like this."

McCready wasn't good at these things. He wasn't sure if he should hug her or try to make her laugh–so he did neither. "So, she's been continuously-"

"Why would they make me again?" Dominique asked McCready, as if he knew the answer. "What if I don't want to be here? What if I'm not who they want me to be?" Back up to the omega reading again. Not good. He hadn't seen something like this happen for a while–and never on anybody of this status. "Why are there all these questions in my head?" she cried. "Why, why, why...I'm so sick of why..."

McCready had seen enough. "I need to go talk with Huxton now," he said to Sofia. "Just...yell or something if you need me." McCready walked down the hallway to the study. He peered in before entering.

Huxton was seated on the corner of a large desk, looking down at a laptop uniview. He glanced up at McCready, motioned for him to enter, then turned his gaze back to the laptop.

"...checking the escorts' camera records," said a chilly, almost supernatural male voice from the uniview. "Will give us a good lead."

"Just make sure that you're the only one who does any investigating," Huxton said. "I'll hold you personally responsible should anyone else within Ordosoft™ find out about this incident."

"Not to worry, sir. Secret's safe with me."

"It better be, Mr. Webber," Huxton said. "It better be. I'll contact you shortly." He closed the laptop and looked at McCready. "I assume you've made your diagnosis?"

"Yeah," McCready said, pulling up a velvet-cushioned, wooden chair. "And if it's what I think it is, it's not good."

"Something has infected her, correct?"

McCready nodded and said, "Your wife's been infobombed, Mr. Huxton."

Huxton paused for a second, considering the possibility. "I was hoping that the mode of infection was going to be one of a less serious nature..." He crossed his arms, placed his finger on his lips. "Are you absolutely sure?"

"Considering her behavior and the range of her FE readings,

I'm pretty sure. There's not really anything else it could be."

"I see," Huxton said, lightly tapping his lip.

"The good news is that, judging from the intensity of the oscillations, I'd say she's peaking right now–which means that the compressed information's on its way out of her mind."

"And the bad news?"

"You're gonna have to wait and see what kind of damage it leaves behind. At this point, you can't really tell–infobombs affect different people in different ways. For some, it's just like getting high–they have all this shit in their head suddenly, but then they sleep it off and they're back to normal the next day. For others... Well, to be honest, it can change them forever. Someone who rarely freeked might become a permanent freeker, and a permanent freeker might suddenly become your most typical alpha-beta. It's hard to predict...and the fact that your wife's a clone only makes the situation that much more unpredictable."

Huxton eyed McCready for a moment, then stood up from the desk and paced over to a tall bookshelf. "How might she have contracted this informational disease?" he asked, staring straight ahead at the hardbound titles.

"Well, one mode of infobomb transmission is through the uniview. She may have been here at Xanadeux, just watching some-"

"Impossible," Huxton interrupted. "If there were some type of viral invasion attempting to enter our systems, Xanadeux would have dealt with it immediately and notified me of the occurrence."

"Isn't it possible the virus could have evaded Xanadeux's detection systems? That is what viruses are created to do."

"And Xanadeux was created to be impenetrable, Agent McCready. *Nothing* can evade its detection systems–it's an impossibility. If she did receive the infobomb through a uniview, I can assure you that it did not occur at Xanadeux." He turned from the bookshelf, facing McCready once again. "What are the other modes of transmission?"

"The only other way I've actually seen it happen is through touch," McCready said. "Someone'll hire a johnny courier, pack their brain with the infobomb instead of the usual data, then have them deliver it to the target via the body's natural electric current. Johnny touches you for a few seconds, and boom–you're bombed." McCready glanced up at the large oil painting behind Huxton's desk. It depicted Mason, looking about the same age as he did now, with Dominique and two brown-haired children, both under ten years old. "I've also heard the Pentagon possesses some kind of laser that can transmit infobombs over long distances, but that's never been confirmed. And I've never heard *any* reports or rumors of a criminal or terrorist organization possessing that kind of technology, so...if your wife was hit with something like that, it would be a first."

Huxton took a deep breath. "I see."

"Sir," announced Xanadeux's hermaphroditic voice over the room's speakers, "Ashley has arrived."

"Thank you, Xanadeux," said Huxton. "Have her come up to the house, and make sure to let her know how pleased we are that she's come by today."

"I'll do that, sir."

When the AI finished its sentence, McCready noticed that there was no sound of an intercom being turned off...meaning Xanadeux was still there–was always there–but just wasn't saying anything. Spooky, he thought. It was like they had an invisible third person in every room. "Mr. Huxton," McCready asked, "did your wife leave Xanadeux at all in the last few days?"

"Yes. She went out to an Eastside mall yesterday morning with some escorts."

"Well, if Xanadeux is as secure as you say it is, then that's when the bombing had to have occurred. I've never seen the information lie dormant for more than a day after transmission, so I doubt it could have happened before then. Did your wife's escorts have cameras on them?"

"Of course," Huxton said. "My head of security is looking into the camera records as we speak." He walked to his desk and poured himself a glass of water from a condensated silver pitcher. "I'll have him send you the information as soon as he's done reviewing it."

"Good. With that, we'll be able to see whether she watched a uniview or came into physical contact with anyone while she was outside of the estate. Then we can begin to piece together information from the biochip records, crossreference it with the visuals, and find out more about what happened. In the meantime, I'd recommend keeping her within Xanadeux, just to be safe. And since whoever attacked your wife is more than likely trying to get at you, you need to take extra caution, too. Until we know more, you should try to stay within Xanadeux. And if you do have to go somewhere, make sure to have escorts with you at all times." McCready looked up at the painting again. "Your children–they're possible targets, too. How old are they now?"

"Adam is thirty, and Ashley is twenty-five."

"And where are they?"

"Adam is currently at a restaurant in Bellevue, with his usual escorts watching over him. Xanadeux is relaying our conversation to him as we speak. I'm making sure that he is well informed, and as long as Adam is prepared, he can take care of himself." Huxton took a sip of water. "Ashley, however, I *am* a little worried about–and that's where you come in. You're my insurance."

McCready didn't like the sound of that. "What do you mean?" he asked.

"My family and I leave for Tibet this Friday, and until then, I would like you to keep an eye on my daughter. She has...shall we say...a talent for getting herself into situations. Therefore, I'd like *you* to insure that the situation happening to my wife does not happen to Ashley."

"You want me to babysit your daughter?" McCready laughed. "Mr. Huxton, you're gonna have to hire someone for that. Even if I wanted to, I wouldn't be able to do it. I'm a Freemon–we don't do 'for-hire' jobs."

Huxton coolly smiled. "You do now."

McCready eyed Huxton over the top of his Obsidians™. "What do you mean?" he asked in a lower tone than before.

"I've already made arrangements with your director, Harold Moore–an old friend, by the way–and he's agreed to grant you a few days off of active leave so that you can attend to my request."

This had to be a joke, McCready thought. Please let this be a joke. I do *not* want to babysit some snobby, stuck up, mall-shopping, designer clothes-wearing, silver spoon-feeding rich girl for the next three days. With my luck, she'll probably be some horrid creature who's had so much plastic surgery she looks like a living Barbie® doll. Definitely a joke, he tried to assure himself, as he pushed his sunglasses back into place. "Seriously?" he asked.

"I'm not known for my humor," Huxton replied.

Shit, McCready thought. He was serious. "So what, you want me to tail her, keep an eye on her...that sort of thing?"

"More than that, Agent McCready–I want you to be her personal escort," Huxton said. "I want you at her side whenever she leaves her residence, and I want you to *personally* make sure that no harm comes to her."

"Can't you get another Freemon to do the job? I'm sure there's someone else who'd be more qualified than me to do it."

"I can," Huxton said, "but I don't want to. I've looked into your records, Agent McCready, and I like what I see. You're a former detective, you've had experience with a number of protection and security services, you're a Freemon–who, I might add, received nothing but accolades and praises from your director... Agent Mc-Cready, you're the perfect man for the job."

McCready laughed and looked away from Huxton. "This is fucked," he said under his breath. He was stuck–you couldn't just say "no" to the head of Ordosoft™. Huxton was used to getting his way, and getting *in* his way was a sure way of going by the employment wayside. "Alright," McCready said, "so say I agree to do this job..." He stared at Huxton. "What's in it for me?"

"For starters, Harold Moore has agreed to give you two weeks paid leave, beginning the moment that we depart from Redmond."

"And for enders?"

"Provided that you do your job properly, I am quite prepared to compensate you for the services rendered."

McCready was starting to warm up to this idea. "Exactly what kind of compensation?"

"Generous."

Well, McCready figured, if you were gonna get fucked anyway, at least money made a good lubricant–metaphorically speaking, of course. "Then I guess you just hired yourself a Freemon." Now he just had to get himself mentally prepared to deal with a bitchy rich girl for the next three days. "So what does your daughter think about this arrangement?" McCready asked.

"Actually, she hasn't made up her mind yet," came a spirited female voice from just outside the study's doorway, "since this is the first time she's even heard about this arrangement."

McCready turned to face the fiery voice, and his stereotypes were instantly reduced to ashes. Ashley Adrianne Huxton, #248-0808-8425. Pyramid glowing orangish-red. Behind the darkened lenses, his eyes widened with surprise. She had no makeup, was simply dressed, wore only a few pieces of jewelry–not at all what he expected. She stood about five feet, eight inches, had long brown hair which gave off an auburn shine underneath the NatraLites™, tiny freckles which dotted her nose and cheeks, and hazel eyes that radiated truth. Ashley was absolutely beautiful. And not in a creepy, cosmetic surgery kind of way–no giant GS tits, no augmented, collagen-injected lips, no carved-up, pointy nose–but in a very real and genuine one. She glowed with honesty.

# ((FREQUENCIES))

"Ashley, dear," Huxton said as he walked over to his daughter, "thank you so much for coming by today." He hugged her with one arm and kissed her forehead.

Ashley accepted his affection, but seemed hesitant to show him any back.

Huxton looked at McCready, motioned towards him, and said, "This is Agent McCready. He's with the Freemon."

Ashley gave him a suspicious look. "Oh, one of the thought police, huh?"

McCready smiled–this was gonna be interesting.

She instinctively smiled back, a warm smile in which her eyes squinted tightly, as if she was gazing at something bright and shining. Ashley extended her hand and said, "I've never met one of you guys before."

"Lucky girl," he said, lightly grasping her hand. Ashley met his grasp with a firmer grip. Nothing rough or unnecessary, just firm. "I wouldn't want to meet one of me," he added.

"I'm sure you wouldn't," she said with eyes still suspicious, though now somewhat curious. She looked around the room. "So, dad–where's Adam?"

"He had an appointment to keep," Huxton said. "He'll be by as soon as he's through conducting his...business."

Ashley walked over to the desk, picked up an empty glass, and poured herself some water. "So what's going on?" she asked. "Adam said she's not doing well."

"No, unfortunately she's not," Huxton said. "Not at all." His expression grew more serious. "We have reason to believe that she's been the target of a terrorist attack."

Ashley covered her mouth. "Oh my goddess... Is she okay?"

"Physically, yes. Mentally...no. Her mind is quite...frail at the moment."

"Adam didn't even mention that earlier..." Ashley's face gave the impression that a thousand different thoughts were running through her head, as the orangish hue on her pyramid gave way to pure red.

"He didn't know yet. I just found out about it myself when Agent McCready made the diagnosis."

"Wow," she said to herself, "this day just keeps getting weirder and weirder..." She paused, looking like she was trying to sort through the thousand thoughts. "So this 'arrangement' you two were talking about...it must have something to do with her attack."

Huxton nodded. "I've assigned Agent McCready to be your security escort until we leave for Tibet on Friday. It's possible that the terrorists may target you also, and I want to make sure that you're not harmed in any way."

"I'd probably be wasting my breath by trying to convince you I'd be fine on my own, huh?" Ashley said.

Huxton didn't reply with any words–he simply smiled.

Ashley glanced at McCready and asked, "You get the same option package?"

"Pretty much," McCready said.

"Well, since neither of us really wants this 'arrangement,'" she said, throwing a playfully hard look over at her father, "I guess we might as well make the best of it–no point in making something negative if it doesn't have to be. We'll just try to respect each other's space..." She looked at McCready. "And go from there."

"Sounds fair to me," McCready said, still astonished that this gorgeous rich girl was so fucking real and down-to-earth.

Ashley stared at the open study door for a moment, her eyes becoming very focused and intent. "I guess I promised Adam that I'd visit her today," she said, walking over to the exit. She paused at the awning, and took a slow, deep breath. Turning her eyes to McCready, she said, "When I'm done with this, I'm gonna be ready to go, okay? Just warning you ahead of time."

Huxton watched her leave, a concerned expression upon his face. "Promise me that you'll keep my daughter safe, Agent Mc-Cready," he said.

Ten minutes ago, McCready would have immediately answered, "I can't make any promises." But now, after meeting Ashley, he wasn't quite so sure how to respond. He thought about what to say, then thought of her. Those eyes. "Yeah," McCready stated in a confident tone, "I promise."

$$\Omega$$

# Chapter 6
# ((Strange Attractors))

*"When confronted with reality's relativistic nature, some
beings experienced anxiety and apprehension, wanting nothing more
than to find someone or something which could define for them what
was to be "real" in their lives and what was not to be. Others,
comfortable with the realization that reality was mutable, relished
the infinite possibilities, and opened themselves to ideas and
concepts which many discarded as impractical, improbable, or
impossible. They perceptively realized that at any point in time, the
impossible could instantly become the possible—and the world could
change overnight.*

Ashley didn't feel like saying much.

As with the other time she had visited her mother's clone,
she left the encounter feeling appalled...sickened by the sight of a
woman who physically resembled her mother in every way, but who
clearly did not have the same presence or essence. Ashley could just
*feel* that the clone lacked her mother's soul, and this was what
disturbed her most. It was so hard for her to look into the eyes of
someone she loved, only to find that the spirit she was accustomed to
seeing was no longer there. The comforting, familiar soulflame had
been extinguished, replaced by something unnatural and wrong.

She kept thinking of demonic possession and that old book,
*The Exorcist.* The similarities were unsettling, especially considering
the current state of the clone. Her mother's shell had been stolen, and
now a confused entity of science was housed within it. Despite what

the technodevils tried to say to the contrary, cloning did *not* restore or replace a loved one–all it did was violate them.

As she and the Freemon walked away from the main house towards the parking area, barely a word was spoken between them. The only time the silence had been broken was when he had muttered to himself that he "wished you could have a fuckin' smoke in this joint." His comment had brought a brief, small smile to her face, but did nothing to dissipate the haunting images of her un-mother's dazed stares and desperate raves. It would have upset Ashley to have seen anyone in a mental state like that–the fact that it was someone who was the exact genetic replica of her mother only made the situation that much *more* upsetting. There were so many emotions she was feeling...so much to think about. And once she flashbacked to the meeting with Brennan, her contemplations only grew deeper...


"Wellor's research revealed to him that all living creatures," Brennan said, watching a mallard fly up from the fountain's pool, "regardless of their form, vibrate at a specific frequency which can be measured upon a spectral bandwidth which he called the LIFE–living incorporate frequency emission–spectrum. Mammalian FE's occupied the upper regions of the LIFE spectrum, bacteria and other microorganisms the bottom, while all other lifeforms were contained somewhere in between. As he continued his research, he found that certain mammals vibrated at the exact same frequency as did human beings–meaning that both were "thinking" at similar FE-activity levels. In fact, some dolphins and primates even registered *higher* on the spectrum than did he, or any of his students or colleagues who agreed to be tested."

"Interesting," Ashley said. "So organisms possessing a brain emanate higher FE's than those who don't, and something else...maybe the number of brain folds in the dolphin's case–also plays a role in the lifeform's position on the spectrum."

Brennan nodded. "Brain folds, genetic differences, the current state of the creature, its past experiences–all of these played a part in its FE reading, and Wellor tested a broad array of subjects and species under many different conditions to better understand the nature of the frequencies. For example, in one experiment, he found that a chimpanzee in a state of stress or agitation tended to have a higher reading than a chimpanzee who was calm and relaxed. Another test revealed that, more often than not, children's frequencies actually *dropped* once they had attended school for a few years. The same was true for any other animal taken from its original environment and placed into a setting which focused heavily on training and discipline." Brennan paused, looking around at the surrounding campus. "I remember Wellor was amazed by one experiment in particular, in which he discovered that a human in a coma gave off the same FE's as certain species of plants. To put it bluntly, a human 'vegetable' was frequentially no different than a cellulose one."

Brennan let out a small, dry cough, and continued, "When Wellor began to extensively test inanimate objects, such as a rock, a piece of plastic, or a cadaver, he found that they radiated absolutely no FE's whatsoever, save for the frequencies emitted by the micro-organisms on or within the object. Only living creatures could register on the LIFE spectrum. And for Wellor, this frequential division of the living and the unliving was pure scientific proof that all life was essentially the same. That the difference between me, you, a dog, a flower–or any other living creature–was merely a matter of degrees. In his view, we are all a living incorporate frequency emission. We are all one. A single electromagnetic wavelength called life."


"You heading home now?" McCready asked.

Lost in her thoughts, it took Ashley a moment to register that he had said something to her. "What?" she hazily asked.

"Where are you off to now? Home?"

"Umm..." she said, still pulling herself from the depths of contemplation, "I...I hadn't really thought about it yet." She looked at him, her eyebrows slightly furrowed, her lips taut around her teeth, then let out a mildly embarrassed laugh. "Sorry I'm kinda spacey right now. I've got a lot on my mind."

McCready smiled–a cunning smile, one that knew it knew things that others never knew. "So I see."

"Oh right, of course," Ashley said. "Your freeker thingy." In her FE research, she had learned that most Freemon's scanners were either housed in a pair of contacts or in some type of visual implants. She gazed at his dark sunglasses, trying to get a good look at the eyes behind. "Your window to the soul, huh?"

"Hardly. Our 'thingys' only measure electromagnetic fre-quencies–just thoughts," he said, as they walked into the canopied parking area. "Nothing as arcane as the soul."

"What if the soul *is* an electromagnetic frequency?"

The same smile again. "With the way modern science can screw around with the EM spectrum? Then things are even more fucked up than I already thought they were." Combined with his tousled black locks, his long green trenchcoat, and his fat oval shades, the smile gave McCready a roguish appearance. Mysterious, intriguing...and strangely attractive.

"Y'know," Ashley said, "you're not at all what I expected a Freemon to be like."

He laughed. "Is that good?"

She thought about the question for a moment, glanced at him from the corner of her eye, then looked back ahead at the antique vehicles. Her lips curved up a little as she replied, "We'll see..."

"Well, if it's any consolation," McCready said, "you're not what I expected either."

She smiled. "Is that good?"

Ashley's Lexus® and a black Chevrolet® pulled up in front of them, courtesy of Xanadeux. "We'll see," McCready said with a grin. "So where to?"

"Where to? I don't know...somewhere away from here, from all..." She motioned to the excessive amount of cars and the multiple Xandys. "...*this*." Though the chauffeurs weren't human, she still felt sympathy for them–shining and detailing all of their artificial lives, forced to wear that synthetic smile upon their faces day after day after day. Ashley wondered if they ever wanted to frown, then wondered if her mother could frown in cryo. She winced at the thought. "Anywhere," she said. "Let's just go–we'll figure it out along the way."

"Alright," McCready said, walking over to the rear of his Polaris™. "You have a preference which car we take?"

"No, not really."

"Then I'd prefer it if we took mine," he said, extending his hand towards the trunk. "More security." Before his biochip had a chance to reach the scanner, the trunk popped open. He stared at it for a moment, still holding his thumb out, then turned his gaze in the direction of one of the Xandys. "Thanks," he commented wryly.

"Hey, Xanadeux," Ashley said, "would you fly my Lex back to my house for me? I'm not gonna need it right now."

The nearest of the car-polishing Xandys looked up from its work. "Of course, Ashley. It would be my pleasure."

"Thanks." Ashley peeked over at McCready, who was still rummaging through the Chevy's® trunk. "Find what you're looking for?" she asked, seating herself on the hood of his car.

"Almost," he said. "Now...where is...ah–here we go." McCready emerged from the trunk with a vest in one hand and a couple of trinkets in the other.

"New toys?" she asked.

"Protection–some things I'd like you to have with you for the next couple days." McCready placed the trinkets on the roof of the car, but kept a hold of the vest. "You have any implants?"

"Besides the mandatory ones?"

"Yeah, other than the freeread and biochip."

"Just these," she said, delicately tugging on her long spiral earrings.

"Pierced ears?" McCready asked, his tone sounding surprised or impressed or some combination of both. "That's it?"

Ashley smiled. "That's it."

"Well, that'll make things a lot simpler. These guys can wreak havoc on certain implants." He handed her the vest.

It was a black, lightweight garment composed of a soft fleecelike material. Two small plastic discs were embedded in the base of it, one on each side of the zipper. Lightly pressing her fingers into the soft fabric, she found that it was packed with thousands of supple, ultrathin strands of filament. "So this must be some type of laserproof vest. Like the ones the cops wear."

"Similar," he said. "But these vests are made specifically for federal agencies. They're a lot more powerful than the ones the city police are issued."

"But they essentially do the same thing."

"Right, the fundamentals are the same–they both create protective emfields around you. But, there's a big difference when it comes to what kinds of attacks they protect you against." McCready picked up one of the devices from the top of the hood and started to tinker with it. "See, the cops' vests only protect against standard police-issue weapons–laser pistols, motor control nappers, etcetera–and that's it. Those things," he said, pointing to the vest "will shield you against reticular nappers, microwave weapons, infobombs, lasers–you name it. If it's an electromagnetic attack, then that emvest should be able to disrupt it."

She thought about how all satellite communications were contained within the EM spectrum, and asked, "Won't it also disrupt my biochip's satellink?"

"Nah, the emfield only extends around your trunk and head,

not your extremities. You can still access your bank accounts and open your locks just like before. The biochip won't be disrupted at all."

Another thought popped into her head: But what about the various effects EMF's could have on a living organism? After all, the vest's field would be emanating from *her* body. "Couldn't the vest also disrupt other things?" Ashley asked. "Like *me*?"

"I sure as hell hope not," McCready laughed, opening his trenchcoat to reveal the vest underneath. "'Cause I'm wearing one, too." Before he closed his coat, Ashley caught a glimpse of the handle of an old steel revolver (which she had previously only seen on the UV), housed within a brown leather shoulder-holster.

"But you don't know for sure," she said. "It's possible that it might mess with the wearer's physiology in some way."

"Well, yeah, of course it's possible," he said, picking up one of the devices from the hood. "It's possible this coat I'm wearing was created with cancer-causing dyes, it's possible that those earrings you have on are picking up mind-altering signals from a planet in the fuckin' Alpha Centauri system–hell, anything's *possible*. You could–" McCready looked up from the device at Ashley and suddenly paused. He had seemed kind of annoyed before, and now it appeared to her like he was trying to make sure that he chose his next words carefully...that if he didn't check himself, he was going to say something that he might regret. "Basically," he said, his tone less uptight than before, "it comes down to this–you get to choose between an emvest that might fuck you up–or a laser that *will*."

"Good point. I guess I'll take my chances with this thing." She ran her fingers along the small discs at the base of the garment. "What do these do?"

"Those are your control knobs. Both of 'em work the same way–push in the center of the button to activate, then turn the dial surrounding it to the desired frequency." He reached his fingers down to the control knobs on his vest. "The one on the right controls your emfield–turning it clockwise will increase the intensity, counter-clockwise will decrease it. I'd recommend you keep it turned to a little past noon–about one o'clock. That should be enough."

She pointed to the other knob on his vest. "And that one?"

"This one," he smiled, "is the 'fashion' button. The vest's fabric is made from optical fibers, so with a turn of the dial..." His green vest slowly changed color through different shades of greenish-yellow, then to pure yellow. "Fuckin' A–you can match with any outfit." McCready turned the dial faster and the vest's color quickly jumped to red. He then turned it all the way counterclockwise, running the entire color spectrum down to deep purple, then to blacks, grays, and finally, whites. "Guess Uncle Sam figured the *Men In Black* needed some color in their wardrobes," McCready said, turning the vest to its previous shade of hunter-green.

Ashley smiled, took off her sweater, and put on her vest. "So I guess I'll be wearing this all the time, huh?"

"Pretty much. You should have it on and activated whenever you leave Xanadeux or your home. From what your dad has told me, your estate is almost as secure as Xanadeux is, so you should be safe from attack either there or here. But outside of those safe zones, you're vulnerable–and that vest becomes your best friend."

"As long as my best friend doesn't resonate my molecules into another dimension," she said, half-joking, as she zipped up the front of the vest. It was a little loose on her, but not so loose that it didn't fit. She rotated the dial until the vest was the emerald hue of her sweater. "There we go. Okay–I'm ready for contraption number two."

McCready handed her a wide, platinum-banded ring which had a clear jewel set into its center. "That should go on your middle finger, same hand as your biochip."

Ashley placed the ring around her finger, but the band was too big to stay on. She examined the gemstone closer, and noticed that it had a small, grippable dial around it. "Is this a twisty-fit?"

"Yup," he said. "But be *extremely* careful as you adjust it. The jewel needs to be centered directly in the middle of your finger–it shouldn't lean one way more than the other. Also, there are four clicks on it instead of the usual two, but make sure not to go past the first two clicks."

"Okay." Holding the ring in place, Ashley twisted the dial one click to the right. She waited a few seconds, until the band had closed to a comfortable fit, then stopped it by clicking the dial again to the right.

"You got it to a snug fit?" he asked. "It doesn't slip at all?"

She tugged on the ring, then shook her head. "No slippage."

"Alright, good. 'Cause if that ring slips even the slightest bit, you could wind up hurting yourself."

"And this is because...?"

"The second two clicks activate the microlaser that's housed inside the jewel."

She looked down at the ring with disbelief, then back up at McCready. "Really? This is a *laser*?"

"Yup. And for its size, its powerful."

Ashley laughed. "A power ring...I feel like Green Lantern®, or what!"

"Yeah, a lot of our stuff feels like superhero equipment."

"I guess so." She turned her palm over to see if there was some type of button on the underside of the ring. No button, but there was a tiny black square which looked like some type of sensor or scanner. "So how does it work?"

"Basically, that sensor you're looking at is the 'trigger.' When the dial is turned to the third or fourth click, all you need to do is make a fist with your thumb tucked in..." McCready held up his hand to show. "...fingernail touching the sensor-square...and the laser will fire. It's not as accurate as a laser pistol, but it doesn't need to be. It's an emergency weapon, and in that type of situation, immediacy takes precedence over accuracy–you just shoot straight ahead at whatever it is that's threatening you, and keep shooting until it's no longer a threat." Ashley felt a pulse of anxiety reverberate through her being, McCready's last words triggering an abrupt recognition that her life really *was* in danger. "The third click will set the laser's intensity to a searing level that'll injure," he continued, "and the fourth focuses it to a cutting level that'll kill."

The novelty of the vest and the ring–and the whole situation in general–had temporarily made everything seem larger than life, as if she were innocuously watching a movie play out before her eyes. But now, as she thought about burning or killing someone with a laser, or someone killing *her* with a laser, the gravity of the situation felt massively heavy. Ashley took a deep breath, and said, "This is all so strange...talking about lasers, and shooting people, and..." She nervously laughed. "...and it's all just so bizarre..." She laid back on the hood of the car, and looked up at the high, conical top of the tent. As she focused her eyes on the center of the cone, the conversation with Brennan came to mind once again...


"When Wellor looked at the world around him," Brennan said, "he saw a planet out of balance, largely due to the exploits of one single species–Homo sapiens. Wellor believed that modern humans had disrupted the Earth's equilibrium by adopting a way of life which encouraged overconsumption and greed, while simultaneously discouraging respect for other cultures and lifeforms. I remember once, him remarking to a few colleagues that humankind, by destroying the living diversity which evolution had taken millions of years to create, was sowing the seeds of its own destruction."

"Makes sense," Ashley said.

"In many ways it does. Yet we're still here, as prosperous as ever, with immortality now looming on the horizon."

"Maybe," she skeptically said. "But what if the effects of our past and present actions still haven't been fully felt yet? Y'know, like when a star burns out...how we're still able to see its light for a while, even though the star itself no longer exists? Maybe right now, human 'progress' is like that star. We're basking in its light, thinking that everything around us is so bright, that we'll be able to play in its glow forever...but we don't realize that the source of the light has already been extinguished. And not until the starlight stops shining, do we finally realize what it is that we've done."

Brennan laughed. "And here I thought *you* were the hopeful one."

"I am," Ashley smiled. "But my hopes don't reside with *this* system we're currently living under. I'm hoping for something more meaningful and true to take its place."

Brennan nodded. "Which is why you're the perfect person to share Wellor's ideas with. He was hoping for the same type of world that you hope for, Ashley. And he believed that hopeful existence could be realized...*if* humankind were to radically alter the schemas and paradigms they used to interpret the world around them. He theorized that if we were to stop looking at ourselves as separate from, or above other lifeforms, and instead began to look at ourselves as part of a diverse, living, interdependent whole–if this was accomplished–then plants and animals would no longer be looked at as merely resources to be exploited, but rather, as equals to be respected."

"Neat," she said. "Sounds like he was a dreamer."

"Indeed he was, Ashley," Brennan said, his face full of remembrance. "And that's why he created the FE technology, in the hopes that it would help others to see the interconnectedness and interdependence of all life. Wellor set out to change the world with his science–and he succeeded." Brennan's expression became grim. "But not in the way he had hoped."


"You okay?" McCready asked.

Ashley slowly sat up. "Mm-hm, I'm fine." She let out a small sigh, then glanced over at McCready. "Have you ever had one of those really, *really* weird days?"

"Yeah," he laughed, "I've had too many of 'em."

"Then you know what kind of day I'm having today." She placed her palms on the hood, slid herself off of the car, and walked around to the passenger side. "You want to tell me about the other gadgets as we fly?"

"Sure," McCready said, slipping a device into his pocket, "no problem. Let me just close the trunk." He walked towards the rear of the car, but before he was even halfway there, Xanadeux closed the trunk. "Alright," McCready said in an irritated tone, turning back to the front of the vehicle. The driver-side door immediately opened. He looked over at Ashley. "And you had to grow up with this?"

Ashley laughed, seated herself inside the vehicle, and allowed Xanadeux to shut the door behind her.

McCready sat down on the driver's seat, his back facing Ashley, his legs placed outside the vehicle. He grabbed hold of the door with his left hand, raised his right hand into the air, extended his middle finger, and panned it around to the Xandys. He then pulled his legs into the car, and made sure to manually shut the door himself.


During the flight, they had decided to go somewhere that was relatively safe and relaxing, but somewhere outside the gates, since they both shared a mutual distaste for the antiseptic ambiance of the gated communities. Ashley suggested they go to Tosh's, an herbal café in the Westside neighborhood of Fremont. Though she hadn't been there in a few months, it still seemed like the best choice possible. She was *very* close with the owner (though they hadn't spoken a lot since their breakup), was friends with most of the employees and regulars, and knew that the café was extremely selective about who they let into the establishment. "Nobody's gonna attack me there," she had told McCready. "It'll be safe." He agreed with the choice, and now, twenty minutes later, they were walking up the sidewalk towards the café. A street musician was leaning against an adjacent building's facade, plucking away at the strings of her worn guitar.

"Have you ever been to Tosh's before?" Ashley asked.

"Nah, I haven't," McCready said. "I don't come to Fremont much. Only when the job brings me here."

"Babylon, Babylon," the musician sang softly, eyes shut tight, head rhythmically swaying with the melody, "your time soon come."

Ashley slowed her pace so she could hear more of the song as they passed by...

*For the voice of change, it floats on the breeze*
*and it speaks of love, and it speaks of peace*
*It tells of a time that must come to be*
*when the truth is the truth, and a lie cannot be*
*So Babylon, Babylon, your time soon come*
*Babylon, Babylon, your time...soon come*

Ashley nodded her head, then said to McCready, "I think you'll like Tosh's. It's got a nice vibe, real kickback."

"Reggae-themed?"

"Yeah. They play a lot of pre-millenial stuff—mostly roots, though they'll also play some dancehall and dub occasionally."

"I like it already," McCready said as they reached the café.

Ashley pulled the front door open, and her nose was immediately filled with the familiar, wonderfully intoxicating scents of the café. Sage and sandalwood incense swirled together with the smoky bouquets of various kinds of cannabis. Fresh-ground coffee intermingled with peppermint and licorice teas. Culinary hints of allspice, cumin, and clove. The aroma was pure olfactory ambrosia.

"Smells good," McCready said.

"*Mm-hm,*" she emphatically agreed, walking to the checkpoint at the end of the hallway. Two men were standing there—one who had his back turned towards them, finishing a conversation with someone inside the café, the other, whom she didn't recognize, was carefully eyeing them as they approached.

"Hey, you," Ashley said playfully to the man with his back turned.

Melloe slowly turned around, a glowing smile upon his face. "Ashley," he said, stepping forward and giving her a warm hug. "It's good t'see you, girl! How you been?"

"I've been good," she said. "I've had some family things I've had to deal with the last few months, but I'm doing well."

"Okay, dat's good," Melloe said, tucking a stray dreadlock beneath his knitted cap. "You dealin' wit' it den." He nodded approvingly as he looked her in the eyes. "Dat's good." He glanced over at the tall, muscular, dreadlocked man standing next to him, then back at Ashley. "Ashley, dis is Bain. He came up from Martinique

95

'bout a mont' ago."

Ashley recalled that Tosh had spoken fondly of a Bain on several occasions–this had to be the same one. "Nice to meet you," she said, extending her fist to Bain's. "I've heard good things about you."

"Likewise," he said. They both twisted their fists, then brought the still-closed hand back to their chests.

"I don't tink I met your friend before," Melloe said, turning to McCready. "I'm Melloe."

"McCready," he said, touching his gloved fist to Melloe's.

"Good to know you, mon," Melloe said. "If you wit' Ashley, then you chill wit' me, okay?"

"Alright," McCready said. He moved his hand over to Bain. "Bain, right?"

Bain nodded slowly. "McCready..." He looked over the Freemon suspiciously as he extended his fist. "Right?"

"Right," he said with a smirk. As before, McCready retracted his fist without bringing it to his chest.

Bain did the same, still cautiously eyeing McCready.

Ashley hoped that she hadn't made a mistake by bringing McCready in here. He *was* a member of the thought police after all, and bringing one of them to an herbal café was sort of like bringing an aardvark to an anthill, since people had a tendency to think freeky thoughts while smoking herb. In spite of the misgivings, she was confident that her intuitions about McCready were correct–that he was someone who, though involved in law enforcement, didn't particularly like the law itself, and wasn't interested in arresting people if he didn't have to. But, she also realized there was a possibility he was just projecting that type of image at her in order to gain her trust. Oh well, Ashley conceded, what's done is done. Time to accept the decision and move on. "Is Tosh around?" she asked Melloe.

"No, na t'right now," he said. "He 'ad to go out somewhere, but 'e should be back in a jif, okay? If you wan', I can tell 'im dat you 'ere when 'e come back."

"Yeah, that'd be good," she said, looking into the café's interior. "It'd be nice to talk to him." As usual, the place was comfortably crowded, filled with familiar faces and positive vibrations. "You ready to head in?" she asked McCready.

"Ready when you are," he said.

"Hold up, mon," Bain said to McCready, picking up a scanner gun from a small wooden stand. "I got'ta check you first."

McCready stopped, turned around and said, "Sure–go ahead."

Bain pointed the scanner at the top of McCready's head, and slowly moved the thin laser-line down his body. His eyebrows lifted as he read the results on the device's small screen. "De scanner's tellin' me dat you loaded wit' all manner a' weapon, mon." His brow furrowed with disapproval. "We na dig dat kind of bumbaklaat 'ere, seen? If you don' got de proper badge, den we got'ta ask you to leave."

McCready reached into his trench, pulled out his badge, and turned it over to Bain.

A holographic Freemon logo materialized into the air as soon as Bain opened it. He picked up a penlike scanner and ran it along the bottom of the badge.

"You need to match it with the biochip?" McCready asked.

"Yah, mon," Melloe said, extending a biochip scanner toward McCready. "No offense, but we got'ta keep de place straight, yunno?"

"No offense taken," McCready said.

Bain studied the information on a nearby laptop, then handed McCready his badge. "Okay, mon," he said, motioning towards the café's interior, "you can go in now."

"Thanks," McCready said.

"There's a booth by the window that just opened up," Ashley said to McCready. "Let's go over there."

Bobbing his head with the upbeat music sounding throughout the space, he replied, "So Jah say."

"What?" Ashley asked, walking past a few of the cushioned wicker couches and their occupants.

"The music," he said. "It's an old Dennis Brown cut–'So Jah Say.' Classic."

"Oh, right," Ashley said, now understanding what he meant. She looked over at the central dance floor to her right, then up at the bar opposite the hallway entrance. The bartender, Frances, immediately noticed Ashley, and they waved at each other with a smile. As she and McCready weaved their way around papasans, tables, and chairs, various people greeted Ashley, some with handshakes or their fists, some with a sup or a nod, others with a simple "hey" or "what's up." Ashley greeted them all back, but made sure not to get caught up in a long conversation with anyone. Not that she didn't want to talk to them, just that she was *very* ready to sit down and relax for a while.

Nearing the booth, McCready said, "I can see why you feel comfortable here."

"Yeah," Ashley said, seating herself on the booth's soft cushioning, "if I'm not safe here..." Meaning conveyed, she let her words trail off, then looked to her right, through the tinted plate glass window which comprised the entire south wall of the building.

Gravity-bound cars driving by, GS cars ascending and descending, a potpourri of people pacing the sidewalk... A section of the city in motion. Watching the different individuals go by, Ashley wondered what each of them were thinking about. Were they hoping for something? Worrying? Dreaming about something? Afraid? Excited? What were they feeling? Whatever it was, she wished them all happiness (briefly thinking of Adam, and how he would always scoff at her for saying things like that), and hoped their innermost dreams were being fulfilled. But, as she studied the sundry faces going by, many of which were broken and downtrodden, she saw that hopes and reality weren't always the same thing. Not yet, at least. She thought of Babylon and the singer's words. Soon.

"People watching?" McCready asked.

More like people *feeling*, Ashley thought. "Sort of," she said.

"I do that all the time. People are so fuckin' weird, all the things you catch 'em doing." He looked out the window. "People are a trip to watch."

"People are a trip to *be*," she said with a small laugh.

"True," he said, nodding his head a few times as he averted his gaze from the window. "Like how we'll comment on how weird people are, while we're sitting there like fuckin' peepin'-Toms watching them, right?" McCready laughed, displaying his barely crooked, off-white teeth.

Ashley smiled. He's able to laugh at himself, she thought. That's a good sign. And his teeth aren't perfect. That's good, too. Cosmetically perfect teeth just wouldn't have fit well with the roguish look. Ashley wondered how old he was. "How old are you?" she asked, as soon as the thought crossed her mind.

McCready leaned back into the booth's cushioning, placing a toothpick between his lips. "How old do you think I am?"

Ashley examined his facial features, trying to find a tell that would reveal his age. Some wrinkles on his forehead, but nothing extreme...same around the mouth. Definitely older than her...but with his sunglasses on, it was hard to make out the eyes. "I can't tell with your shades on."

"Alright." McCready removed his sunglasses and set them down on the table. Ashley was surprised how different he looked without them. Far from roguish, McCready now looked...the first word that came to her mind was "vulnerable." His dark brown eyes reflected a sort of sadness...or hurt. Not at all weakness, but *deep*ness. A depth that he kept hidden away from the world, almost like the shades were a slick veneer to protect the feeling eyes beneath. "How's that?" he asked.

"...better," she quietly said, staring into his eyes. They reminded her of a literary cliché, the one about pools so deep you could drown in them. Ashley felt her face getting flushed and decided she better get back to the task of determining his age. She looked down at his ungloved hand. It appeared rough, like it had been worked for at least thirty years. Crow's feet around the eyes, but as with his forehead, nothing extreme...definitely not forty. "Thirty-three," she said.

"Close."

"Thirty-five."

"Bingo. You got it."

She smiled, and asked, "So how old do you think I am?"

"Twenty-five," he answered without hesitation.

"Wow," Ashley laughed, "first try. Lucky guess?"

"Nope–ancient secret."

"Which is?"

He coyly smiled, as one of the café's waiters approached the table. "Ask her father."

Ashley shook her head and laughed, then looked up at the waiter. "Hey, Joseph," she said to the young man, whose tight braids had colorful wooden beads near their ends.

"What's up, Ashley," Joseph smiled. "Long time no see."

"Yeah," she agreed, meeting her fist with his, "it's been a while. You changed your hair."

Joseph shrugged his shoulders as he took a pull from his spliff. "It's jus' a likkle suh'em suh'em, yunno?"

"I like it a lot," Ashley said. "It fits you."

"Okay, thanks," he said with a quiet smile.

"Joseph," she said, "I'd like you to meet my..." She paused, trying to think of the proper word. Glancing at McCready, she smiled, then looked back at Joseph. "...friend, McCready."

McCready held out his fist like he'd been doing it for years.

Joseph laughed. "You know de greetin'? Yah, mon," he said as he touched his fist to McCready's. "Nice to meet you."

McCready brought his fist back to his chest, nodded his head, and earnestly said, "You too, Joseph."

"Yah, mon. Notin' better den people connectin', yunno? One

love." He swayed with the music, and asked, "So you two in de mood to smoke de canny, eat some food, 'ave a drink...?"

"I wouldn't mind a beer," McCready said.

"Sorry, mon. We na serve de poison 'ere. Bad vibes, yunno?"

"Fair enough," he said. "Give me a latté then–triple short."

"Sure. Anyting else?"

"You probably don't allow cigarettes in here, right?"

"No, mon," Joseph said. "De only tobacco we 'ave is de leaf on a blunt. Dat's it."

"Just the latté then."

"Okay, sure." To Ashley, he said, "You smokin' today?"

"Hm-mm," she said, shaking her head, "it's too early for me. I can't smoke until the sun goes down." Wait, she thought, that's not fully the truth. "Except sometimes when I'm exercising–then I do it in the daytime. But anyways, I would like a chamomile-sativa tea, please. With some honey. And a small bowl of potlikker. That's it." She laughed. "Please."

"Sure, I'll be right back." He walked towards the bar.

"Potlikker?" McCready asked her. "What the hell is that?"

"Stewed greens, basically," she said. "Mostly collards and mustards...sometimes kale. It's yummy."

"I'm sure it is," he said, "but that's a weird fuckin' name. Sounds like a word for the guy who always gets stuck with the leftovers–the pot licker."

Ashley laughed at the absurdity of his remark. "I'm sure that's not what it means. I think it's a Jamaican word, actually."

"Is that what these guys are?"

"Uh-uh. Most everyone who works here is either from Dominica or Martinique. Tosh grew up on both islands, and he brings family and friends up here to work in the place."

"That's cool," McCready said.

A new song began to play on the soundsystem, one that she recognized but didn't know the name of. The volume increased, and the thumping drum beat vibrated up from the ground through her body. The sensation felt neat...sort of tingly. "I like this song," she said, playing the tabletop like a drum. "It's Bob Marley, isn't it?"

"Yup, when he was still with the Wailers. 'Rastaman Chant.' Yeah," he said, nodding his head to the beat with a smile, "this song's the cut, right here."

McCready looked so lighthearted and content right now, as he sat there enjoying the music, watching people express themselves on the dance floor...almost like he was experiencing something new. Like he didn't get to experience happiness very often. The look on his face made her think of a man who had been carrying a heavy burden for a long time, and had finally gotten a chance to set it down and relax. Maybe she was just reading into things (she knew she had a tendency to do that), but that was what she was sensing. Plus, she just couldn't see a job that involved busting people for their thoughts as being very conducive to a joyful mindstate. Peaceful moments for a Freemon must be few and far between, she thought. Why would someone want that kind of lifestyle? Why would *he* want it? She wanted to know more. "What made you decide to become a Freemon?"

McCready thought about the question for a few seconds before answering. "It's funny," he said, "'cause in a way I never really decided to become one. It's more like it happened to me."

"What, they recruited you?"

"That's one way of putting it. Drafted–that'd probably be even closer."

"That sounds creepy," she said. "So you didn't have any choice in the matter?"

"Well, I had a 'choice,'" McCready said, using his fingers to make quote marks. "I gotta choose whether I wanted to be placed in a job that completely isolated me from other people, or apply for a job that gave me clearance to think and discuss freeker thoughts. It was a lesser of two evils kind of thing. I chose the one that would allow me the most freedom."

"But why not something else? Something less..." she paused, thinking of the proper word. "...oppressive. Why the Freemon?"

"Because it was the only way *I* was gonna get clearance, sweetheart," he said. "'Cause I don't come from money, I don't like academia or politics, and I abso-fuckin'-lutely loathe corporate bullshit. The Freemon were my best option. By far."

She still couldn't understand why anyone would want the job. "Okay, but you said that you chose the Freemon because it gives you freedom. If you like that ideal so much, then doesn't it bug you to take away someone *else's* freedom?"

McCready laughed. "Do you always interrogate people when you first meet them?"

Ashley smiled, shrugged her shoulders, and replied, "Only if they interest me. Don't give me an answer if you don't feel like it."

"I won't," McCready said bluntly. "But I don't mind answering your question." He placed his toothpick into an ashtray and picked up a fresh one. "If you want to know the truth, it *does* bug me to fuck around with people's lives. I hate it. It's fucked up. But that's what this society does–it makes you a part of things you don't want to be a part of. And yeah, I'm more directly involved in the fucked up shit than a lot of people are, but c'mon, let's face it–indirectly, we're *all* a part of it, aren't we?"

He leaned forward, smiling devilishly. "I mean, you can *try* to pretend that you're not–but you still are. 'Cause every time you spend some cash or pay your taxes, you're keepin' the economy run-ning–and that means you're supporting some kind of oppressive shit you don't want to. Whether it's death squads in Columbia or riot cops in Rainier Valley, *your* taxes are payin' for it. And the fucked up thing is, the only *real* way to rebel is to stop paying taxes and stop spending–but then you're gonna starve or end up in the workcamps. And then what good are you?" McCready leaned back, shaking his head. "I'm tellin' you, sweetheart, whoever designed this system was a fuckin' genius. They created their society like one big, gigantic prison that you can't even see, let alone escape from. And I'm trapped in it like everyone else. I don't like my job, but it keeps me fed. I'd do something else if it was a different world, but it's not, so I don't. That's the unfortunate reality."

"That's the reality for *now*," Ashley said, tracing a spiral on the tabletop with her finger, "but it'll change eventually. It's all just a matter of time..." She stared at the imaginary symbol and smiled with angelic assurance. "And time doesn't really matter."

Walking up to their booth with a tray in his hand, Joseph said, "Okay, 'ere's your orders."

"Thanks, Joseph," Ashley said, picking up her mug of tea and sniffing its fragrance. "It smells wonderful."

Joseph smiled. "Good. Let me know if you need anyting else, okay? Enjoy."

Ashley brought the rim of the mug to her lips, gently blew on the surface of the tea, and took a few careful sips. The flowery blend of warm, sweet liquid felt soothing as she swallowed, suffusing her self with a sensation both calm and inspiriting. "Perfect," she said.

McCready stuck his finger into his latté, quickly pulled it out, and said, "Too hot."

She smiled, savored another slow sip, and set her mug down. The chamomile aftertaste reminded her of childhood...of morning teas with her mother. Good memories, ones which could never be tainted by the wrongs of the present. Her thoughts moving from the past to the now, she asked, "So what exactly happened to the clone?"

"You mean your mother?" McCready said.

"*No*, I mean the clone of my mother." She swirled the cloth teabag around in the mug. "What happened to her?"

"Well, we still have a few things to check out and verify, but all the signs are pointing to an infobombing."

"Hmm," she said, cupping her hands around the tea, "mental graffiti, huh?" She thought about the things her un-mother spoke about during the time they spent together. "That would explain why she's freeking out so hard. The bomb probably had something in it to make her insecure about being a clone."

"Right," McCready said. "Either it was specifically created for her–which is the worst case scenario for your father, since that would mean someone hostile to your family knows your mother's been cloned–or the bomb contained some type of uninhibitor. One that unlocks a person's deepest fears, whatever they may be. And typically, most clones fear they're not real people–that they're something less than human." He pulled out a pack of cigarettes and set them down on the table. "Which is exactly what she's freeking about."

"True," Ashley said. "Either way, the whole situation's messed up. I feel so bad for that woman...it must be so hard, y'know? It's bad enough that she has to try to be someone who she's not, but then to have some kind of infobomb make everything even more confusing..." She shook her head, her mouth frowning down at the corners. "It's just messed up. I wish things were different."

"Yup," McCready said. "I know. It's an insane fuckin' world."

"It's definitely that," Ashley said, pulling the bowl of potlikker in front of her. Taking a deep breath, she closed her eyes, bowed her head, and said a silent prayer over the food. She then opened her eyes, and picked up her fork.

"That's a small?" McCready asked, eyeing the large serving.

"Mm-hm," Ashley said, taking a bite. "Big, huh? You want some?"

"Nah, I'm trying to save room for dinner later to-" He paused for a moment, and asked, "Are you going out tonight?"

"I wasn't planning on it. Why?"

"I just realized that if you're not staying at home or at Xanadeux, then I need to cancel some dinner plans I had for tonight."

"Oh, don't worry, you won't need to cancel your plans. All I want to do tonight is kick back at home, relax, and sort through everything that's happened today."

"You sure?"

"Yeah, I'm sure."

"You don't need me around tonight or anything? You're gonna be okay?"

She smiled. "I'll be fine. Thanks, though."

"No prob." McCready shook a cigarette out of the package. "Well, the ol' nicaddiction's calling." He stood up and put on his sunglasses. "I'm gonna step outside for a sec and have a smoke, alright?"

Ashley picked up the crumpled, green and white pack of cigarettes from the table. "Old Skools™?" She glanced up at McCready with a skeptical eye, holding the pack out towards him. "You actually smoke these?"

"Yup." He took the package from her hand with a smirk.

"Do you know they lace those things with ammonia so your lungs'll absorb more nicotine?"

"Yup. There's a bunch of other shit in 'em, too. Freon, pesticides... I even heard they grow their tobacco in uranium-enriched soil." He looked at the cigarette. "Filthy habit. I wouldn't recommend taking it up."

"Oh, I won't," she said. "Not again. I already quit once, and I have *no* desire to get hooked again."

"What? And miss out on that terrific, liberating feeling of constant nicotine withdrawals?" McCready smiled sarcastically. "Suit yourself, sweetheart. I'll be back."

Ashley took another bite of the greens as she watched him slither his way through the crowded café. McCready effortlessly blended in with the scene, giving no indication that he was who he was...a snake in the grass, slippery, slick, and sly. As he passed out of sight through the hallway, she laughed to herself at how this cynically facetious character had suddenly popped into her life... Then laughed harder at the fact that she was finding him attractive. She reflected back on the strange twist of fate which had thrown them together–an attack on her mother's clone–then thought about her conversation with Brennan and all of *its* many implications. She thought about coincidence and destiny, chaos and synchronicity.

And marvelled at the mysterious, wild ways in which life weaves its intricate web.

# Chapter 7
# ((Existencia))

*Thus, if something unwanted or undesirable were present in their
reality, they effected change so that the problem would cease to exist
within their own personal sphere of influence. When others did the
same, the problematic force exerting itself upon their shared world
either diminished in strength, or–if the sphere of influence had
spread far enough–ceased to exist at all.*
*Likewise, if something vital or necessary was absent from their
reality, they actively sought to fill this hollow space, and put into
their lives that which was previously missing."*

"Unh...ah...almost...unh...there..." Ignacio said with deep, heavy
breaths, sliding his damp palms down the inside of her soft, slender
thighs. "...ahunh...almost..."

Raquel opened her legs wider at his touch, braced her arms on
the mattress, and pressed herself down harder on top of him.
"You...mhnh...wanna pull out," she asked, turning her head and
looking back at him, "or do you...want to...mmh...come inside me?"

"Don't...don't play...Raquel..." he said with a small laugh.
"You... unh...you know what I want."

She smiled, turned her head back around, and slowly moved
her hips in strong, wide, circular motions.

Ignacio tightly clenched his molars. His hands reached the
base of her thighs, and he felt her groin muscles tensing with each
puissant gyration. He moved further inwards, until his hands were
touching the moist, warm area where the two of them were joined

together. "Ounh...keep going..." he whispered forcefully through his teeth, rubbing his fingertips in her wetness. "Don't stop...I'm...ah... about to..."

"I know, sweetie," Raquel said, increasing the rapidity of her gyrations to an almost unbearable speed, "mmh...I can feel you."

Ignacio leaned back against the bed's pillowed headboard and looked up at the ceiling fan, whose spinning motion seemed to perfectly match Raquel's. He rubbed one of his sticky, wet hands along his mouth and nose, breathed in the sweet, sexual scent, and closed his eyes. He briefly imagined that it was Essence on top of him, then focused back on Raquel. "Ouhn...so close..." Ignacio moaned, trying to hold back his climax as long as possible.

When the irresistible pressure became too much, he reached his hands up to her ass, squeezed it firmly, and released his orgasm. "Ounhhhndios," he vigorously sighed, thrusting himself deeper into her with each climactic pulse. "I love you...ounhh, god...I love you, Raquel."

Smoothly moving her hips in unison with his final ejaculations, Raquel whispered, in a barely audible tone, "No you don't." When he was completely finished, she reclined onto his chest, making sure to keep him inside of her. Laying the back of her head just above his collarbone, she looked up at him and said, "The only time you say you love me is when you're coming."

He ran his fingers through her short, dyed-blond hair. "Maybe that's the only time I tell the truth."

"Maybe." She quickly wiggled her hips. "And maybe I know you better than that."

"Aaah!" Ignacio shouted with a laugh. He playfully pushed her off of him, on to the other side of the king-sized bed. "¡Cuidado, chica–that's ticklish!"

"I know," she said, crawling back over to him. "That's why I did it." She straddled him, lightly moved her fingernails through the hair on his chest. "Love's a special word, Iggy. You shouldn't use it unless you mean it." She sharply tugged a few of the hairs, just to emphasize her point.

"Ow!" he said, firmly grabbing one of her tiny wrists. "Okay, Raquel." He laughed in a bothered manner. "Enough. Damn..." He shook his head as he released her wrist, then reached over to the nightstand and picked up his rum and Coke®. "Why you bein' like that? ¿Qué pasa?"

Raquel shrugged her shoulders.

# ((FREQUENCIES))

"You're not gonna tell me?"

"Why should I? You already know."

She was right–he did know. One person had begun to actually feel something for the other, and their little love game had become unbalanced. But Ignacio didn't want the game to end. Not yet. "You don't think I love you, do you?" he asked.

Raquel looked at him with her yearning, innocent eyes. "You say you do, but you don't really mean it."

Leaning forward and seductively sucking on her dark brown nipples, Ignacio asked, "How can you be so sure that I don't?"

"Because." She gently moved his head away from her breasts.

"Because why?"

"Because if you did love me, you wouldn't only be coming *here* to see me." Raquel leaned over him and affectionately kissed his upper lip. "And you wouldn't want to pay me for my sex anymore..." She moved her kiss to his forehead. "...you'd want to earn it." She brusquely rolled off of him, stood up, and walked over to the dresser at the opposite end of the room.

That hurt him. The truth usually did.

Ignacio knew that he wasn't in love with her, but somehow it had comforted him to pretend he was. He'd bring her gifts, buy her things, shower her with compliments–do all the things that he never did for his wife. And Raquel invariably enjoyed the attention, always playing along with the charade. Up until today, that is. Now she had suddenly called him out, and their shared illusion had been abruptly shattered, like a ceiling mirror falling hard to the floor. There was nothing left for them to do but pick up the pieces...and try to avoid cutting themselves in the process. Ignacio took another sip of his sugary-sweet drink. "Chica," he said, in as soft a tone as he could, "come back here."

Her back turned towards him, Raquel picked up the thin silver watch he had given her from atop the dresser. "Your time's almost up." She set the watch down, then turned around to face him. He looked over her naked frontside, at her slender figure, her trimmed, brown pubic hair, her small breasts–and when his gaze had reached her youthful, almost childlike face, he saw the hurt in her eyes. The illusory shards had made their first cut. Raquel placed her hands on her hips and numbly asked him, "Are you done? Or do you wanna fuck me again?"

Though he didn't want it to, an erection rose up at the suggestion. "Aw, c'mon, Raquel..." Ignacio said, trying to push it back down.

107

"Don't be like that. You know I care about you."

"No, Iggy, I don't," she said, moving to the bathroom. "I don't know what you feel about me. You buy me all these gifts, you tell me you love me..." She pulled some toilet paper off the roll, folded it neatly, and started to wipe herself with it. "...and you make me feel special. And wanted. And sometimes I actually even let myself enjoy the sex I have with you." Her voice cracked a little, as she said, "I start thinking, 'Hey, maybe this guy really *does* care about me...maybe I should give him a chance.' And so I start letting down my guard, and I start believing that you're gonna be the one who helps me get out of this degrading shit-job." She threw the semen-soaked wad of tissue into the toilet, struggling to hold back her tears. "But then you pay me and leave, and everything gets all fucked up again." Her tears began to flow, and she quickly shut the bathroom door.

It didn't matter, though–Ignacio could still hear her crying. He sat there and listened to her for a few seconds, but the weeping started to make him edgy. It was making him feel guilty–and he hated guilt. Because guilt had the power to turn the strongest of men into the littlest of bitches. Why'd she have to pick today to pull this shit? he asked himself. After spending the whole day at the riot scene, all he had wanted to do was come here and release some tension–but now he was even more tense than when he first arrived.

Ignacio placed his legs over the edge of the bed and gulped down the rest of his drink. "Dios," he cursed under his breath, "forty-seven years old and I'm gettin' involved with a four-year old." It was easy now, in retrospect, to see that he should have played his game with one of the other girls. Midori or Katrina. Desireé. Even Lara, as loco as she was, would have been a better choice. But, despite her age–or perhaps because of it–he had chosen Raquel. The four-year old. Cloned and genetically accelerated to the age of fourteen by an abusive mother, granted emancipation by the courts at fifteen, illegal prostitution until her eighteenth birthday, now a legal prostitute here at Deep Heat massage parlor. Not exactly the best choice for mind games, he admitted to himself.

Deciding that he'd better get out of there before he had to face Raquel again, Ignacio stood up to leave. He looked around for his clothes, then grumbled, "Aw, no," with the realization they were inside the bathroom. With Raquel. Ignacio felt like hitting some-thing. But, as hard as it was for him to do, he managed to suppress the fire. For now. He walked over to the bathroom door, waited a few moments, then pushed it open. Time to face the unhappy music he'd helped to compose.

Raquel was still cleaning herself, one leg up on the rim of the tub, the other on the linoleum floor. "Jeez," she said as she looked down at the off-white piece of toilet paper, "you sure did come a lot."

Normally a comment like that would have elicited a humorous response from him. But now wasn't the time. He needed to choose his words carefully; make sure that he calmed her down so he could get the hell out of there without any more emotional backlash. "Raquel," he kindly said, placing his arms around her waist, kissing her on the cheek, "I'm sorry, baby. Honestly."

"You're just saying that 'cause you don't like it when I cry."

Ignacio turned her around, placed his hand under her chin, and lifted her head so her eyes met with his. "That's not true, chica," he lied. "I *am* sorry." He smiled, kissed her softly on the lips. "I never meant to hurt you." At least *that* was true, he rationalized. He hadn't set out to bring her distress, he'd just wanted to play around a little. "What can I do to make things better?"

"I don't know, Iggy," she said, hugging her wet face to his chest. "I wish I did."

Ignacio glanced down at the pile of clothes to his left. "Here, Raquel," he said, gently breaking her embrace, "why don't you put some clothes on." He picked up a few pieces of her clothing, and extended them towards her.

"Thanks." She placed the clothes on top of the sink. "But I'm not gonna need 'em right now. I wanna take a bath first." She wiped her eyes. "A really hot one. And I just wanna sit in the water and think."

"That'll be good," Ignacio said, as he gathered up his clothes. "You'll feel better after that."

"I doubt it," she said. "But I'm gonna try anyways." She reached over and turned on the tub's faucet. The steaming water began to flow.

Ignacio couldn't think of anything else to say–so he didn't. There was silence for the next minute or so, as he put on his clothes and got dressed, and she sat there atop the toilet, her head buried in her hands, letting out the occasional, exhausted sigh.

The silence was finally broken when Raquel said, "I don't think you should see me anymore."

He was surprised to hear her say that. "Are you sure?" he asked, feeling an unexpected need to confirm her statement.

"I think so," she said, swirling two of her fingers in the hot water. "Yeah."

He was even more surprised when he found himself wanting to talk her out of the decision. Zipping up his Levi's®, he told her, "Maybe we should just wait a while–take some time off from each other. Then I'll come by and see you in a few weeks." What the hell are you saying? he asked himself. You got the perfect opportunity to leave and make a clean break from this bullshit–so why aren't you taking it? "How's that sound?" he asked.

She looked up at him with those same yearning eyes, shook her head, and said, "I'm sorry, Iggy..." She wrapped her arms around her naked self. "But I can't do it anymore. Not like this."

As he finished putting on his jacket, Ignacio once again found himself at a loss for words. His mind was screaming at him to say goodbye and be done with her, but something else–he would have said his heart, if he wasn't in such denial–was pleading with him not to let her go. What to do? he wondered. More confusion. And what to say? More tension. "What if..." Ignacio tried to stop himself, but he couldn't. "What if we made things different?"

Raquel gave him a confused look. "What do you mean?"

In his head, all he heard was "Don't say it!" But what he said was, "What if I didn't come here anymore–and we started seeing each other outside the parlor?" He paused, feeling sick to his stomach. "...and I stopped paying you."

With an incredulous laugh, she asked, "Why would you wanna do that?"

"Because..." The painful truth rose up inside him like bile, and he spit up the words, "...I need you, Raquel."

She intently studied his face, then slowly turned away from him, saying, "Oh, jeez..." Watching the steam rise from the tub, she added, "You really mean it."

Feeling like a little vulnerable bitch, Ignacio tramped out of the bathroom, cursing at himself as he left.

"Iggy, wait!" Raquel shouted, following after him.

He stopped, but didn't turn to face her.

"Iggy," she said. "C'mon, look at me." She tugged on his jacket. "Please?"

Ignacio reluctantly turned around, defeated. He looked her in the face, but didn't connect eye to eye.

"Sweetie..." She reached her hand around the back of his neck and caressed him.

# ((FREQUENCIES))

He drooped his head, closed his eyes, allowing her cool hand to soothe his fevered skin. The emotional turmoil churning inside of him began to subside, and for a brief moment, he felt a rare sense of peace and clarity. He saw things for what they were, and actually confronted the issues which haunted him, rather than repressing them. He thought about his irreverence and utter disregard of Irena's faithful love and devotion; the lack of time he dedicated to his two beautiful little girls; the prostitutes he frequented, and how he would *never* want Aurora or Esperanza to experience the things that those girls did; the feelings he had for Raquel, and the love for her that he pretended was make-believe... The sudden lucidity nearly made him weep, but he firmly held back the emotions, erecting the wall of repression which had just been torn down. He pulled away from her comforting embrace and stammered, "I...I gotta go, Raquel," then walked towards the door.

"Iggy...?" she asked him.

He looked back at her, but didn't say anything.

"My number's listed..." She smiled uneasily. "If you ever wanna make things different."

Ignacio nodded, opened the door, and quickly left the room. Walking down the magenta-colored hallway, past the numbered front doors of the parlor's other rooms, he didn't allow himself to look back. Not even once. Because he knew that even the fleetest glance over his shoulder would send him running, right back to the solace of that little womangirl's loving arms. That fact, he couldn't stand. Or understand. He clenched his fists and ground his teeth.

The fire inside had been stoked once more.

By the time he reached the parlor's smoky lounge, he was inebriated with negative emotions. A volatile cocktail was being mixed within him—one part anger, one part embarrassment, and one part confusion. With a twist of hurt pride. Ignacio walked over to the bar, and said to the bald bartender, "Ey, Charlie—pour me two shots of Bacardi®. 151."

"Sure thing, Mo," Charlie said. He set a pair of shot glasses down in front of Ignacio. "Everything okay?"

Ignacio downed the shot as soon as Charlie was finished pouring. Clearing his throat, he replied, "Bueno."

Charlie poured the other glass full. "Raquel treat you good?"

"Bueno."

As Ignacio finished his second shot, one of the nearby customers twisted around on his stool and faced them. He was dressed

111

in extravagant, expensive clothes, looked to be in his late twenties, was surreally ripped (definitely hypersteroids), and had a number of tattoodecals on his face, neck, and forearms. Ignacio had never met him before, but he'd heard about him. They called him Tattoo, and he was known around town as a mid-level amp dealer. Not one of the underworld's big boys, but he was doing his best to become one.

"You guys talkin' 'bout Raquel?" Tattoo asked in a hoarse voice. Without waiting for an answer, he looked at Ignacio and said, "That bitch is hunny, fool. No joke, she can fuck." He turned to his shorter, less muscular drinking buddy. "Ain't that right, Z?"

"I'm sayin'!" Z said with a laugh, giddily raising his mug of stout into the air.

With the extra alcohol burning its way down his gut, the volatile cocktail had now become a Molotov cocktail. Ignacio had the fire–now all he needed was to be thrown. "What'd you just say?" he asked the tattooed man.

Tattoo turned back towards him. "I said she can fuck." Noticing the anger in Ignacio's face, he laughed and said, "You need an ear implant, old man, or what?"

"Let it slide, Mo," Charlie said. "He's just playin' around."

"I ain't playin'," Tattoo said to Charlie. "So don't speak for me." He glared at Ignacio, his expression warping into a formidable screwface. "I asked if you needed an implant. Do you?"

"What I need, cabróna," Ignacio said, "is for you to take a swing at me. Then I can beat the fuckin' living shit out of you."

Tattoo bared his teeth. "I don't know what you're smokin', pancho, but you better jet while you still got the chance." One hand holding on to his glass of ale, he started to reach the other down to his waistline.

"What, you got a weapon in there?" Ignacio asked. "Keep goin' for it, bitch–see what happens."

Tattoo stared at Ignacio for a long, slow moment...then made his move.

Before Tattoo had the chance to even *touch* his weapon, Ignacio had already landed two strong, lightning-like punches to his face–one on the bridge of his nose, the other on the right side of his jaw. Tattoo's glass of ale began to fall to the ground...

And
the
world
started

# ((FREQUENCIES))

to

    move

      in

        slow

          motion.

When Ignacio allowed his cybernetically enhanced reflexes to work at their full capacity, it was like time slowed down around him. His movements became so fast, the motion of nearly everything else came to a crawl. The ale spilling out of Tattoo's glass looked more like amber mercury, while the spray of saliva coming from his mouth appeared as individual droplets of spittle. Ignacio could clearly see the flattened skin and cartilage of the drug dealer's nose rebounding back from the previous blow. As he gradually fell off his barstool, Tattoo made a futile attempt to raise up his hands and protect his injured face.

Ignacio swiftly hit him three more times.

The first punch landed on the same side of Tattoo's jaw as before–only this time the mandible shattered. The next two punches were aimed directly at his eyes, Ignacio's thick metal rings easily splitting open the thin skin surrounding Tattoo's sockets. The dealer's motion towards the ground increased a bit with the extra force, but Ignacio still had time to forcefully slam the side of his fist down on Tattoo's forehead.

The first few drops of ale splashed onto the barroom floor in photographic fashion, just as Tattoo's bloodied face was about to join them. But before his head could touch the ground, Ignacio pretended Tattoo's skull was a soccer ball and he was a goalie about to drop kick. His steel-toed boots smashed into the now-unconscious man's mouth, scattering his teeth across the floor like ivory pebbles.

The ale glass shattered loudly, as it and Tattoo's head finally hit the ground. Ignacio slowed himself down...

And

the

world

returned to normal speed. He quickly looked over at Z, gave him a sup, and said, "You got next?"

Z, whose pudgy, rounded face displayed an expression of utter shock, shook his head "no" at a very frenetic speed.

To the bartender, Ignacio said, "Sorry, Charlie. I apologize for the mess. Just put it on my tab."

"Uh, yeah, Mo," Charlie said, eyes wide open. "Right. Sure."

Ignacio reached down to Tattoo's waistline and pulled out a small laser pistol. "Illegal," he said to himself, relieved that he now had legal grounds for thrashing the man so badly. He looked at Charlie and held up the piece. "In case this bad boy tries to press any charges, I'm showin' you the weapon. You're my witness that he was threatening me with this." He looked over at Z. "You, too. And since nobody wants the cops to come sniffin' around here, let's leave 'em out of this. I'm not involving the law unless he does."

Coming around the bar with a towel, Charlie said, "I don't think he will, Mo." He started wiping the blood, ale, and broken glass from the floor, quickly turning the white cloth a deep burgundy color. "But you better be careful next time you come 'round here. He's gonna be lookin' for payback."

"He'll regret it if he does," Ignacio said. "I went easy on him this time–next time I won't." He looked at Z again. "You let him know that, too, chubby. If he tries to pull any shit..." He pulled out his Freemon badge, showing it to Z. "He's gonna find himself in a coma."

Z nodded as he stared down at his fallen friend. "Shit, dude," he mumbled, "I think he already is."

His enhanced metabolism now fully slowed, Ignacio began to feel tired. And lethargic. And most of all, hungry. He always needed to fuel up after using his enhancements, which ate up his body's energy quicker than a starved man at a buffet. He was eager to get home to dinner. Slipping the laser pistol into his jacket, he said, "I'm outta here, Charlie."

"I'll be seein' you, Mo."

The other occupants of the lounge murmured and whispered amongst themselves, all watching Ignacio as he walked out of the dimly lit establishment. Outside, the sun was still shining brightly, though now it was setting on the horizon. He moved through the Pioneer Square crowd, over to the curb where his Harley-Davidson® Skyhog™ was parked. He fired up the hoverbike's engines, put on his black, visored helmet, and flew off towards his Queen Anne home.

Ignacio quietly let himself in, and headed straight for the bathroom. He knew he reeked of booze, sex, and violence, and wanted to clean himself up first before facing his family. Luckily, Irena and the girls were in the back of the house preparing dinner together, and he was able to hop into the shower unnoticed.

As he stood there under the water, letting the cool, brisk

spray wash over him, Ignacio lost track of the time. He may have been in there for ten minutes, maybe even twenty or thirty. He wasn't even sure. And he didn't really care. The cold, anesthetic temperature numbed both his body and mind, and for the first time all day, he didn't think or feel anything. No emotions to wrangle with, no plaguing thoughts to ponder. He blanked out into a desensitized heaven. A meperidine bliss.

Until there was a knock at the bathroom door.

Descending back to the realm of the senses, Ignacio asked, "Yeah?"

Irena opened the door halfway, popped her head in, and said, "Baby, Marc's here–and the food's done."

"I'll be right out, Irena. Gracias."

Ignacio stood there and enjoyed the coolness for a few more seconds...then slowly turned the water off. After putting on a pair of Calvin Klein® boxers, Ignacio looked at his exposed upper body in the mirror. He touched his stomach, where a thin, recently formed layer of fat now covered what used to be a six-pack. It was still as strong as it used to be–which he confirmed by firmly poking one of his fingers into it–but it no longer looked the same. His reflection looked disappointed. In response, he flexed both of his muscular biceps, then his triceps and forearms, relieved to see that they still looked as strong as ever. In fact, the extra weight he'd gained actually made them appear even bigger. Same with his chest. The reflection gave him a confident nod of approval. He smiled at it, rubbed some gel through his thin charcoal hair, and threw on his threads.

He was about to toss his dirty clothes into the hamper, but then abruptly stopped. He brought the garments to his nose and sniffed them. Ignacio couldn't smell Raquel on the clothes–but he knew Irena would be able to. Women always had that uncanny ability to sense each other's scents. He moved to the bedroom, over to the washing machine set into the wall, put the laundry in, and started the cycle. Evidence dismissed.

Ignacio exited the bedroom and breezed into the spacious living room. McCready was seated on one of the brown leather couches, the children sitting next to him on the carpeted floor. All three of them were watching some loud, colorful cartoon on the holoview. "¡Patrón!" Ignacio announced.

McCready stood up. "Hey, Morris." They clasped their right hands together, hugging each other with their left arms. "Thanks for having me over."

"De nada. I'm glad you could make it."

"So am I." McCready smelled the air. "'Cause, man, I'm tellin' you, it sure smells hella good in here."

Ignacio smiled. "It does, doesn't it?"

"Papá, move!" Aurora shouted, tugging on her father's pant leg. "You're in the way! I can't see the show!"

"Ay, okay! Calm down, mi hija!" Ignacio laughed. "I'm moving!" He looked at McCready with mock disbelief. "I tell you–these girls, man, they're spoiled. Think they're the queens of the castle."

"We don't think that," Esperanza said in a sassy tone. "*Mom's* the queen." She smiled. "We're the princesses."

Ignacio looked at McCready and laughed. "Princesses."

An especially loud commotion started to occur on the holoview, drawing all of their attention towards it. On the projected, 3-D screen, an anthropomorphic cat in a suit was shooting a laser pistol at some villianous-looking Asian soldiers, who were firing back with lasers of their own. The bright colors from the show lit up the entire room with their light.

"What is this?" Ignacio asked the girls.

"Katmandu," said Aurora.

"Katmandu?" he asked, as the cat threw some shuriken which looked like little spinning wheels. "This show beamed from Tibet?"

"Nah," McCready answered, "it's an American show. That guy," he said, putting his gloved finger through the cat's holographic head, "is Kat Mandu. He's like a Buddhist James Bond." He watched for a few seconds, then said, "He gets sent on all these missions by the Dalai Lama's preserved brain. He mostly fights a lot of Chinese terrorists, but there's always this larger quest of him seeking out an ultimate weapon called the Lotus Flower."

"And he does Tantric sex rituals with Shikta," added Esperanza. "She's his partner."

McCready laughed. "And he does that, too."

"Isn't there something else you guys could watch?"

"No, we *like* Kat," Esperanza said. "And Lery Vast comes on sometimes during Kat's show."

Now *that*, Ignacio had seen before. It was hard to miss *The Lery Vast Moment*. It ran on different channels, at random times of the day, for various lengths of time. Sometimes it lasted for a second, sometimes a few minutes, but it always contained something different each time. The show was so random that it never had recurring characters, and rarely even had a theme. It was never listed in any of the channel guides, so viewers had to try to look for patterns of when and where it appeared if they wanted to try to tune in or set their UV's on record. The unpredictability of the show made it a huge hit, and people would sometimes sit in front of their univiews for hours on end, all in the hopes of catching a new *Lery Vast*.

"Yeah, and last time," Aurora said, "they had a lion on it, and then he ate a deer an' then-"

"It wasn't a *deer*, 'Rora," said Esperanza. "It was a gazelle."

"Yeah," Aurora continued, "an' then he ate the 'zelle, an' then he turned into this big, big, big building, an' then there was this blue light, an' then the building fell over and crashed." She took a small breath. "An' then that was it."

"Okay, everyone," Irena said from the kitchen, "time to eat."

"Papá, can we eat out here?" Aurora pouted. "Pleeese?"

"Don't you want to eat with all of us, 'Rora?" he asked.

"Yeah," she said. "But I wanna watch Kat more."

"Even though Marc came over?"

"Papá, Marc *always* comes over."

"And he already promised he'd have flan with us out here after dinner," chimed Esperanza. "So we'll still get to see him anyway." She smiled her princess smile at him and McCready.

Ignacio looked over at McCready, who shrugged his shoulders and said, "I did promise 'em that–though I didn't know it was gonna be used as evidence in their dinner defense."

"Okay," Ignacio said to the girls, "but you need to go and get your food yourselves. Mommy's done enough work already."

"Yay!" Aurora excitedly bounced up and clapped her hands, hugged Ignacio's leg, and ran off to the kitchen.

"Gracias, Papá," Esperanza said, following after her younger sister.

Ignacio sighed. "Am I too lenient with them?"

"Nah, man," McCready said, "they're your kids. It's alright to pamper 'em sometimes. And you can tell in their faces they appreciate it."

As they entered the kitchen, Ignacio looked at his daughters' facial expressions, smiled at McCready's words, and nodded his head.

"You guys can sit down," Irena said as she served the girls. "Your food's already on the table."

"Thanks, Irena," McCready said, taking a seat.

Ignacio stood there for a moment and appreciatively gazed at his wife. Though he wasn't faithful to her, he did love her. And she was still so beautiful. Thirty-seven years old, and she looked like she hadn't even reached thirty yet. He walked to Irena, gave her a kiss on the head, and warmly said, "Gracias, baby. Te amo."

"Te amo, tambien," she replied, her attention still focused on the girls. Aurora started to leave the kitchen and Irena said, "Aurora, wait!" She held out a placemat towards her daughter. "You need to eat on top of this so you don't dirty the carpet."

Aurora grabbed the placemat and ran off to the living room.

"Esperanza," Irena said, "make sure she doesn't spill, 'kay?"

"Yo prometo, Mamá," Esperanza said.

Irena took a deep breath, sighed heavily, looked at Ignacio and said, "Finalmente–comemos."

"Sí," he agreed with a laugh, as they both joined McCready at the table.

"Thanks again, guys, for having me over," McCready said. "This is a real treat. I appreciate it."

"You're welcome, Marc. It's nice to have you over." Irena looked at both of them, smiled, and said, "Let's eat."

McCready immediately took a bite of the chicken molé. A smile appeared across his face as he chewed, and he said to Irena, "This is incredible, sweetheart. I'm in heaven."

She laughed. "I don't know about *that*, but thank you."

"No, thank *you*," he said, taking another bite. "And honestly, this is probably the closest I'*m* gonna get to heaven."

Ignacio laughed. "This is really good, baby," he added.

"Thanks." Irena licked her lips and gave him a peck on his cheek.

"So, Ignacio," McCready said, "what was the deal with the riot? What happened after I left?"

"Not too much, really," he said. "We conducted a general sweep of the area, turned up some more freekers...that was about it. Most of 'em surrendered without a fight, though there were a few of 'em we had to tussle with." He sipped on a spoonful of sopa. "The cops made a bunch of arrests once they got inside people's apartments–mostly drug-related stuff, though I think they found some illegal weapons, too."

"You guys find any evidence about what caused the riot? I mean, other than the cops' hit parade?"

"No, nothing turned up there," Ignacio said. "But when we got back to HQ, Takura had checked into that sector's ambient frequential records. Apparently, there was some type of large-scale EMF transmission that hit the infected area right before the riot started."

"What, like a giant infobomb?"

"We thought that at first, but Takura said the transmission's frequencies more resembled some type of alpha-wave inhibitor. His theory was that the EMF's had countered the UV's normal alpha-wave transmissions, and since the people were so pissed off about what had happened with the cops, the absence of the calming waves caused them to freek out."

"Interesting," McCready said.

"Then that's probably also what happened in Vancouver," Irena said.

"Vancouver?" McCready asked.

Irena nodded. "The news said that something similar happened in Vancouver yesterday."

"Then something big's goin' on here," McCready said. "That's right down I-5–the proximities are way too close for them not to be related."

"That's what the bureau thinks, too," Ignacio said. "They're flyin' two DCC agents into SeaTac in the morning. They're gonna work with us to figure out what's goin' on."

"Well," McCready said, "the next few days are sure gonna be interesting, aren't they?"

"Looks that way, patrón." Ignacio scooped up some rice with his fork, then said,"Ey, so what did you end up doing at the skyland? Takura said it was about a butler or somethin'."

McCready hesitated briefly, and said, "Yeah, it was just some guy who was trippin' out on his servitude. His boss had me look over him, ask him some questions, tell him his options...shit like that. It was boring."

"They called you from the riot just for that?"

"Yup. Go figure." That didn't make much sense. Ignacio had a feeling that McCready was holding something back, but didn't want to press him on it. Not now.

"Mommy!" yelled Aurora from the living room. "C'mere!"

"What do you need, baby?" Irena asked.

"I spilt my drink!"

"It wasn't my fault!" said Esperanza.

Irena laughed, and started to get up from the table.

Ignacio touched her hand. "You want me to handle it?"

"No, I'm already up," Irena said, "I'll get it."

Watching Irena exit the room, a look of fond affection appeared in McCready's eyes, and he said, "You're one lucky man, my friend–'cause that is sure one special woman."

Ignacio knew McCready had something of a crush on Irena, but it had never really bothered him since he knew the younger Freemon would never disrespect his familial boundaries. And in a way, the attention to his wife flattered Ignacio, and also served as a frequent reminder for him to appreciate what he already had. He nodded at McCready's comments and said, "Sí, I'm very lucky, patrón." Taking another bite of his dinner, he looked back at the living room, made sure that Irena wasn't finished with the girls yet, and said to McCready in a hushed tone, "One thing I want to tell you about, Marc–but don't say anything about this to Irena."

McCready leaned forward and whispered, "Yeah, sure, man. What is it?"

"Earlier today, when I was at Deep Heat, I roughed up some blud named Tattoo–a middle-man amp dealer. Not a big boy, but I know he's got some back." He glanced over his shoulder at the living room, then continued, "If anything happens to me in the next few days, I want to make sure you know who to look for. I doubt shit's gonna go down, but I'm lettin' you know about it just in case."

"Alright, yeah. I'm glad you told me." McCready's face showed concern. "You don't think we should maybe just get him first?"

"No, no," Ignacio said. "I don't want to draw any extra attention to me being at the massage parlor. Everything should be chill, patrón, don't worry."

"Alright, Morris, if you say so...though I-" McCready stopped his words, and casually leaned back in his chair.

"Those girls are a handful," Irena said with a laugh, as she rejoined them at the table. "But at least that's done with. Now we can relax and finish our dinner."

They all began to eat again, but were quickly interrupted when Esperanza asked, "Mamá? Can we have dessert now?"

Ignacio, Irena, and McCready all looked at each other for a moment. And then they laughed.

Together.

Δ

# α

# Chapter 8
## ((The Invisible Hand))

*"The reality-masters did their very best to ensure that enlightened*
*individuals lost confidence in their own abilities.*
*Fear, terror, doubt, complacency, confusion...these were but a few of*
*the techniques exploited by them in order to destroy one's trust in*
*oneself. Diabolically, the masters took advantage of the fact that*
*without any confidence in self, the individual could achieve*
*nothing...and nothing could never be a threat to their control.*
*What could be a threat to them, and which they tried at all costs to*
*prevent others from truly knowing, was the fact that with full self-*
*confidence, the individual could achieve everything and anything,*
*for being in touch with oneself was akin to godhood.*
*And wasn't it God's hand which created the world?"*

Lifting the cup and saucer from the breakfast room table, Mason
asked, "And, gentlemen, what were the results of these findings?"

On the large uniview embedded in the wall before him, were
the images of Mr. Webber and Agent McCready, each occupying one
half of the currently split-screen. The Wednesday afternoon sun was
just beginning to burn through the gray, overcast sky, and through the
breakfast room's glass doors, a few scattered patches of sunlight could
be seen dotting the lawns and gardens outside.

"Camera records revealed Mrs. Huxton had no prolonged
exposure to a uniview screen," answered Mr. Webber, the edges of his
implanted, metallic-red goggles glinting brightly from a nearby light
source. "Mall uniview records showed no anomalous transmissions

during her visit." The gogs' rounded lenses constricted momentarily, then dilated as the glint disappeared. "Eliminates possibility of infection via uniview. Suspect usage of a time-delayed information release so as not to attract immediate attention. Passed through physical contact with your wife."

"I take it then, that you know who the attacker was?"

"Camera records revealed six possible suspects," Webber said. "Narrowed to three after biochip search. Freemon can tell you more."

Mason took a sip of espresso, and looked at Agent McCready.

"Late last night," said McCready, who was seated on his living room couch, "I went down to HQ and looked into your wife's biochip data." Behind him, above the couch, hung a framed Marilyn Monroe print by Andy Warhol. "From the camera records that Webber sent to me, I was able to note the times in which your wife came into physical contact with someone, then match that up with her biochip's medical data." McCready opened a can of Folger's® latté, took a drink, and continued, "At 3:36 on Monday afternoon, there was a sudden increase in your wife's cardiovascular and electrodermal readings. Also at this time, her freeread showed a lowering of amplitude and an increase in frequency. Since her bioreadings were normal and steady up to this point, we can safely say this was the time the information unloaded itself. But, as Webber said before, it was a time-delayed burst of information–a type of infobomb that's biologically untraceable until the moment it actually attacks and releases itself–which means that the time she contracted the infobomb isn't the same time as when her bioreadings jumped."

Mason nodded. "And therefore you can't simply match the time of her abnormal readings with one of the incidents of contact."

"Right. In this case, infection and effect aren't simultaneous. So basically, your wife's bioreadings can't tell us *who* did the attack, but it can tell us who didn't." He took another drink of his beverage, and said, "Since three of the people she came into contact with touched her *after* the abnormal bioreadings, we can eliminate them as possible suspects. That leaves us with three possibilities–a store employee who she'd come into contact with several times before, another who she'd never met, and one of her escorts."

"Mr. Webber," Mason said to his head of security, "which escort is he referring to?"

Adjusting the speakerlike implants which served as his ears, Mr. Webber replied, "Benjamin, sir. Currently detained and being questioned. Interrogation to be conducted by myself at the conclusion of this conversation."

"Very good," Mason said. "Now, Agent McCready, these other two suspects–what information have you gathered on them?"

McCready picked up a remote, pressed a few buttons, and three faces–two males and one female–appeared in the lower corner of Mason's screen. "The person who she'd had previous contact with is Candace Wilson," McCready said, as the border around the attractive female's photo began to glow, "an employee at the cosmetics department at Nordstrom®. Her files show no record of the type of memory augmentation that's required to hold an infobomb, and her only surgeries have been a tit, ass, and nose job. I checked into the possibility of an illegal operation, but her biochip doesn't sense the presence of any non-documented implants or alterations." He highlighted the photo of a clean-cut Latino man. "The other suspect, Antonio Jiminez, works at Ben Bridge® jewelers. He's had some brain modifications in the past–a few memory improvements and an implant that regulates a tic he gets when he's nervous or anxious. I'd say him and your escort are the most likely suspects, since what's his name–Benjamin–used to be a professional johnny courier. Either of them could have had the infobomb uploaded into their heads."

Mason placed his finger on his lip. "Agent McCready, when a courier transfers his data to another source, isn't there some indicator of this...informational release in his bioreadings?"

"Usually, yeah."

"Then can't you check the two suspects' bioreadings for that day, look for the indicator, and determine which one did it?"

"Nope, not with this kind of infobomb. As long as it's dormant, the biochip can't detect its presence. And unfortunately, when it's sitting inside the courier's head, it's dormant–same thing when it's transmitted. The biochip's basically useless until the information exposes itself."

"I see," Mason said. "Then what will be the next step?"

"Well, next we'll do some data mining into the suspects' activities over the last few months–who they've come into contact with, where they've been, what they've bought, what they've watched, etcetera. That should give us some good leads. Webber's interrogation should give us some more information, too."

"Most certainly it will," said Mr. Webber. His mouth widened into a macabre smile which revealed the sharp, metallic teeth underneath. "Interrogation of the other two suspects surely would as well."

"Not just yet," Mason said. "Let's find out more about them first."

"Legal concerns?" asked Webber.

"No–future concerns." Mason picked up a croissant from the large platter of fruits and pastries atop the breakfast table. "Because it seems extremely improbable to me, Mr. Webber, that one individual planned this attack all by themselves. This entire situation *reeks* of conspiracy." He portioned off a tiny piece of croissant, placed it in his mouth, and carefully chewed. "And if there *is* a conspiracy afoot, then I want it–and every single one of its members–eliminated." He swallowed. "Completely."

"Reasoning that one of the suspects might lead to a larger organization?"

"Precisely, Mr. Webber."

"That's not a bad idea," McCready said. "But if Benjamin turns out to be the attacker, then you're not gonna be able to do that–'cause now he knows you know. Why the different approaches?"

"Because I will not tolerate defection or betrayal within the upper ranks of Ordosoft™, Agent McCready. Treachery is a weed which must be pulled immediately, lest it should spread and grow throughout one's entire garden." He set the croissant aside, and picked up a few champagne grapes. "Besides, after spending a few hours with Mr. Webber, I am *quite* confident that Benjamin will be eager to tell us everything it is that he knows."

"Alright. So are you wanting me to carry out the data mining on the other two suspects, or is Webber gonna do that?"

"Mr. Webber will conduct the rest of the investigation, then consult with you on his findings. I want you to be available to give full and complete attention to Ashley's safety–and conducting a thorough investigation would prevent you from doing that." He looked to the other half of the screen. "Mr. Webber, I want you to assign two–and only two–other Ordocops™ to this case in order to assist you with the detective work. Do not tell them anything about the attack, merely inform them that we are conducting an investigation into the lives of these two individuals. Contact me should you find something of significance, otherwise...I'll be contacting you. That will be all for now, Mr. Webber."

Webber bowed his head, then his half of the screen quickly shrank in size until it disappeared completely. McCready's image enlarged, filling up the rest of the screen.

"So tell me, Agent McCready," Mason said, making sure his

vocal intonations sounded a bit less formal, "how are things going with Ashley?"

"You mean how is her safety, or how are we getting along?"

"The latter–I already know that she's safe."

"Well, I haven't pissed her off yet, she hasn't pissed me off yet...so I'd say things are going pretty damn good." He lit up a cigarette. "And actually, in all honesty, I'm enjoying my time around her. Your daughter's a real sweetheart, Huxton."

"I'm pleased to hear you say that, Agent McCready. Though I knew you'd both be reluctant at first, I had a feeling that you two would enjoy each other's company once you got to know each other. You are, shall we say...of like minds."

McCready let out a small laugh. "That's one way to put it."

"Yes, and I believe that because of this, Ashley will come to respect you a great deal." Mason then said, in the same voice he used for sensitive business negotiations, "And that means that you could have a positive influence on her."

McCready smiled. "My influence has been called a lot of things, Huxton, but I think you're the first person to ever label it as 'positive.'"

Mason smiled back. "With Ashley, I believe it will be. You see, Agent McCready, despite my best efforts, my daughter has never been interested in becoming an integral part of Ordosoft™. She has an irrational...fear, so to speak–a trepidation of structure and order. You, on the other hand, obviously respect and appreciate these values, or else you wouldn't be in the line of work that you're in now."

"Not necessarily," McCready said, leaning back in his couch. "Maybe I'm just too lazy to find another job."

"Perhaps," Mason said. "But I doubt it. I think you have more respect for order than you're willing to admit. Otherwise, the duties required of a Freemon would have pushed you away from the job a *long* time ago." He lifted his eyebrows. "Am I wrong?"

McCready took a few more draws from his cigarette, saying nothing in response.

"As you spend the next few days with Ashley, Agent McCready, I would ask that you please keep this in mind. " Mason picked up a shiny red apple, and polished its skin with a cloth napkin. "If you can influence her in any way toward seeing *our* point of view more clearly, it would be most appreciated. As a matter of fact, I would consider it a great favor." He took a bite from the apple, then dabbed his mouth with the napkin. "And those who do me favors always seem to meet with fortune and prosperity." Mason smiled, replacing the barely eaten apple onto the silver platter. "Please tell Ashley I said hello when you see her. I'll speak to you again shortly, Agent McCready. Good day." He severed the connection, and the Freemon's image morphed into the Ordosoft™ logo.

"Marcel," Mason announced to his butler, "I'm all finished with this." He motioned to the replete platter of food. "You can dispose of it now."

"Right away, sir," Marcel said.

"Where is Dominique?"

Picking up the silver platter, Marcel said, "I believe she's in the garden, sir."

Mason looked out through the glass doors. "I don't see her, Marcel. Are you sure?"

"Excuse me, sir, I should have been more specific. She's in the *west* garden."

"And was she going out for a walk, or was she actually going out to garden?"

"Considering her attire, sir, I would say she was going out to do some gardening."

"Good," Mason said, nodding his head. "That's a very good sign, Marcel. Dominique always loved her gardening so."

"She did, sir." He coughed. "Or rather, she *does*."

"Indeed. I'll be in the west garden should you need me." Mason stood up and walked out onto the veranda. He soon spotted Dominique, who was bent over on her knees, digging through a flower bed. His heart fluttered at the sight, as he recalled fond memories of his wife before her rebirth. He simply stood there for the next couple of minutes, watching her do that which she had always done. The familiarity was comforting, and it was showing itself at a most opportune time.

Since the infobombing—even before that, now that he thought about it—Mason had gradually been losing faith that the reborn Dominique could ever take the place of the original. Though he knew the rebirth wasn't always going to come along smoothly, he had expected that Dominique's innate characteristics would eventually start to emerge and manifest themselves. However, as hard as it was for him to admit, the painful truth was that she was clearly turning out *not* to be the same person as before. I might as well be married to a complete stranger, he had caught himself thinking yesterday. But now, seeing this integral part of Dominique's personality appear, he was suddenly filled with a newfound hope; invigorated once again with the refreshing belief that, yes, things could be as they once were before. The joyful past could once again become the present.

He strolled over to his wife and announced, "Good afternoon, dear." He bent down beside her, affectionately placing his hand on her back. "Enjoying yourself?"

She let out a frustrated sigh and stuck her spade into the dirt. "Dear?"

Dominique turned around, a defeated smile upon her face, and said, "I hate this."

"What...what do you mean?" he asked, standing back up.

Dominique held up her soiled hands. "*This*," she said. "I'm all dirty, I feel sweaty..." She wiped her forehead with her arm. "And there's all these bugs that keep getting on me. I don't think I like gardening. Not at all."

"But gardening is something you love, Dominique. You always said that it helped you to relax and clear your mind."

"That's what Sophia said, too, so I decided I'd come out here and try it. I thought it might help me be who I'm supposed to be." She shook her head and scattered some dirt with the back of her hand. "But it's not working. I just don't like it, no matter how hard I try."

Mason's heart sank within his chest. All the newly hatched hope which had been steadily growing inside of him had rudely and abruptly been squashed back down, and now its crushed and mangled remains were writhing within, metamorphosizing into an entirely different emotive creation—one born of anger and rage, of bitterness and resentment. The right side of his nose started to twitch, he felt his blood pressure rise, his entire body began to violently shake. Mason breathed out heavily through his nostrils and clenched both of his fists. He looked down at the pathetic little creature seated at his feet, and it was all he could do not to strike his hand across that sickening, ungrateful face of hers. "You make me *sick*," he said disgustedly, spittle forcefully escaping from his mouth through the front of his teeth.

Her expression immediately went from frustration to despondency. "Please don't say that, Mason. I'm trying to be who you want me to be." A whimper sounded from somewhere deep in her throat. "Really, I am. I'm trying."

Mason stared at her with wrathful eyes. "Then try harder." He turned away from her and stormed off to the house. Upon entering the dining room, he stopped, his mind awash in confusion, and tried to figure out what to do next. He was too angry to conduct any type of productive business affairs–and besides, he'd already delegated the day's duties in order that he could spend time with Dominique. But now the last thing he wanted to do was be around that pitiful creature. He needed to get away from here, from her...from it all. He needed to escape.

Mason unclipped his Nokia® from his belt, touching a button on its side. "Connect me to Burke."

Seconds passed, then the tiny screen lit up with the image of his chauffeur. He was presently not in uniform, since Mason had told him earlier that he could take the day off. "Yes, sir?" he asked.

"Meet me at the front of the main house. Now."

"I'll be right there, sir." Burke grabbed his coat. "Change of plans?"

"Yes," Mason said. "It appears that I will be needing to leave Xanadeux today, after all."

"To Redmond?"

"No," he replied. "The Invisible Hand."


As Burke landed the limousine on the roof of the monolithic Bank of America® Columbia Tower, Mason tranquilly opened his eyes, and slowly brought his head forward from the seat. The Diazecalm™ had now worked its way into his system, and he was finding the drug's effects not at all unpleasant. The anger had been quelled, and the desire to lash out quenched. He was once again able to see things clearly and rationally, now that the previous, illogical emotions had been chemically banished from his being. He still was not satisfied with his wife, but he was no longer furious with her. Blind fury would solve nothing. There were ways–orderly ways–to remedy the situation. And after today, he vowed to explore those possibilities.

"Open door," Mason said. He stepped out into The Invisible Hand's parking lot, then walked up to the driver's side window. The tinted glass rolled down, and Mason said, "I'll be in contact via my cellphone. You needn't wait for me up here, but make sure that you're available to leave on my word."

"Will do, sir," Burke said.

As the limo ascended into the air, Mason walked toward the center of the tower's roof, to the gigantic plexiglass pyramid which served as the Hand's point of entry. He was greeted by two armed guards, both of whom he recognized.

"Good afternoon, Mr. Huxton," said the human member of the pair.

"Good day, Lex." Mason reached into his pocket and pulled out the transparent ID card which only members of The Invisible Hand Society™ were issued. "And a good day to you, too, Smith."

"Thank you, sir," replied the android, whose design was so flawless, one could not tell from appearance alone whether or not he was human. He held up his right hand, palm facing out toward Mason. "I'm pleased you could join us today." In the center of his palm, tattoodecalled into his genetically engineered skin, was the image of a pyramid with thirteen tiers. Levitating at the top of this pyramid, was a glowing, illuminated eye, framed in a triangular shape. Curving in a semi-circle around the lower part of the pyramid, was a rippled banner which contained the words: "NOVUS ORDO SECLORUM."

Smith said, "It will be just a moment while I verify your card." The ID was then magnetically sucked from Mason's hand, it quickly shot over to Smith, and affixed itself onto his tattoodecal. Both the android's hand and the transparent card's physical structure started to undulate upon contact, their visibility becoming unsteady in synchronization with the wavelike motions.

A holographic replica of the tattoodecal shimmered into being, directly between Mason and Smith, just as a small bulge appeared beneath the android's skin, directly in the center of his forehead. The skin grew tauter and tighter until it finally split open–cleanly, with no blood–revealing the bulge beneath to be an oversized human eyeball whose iris had a pale blue pigmentation. White light emerged forth from the third eye's pupil, entered the eye of the pyramid, and dispersed out into a spectrum of primary colors which bathed Mason's body in a bright prismatic glow.

A few seconds passed, the eyeball blinked, and the white light ceased emitting. "All finished now, Mr. Huxton." The skin grew back together over the eyeball, the bulge receded, the hologram vanished, and the ID rematerialized. "Thanks for your patience."

"Of course," Mason said.

The Plexiglas® pyramid's triangular double doors swivelled open behind Smith. He handed Mason his member card, and said, "Please enjoy your visit."

"Thank you, Smith. I will." Mason entered the pyramid, headed straight to the circular glass elevator, and stepped onto a GS platform which was very similar to the one at his Redmond office, only much larger in diameter. He looked up through the elevator's clear roof, through the transparent tip of the pyramid above, and gazing at the now-blue sky overhead, he commanded, "Down."

The platform started its descent, but Mason's eyes remained fixed upon the refracted heavens above. He continued to watch until the opening had fully closed and the daytime sky could no longer be seen. With the natural lighting gone, the elevator's LEDs turned on, and the entire tube began to glow with a soft blue hue. After passing through the scintillating stratum of shock-absorbent Gelaform® which served as a security buffer between the roof and the establishment, the LEDs emitted a reddish light, and mere seconds later, Mason was inside of The Invisible Hand.

It was a unique and amazing place–huge, circular, and multi-tiered, like a coliseum stretched vertically so its rows could become floors. The transparent elevator tube was positioned in the exact center of the enormous area, allowing one to take in a full 360-degree view of the Hand's many levels as they descended into it. There were a total of thirteen floors, each with their own different theme, each spaced exactly 33 and 1/3 feet away from the tube. All but one were visible to the elevator's occupants, and, barring the ground floor, none could be reached via the entrance tube. This panoptic design ensured that one would not feel watched as they entered the Hand, but rather, allowed *them* to feel like the watcher.

Dropping down to the Las Vegas-like eleventh floor, Mason looked out at the members who had decided to spend their afternoon gambling, and considered that as one of the activities he might like to engage in today. On the ninth level, comprised mostly of private rooms, he could see numerous alluring women and men parading along the outer hallway, all dressed in revealing or eye-catching attire. Down further, he reached level seven, where members were hooked up to various kinds of hard, soft, and wetware, then level six, whose inner parts were concealed by a surrounding black wall, since every member had agreed that the fetish floor should be the one level which remained *completely* private from the elevator's view. After passing the second floor, which served as the Hand's cigar bar and smoking area, the platform reached the bottom level.

The elevator doors opened quietly, and Mason stepped out into the noisy, bustling area. In addition to being the portal to the Hand's other levels, the ground floor acted as the establishment's lobby and main social area, where fellow members of the society could hobnob and mingle with each other at the many themed bars which were spread about the capacious space. There was a wide selection of lounges and saloons to choose from, each one spotlighting a different era in American history. Mason had his own particular favorite–the one which harked back to the roaring twenties. It had a nice atmosphere, pleasant music, but most importantly, it served the Hand's most extensive collection of vintage ports and sherries.

With a tug of his coat, Mason made his way over to the lively, buzzing speakeasy, and took a seat in one of the velvety antique chairs not too far from the bar. Now that he was inside, he could no longer hear ambient sounds from the lobby, only the music and commotion emanating from within. Though there were no walls lining the speakeasy's perimeter, a barrier of white noise surrounded the entire section, giving one the aural impression that they were in an enclosed space. It was possible to look around at the nearby lounges and see the occupant's actions, but one could not hear their conversations, nor listen to that section's music.

As Mason loosened his tie, he was waited upon by an attractive woman dressed as a flapper.

"Hey, Mr. Huxton, how are ya?" she cheerfully asked in her high-pitched voice.

"Very well, Holly, thank you." And though he didn't really care, he asked, "And how are you today?"

Her face lit up, bright like gaudy Christmas lights. "Better now–thanks for askin'! You're the first person who's asked me that all day." As Mason's eyes and mind wandered about the room, she continued, "Y'know, sometimes it can feel like people don't even care about'cha at all. They treat ya like you were just an object–like you were workin' on level six, or somethin'!"

Trying to keep himself occupied while she delivered her terribly uninteresting soliloquy, he moved his eyes to her chest, and was able to mildly excite himself by focusing on the curves of her ample breasts, which were blatantly showing their shape through the satiny fabric of her top.

"It's so nice to see you're not like that, Mr. Huxton."

He smiled, and dryly said, "Yes."

"So what can I getcha today?"

"Your finest tawny port," Mason replied, the Diazecalm™ greatly helping him to maintain his civility. "Please."

"Right away," Holly said, then mercifully took her chipper presence away from him.

Mason looked around the vicinity of the speakeasy, at the

waiters dressed like mobsters and the old dusty bottles displayed upon the bar's wooden shelves, then shifted his gaze up to the thirteen levels towering above him. As he was staring at a figure leaning on the wrought-iron railing of the ninth level, he heard his name being called.

"Mason!" came the voice of Thomas Locke from behind him.

"Hello, Thomas," Mason replied, turning his head to face the large, corpulent man. "How are you today?"

"Quite well, thank you." Barely managing to squeeze his obese rear end into the chair next to Mason, he asked, "And yourself?"

"Well, also," Mason said. "Are you just getting here?"

"Yes, as a matter of fact. I arrived a few minutes before you did. Helped myself to some Dom Pérignon®," he raised his glass as if he were giving a toast, "saw you over here, and decided to come and chat before I indulged into the Hand's *other* pleasures." He laughed, causing his double chin to quiver in an odd sort of way, then took a hefty sip of the alcohol. "Aaaah, that hits the spot nicely."

Holly walked up to Mason, and handed him a full glass of port. "There ya are, Mr. Huxton."

"Thank you." Mason cupped his hand around the base of the glass, swirled it slightly, and brought it to his nose for a careful sniff. "Put the charge on my account, please." He took a small sip, judged its flavor, and smiled. "And give yourself a generous tip, my dear."

"Thanks, Mr. Huxton! Let me know if ya need anything else!" She whirled around, and whisked back to the bar.

With hungry, predatory eyes, Thomas said, "Peppy little thing, isn't she?"

Mason nodded. "Quite."

"And she seems so innocent..." Thomas smiled diabolically. "So ready to be defiled." He licked his lips, then finished off his champagne with another large gulp. "What ungodly acts I could show her, Mason."

"I'm sure," Mason said with a smirk, knowing how much his contemporary enjoyed engaging in the iniquitous. After all, as president and CEO of Cytherea™, an extremely lucrative enterprise which specialized in pornographic products, it was Thomas' *job* to immerse himself into the world of sin. But for Thomas, it was much, *much* more than an occupation. From allowing himself to become grossly overweight (he believed it was a show of respect to some god of gluttony which he worshipped), to partaking in the lewdest activities available at the Hand, it could veritably be said to be a lifestyle.

Thomas laughed heartily at Mason's response, set down his glass on a nearby table, and said, "Speaking of ungodly acts, which one brings you here today?"

"A rather tame and uninteresting one, I'm afraid." Mason took a sip of the port. "Level seven."

"Ever the man of technology, eh, Mason?"

"Indeed."

"Well, even on level seven, there's plenty of naughty things for you to do. In fact, we just supplied it with a couple of new, *ultra-intense* sexsims about a week ago. One of them," he said, excitedly leaning forward and lowering his voice, "can even make you have multiple orgasms."

Unimpressed, Mason said, "That's nothing new, Thomas. There are already some up there that can do that."

"Yes, but how many of them can guarantee to make you orgasm at least *thirty* times per session, hmm?" Thomas leaned back with a smug look on his face.

Mason nodded, his eyebrows raised. "Yes, that certainly is something new, isn't it?" He let out a small laugh. "But, no offense to your impressive new device, I will be engaging in activities of a less...shall we say...arousing nature."

"To each their own, my friend. As for myself..." Thomas carefully squeezed himself out of his chair. "...temptation calls. Are you going up yet?"

"Yes, actually. I'll join you on the elevator."

"Excellent."

They walked out of the speakeasy, toward one of the elevators which granted access to the upper floors. On their way, they passed by a saloon reminiscent of the late 1800's, a hyperbar which paid homage to the 2020's, and a tavern which carried a Revolutionary War theme.

Reaching the elevator, Mason asked, "Which level will you be going to today, Thomas?"

"The sixth." Another diabolical smile as they stepped into the empty car. "Of course."

"Of course," Mason said. "Sixth and seventh levels, please." The elevator started its smooth ascent.

Thomas said, "Now, if memory serves, you've never been up to level six, have you?"

"No, I haven't."

"Oh, you really should take advantage of this level some

time, Mason." He slowly rubbed his palms together. "I guarantee that once you've tasted its impure nectar, you'll always be coming back for more." He smiled. "Your world will never be the same."

That's what I'm afraid of, Mason thought. "I'll consider it, Thomas," he lied, as the elevator came to a stop.

The doors parted open, revealing a short hallway with a large black gate at its end. Thomas stepped out of the elevator, and walked down the hall.

The dark gate raised up into the ceiling, allowing Mason to catch a fleeting glimpse of a horrid gengineered creation, the likes of which he had never seen. It was essentially two men, grown together like Siamese twins, dressed only in black, metal-studded leather. One person stood upright, while the other was connected such that their shoulders were the other person's pelvis, causing their body to extend out horizontally in a manner resembling a centaur. The lower person had no arms, and his head protruded out just above the other's privates. The upright one, who was wearing a studded leather mask, was holding a whip in one hand, and with the other was grasping the lower person by his hair, forcing him to give themselves fellatio.

Thomas looked back at Mason. "Sure you don't want to join me, old boy?"

"Quite," Mason said.

The doors closed, and the car started to move again.

Reaching the seventh level, Mason headed straight toward his destination. He walked through the floor's wide array of VR machines, past the immersibles and the sexsims, to the area where the MUDs could be accessed. There were rows of private rooms, placed not too close together, extending all the way back to the far wall. Many were occupied, but with a brief stroll down one of the hallways, Mason was able to find an available room. It contained within it a black easy chair, a small coffee table, a couple of floor plants, and little else. The lighting was low, and there was the faintest hint of classical music coming from a hidden speaker.

Mason closed the soundproof door behind him, slipped out of his shoes, sat down in the easy chair, and relaxed his arms upon the rests. A lightweight headset emerged from the top of the chair, gently placing itself atop his head.

His eyes were now covered by thin wraparound gogs, his ears enclosed by form-fitting surround speakers. A mini microphone curved around from the right side of the headset, perfectly positioning itself in front of his lips. After he set his feet onto the cushioned,

135

pedal-like rests at the base of the chair, two small compartments opened beneath his hands. He put his palms into the opening, and placed his fingertips inside ten thimble-shaped devices. Retracting his hands from the compartment, the wireless tipsets still on his fingers, he said, "Voice-rec on."

The previously transparent lenses filled up with light, and now all he could see before him were the images transmitted via satellink. At first, nothing but a blue void, giving him the sensation that he was floating around in a sea of nothingness. A combination ocean/static sound played through the speakers, adding to the vacuous effect. The Ordosoft™ logo appeared from a vanishing point far in the distance, then quickly shot forward, directly at him. Just as it looked like the logo was going to hit into him, it swiftly veered to the right, and zoomed past him with a whoosh. Behind him, he could hear it moving over to the left, then it shot past his ahead again, stopped a few feet in front of him, and morphed into The Invisible Hand's logo–a black outline of a hand, its palm facing out, with the triangular, illuminated eye design set into the negative space of its interior.

"Welcome to The Invisible Hand," said a pleasing female voice which seemed to be emanating from everywhere around him. "Please select your destination." Various shapes, designs, and iconic graphics appeared–some slowly materializing into view, others popping up out of the void's thin air, a few growing larger from a small speck–then hovered there before him in the bluish vacuity.

Now that the Hand's computer had accessed his identity, Mason was able to look down and see his arms, body, and legs, all virtually rendered to perfection. He pointed his finger toward the icons, pushed forward on the pedals, and started to move straight ahead through the void. The specific graphic he wanted to reach was a bit to his right, so he moved his finger slightly in that direction, and his virtual body followed suit. Reaching the MUD icon–which depicted four circles in a squarelike shape, each one linked to the other via six, solid black lines–Mason eased up on the pedals, and his motion came to a stop. He raised his hand before the icon, pointed his index finger, and quickly tapped forward two times.

"Thank you, Mr. Huxton," said the omnipresent voice. "Now accessing multi-user domain." The icon transformed into a black hole, which proceeded to grow larger in size until it completely enveloped him. Mason then found himself inside of a spacelike dimension filled with stars, planets, asteroids, and other types of celestial bodies.

Floating directly in front of him, were the six avatars which he most frequently used in this domain. "Please select an avatar for this session," the voice said.

Mason moved his finger along the row of iconic identities, past the one that looked like himself, past one which resembled a figure from a Duchamp painting, past another which resembled King Arthur, then stopped when it was pointing at the one depicting a simply dressed, very ordinary, thirteen-year old boy. He double-tapped the avatar, it rotated in place for a moment, then it moved forward, morphed itself around him, and he became it.

"Where would you like to go today?" the voice asked. Different portals opened up in the space around him, each one a gateway to the virtual domain visualized within.

Mason double-tapped his finger over the portal showing a beautiful ocean beach. The portal increased in size, zoomed toward him, and he was instantly transported into the picturesque scene.

As he gently floated down from the overcast sky, he looked over the peaceful domain below. On his right, a calm, grayish-blue ocean, with waves no more than a couple of feet high. A few seastacks, ranging in height from approximately ten to thirty feet, jutted up through the water, their flora-covered tops providing a welcome refuge for the environment's avian occupants. To his left, a vast, ancient evergreen forest, growing all the way up to the fringes of the brown sand beach. Directly below him, driftlogs and seaweed were randomly scattered about, as were the assorted tidepools which were just now beginning to reveal themselves. A menagerie of avatars occupied the sandy shores, some playing or talking together, others simply sitting alone and enjoying the spectacular view.

Once his virtual body had touched down on the beach, Mason began to roam around the coast in search of familiar faces. Being that he was such a frequent visitor to the domain, it didn't take long for him to find some.

"Jeremiah!" waved Anna. She was presenting as a scanned image of herself, dressed in worn summer clothing. "You made it!"

"Anna!" Mason said excitedly, his avatar voice sounding altogether different from his real one. He waved back, and briskly made his way over to her and Demetrius.

"We didn't think you were going to make it today," she said.

"Neither did I. But I managed to get more work done than I expected." Mason sat down next to the two them. "And my supervisor is quite...chill about being telepresent. She doesn't care about set hours, provided that I get all of my work done."

"You're lucky, Jeremiah." Demetrius was presenting as his usual avatar–an oversized bronze mask which was a caricature of the sun, set atop the scanned image of a statuesque body. "My bosses are so anal about set hours. We have to be telepresent even if we don't have anything to do. It's so stupid." He shook his head, the dull sunlight glinting off of his shiny metal face. "It doesn't make any sense."

"That's because it's a job, Dee," Anna laughed. "They're not supposed to make sense."

Demetrius laughed, the wavy sunray designs around his head moving in unison with his voice.

Mason laughed also, though he didn't really agree with her statement. He could think of *lots* of reasons why jobs made sense–but that was Mason, not Jeremiah. Jeremiah *would* understand what she was saying, because he was one of their kind, and he knew what they went through. So he continued to laugh, and as he did, he began to understand and agree with what she said. He became one of them.

He became Jeremiah.

And that was what he enjoyed about this place so much–he could be someone else, and escape from the stressful corporate life which he lived every day. Here, there were no business meetings, no agendas, no deals to be made, no ulterior motives behind every word spoken–here it was simple. Simple people discussing simple things in simple terms. Jeremiah loved it here. It was the world to him, literally all he lived for.

"It would be nice if they did, though," Demetrius said as he finished his laugh.

Jeremiah smiled. "It would be even nicer if there *were* no jobs."

Anna nodded. "You can say that again."

Jeremiah watched a wave crest, and as it crashed back down with a lovely splash, he said, "Then we could sit around and talk . like this all the time." A seagull flew across the horizon, circled around one of the tall seastacks, and landed on top of it. "Without worrying about having to go back."

"Maybe it'll happen someday, Jeremiah," Demetrius said. "You never know."

For a few moments, there was nothing but the sound of the ocean, the birds, and distant voices. Then Jeremiah said, "I just realized...where's Noelani?"

"She should be back any time now," Demetrius said. "We IM'd her when you got here, and she said she'd be coming right up."

"But you know 'Lani," Anna laughed. "'Right up' could be a while."

"Oh," Jeremiah said, "she's in the ocean, is she?"

"You got it."

"And presenting as a mermaid?"

Anna nodded.

Jeremiah laughed. "Then it certainly will be a while before she comes up." He ran his fingers through the sand, and said, "Maybe we should all join her. It *is* beautiful down there. The reefs, the fish, the seals..."

"Sounds like fun," Anna said. "What do you think, Dee?"

"I'm game. That way, we-" Demetrius suddenly stopped, his sunny face showing a look of concern.

"What is it?" asked Jeremiah.

"Behind you," Demetrius said. "Look, Anna, that weird thing is back again."

Jeremiah turned his head, and saw a thin, shadowy, humanlike figure approaching them. Its entire structure was shaking and vibrating at an incredibly fast rate, as if a filmmaker was shooting a scene of someone having an intense epileptic seizure, but was making constant, jerky motions with the camera themselves. "That certainly is odd looking," Jeremiah said.

"It's not just the way it looks," Anna said. "That thing gives off some really weird frees. It'll just stare at you with these creepy faces..." She watched as it came closer. "It should go to a different domain."

"Like one of the goth realms," Dee said.

"The goths aren't *that* scary," Anna said with a nervous laugh. "It would creep them out, too. That thing belongs in a Lynchian domain."

"I guess we'll be finding out what it wants," Jeremiah said. "Because it's most definitely coming our way." A few seconds later, the creature had reached them. Though it was still vibrating quickly, its proximity allowed him to see a better detail of its features.

It had a very thin and elongated physique, with fingers that ended in sharp points. Its entire body was made purely of shadow, with no marks, designs, or clothing upon it. And then there was the head–a shadowy, featureless shape which flashed sick and disturbing images across its face. They appeared quickly, without warning, then disappeared before the mind had a chance to fully understand what it was that it just saw.

139

The shadow creature stood there before them, not saying a word. The only noise emanating from it was the strange buzzing sound which accompanied its vibratory motions. Then across its face flashed the silent image of a blood-spattered woman screaming in terror.

"Why don't you just go away?" Anna said. "What do you want?"

The creature's head tilted to one side. A flash of a hanged-man's upper body, his neck grotesquely twisted, his tongue hanging out of his mouth. Its head returned upright, then it slowly raised its hand forward, its long, pointy index finger uncurling toward Jeremiah. "Him," it said in a voice composed of the same vibratory sounds as its motion.

Shocked, Jeremiah asked, "Me?"

"Jeremiah?" asked Anna.

Buzzing laughter. "There is no such person here." Mason's face flashed across the creature's head. "Jeremiah is the figment of an unhappy rich man's imagination."

Demetrius looked at Jeremiah. "What's he talking about? Do you know him?"

"I've never met him before in my life," said Jeremiah.

A flash of the Ordosoft™ logo engulfed in flames. "But you know what I'm talking about, don't you, Mason?"

Jeremiah wasn't sure how to respond. His world of escape was beginning to break apart and crumble, and he was afraid. He didn't want to lose it *or* his friends. Panicked, torn between two identities, he could only think to ask, "What is it that you want from me?"

Flash: a human skull, imploding. "Many things," it said. "I want your friends to know the truth about you. About how you've lied to them all this time, pretending to be someone else." Flash: A horribly disfigured man placing a skinned human mask upon his face. "I want your inane fantasy to come to an end."

"Mason...?" Demetrius said. "Mason Huxton?"

With sadness and confusion in his eyes, Mason/Jeremiah looked back at Demetrius, but said nothing.

"Yes," the creature said, "Mason Huxton." Flash: Mason's face again, a crown of barbed wire atop his head, rivulets of blood dripping drown from the wounds. "One of the kings of the world, virtually slumming it with the commoners." It buzzingly laughed, feeling to Mason like a bumblebee entering his ear canal. "Melodrama at its best."

"So what if he *is* Mason Huxton?" Anna said. "Guess what,

weirdo? I don't care! I'll accept him for who he is here, no matter what he is out there!" She picked up a handful of sand and threw it at the creature.

The grains passed harmlessly through its body, true to its shadow form. Across its face, a flash of a woman digging her eyes out with her fingernails.

"Go away!" Anna shouted. "Nobody wants you here! Don't you understand?! You failed! You didn't accomplish anything!"

"Ah, but I did." A flash of flesh being violently ripped from someone's face. "Whether or not you accept him is irrelevant. What matters is that he can never face *you* again." It turned to Mason with a flash of the same face, flesh completely gone, musculature now being torn apart. "The illusion is gone—it can never be the same for him." Flash: The final muscle torn, now just a skull. "Can it, Mason?" Flash: The skull, imploding.

Mason stood up, calmly dusted himself off, and boldly stared down the creature. "I can assure *you* that it will never be the same." Outside of the beachworld, he said, "Command: Alert security."

A flash of Nazi stormtroopers marching in perfect unison. "Trying to call the Gestapo?" the creature asked. "It's going to take them a while to get through my walls of fire and ice." Flash: A little girl burned with napalm, running from a village with tears in her eyes. The creature turned to Demetrius and Anna. "Leave now, or I'll infect your brains with informational pus."

Anna and Demetrius looked at Mason, unsure of what to do.

"Do as he says," Mason told them. "I'll be fine."

Anna hesitated, but Demetrius grabbed her and said, "Let's go, Anna!" She looked at Mason's Jeremiah avatar for a long second, then they both faded away.

The next instant, water from the ocean rose up, tsunami-like, and rapidly headed toward them. Mason stood his ground, confident that his avatar could handle the impact. But rather than crashing down, the wave curled over them and shaped into a dome, creating a pocket of sand and air within a raging sea. Ocean swirled about, the sounds of rushing water everywhere, then suddenly silence, as the water slowed down and froze into ice. The inside layer of the dome ignited, blazing with a fire which wouldn't melt the frozen saltwater. It was an impressive icewall/firewall combination, different than any Mason had seen before.

Outside of the domain, he said, "Command: Assume Arthur avatar." Within the domain, he transformed into a likeness of King

Arthur, complete with crown, armor, and sword.

"An old-fashioned duel," the creature said. A flash of two knights jousting, one being impaled through the sternum by the other's lance. "Goody."

Mason raised Excalibur into the air, and grasped its hilt with both hands. "Let's have at it then, creature." He swung the enchanted blade at the shadow, but its body unformed in the very place which the sword was going to connect with. As the weapon passed through the open space, the creature quickly reformed, and readied for attack.

Flash: A surgeon's scalpel, slicing open a pale man's chest. The creature lunged forward with its long, sharp fingers and slashed Mason's chest, causing bright blue sparks to fly off his armor.

Unfazed by the attack, Mason swung his sword another time, but the creature simply unformed and formed once again.

They circled each other cautiously, both combatants trying to predict the best moment to strike. The creature acted first.

Another lunge, this time at Mason's face. A flash of the back of JFK's head being shot out, blood and brains spraying out like mist. The claws hit an invisible barrier before they could touch him, and the creature immediately retracted its wounded hand.

Mason stepped in and swung for its neck, but the creature quickly ducked.

Still crouched down, it crawled back a few steps, and said, "Die." Its face flashed the bomb at Hiroshima, then a mushroom cloud exploded around Mason.

The cloud lifted, and Mason stood there, unscathed. "You forget I know Merlin." He pointed the tip of his sword at the creature, and blasted out a shotgunlike spray of blue photonic particles.

The shadow instantly collapsed, its body becoming corrupted with the blue Excalibur virus, its vibrations gradually slowing down and shifting into focus. Its head, however, remained the same, buzzing as fast as it was before. Flashing the image of American troops pulling out of Vietnam, it asked, "You think you've won, don't you?"

"Considering that you're lying there, crippled," Mason said, coldly staring at the creature, "I'd say 'yes.'" He looked up above, at the slowly dissipating dome. "And if I were considering the fact that security is already working its way through your walls, I'd respond with an emphatic 'yes.'"

Flash: A whipped and bloodied slave, breaking his chains and escaping. "I'll already be gone by the time they get here."

"You think, do you?"

142

# ((FREQUENCIES))

"I *know*." Across its face appeared images of the bombing at Pearl Harbor, then its head levitated from its corrupted body, and hovered there in the air. "You've heard the saying, 'lost the battle, but won the war?'" A flash of Adam's face.

Mason's expression grew dead serious, butterflies of dread fluttering within his stomach.

Flash: Adam's face, colored purplish-black, fat and bloated from the effects of decomposition. The beheaded creature said, in that horrible buzzing voice, "You no longer have a son."

Then it vibrated even faster, dispersed itself into tiny fragments, and disappeared altogether.

## α

# Ω

# Chapter 9
## ((Vicissitudes))

*"To simply live one's life was an impossibility.*
*Life was not a simple thing.*
*Complex and convoluted, it was the universe in microcosm, rife with*
*infinite turns and twists, some expected, others not.*

Twilight in the Emerald City.

Across a sky stained with violent reds and redolent violets, the Polaris™ flew on automatic, due east to Issaquah. Its windows rolled down, A Tribe Called Quest's "Can I Kick It?" playing loudly on its stereo, it weaved its way through the numerous holographic billboards which covered the city's skyscape, as the adsats overhead began to brightly display their graphics and slogans.

McCready gazed up through the Chevy's® roof at the commercial constellations above, and asked, "N.J., am I still on hold, or did we get disconnected?"

"You're still on hold, Marc," said the cartoon Marilyn, currently wearing a black see-through dress from *Some Like It Hot*, "though you have been waiting an unusually long amount of time. Would you like me to disconnect and call him back?"

"Nah, that's alright. With the kind of day he's had, I'm sure that'd only piss him off more. I was just curious. Keep holding."

Twenty seconds passed, the volume of the song lowered, and he heard the voice of Mason Huxton ask, "Agent McCready?"

Averting his eyes from a chip-shaped Doritos® adsat, McCready looked down at the uniview, raised his seat forward, and said, "Yeah, I'm still here. What's up? How is he?"

"Thankfully," Huxton sighed, his voice showing signs of both weariness and relief, "much better than before. He's still groggy from the concussion and the pain relievers, but his memory appears to have fully returned."

"No permanent damage?"

"The doctors don't think so, no. The MRI's showed no bruising or tearing of the brain, and the other diagnostics yielded positive results as well. He'll be bedridden for a while, but they're expecting a full and complete recovery."

"That's good to hear. 'Cause I gotta admit, after I saw the video..." McCready's voice trailed off as he recalled the streetcam images of the incident: Adam Huxton emerging from a limo, surrounded by two Ordocops™ and two Xandys. Taking a few steps from the car, he's suddenly grabbed and shielded by one of the Xandys, then pushed by the other, just as a full-size truck comes barreling into the entire entourage. Two Ordocops™ and one Xandy are brutally crushed underneath the speeding vehicle, as the android-shielded Adam goes flying over the grill, smashes into the windshield, and falls unconscious to the hard concrete. "...I was expecting worse news."

"Yes," Huxton said grimly, nodding his head, "so was I... It's frightening to think what would have happened had Xanadeux not been there to take the brunt of the blow."

Your son would be roadkill right now, McCready thought, feeling no fright whatsoever at the notion. "Well, at least it *was* there, so you won't even have to consider the alternative."

"True enough, Agent McCready." Huxton glanced back over his shoulder, allowing McCready to catch a glimpse of Adam lying in a hospital bed, his face badly bruised, his entire right arm housed within an exoskeleton. "Yet when one's child is involved, one can't help *but* think of the alternative."

"I guess I wouldn't know." An ambulance flew past McCready, its annoyingly loud sirens temporarily drowning out all other sounds. As the vehicular wailing faded away, he asked, "So did the OFT's end up matching with the biochip data?"

He nodded. "Only the owner had been in the truck recently."

"And you've already detained and questioned him?"

"Yes, but it was quickly apparent he knew nothing," Huxton said. "Moreover, his biochip showed that he was clear across town at the time of the attack, and there are numerous witnesses to corroborate the data."

"Hmm. Definitely a remote attack then. They must've jacked the truck's CPU and homed it in on Adam's biochip." He rubbed his thumb against the grain of his stubbly chin. "Which means there should still be some type of cybertrail from the truck back to the location where the attack was programmed."

"There should be, yes," Huxton said. "But the unfortunate truth, Agent McCready, is that these terrorists appear quite adept at covering their tracks. So much so, that not even Xanadeux has been able to follow their trail."

Not even Xanadeux, McCready thought mockingly. Huxton spoke about the androidal creation like it was a fuckin' god or something–like the AI was perfect, without any limitations or faults. But McCready had learned long ago that nothing was perfect. Not people, not places, not things. Not even God. "How long has he–or it–been looking into the case?" he asked.

"Ever since the attack occurred."

That would be about five hours now, McCready thought. Plenty of time for a good cracker to break some of the codes the terrorists were hiding behind. "And Xanadeux hasn't found out anything on your attack either?"

Huxton shook his head as he slowly blinked his eyes. "No."

"Have you considered the possibility that Xanadeux might be involved in the attacks?"

Huxton scowled. "I don't consider the impossible, Agent Mc-Cready. Xanadeux would never bring harm to myself or my family."

McCready couldn't help but let out a small laugh at Huxton's close-mindedness. Discussing Xanadeux with him was like trying to discuss the Bible with a Jesus freak–no matter what you said to them, no matter how logical, they'd always retreat back to some bullshit argument about how the Book is always right. Fuck the facts. "It's not impossible, Huxton," McCready said. "It's been known to happen in andys who've been programmed with emotions. They get jealous, angry, sad, depressed... Just like anyone else."

"Not Xanadeux," Huxton said. "My father created it to be perfectly loyal." He solemnly stared at McCready. "And it is."

"Alright, if you say so," McCready resigned, not interested in wasting any more breath on Huxton's faith-clogged ears. "But let me make one suggestion."

"Certainly. Go ahead."

"Let someone else get a crack at finding their trail. A human."

"I take it you have someone in mind?"

"Yeah. Takura."

"Your fellow agent?"

"Right."

Huxton placed his finger on his lip, contemplated for a few seconds. "He's that good?"

Without hesitation, McCready said, "Are corporations greedy?"

Nothing but solemnity from Huxton. Then a subtle expression, something faintly resembling a smile, and he said, "I'll contact him immediately."


Now that Huxton, his son, and his wife had all been attacked, McCready knew that the head of Ordosoft™ wasn't going to be taking any chances with his daughter's safety. So when he reached Ashley's estate and found an assortment of Ordocop™ vehicles and personnel–some ground-based, others airborne–stationed around its perimeter, he wasn't in any way surprised. Impressed maybe, by the sheer number of units armed and equipped to protect one single woman–but not surprised. This was the daughter of one of the richest men in the world, for Christ's sake. Of course he'd use his corporate army to protect her. Especially, McCready decided, if his daughter happened to be Ashley. Funny thing was, rather than having their hands full with terrorists, the Ordocops™ were instead having to deal with the flock of news crews which had vulturically descended down upon Ashley's Issaquah residence, eager to snatch up a fresh tidbit of morbid news.

Which didn't surprise him either–the buzz always grew quickly when a publicly accessible streetcam caught something scandalous or disastrous happening to someone famous. By now, the grisly images of Adam's assault had been repeated, replayed, uploaded, downloaded–fuck, McCready thought, probably even masturbated to–thousands of times all over the uninet. And once word had gotten out that the security around Xanadeux and Ashley's place had been significantly beefed up, not even Mason's influence could prevent the media from sighting their new target.

The story of the day had been found, and the news scavengers were hungry. There were the skyvans and Zoomcams™ of *Inside Edition*, *Eye Spye*, and the other tabloids, all carefully circling the area, making sure not to infringe upon the no-fly zone above Ashley's estate. Local reporters, representing every station from KIRO to

KOMO, were on the ground, incessantly picking at the Ordocops™ for more juicy information. Even CNN®, MSNBC®, and the internationals were there, their sleek, self-contained RCC spheres whizzing to different locations around the area. All of the commotion and chaos reminded him a little of the riot. Except in this case, people were being kept *out* rather than in. And, McCready thought, when it's all said and done, the reporters get to go *home*.

After receiving clearance from the Ordocops™ to enter the estate, McCready had the Polaris™ do a quick flyby of the arboreal area, just to make sure that nothing unusual was going on. Not that he could see much from above, since her residence was literally overgrown with herbage and foliage–to the point that typical aerial reconnaissance was pretty much futile–but he made the token attempt anyway. Not surprisingly, the quickie inspection revealed nothing of a sinister or threatening nature. What it *did* reveal, he realized as he passed over her house–which was composed entirely of pyramids, cylinders, and spheres–was that eccentricity must be a trait that W.A. Huxton had gengineered into all of his offspring. Either that, McCready laughed to himself, or they were all an example of what happens when you have too much money on your hands. You end up building weird shit like floating castles and homes with fucked up geometrics.

Passing over the parking area, McCready said, "N.J., connect me with Ashley." He pulled out a Kamel®, placed it between his lips. "And go ahead and park over there by the green Lex."

Seconds passed. The cartoon Marilyn tapped her fingernails on an art deco table she was sitting at. No answer.

The Polaris™ set itself down behind Ashley's Lexus®. "There's currently no response, Marc. Would you like to leave a message?"

"Try again," McCready said, his tongue moving back and forth along the butt of the cigarette. "And make sure she knows it's me."

More seconds passed.

Marilyn took a deep breath, then exhaled impatiently.

Still no answer.

"Aw, fuck," McCready grumbled, uneasily shifting in his seat. He had just spoken to Ashley about twenty minutes ago. Had she suddenly left? he wondered. Unlikely. She had told him that she'd wait there until he arrived. Then why wasn't she answering? "N.J.," he said, "is Ashley even in the house?"

Marilyn looked through a pair of binoculars. "Her biochip says she is, but she's still not answering."

The cigarette wavered between McCready's lips, its motion moving quicker with his thoughts. Had something happened since he spoke with her? Could the terrorists have made their next move? When the next question, "Is she in danger?" passed through his mind, he was out of the car, quickly walking through the jungly garden pathway which led to her house. With his palm touching the cold steel handle of his holstered Colt® Python®, McCready emerged from the tall vegetation and trotted to the front door. He activated his emvest, causing a momentary ripple in the visual space around his upper body, then touched his hand on the callscreen. "Ashley?" he asked. "You there?"

On the callscreen's oval monitor, nothing but an animated spiral, hypnotically swirling round and round to infinity.

Ten more anxious seconds passed.

"Ashley?!" McCready called out. He touched his wristcom, drew his .357 with his perspiring left hand. "N.J., I need you to scan Ashley's biochip for location and vital signs. Now!" Pounding his fist on the wooden front door, he yelled, "Ashley?! Are you in there?!"

"Marc?" said the cartoon Marilyn.

"Yeah?" he asked, snapping a mini plasma torch off his belt. "What've you got?"

"Ashley is in the lower portion of the house," N.J. said, just as McCready aimed the torch at the door, "and her vital signs and frees are perfectly normal."

He lifted his finger off the "fire" button. "So she's fine..."

"According to the biochip readings, that's correct."

"Well where the hell is she then?" he blurted out.

"She's currently moving through the house in a southerly direction, toward her callscreen. In fact, she should be making contact with you right...about...now."

Within the monitor's oval frame, the spinning spiral morphed into a curious and slightly confused Ashley. "What's going on?" she asked. "Is everything okay?"

"That depends. Are *you* okay?" McCready asked, the tone of his voice falling somewhere between concern and irritation.

Ashley gave him a funny look. "Uh...yeah."

"Then why didn't you answer the UV?"

"I turned it off," she said. "I was meditating."

Meditating, he thought. Of course. "I wish you would've told me you'd be doing that. You could've saved me some adrenalin." He holstered his Colt® and adjusted his trenchcoat.

"Sorry about that," she said with a laugh. "I just figured you'd come up to the door without calling first." Reaching her hand towards the callscreen, she said, "I'll be right there."

The screen morphed back into the psychedelic spiral. McCready placed his hands in his pockets, looked around at the giant evergreens which filled the southern part of the estate. As his eyes moved from the base of their fat brown trunks, all the way up to their towering, needled tops, he was relieved to see that the forest had grown together thick enough so that its canopy practically covered the sky above–meaning that his "rescue" probably hadn't been caught on camera by one of the skyvans. That would've been all I needed, he thought. To spend my fifteen minutes of fame being known as the dumb fuck who made the world think another attack had happened. Hearing the twist of the doorknob, he turned back around.

"Hey there, Mr. Action Hero," Ashley smiled. "Come on in."

"Action hero," McCready said with a droll laugh, stepping into the cylindrical entrance hall. He looked over the curved, ivy-covered walls and ceiling, which appeared to be composed entirely of an electrochromic, plexiglass-like material. "Interesting place you got here."

"Like it?" she asked.

Be diplomatic, he had to remind himself. "It's different."

"Yeah," she said as she locked the door, "it is. That's what I love about it. Most Western architecture is so harsh and angular." Drifting over to the wall, she softly ran her hand along its rounded surface. "I wanted something that was gonna be more curvy and smooth..." Her fingers caressed the vines of ivy. "Something a little more natural, y'know?"

He acknowledged her statement with a few nods, continuing to scan his eyes over the hall. "Who did the design?"

"My mom and I," she said, cradling one of the green, spade-shaped leaves in the palm of her hand. She stared at it for a moment, her thumb circling gently round its soft edges, then smiled nostalgically. "We did it together."

"You an architect?"

"No, my mom is...was." Ashley laughed uncomfortably, shaking her head. "Is." She moved past him, further down the long hallway towards another oval door. "I did a few rough drawings, told her what I wanted...but she was the one who designed it."

Ashley took in a strong, bittersweet breath. "She was the one who made it real."

Sensing the hurt in her voice, McCready was tempted to say something comforting to her. He knew firsthand what it was like to lose a parent, and remembered how shitty it felt. But he wasn't very good with caring words, and he couldn't really think of the right thing to say. And he didn't want to think about his dad right now anyway–so he opted for small talk. "Must've been a lot of work."

"Yeah, it was," she said as she reached the northern door, this one less of a throwback than the other. "But she did it. She's amazing." Pressing her thumb onto a biochip scanner, she spoke the words, "Forty-two," and the oval door slid open with a hiss. "Oh yeah–there's one rule before you come in," she said.

"What's that?"

She pointed to her bare feet. "You gotta take your shoes off."

"Nah," he said, figuring she was kidding with him. Glancing down at his Timberlands®, he saw a few pairs of her shoes lying on the floor. He looked back up at her. "Really?"

"Yeah," she laughed. "Really."

"Alright," he said reluctantly, "just don't blame me if the CDC tries to place your hallway under quarantine."

Ashley rolled her eyes and smiled. "I'm sure your feet don't smell *that* bad, Agent McCready."

Slipping his feet out of his tims, McCready followed Ashley through the oval doorway, into another segment of the house–this one a huge spherical room filled with more books than he'd ever seen, more plants than he'd ever want, and more art pieces than he could probably ever afford. The door hissed shut behind him, and he asked, "So how are you holding up through everything?"

"Okay, I guess," she said, pushing aside a beanbag ottoman with her foot. "I mean, considering my family's being terrorized and there's a media circus outside my house." She walked over to the east side of the sphere, where a spacious, covelike kitchen area was located. "Do you want something to drink?"

"You got anything with caffeine?" he asked, examining a tall spiral staircase which curved through the domed ceiling into another room above.

"I'll check." She touched a sensor on her cylindrical refrigerator, turning its opaque surface transparent. "Looks like your only choices are between a green tea brew...and..." She laughed. "A green tea brew. That's it."

151

McCready moved over to the counter which separated the cove from the rest of the room. "If it's got caffeine," he said, sitting down on one of cushioned stools, "I'll take it."

Ashley opened the brew and set it down on the countertop before him. "There ya go. Caffeine."

"Thanks." McCready removed his shades and took a swig.

"You're welcome." Ashley turned the fridge back to its previous opaqueness, then served herself some water from the spigot of a green ceramic cooler. "Y'know, Agent McCready," she said, her face growing contemplative as she leaned against the counter, "right now...I think the reason I'm doing okay through all this, is because it kinda feels like I'm living in a dream. Or dreaming while awake...something of that nature." She sipped the water. "It's kinda like everything's real, but at the same time it's unreal, y'know?"

McCready nodded. "I know the feeling. Like you're watching this incredibly intense fuckin' movie...called your life."

Ashley smiled. "Exactly." She rounded the counter and seated herself on the stool next to him. "These last few days," she said, her legs brushing against his as she placed her feet onto the contoured chrome footstool, "the last few months, really...so many major things have happened, it's like now I'm just *expecting* that the next day's gonna bring something deep with it. Almost like I'm not surprised anymore if my dad or my brother gets attacked...or if I'm suddenly told about all these things I never knew." She rotated her glass in place on the countertop. "But not in a numb way, y'know? It's more...it's more of an understanding that everything happens for a reason...and each person's placed here for a purpose."

"Destiny," he said.

"Yeah," she said, "destiny. And fate, synchronicity...all those things. The way everything just kinda falls into place the way it's supposed to, when it's supposed to." She took another sip of the water, the simple act somehow appearing very elegant and attractive to him. "It's like how when you read something, it means you were always meant to be introduced to those ideas, or when you hear about something, it means you were always meant to know about that information. Or when you meet someone..." Her eyes locking with his, him feeling a rush. "It means that you two were always meant to experience each other." She smiled warmly. "How could it be anything else? Things happen the way they're supposed to, and it's just a matter of us deciphering their meaning." Turning her eyes to the giant skylight which comprised half of the dome's ceiling, she said,

"And right now, with all these things that've happened lately...I think life's trying to tell me something, Agent McCready. It's trying to bring something out of me. I'm not sure exactly what..." She looked back at him. "But it's something."

Before McCready had a chance to respond, he suddenly heard an odd noise. "What the hell was that?" he asked, perking his head up as he instinctively reached down for his napper.

"What the hell was what?"

"That noise..." McCready stood up, and cautiously moved towards the spiral staircase. "Coming from upstairs–sounds like a voice. And movement."

"Oh, *that*," Ashley said, exhaling with relief. "It's probably just Don waking up."

"Don?" McCready stopped his progress, turned around. "Who's that, your boyfriend?"

She laughed. "No, *Dawn*. D-a-w-n. Female."

"Your girlfriend?"

"My just-friend," Ashley said, still laughing, as she moved to the base of the staircase. "You sure are curious."

"Have to be," he smirked. "It's part of the job description."

"Of course." Looking up the stairs, Ashley called out, "Dawn? You up?"

"Yes, no thanks to you," answered a feminine voice. "I thought you said you were going to wake me up when you were done meditating."

"I was," Ashley said. "But I got kinda sidetracked."

A slender, curvy, strikingly attractive redhead walked down the staircase. "You, the chaos queen? Sidetracked?" She slipped a cellphone into her purse. "I don't believe it."

"Yeah, right," Ashley said playfully. "How was your catnap?"

"Divine," she replied. "Your bed is *so* absolutely amazing, sweetie. I want one of my own–kitties and all." Reaching the base of the stairs, Dawn gave Ashley a hug and a kiss on the cheek. "Thanks for letting me sleep, Ash. I needed it."

"You're welcome. Thanks for keeping me company."

"Isn't that what best friends are for?" Turning to McCready, Dawn said, "Now, you must be the dashing secret agent I've been hearing about." Something vaguely familiar about her, but he couldn't quite place what it was. She daintily offered him her jewelled and manicured hand, and said, "I'm Amanda."

"McCready," he said, lightly grasping her soft, perfumed fingers, his thumb touching a few of the small implanted epigems. "Nice to meet you."

"The pleasure's mine," she said.

"So should I be calling you Amanda or Dawn?"

"Amanda." She looked over at Ashley with mock irritation. "Only Ash still calls me Dawn."

Ashley laughed. "That's 'cause Ash still remembers when you wouldn't *let* anyone call you Amanda." To McCready, she said, "This would be *before* she went to Hollywood."

Familiar face, Amanda, Hollywood—now it clicked. "I thought I recognized you," McCready said. "Amanda Knight?"

"In the flesh. You're familiar with my work?"

"I've seen a few of your films, yeah. Think I also did an interact that you starred in."

"And what'd you think?"

His hands in his coat pockets, he shrugged his shoulders. "Not bad."

Amanda raised her carefully trimmed eyebrows. "Not good?"

"Not really."

She burst out into laughter. "Ooh, I *like* it. A man who speaks his mind. Got any plans for tomorrow night?" she jested.

McCready and Ashley made eye contact, and he replied, "'Fraid so."

"Too bad," Amanda smiled. "Maybe next time." She looked at Ashley. "Well, my dear, I should be heading home now. I want to make sure I have time to take a shower and freshen up a bit before the gathering."

"Mm-kay. Let me walk you out." Ashley picked up a light coat from the back of a futon. "I'll be right back, Agent McCready, okay?"

"Alright," McCready said. He walked over to the counter, picked up his drink, and started to saunter around Ashley's pad.

Following the sphere's raised outer rim in a counterclockwise direction, he browsed the various masks, artifacts, and plants hanging upon the curved walls. Each item, including the living ones, exuded an air of antiquity, making him feel like he was walking through a museum or gallery rather than a home. Passing by the mouth of another cylindrical hallway—this one leading to some sort of large empty room with hardwood floors—past more antediluvian wall decorations, he reached the entrance to a stairwell. He peeked his head in and looked up. There were tons of steps, spiraling all the way to the top of the tall vertical shaft. It was currently lit so that it gave the appearance of ascending into a black infinity. If he was remembering the details of his flyby correctly, this would have to be the tower which had the Kremlin-looking thing on the top of it, since that structure was the highest point on the estate.

McCready took a sip of his brew and continued along the outer rim of the sphere, towards a curved sliding glass door which led out to the back part of the estate. As he neared it, he began to peer outside–and could have sworn he saw something flash by.

Something human-sized.

Moving swiftly to the door, McCready snapped a mini Maglite® off his belt and shined it through the glass, around the dimly lit backyard area. Nothing but foliage, fountains, and the shining eyes of a few nocturnal animals. Wondering if it was just his imagination, he checked the label of the brew he was drinking to make sure it was only green tea and not one of those mind-fucking Psilobrews™. Two yin-yang lizards, and the words, "Sobe®." Definitely only green tea. McCready took another look around the area. Nothing. He replaced the flashlight onto his belt, conceding that the flash was nothing but his eyes playing tricks on him.

Turning from the glass, he stepped down from the outer rim, into the sunken, center part of the sphere. It was filled with low-to-the-ground furniture such as futons, beanbags, and love seats, all looking like they'd been arranged by a tornado rather than a person–very chaotic, but just like Mother Nature, there was a certain underlying pattern to the design. Scattered amongst the furniture, in an equally random way, were different types of artistic tools, including pencils, pens, sketchbooks, musical instruments, and laptops. He kneeled down by one of the wire-bound sketchbooks, and began to flip through its contents.

Predictably, it contained a lot of abstract stuff–spirals, dots, wavy lines, trippy alphanumerics, and the like. Unpredictably, it also contained a lot of carefully rendered, painstakingly detailed drawings of people, animals, and structures. Her artistic range was impressive, and when he had reached the end of the sketchbook, he found himself drawn to look at more. He picked up another spiral-bound book, this one smaller in size, and perused its contents. Few pictures this time–it was filled mostly with writing. Not wanting to invade her privacy (somehow it seemed to him that words were more personal than pictures), McCready skipped further ahead to see if there were any other drawings.

No more drawings, but he did find a page of writing that he couldn't help but take notice of. On one of the book's creme-colored pages, in big, bright red letters, it said:

# WHERE IS ADRIAN WELLOR????

His face grew gravely serious as he looked up from the book. Adrian Wellor? Why the fuck was Ashley asking questions about *him*? And more, how did she even know about his existence at all? As far as McCready knew, all of Wellor's personal files, and any references made to him, had been edited out of the uninet's databases. The only place where information on him could be found was within the private and secured data banks of the upper-level government agencies, such as the Freemon or the NSA. And even then, the info was pretty scarce—all the files said was that Wellor was a scientist involved in the classified creation of the freereads, who then began to engage in terrorist activities. Soon after that, he completely and utterly disappeared, but since his body was never recovered, he was presumed to still be alive. Even to the present day, Wellor's capture—or the obtaining of any information which could lead to his capture—was considered a top priority. McCready looked back down at the enigmatic page. So what exactly did Ashley know? And what the hell was he going to do about it?

Just then, out of the corner of his eye, McCready saw the flash of movement again. He quickly turned his head to the door and was startled by what he saw.

Standing there, staring at him through the glass with that hideously inhuman face, was one of the Xandys. Not motioning or moving—just staring.

And then he heard the oval door hissing open, and Ashley saying, "Sorry to keep you waiting, Agent McCready."

He swiftly closed the notebook, whipped his head in her direction, and tried his very best to appear calm and composed.

Not paying much attention to what McCready was doing, Ashley took off her coat, and continued, "You get me an' Dawn together, and we can start talking for hours."

"Ah...right." McCready furtively dropped the notebook onto a beanbag. "I know how that is." He looked back at the sliding glass door. Xanadeux was gone from sight. "Did you know there's Xandys running around your backyard right now?"

"Mm-hm," she said. "My dad sent a few of them here for security. Did you just see one?"

"Yeah, one of 'em was just standing there outside your door, staring. It split when you came in." McCready walked towards Ashley. "I hate those creepy little fuckers."

"I guess I'm kinda used to them," she said, beginning to ascend the spiral staircase. "But I could see how they'd be creepy."

"Where are you going?"

"To my bedroom. I'm gonna throw on something else before we go out."

Placing his hand on the staircase's polished wood railing, he looked up at her and asked, "We're going *out*? You really think it's safe to be going out on the same day that your brother and father got attacked?"

Ashley stopped her motion and looked down at him through the steps. "Maybe, maybe not. But neither is here, really. If they wanna attack me, they're gonna find a way. And besides, I don't want to feel like I'm trapped in my own home. If this wasn't happening, then I'd be going out tonight."

"But this *is* happening."

Ashley laughed. "Oh well, then." She continued up the stairs. "I'm not gonna live my life in fear."

Brave words, he thought, walking to the counter and setting down his empty bottle. Or maybe it was something else. Maybe she didn't have anything to fear because she knew she wasn't going to be attacked. If she was asking questions about known terrorists, who was to say she wasn't somehow involved in the attacks on her family? She did seem to be handling it awfully well. Maybe Huxton had been on to something after all...

Though Ashley didn't know it, her father had hired McCready not only to protect her, but also to keep an eye on her activities. Mason knew how angry she was about the situation with her mother, and reasoned that there was a remote possibility that Ashley had something to do with the attack on the clone. Unlikely, he had said, but possible. McCready had doubted the scenario from the beginning–especially after getting a chance to spend some time with Ashley. But now he wasn't so sure. He certainly didn't *want* it to be true. Ashley was the most phenomenal woman he'd met in a long time. Maybe ever. And he was looking forward to getting to know her better. But now he had to seriously consider the notion that she was a terrorist herself, and that bothered him. Hella.

"Okay," Ashley said, coming down the stairs dressed in . fitted black pants and an orange silk top. "I'm all ready to go."

"I'm glad someone is," he muttered to himself, thinking about earlier, when Huxton had told him–in his polite, corporate, double-speak way–that it would be McCready's ass if he let her go out tonight and something were to happen to her. Ashley grabbed a jacket as they converged towards the oval door. "You realize what'll happen to me if something happens to you tonight?" McCready said.

"Do you realize what'll happen to *me* if something happens to me tonight?" She let out a short, exasperated sigh as she opened the door. "It's not like I have this burning desire to get attacked, or what." She walked out of the sphere, into the cylindrical hallway. "I'm just trying to retain *some* semblance of my normal life through all this craziness, okay?"

"Alright, alright," McCready said with a laugh. "No need to get your feathers ruffled." He pulled out his shades. "So where are you planning on taking us?"

Reaching the throwback door, Ashley said, somewhat antagonistically, "I don't know. Maybe to get something to eat. Then I might catch up with Dawn at the gathering. I'll just have to see how I feel." She opened the door, and said, "After you."

"Thanks," McCready smirked. He stepped out into the cool night air. A breeze was blowing from the west, slightly moist and altogether refreshing. And though there weren't any gray clouds yet, it felt like rain was on its way. "You got your emvest on?"

"What do you think?" she replied, walking past him.

"Honestly, sweetheart," he said, following her down the garden path towards the parking area, "I wouldn't be surprised either way."

Without stopping her motion, Ashley turned towards him, opened the flaps of her chestnut brown jacket, showed him the emvest underneath, and turned back around.

McCready smiled mischievously. There was something about getting under people's skins that he enjoyed–particularly when he was attracted to them. "Anyone ever tell you how cute you are when you're angry?" he asked as they reached the Chevy®.

Walking around to the passenger side, Ashley faced him, looked at him with disbelief, and said, "You didn't just say that."

"I did," McCready said.

She stared at him for a few more seconds, trying her best to keep a serious face. Then she reluctantly smiled, and started to laugh.

# ((FREQUENCIES))

"You're crazy, Agent McCready, you know that?"

"So I've been told, sweetheart," McCready said as they got into car, "so I've been told."

Still smiling, she gave him a little nudge on his shoulder, and added, "But you're crazy in a good way."

A different, rarer kind of smile this time. McCready placed his thumb on the ignition pad, spoke his password, then suddenly realized that the last thing in the world he would have wanted to say at that moment was something as impassive and indifferent as "whatever."

"Good evening, Agent McCready," the car said.

"N.J.," he immediately stated, "change password."

Marilyn snapped her fingers, and with a swirl of animated magic, her white dress transformed into the skimpy, coin-draped outfit of a Persian belly dancer, while her 1950's backdrop was replaced with the desert cave from *Ali Baba and the Forty Thieves*. Clicking her finger-cymbals together, she said, "Please state your new password now."

Not really sure exactly *what* he wanted to change his password to, McCready simply glanced over at the beautiful, entrancing woman seated next to him, took in the moment, and said the first thing that came to his mind.

"Fuckin'-A."

Now that was more like it.

$$\Omega$$

# Chapter 10
# ((The Gathering))

*And just as the universe itself, life's space was filled with millions of celestial bodies, each one wholly unique unto itself, a miraculous creation unlike any other.*
*Some were like planets, birthed in the same solar system. They orbited the same sun, shared similar traits, and produced corresponding frequencies which allowed them to resonate in harmony with one another. And while every planetary body had its own origins and evolutions, and each spun at their own individual rotations, they were all drawn together by the same guiding light.*

Two hours later, having enjoyed a relaxing dinner at the most fabulous restaurant in the entire world, they sat together in satiated silence, the  Polaris™ smoothly carrying them through the nighttime skies above downtown Seattle.

The moon nearly as full as her stomach, Ashley stared out at the silvery satellite, allowing her eyes to bask, unfocused, in its lovely luminescence. "Goddess," she said dreamily, both hands resting atop her tummy, "I love Ethiopian food."

McCready, who was lazily reclined back in his seat, his eyes closed, said nothing in response.

Music played softly through the car's speakers, something old and beautiful. A woman, her voice deep and rich and full of soul, backed only by the subtle strings of a piano and the occasional brush on a drum, singing about flying to the moon and playing amongst the stars.

"That food *was* pretty damn good," McCready belatedly agreed, before slipping back into contented quietude.

For the next few minutes, neither of them said a word.

Ashley continued to space off into space as she listened to the ethereal voice sing about her desire to sing. It was a peaceful moment, during which Ashley wasn't worrying or thinking about the fact that she could possibly be in mortal danger, or that she could be attacked at any time. None of that mattered, because right then, she was warm and full and comfortable and everything felt okay.

"Who's singing this?" she asked, watching a thin veil of cirrostratus clouds pass over the moon.

"Sarah Vaughan," he said.

"Her voice...it's so pretty, isn't it?"

"Yup."

"It's like she's an angel," Ashley said, as a prismatic halo formed around the moon.

"Amen," McCready said, and they both lapsed into silence once again.

When the song came to a close, McCready yawned, raised his seat forward, and said, "Well, if you're still planning on going to that gathering shindig, I guess we might want to start heading over there."

"Yeah," she said, somewhat disappointedly, "I guess so." Her watch said it was already half past ten...right about the time she'd told Dawn that she would meet up with her. Ashley was almost tempted not to go, but then she remembered that Dawn had mentioned that Seer would be there–and she definitely wanted the chance to talk to him about Wellor. Seer tended to know about all kinds of things–above *and* underground–and could probably shed some light on some of her questions.

"N.J.," McCready said, "stop cruising."

The Marilyn Monroe toon's old-fashioned low rider bounced up and down on its raised shocks a few times. "Where to next?" she asked, in that marvelous voice of hers.

"Over to–" He looked at Ashley. "Where to again?"

"Third and Bell," she said. "The Tiger's Lair."

"The Tiger's Lair," he repeated to the car. "Third and Bell."

Marilyn raised her hand to her head, saluted them, then turned off of the cruising strip and headed in a new direction.

Ashley giggled and said, "I love your car's avatar, Agent McCready. She's so adorable."

He smiled. "Thanks. I dig her, too."

"What site did you get her at?"

"None. A friend of mine at the bureau designed her for me. Same guy who's working on your family's case now."

Looking ahead at the approaching Space Needle, Ashley asked, "So what *is* my family's case right now, anyways?"

"What do you mean?"

"I mean, like, what do you guys think is going on? What's your theory behind the attacks?"

"Honestly, Ashley," he said, rolling a toothpick from one corner of his mouth to the other, "I think everyone's pretty much in the dark right now. Nobody's issued any demands, no one's claimed any responsibility, and last I heard, we didn't even have any solid leads. At this point, all we know is the obvious–someone has it in for your family. Beyond that?" He looked at her, the toothpick rolling back to the opposite corner. "We know jackshit."

As the Polaris™ flew by the Needle, she said, "Well, what about these riots that are happening around Cascadia? Couldn't they have something to do with the attacks?"

"It's possible. But I doubt it."

Ashley stared at him for a second, expecting him to explain further. Realizing that he wasn't going to say any more without some prodding, she prodded, "And this is because...?"

"Because other than the fact that they both started happening at the same time, I'm just not seeing a logical connection between the two. It'd be one thing if the rioters were destroying some kind of commerce or infrastructure, or if they were trying to get behind the gates–*then* I could see there be some type of connection. But all they're doing right now is fuckin' up their own neighborhoods and getting themselves arrested and killed. That's not posing any kind of threat to the system–that's doing it a fuckin' favor." McCready shook his head and let out a frustrated laugh, then paused momentarily. "But those attacks on your family," he said, as the car descended down towards the street, "that's some shit that's gonna *freek* the establishment out. That's a real threat, right there–'cause if they can get to Mason Huxton, then that means they can get to *anyone*."

Stopping its motion above a BMW® parked curbside in front of the Tiger's Lair, the car asked, "Marc, would you like me to find a parking space?"

"Nah, N.J.," he said, "I don't want you parked while we're in there. You need to be ready to respond at a moment's notice."

"Where would you like me to let you out at?" Marilyn asked,

blowing him an animated goodbye kiss which fluttered through the
air like a crimson butterfly.

"Drop us off at the corner up there." The Polaris™ moved over
the row of parked cars until it reached the tow-away zone at the end
of the street. "You ready?" he asked Ashley.

She smiled. "Ready as I'll ever be."

McCready touched his gun, patted a few different places on
his belt, and said, "Alright. N.J.–open door, driver's side." He looked
at Ashley. "I'll come around to let you out."

From inside the car, she watched him carefully scope out the
area as he stepped into the street. He rounded the front of the vehicle, took one more cautious look around, then spoke into his wristcom.

The passenger door immediately opened. McCready stood
there, his hand extended towards her. "Alright, let's go."

Ashley grabbed hold of his gloved hand, allowing him to
help her out of the Polaris™. "Thanks," she said. "Everything seem
okay?"

"Yeah," he replied, watching a group of rowdy crossbreeds
pass by them, the wolfen member loudly howling up at the moon.
"Relatively speaking." He touched his wristcom. "N.J., shadow us
until we get into the club, then circle the block 'til further notice."

As they started to walk down the sidewalk, the Polaris™
rose up about twenty feet, and slowly followed overhead.

"See that Benzy over there?" McCready asked, supping his
head towards a dark green Mercedes® parked up the street.

"Mm-hm," she said. "Looks like an unmarked Ordocop™ car."

"It is. There's a few more of 'em parked back there," he said,
pointing his thumb in the opposite direction. "They've been tailing us
ever since we left your place."

She glanced over her shoulder. "I guess just you isn't enough
anymore, huh?"

"Nope," McCready said, taking the lead as they reached the
entrance to the Tiger's Lair. "Not anymore."

"Sorry, guy," said one of the stylish bouncers, extending a
baton in front of McCready's path. "You gotta be on the list."

"He's with me, Rachel," Ashley said, stepping out from
behind McCready.

"Ashley," the sable-haired woman said in a surprised tone.
"I...I didn't think you'd be coming tonight. What with, you know–"
She cleared her throat. "The stuff on the news."

Ashley nodded. "Yeah, I didn't think I'd be coming down here either. But Amanda talked me into it."

"You're blowing this way out of proportion," said the other bouncer into her cellphone. "Oh, please. Like I'm suddenly gonna turn bi overnight?"

"Hey, Glyn," Ashley whispered to the orange-haired woman, just loud enough so she could hear.

Glynda looked up from the screen, waved one hand, mouthed the words, "Hi, Ashley," then went back to her conversation. "What are you talking about, Sera?" she asked. "It was platonic. Pla-tonic. Does that word even *exist* in your vocabulary?"

"It's her girlfriend," said Rachel. "She's a bit possessive."

"I guess so," Ashley said. "Oh yeah, Rache, by the way–this is McCready."

Shaking his hand, Rachel asked, "You the bodyguard?"

"You could say that," replied McCready.

"You look like it," Rachel smiled.

"Is Amanda already here?" Ashley asked.

Rachel shook her head. "Not yet."

"Fashionably late, as usual," Ashley said, moving towards the revolving entrance door. "Well, tell her that I'm here, okay?"

"You got it," Rachel said. "Take care of yourself, Ashley."

"Thanks, I will." Ashley stepped through the revolving door, into the bustling club's smoky, Indian–motifed foyer.

"Welcome, Ashley," said the tall, dark and handsome door-man, extending his hands towards her. "I'm glad you could make it. How are you?"

"I'm okay, Raj," she said. "Thanks."

As McCready came through the door, a few of the casually attired members of security moved forward to inspect him.

"Raj," said one of the burly guards, "he's projecting some kind of emfield that's disrupting the revolver's sensors. And she's got an emvest on." He looked at Ashley uncomfortably. "Hi, Ashley."

"Hey, Ally," she said.

Raj looked at McCready, his eyebrows raised. "Well?"

McCready handed his badge over to security. "Agent Marc McCready, Freemon. I've got clearance for everything. So does she."

Ally examined the badge and hologram with a handheld scanner, then said, "He's legit, Raj."

"Good." Raj extended his hands. "Welcome to tonight's gathering, Mr. McCready."

"Thanks," he said, shaking Raj's hand with his gloved one.

# ((FREQUENCIES))

Raj eyed him curiously. "Why am I not sensing a biochip?"

McCready raised his left hand. "'Cause it's in this hand."

Raj smiled. "Better." He released his grip, looked at Ashley and McCready, and motioned his hand to the surroundings. "Please enjoy yourselves tonight."

"Thanks, Raj." She and McCready moved into the spacious foyer, past tall, colorful statues of Vishnu, Brahma, and Shiva. "You wanna get a drink before we head in to the gathering?" she asked.

"Yeah, sounds good." As they walked towards the ornately decorated bar, McCready said, "What setting is your emvest at?"

"Umm..." she said, grinning guiltily. "None."

"What?"

"I actually haven't turned it on yet."

McCready looked at her, dumbfounded. "Well turn it on already. It's not gonna do you any good unless it's activated."

"I know, I know," Ashley said. She reached down, placed her fingers on the tiny knob, and hesitated. "You really don't think it's gonna disrupt me?"

McCready laughed. "Just do it, Ashley. C'mon, you'll be fine. I promise."

"Okay," she reluctantly said. Giving the knob a half-turn, everything around her rippled and waved, the world suddenly turning into a gigantic funhouse mirror. "Whoa..." she said, grabbing hold of McCready. "I think...I think I just got disrupted."

"You're fine," he reassured her. "The effect's only temporary."

"Damn, dude," she heard a male passerby say, "that chick looks *curbed*."

"Okay..." Ashley said, letting go of her grip on McCready's trenchcoat. "The world is becoming solid again."

"Good." As they approached two empty seats at the end of the bar, McCready shook his head and started to laugh.

Smiling, she said, "What are you laughing at?"

"The look on your face," he said, seating himself on a plush tiger-print barstool. "That was fuckin' priceless. You really looked like you thought your molecules were about to scatter."

"You could of warned me that was gonna happen!" Ashley laughed, giving him a push. "Mr. 'don't worry, you'll be fine.'"

"Did I lie?" McCready asked, turning his palms up. "Are you alright?"

"I guess," she said. "As long as my brain waves aren't all scrambled now."

Gazing directly at her, his face turned dead serious. "Actually, now that you mention it..."

"What?" she concernedly asked.

"Your frees *do* look a bit odd right now."

"Really?"

"Nah." He smiled. "I'm just fuckin' with you."

"You smartass," she laughed, tossing a coaster at him. "Now seriously, though–everything looks normal?"

"Yeah. Seriously, Ashley. Your frees look perfectly normal. If some kind of scrambling effect had happened, I'd be able to tell." He placed his hand on her shoulder, lightly massaged it, and smiled. "So relax, alright? You're fine."

Though she wasn't entirely convinced–after all, no matter how advanced a technology was, it could never take *everything* into account–his touch at least comforted her. She smiled back, nodded her head, and said, "Okay. But if the world starts to liquify again..." She pointed her finger at him. "You're in trouble."

"Fair enough," he said, pulling out a pack of Old Skools™ as the bartender, dressed in an orange and black silk outfit, approached them.

"Good evening, Ashley," he said. "What can I get for you?"

"Hey, Rowan," she said. "Could I have a little glass of the anise liqueur, please?"

"Of course." To McCready, he asked, "And you?"

"Kahlúa® and cream. With a double shot of espresso."

Rowan nodded. "I'll be right back."

McCready lit up his cancer stick with an old-fashioned flip-top lighter, then took in a slow, deep draw. "This place seems cool," he said, exhaling the noxious fumes as he took a look around. "Music's good."

"Mm-hm," she agreed, subtly moving her body to the Indian music's mystical rhythm.

"Mind you, I can't understand a fuckin' word of it," he said. "But it sounds cool."

Ashley smiled. "I can't understand the words either." She picked up another tiger-adorned coaster, twirled it between her fingers. "But that's what makes music so powerful. It transcends language barriers...and logic barriers, and all the other mazy bullshit that our minds get trapped in. It gets down to the core, y'know? The *real*, the feel, the primal..."

"The funk," McCready said.

166

She laughed. "Yeah. The funk. I like that."

"Here you are," Rowan said, setting McCready's cloudy drink onto the counter. "And..." From a gorgeous, blue crystal decanter which reminded her of an Egyptian perfume bottle, he poured a small amount of clear liquid into a port glass. "There you are."

"Thank you," Ashley said, making sure to make eye contact with him.

"Yeah, thanks, man," McCready chimed.

"Of course," Rowan smiled.

Picking up both the glass of liqueur and her train of thought, Ashley said, "Yeah, music is *so* powerful. If there ever is gonna be any kind of true revolution—or evolution, deevolution, whatever you want to call it—music is definitely gonna have to play a part in it."

"In what way?"

"In a lot of ways," she replied.

"Like?"

"Well, for one, it's about the only thing that can still *physically* bring people together. Which is pretty amazing when you consider how much of our lives are spent in isolation, immersed in the uniview or some other kind of convenience technology. I mean, yeah, we're always *tele*communicating with each other, and we're always virtually interacting with each other, but it's just not the same as being physically together. There's so much more energy created when five hundred people are in a club, than when five hundred people are in a MUD, y'know? It's a completely different phenomena. Like night and day." Ashley took a sip of her licoricey drink, and said, "So I just think there's an incredible amount of power in something that can still draw our energies together like that. Which is what music does. Just look at here—it's a perfect example. Most of us are total strangers, yet we're *physically* gathering together, united through music. Same with any other club or concert."

"Alright, I can see what you're saying." He took a drag from his cigarette. "But I think you're overlooking something."

"What's that?"

"The fuck factor."

"The *what*?" Ashley asked.

"The fuck factor," he said. "Sex. I bet you half the people in here could give a clone whore's ass about the music, let alone a revolution. They're just comin' here to find someone to shag."

"Yeah, of course," Ashley said. "I'm not overlooking that though—I think that's part of it. 'Cause right now, humanity is in serious danger of losing its physicality and its senses." She laughed. "Losing its senses...that's fitting. Anyways, sexuality is one of the *major* advantages of physicality–and a great persuader for not giving up our physical existence to a virtual one."

McCready touched his glass to Ashley's. "Well, amen to that, sister."

Ashley smiled, and they both took a drink. Licking her lips, she said, "Yeah, at this point, I just see music and sensuality and anything that allows us to have fun and feel each other's vibrations as being part of the same cause. Anything that touches our souls, taps into our collective unconscious, and lets us know we're *alive*." She took a deep breath. "'Cause in this cold, apathetic world, just feeling alive and being happy and knowing hope..." She stared straight into the centers of McCready's sunglasses. "That's a revolution in itself, wouldn't you say?"

The end of McCready's cigarette flared up brightly. "I hadn't really thought of it that way. Makes sense, though."

"I think so," she said, waving to some friends across the room. "And I think that's why socialism and communism, and so many of the other so-called revolutions failed in the past. They weren't really changing the vibe at all, y'know? They were too logical and stiff and serious...all stuck up in the same old, tired paradigms they were claiming to replace. I mean, c'mon, what's the point of a revolution if you're not having fun while you're doing it?" The glass stem between her fingers, she rotated the cup in her hand, counter-clockwise, and said, "It's just time for something new–and I mean *completely* new. New signs, new symbols...new everything. Something that's beyond words, something so new and *so* different, that this restrictive English language can't even describe it." She raised the glass to her lips. "*That's* what I'm ready for."

McCready let out a puffy cloud of smoke, and coolly said, "Your thoughts are fuckin' beautiful."

She laughed, unsure of how to take the comment.

"No, I'm serious. They are. Literally. When you were just talking there, the color patterns were shifting and swirling in this hella cool way," he said, his hand moving in smooth, wavy motions, the cigarette's embers making Mobius-strip tracers in the club's low lighting. "It was fresh."

"Huh. That's interesting. I hadn't ever thought about the frees being aesthetically appealing."

"Well, I don't think most Freemon think so, but at least it's

168

always been that way for me. It kind of feels like I have this personal, sorta psychedelic light show happening right in front of my
eyes. And since everyone's thoughts are different," he said, blowing
out a few perfectly formed smoke rings, "and their thoughts are
always changing," he continued, blowing a thin stream of smoke
through the widening rings, "it never really gets boring to watch. It's
like seeing each person paint their own frequential art piece." He
pointed his two cigarette-holding fingers towards her. "And you just
painted a masterpiece."

"Thanks," she said. "So what'd it look like?"

"A lot of reds. Crimson and rose swirls. Splashes of deep
orange here and there. Very wavy, very soothing."

"And now?"

"Still wavy and smooth," he said. "But now you're using more
yellows. A few lush greens. It's a nice composition."

"Wow..." she softly said, marvelling at both the technology
and the breadth of its user. "You must be so interesting. I mean," she
quickly corrected herself, "that must be so interesting. To see people's
thoughts like that."

"Yeah, it is," he said. "But it all gets fucked up once I have
to arrest someone based on their painting." He let out the same frustrated laugh as earlier in the car. "This world's fuckin' nuts, Ashley."
He stood up and downed the rest of his drink. "Damn good drink."
He slammed the empty glass down on the bar, then wiped his mouth
with the back of his hand. "So we heading into this gathering place,
or what?"

"I guess so," she said, standing up from her seat. "I wanted
to wait for Dawn, but now I'm wondering if she's even coming." She
looked around the foyer, but saw no sign of her often-flaky best friend.
"Okay, let's go." As they walked away from the bar, towards the
hallway leading to the auditorium, she asked, "You ever taken part
in a gathering before?"

"Nah." He snickered. "I've had to raid a few, though."

Ashley looked at him, a bit concerned. "You're not gonna pull
any of that kinda shit tonight, are you?"

"Hell no, sweetheart. I'm off duty." He nodded at a dreadlocked white guy walking by. "Right now, as long as it's not threatening you, I don't give a fuck *what* people want to think or do."

"Okay, good," she said, as they entered into the gorgeous
rounded hallway, which was covered with a painted montage of
Hindu and Indian images. Feeling the low bass throb of the

gathering's music beneath her feet, she noticed two people she recognized emerging from the auditorium's entrance. "Kaya, Gus," she said. "What's up?"

"Hey, Ash," Kaya said, giving her a warm hug.

Gus nodded at Ashley, his bearded face barely visible beneath his cloak's shadowy hood.

Ashley nodded back at him and smiled, then Kaya asked her, "You goin' in to watch Seer?"

"Is he already on?"

"Yup," Kaya said, rubbing a nub of her hair between her fingers. "We just got done doin' our thing with him. He's on his last few songs now. You better get in there if you wanna catch him."

"Yeah, I will," Ashley said, beginning to walk towards the auditorium once again. "Thanks. I'll see you guys in a bit, okay?"

"Yeah, we'll be around," Kaya said.

"The hooded guy always that talkative?" McCready asked.

"Usually," Ashley said.

Reaching the auditorium's entrance, which was framed with an outline of the Taj Mahal, the painted door hissed open, instantly letting out the lively, infectious music coming from within.

"AaaAHHHH," the song's voices said, rising to a rousing crescendo. "Freek out!!"

As they entered into the pulsing, red strobe-lit space, the song's voices echoed out, and a raw, thumping beat began to drop.

"That's nasty," McCready said.

"Yeah, it is," she agreed, her body already starting to bob with the beat.

The place was packed. But not so crowded that there wasn't space to move around freely–which was how the gatherings were always organized, since the emphasis was as much on the crowd as on the performers. People were dancing in all kinds of different ways–a quick glance showed breakdancing, salsa, capoeira, jazz, triballet, and numerous freestyles–while others had formed drumming circles, or were just tapping out some drum rhythms by themselves. There were some who were just watching the performance, others who were talking, laughing, or smoking weed, and a few stray souls who were simply walking around the place in a complete, drug-induced daze.

The gatherings were something which had always fascinated Ashley, since they were essentially a refuge where the wealthy, well-off, under-forty crowd could come together, cut loose, and get freeky. It was an outlet for those who had clearance; an outlet for the minority of successful people–doctors, lawyers, actors, artists, professors, scientists, rich kids like herself, etcetera–who weren't quite satisfied with life behind the gates. Here, they could satisfy their rebellious urges in a legal, commercial way (membership in a gathering circle was *very* expensive) which wouldn't threaten the overlords of society. And usually, the outlet worked. Everyone would get all riled up one night, half-heartedly talk about change and revolution, then go back to work the next day, not say a word about it to any of their coworkers, and forget the whole experience altogether. Then they would come back next week and repeat the same cycle all over again. Harmless fun for the well-to-do.

Occasionally, though–and in her opinion, not enough–they actually *were* a rebellious event, toeing the line between subversity and stability, and sometimes even crossing over it. Ashley had been to a few gatherings where she could sense a mass awakening happening; where a new vibration was beginning to take hold. But unfortunately, those also tended to be the ones that got raided, since too many people started emitting similar, "dangerous" frees. These truly subversive gatherings were most likely to occur when the organizers brought in underground acts from outside the gates, rather than the safe, bubble gum fare they were supposed to bring in. When those acts came through, the vibe got *real* interesting.

And right now in the Tiger's Lair, the underground was representing in full.

Seer stood atop the jungle-motifed stage, wireless mic in hand, energetically pacing back and forth from one side to the other. He currently looked like a young, six-foot African-American man with a skully, dressed in tiger-striped fatigues and black Karl Kani® boots–much different than the last time she had seen him, when he had appeared as an older, shorter Native-American, attired in a traditional Makah outfit, performing the ancient songs of that aboriginal tribe.

Ashley had no idea what Seer *actually* looked like, since he always wore an ever-changing hologram over himself. But his voice, which was very strong, resonant, and somehow able to be simultaneously combative and peaceful, was something that she could always recognize. Walking closer to the stage, she began to listen to his lyrics...

*Just kickin' this verse*
*thoughts disperse*

171

rhymes' gettin' freeky and they gonna get worse
'cause I'm comin' to the spot
makin' it hot
as I
inoc-
ulate ya dome
'gainst that wack propaganda that be flowin' through ya home
on the unie
you need
to check the time
'cause there ain't no time to be walkin' 'round blind
so
now
just
take a look around
what's goin' down?
riots goin' on seem to me like a clown
a dis
and now
I-an'-I 'bout to get pissed
disturbed
a word
of advice to all'a y'all
wake ya ass up there's about to be a fall
'cause these devils be tryin'
these devils be lyin'
sayin' it's the people
when it's them who's connivin'

"This is trippy," McCready said in Ashley's ear. "This guy's rappin' all this freeky shit, but his freeread is showing something completely different."

"So what's that mean?" she asked.

"I'm not sure," he replied. "That's what's trippy. His free-read must be malfunctioning or something."

"Maybe he just knows how to control his thoughts," she said.

"Yeah, right," he scoffed. "The day people figure out how to mentally fool the freereads is the day this society comes to an end."

Ashley simply smiled, said nothing in response, and focused her attention on Seer again.

# ((FREQUENCIES))

*'Cause me na waan be on de uniview*
*steal ya soul like de devil go t'hell when it's tru*
*so me neva gon' be on de uniview*
*I say me neva gonna be on de uniview*
*me neva gon' be on de uniview*
*I-an'-I stay undaground whatcha gonna do?!*

Seer slammed his mic to the ground, and a raging fire began to burn around him. The strobes started flashing faster, the flames consumed his physical form, and he was reduced to ashes in a manner of seconds. A fiery phoenix rose from the conflagration, up to the ceiling, and exploded into a glorious blaze, leaving behind the words **"SAY WHAT YOU SEE"** in its flaming wake. Then the lights went out, dropping the entire room into complete darkness, save for the flickering letters overhead.

When the lights came back on–no strobes this time, now a steady, dim blue–Seer was nowhere to be seen.

As "The Freaks Come Out At Night" began to play loudly through the soundsystem, holographic designs started to float in the air. "That guy just completely disappeared," McCready said.

"I know," she said disappointedly, realizing she probably wasn't going to get a chance to talk to Seer tonight.

"That's fuckin' weird," McCready continued. "I had a bead on him even while he was burning up. Then his freeread turned to static once the lights went out." He looked at Ashley. "And now he's completely gone. I don't get it."

"Yeah," Ashley said, scanning her eyes over the ends of the stage, hoping to find some sign of the musician, "Seer's a mysterious guy." She was about to give up, when she caught a glimpse of a familiar face–ponytail, Chinese, handsome–one she'd seen Seer use before. "I'm gonna go say hi to someone real quick," she said, beginning to move away from McCready. "I'll be right back, okay?"

"Wait," he said, grabbing a painful hold of her wrist.

"Ow!" she shouted. "What the hell are you doing?!"

McCready immediately let go, a startled look on his face. "Sorry, I-" He raised his gloved hand and flexed it. "The bionics... They're imprecise. Sorry."

Ashley looked back to make sure she could still see Seer. He was virtually in the same place, now talking to a few people. Turning back to McCready, she rubbed her sore wrist and said, "It's fine. What'd you need to tell me?"

173

He laughed uncomfortably. "Nothing, really. I...I was just gonna tell you to be careful. And watch out. That's it."

Sensing his sincerity, she smiled. "I will. Thanks." She then turned away from him and briskly moved through the crowd, to the far end of the auditorium where Seer was standing.

The moment she reached him, Seer looked at her and said, "Ní hao, Ashley."

"Ní hao," she replied. "Could I speak with you alone for a minute?" She smiled, somewhat apologetically, at the man and woman he was talking to.

"One moment," Seer said. To the Asian couple, he said something in Chinese that she couldn't understand.

They both nodded and smiled, then the woman said, "Wo dong le."

Seer smiled. "Xiexie. Hui jian." He looked at Ashley. "Let's move over here."

"I'm sorry to interrupt you," she said, following him to a less populated section of the club, "but I'm trying to make sense out of something that happened to me yesterday, and I really don't know who else to talk to."

"Apologies are unnecessary," he said. "We do what we must." He stopped his motion, placing his hands in the pouch of his robelike outfit. "What is it that happened?"

"Okay," she said, gathering her thoughts together, "yesterday...I met with a former professor of mine at the U-dub, and he told me about this man named Adrian Wellor."

Seer stared deeply into her eyes, as if to gauge her intentions. "The professor's name—what was it?"

"Brennan."

Seer cocked one of his eyebrows. "*Michael* Brennan?"

"Yeah," she said, noticing that a few of the Ordocops™ were now discreetly patrolling the auditorium, maintaining their watchful vigil on her. "Do you know him?"

His eyes glancing to where Ashley's had been, he said, "I know that he speaks with a forked tongue."

"He seemed sincere."

"The devil usually does. What did he tell you?"

"He said that Wellor created the freeread technology, not him. And that Wellor never intended it to be used in *this* way," she said, touching her forehead.

Seer nodded a few times. "What else did he say?"

174

"Well, basically he said that he stole Wellor's idea, then warped it into what it is now by forming a commission..."

"The Brennan Commission," Ashley said, moving a few strands of her hair behind her ears. "I read about that in my research. That was where you formed the committee to study human FE's, right?"

"Correct," Brennan said. "After Wellor completed some of the initial prototypes, I suggested we form a commission to study the full implications of the technology and its possible applications to society. The government eagerly agreed, authorized myself and others to begin the task, and allocated us the necessary funding to see it through." He turned his head from the fountain, as a strong breeze blew some spray into his face. "As you can imagine, Wellor was quite thrilled when he heard the news. He thought his greatest dreams had been realized... I still vividly recall him coming up to me, hope and excitement gleaming in his eyes, thanking me for setting the wheels in motion." He paused, wrinkles of guilt forming around the corners of his eyes. "But his excitement soon turned to horror, when he realized the commission was only interested in mapping the human FE spectrum, and that we had no interest whatsoever in studying the interconnectedness or interdependence of all life. Which, as you know, was the entire motivating force behind his scientific endeavors."

"Goddess," Ashley said, "he must have been so angry. What did he do? Did he take his story to the media?"

"He couldn't."

"Why not?"

"That was the catch, you see. When we formed the commission, we placed it under the protection of national security. Therefore, all of its members had to sign a contract of confidentiality in order to become part of the group–which meant that the unauthorized disclosure of *any* information pertaining to the commission's findings was considered to be an act of treason."

"And Wellor agreed to this?"

"Naturally. If you had created a technology around which an entire commission was being built, wouldn't *you* want to be part of it?"

"Yeah, I guess," she said, feeling a hint of the frustration which Wellor must have felt. "I mean, I would have wanted to be a part of it, but still... I don't think I would have signed the contract. It would have seemed suspicious to me."

"I don't doubt that it would have. But Adrian did not share

your distrust of the government, Ashley. He believed in America and its institutions, and he believed in academia. And more than anything else...he believed in me. He trusted me with all his heart." Brennan paused, his teeth grinding together uneasily. "And why shouldn't he have? I was his mentor, for God's sake. I was supposed to be the one person he could trust above all."

"So why did you betray him then?"

"I was cold, power-hungry...weak," he said. "And the temptation was too strong for me to resist. I saw an opportunity to impact the world, to cement my place in history. So I took advantage of it, and devised ways in which I could legally take control of Wellor's creation."

"Like the contract."

"Yes, that was one of the final steps, but there were many others leading up to it. And because I was his mentor, they weren't very hard to put in motion. He greatly respected my opinion, and therefore it was a rather simple task to influence his choices in one direction or another. All I had to do was lie to him."

"Wow," Ashley said flatly. "You sold your soul, Professor Brennan."

"If only you knew," he said under his breath, his eyes turning towards the ground.

There was silence between them.

Ashley stared at him, amazed at the evil this seemingly gentle man had once committed. Granted, everyone had their dark side, but raping someone's idea and then knowingly turning it into a device which raped people's thoughts... That wasn't a dark side, that was a *demon* side.

Breaking the silence, Ashley asked, "So what happened to Wellor?"

"I have no idea," he said, still gazing at the concrete.

"You must have some idea."

"I wish I did." He looked up at her. "But the truth is, I don't. The last time I even saw him was at the turn of the century, shortly before the committee's end. By that time, he realized that his ideas had absolutely no hope of ever being implemented. So one day, he politely threatened to expose us all, and quietly excused himself from the meeting. We immediately sent FBI agents out to his residence to detain him–but he never showed up." He twisted his cane around in place. "And we've never heard from him since."

"Nothing?"

# ((FREQUENCIES))

"Nothing substantial," he said. "Since this was before the Frequency Emissions Act, he was never biochipped, so we were never able to track his movements. We assume that he's dead, but his body has never been recovered to confirm it. It's an enigmatic situation, to say the least."

Ashley thought about his response, then remarked, "You said nothing *substantial*. What did you mean by that?"

He smiled. "I did say that, didn't I? Well, since his disappearance, various rumors have surfaced from time to time concerning his existence and whereabouts. I've heard some colleagues say he simply assumed another identity and lived out a normal life, and I've had others tell me that he committed suicide in a remote part of the world. Yet others have said that he went underground, and is still currently plotting his revenge against us. But none of these rumors have ever been substantiated. The truth of the matter is, even to this day, the question of what happened to Adrian Wellor remains a complete and utter mystery to us."


"And that's essentially what he had to say," she finished. "Though I'm not exactly sure what to make of it."

His arms folded, his chin resting on his right hand, Seer thought for a moment. "This is odd," he said.

"Tell me about it," she agreed.

"He told you the truth...which I find much more suspicious than if he had told you a lie. What were his reasons for revealing this information to you?"

"He said that it was his way of making amends. He hoped that by telling me, Wellor's dream wouldn't die with him."

Seer smiled, placing his hands back in his pouch. "He needn't worry."

"Why not?"

"Wellor's dream is in no danger of dying."

"Meaning that Wellor's still alive?"

"Meaning that-" Seer paused, his eyes darting quickly to the auditorium's entrance and back. "I can tell you this much, Ashley," he said, as the previous song seamlessly blended into another much darker in tone. "What was once a dream, shall soon become reality."

A cryptic response, but it conveyed the message...and further confirmed what she'd already been feeling. Change was on its way. "That's what I wanted to hear," she said.

177

"For now though," Seer said, "you should be most concerned with the Presence."

"The Presence?"

"The entity that's attacking your family." He looked towards the entrance again, this time his gaze remaining fixed. "It's a powerful ally, but its methods are crude and reckless. You're likely to get caught in its path, simply because of your heritage."

Ashley glanced in the direction he was. Six people, whom she'd never seen at any gathering before, were standing together, looking at her and Seer. Two women, two men, and two crossbreeds, all very starchy and rigid–obviously not here to enjoy the vibe.

Watching them, she asked, "So what should I do?"

"Stay alert," Seer said, as the six individuals began to walk towards them, the shapely, ebony member of the sextet taking the lead.

Ashley's heart started to race. She looked around for Mc-Cready or the Ordocops™, but then the lights suddenly dimmed to a deep purple, and she could no longer make out any faces in the crowd.

"Be prepared." Seer's image started to flicker and blink, like a uniview rapidly changing channels.

The attractive female, who was clad in glossy, black, skin-tight plastic, continued to move forward.

Ashley breathed in deeply through her nose, placed her fingers around the twisty-fit, rotated it–twice–then turned her em-vest up to full power.

"And expect the unexpected." Seer flickered, flashed, and blinked out of existence. "I'll find you," his invisible voice said, then she felt a rush of air as he left her presence.

One of the crossbreeds immediately turned into a blur, racing in the direction she had felt Seer move in. A split-second later, the mustached, Latino member of the group did the same.

"Stay where you are!" the woman commanded, pointing her outstretched arm at Ashley.

"Freeze!" yelled an Ordocop™, as he and the other two under-covers drew their laser pistols on the quartet. "Don't move!"

"This is governmental jurisdiction!" shouted the older, salt-and-pepper-haired member of the quartet. He and the Asian woman pulled out their pistols and faced the Ordocops™. "Lower your weapons and back off!"

The crowd was quickly becoming alarmed, the ominous music felt like it was getting louder.

Ashley instinctively started to retreat, walking backwards while still facing the threatening woman.

"You think I'm playin', girl?!" A pulse of clear energy shot out from the woman's hand, straight at Ashley's head, and burst into a spectrum of color just a few inches from her face.

Ashley shielded herself as the colors dissipated, the funhouse mirror effect happening once again.

Lasers began to fly as the Ordocops™ and the government agents started shooting at each other indiscriminately. The crowd panicked, people went running everywhere. Order's chaos descended upon the club.

"Her emvest's too strong!" the iridescent-eyed woman shouted above the cacophony. "Time to get physical! Rex!" She looked at the short man-creature who was crouched next to her in a feral manner, pointed at Ashley and screamed, "Sick her!"

Rex bounded towards Ashley in an apelike fashion, as the woman turned to the Ordocops™ and exchanged fire.

"Oh, shit," Ashley whispered, raising her fist at the incoming crossbreed. She fired the laser on her ring, but it harmlessly reflected off his chest in an emvestial display of colors. Just as Rex was about to reach her, she remembered that emvests protected only the head and trunk, and aimed towards his legs.

The same flash of colors at his knees, and Rex had grabbed a tight hold of both of her hands, while his simian feet latched onto her ankles. "Nice try, lady," he gutturally said, his wet snout glistening with his mouth's movements, "but my entire body is an emvest. And now that I'm inside *your* emfield..." His eyes started to glow an indigo hue. "Say good night."

A thunderous gunshot suddenly rang out, spraying a mist of blood into the air. The flesh on Rex's arm ruptured violently, revealing beneath it a silvery alloy. He didn't scream or release his grip on her, but merely looked in the direction of the gunshot.

Ashley did the same.

McCready calmly walked towards them, his smoking revolver aimed at the simian man, and said, "Let her go now, you fuckin' Cro-Magnon–or I'm puttin' the next one in your fuckin' head!"

Ashley struggled, but she couldn't break free of the crossbreed's powerful grip.

"I call your bluff, McCready!" Rex said, his eyes still aglow. "You're out of your jurisdiction!"

"Last chance, fucker," McCready said, keeping his aim and

Joshua Ortega

closing his ground.

Rex's orbs grew bright red. Twin lasers shot from his eyes at McCready's gun, but a kaleidoscope of colors formed around the antique weapon. "What?" Rex said, then a bullet split open the flesh on his forehead, sending streams of blood into his glowing eyes.

Ashley backed her head away from the gore and dry-heaved.

"There's an emfield in the handle, dumbfuck." McCready fired another shot into Rex's face, bursting one of his eyeballs into a whitish goo.

Rex let go of Ashley and rushed at McCready with a furious primal scream, its long, hairy arms flailing wildly about.

Unruffled by the showy display, McCready shot off two rounds into Rex's chest, temporarily slowing the creature's progress. As Rex started to move again, McCready swiftly reached down to his belt, grabbed hold of something small, and threw it towards Rex like he was tossing a mini Frisbee®.

Rex immediately lifted off of the ground, his body becoming weightless, but his motion continuing towards McCready.

As Rex struggled to remove whatever it was that had been attached to him, McCready rushed forward, cocked his bionic hand back, and delivered a crushing blow to the creature's bloodied face, sending it backwards through the air at an unreally fast speed. Its motion didn't cease until it had slammed into the auditorium's wall, located about twenty feet from McCready's fist.

"That's not gonna stop him for long," McCready said. "Let's get out of here."

"What the hell's going on?!" she said, moving towards McCready as she looked back at the Ordocop's™ battle with the government agents–a conflict which the corpos were obviously losing.

"I don't know," McCready said, as they started to run up the stairs leading to the verdant, hothouse stage, "but now's not the time to find out!" Weaving their way through the Indian foliage, they rapidly proceeded backstage in search of an escape route. "There's gotta be an exit here somewhere!" he shouted, hopping over the musical equipment scattered about. To his wristcom, he said, "N.J., show me a blueprint of this place with my position and lock on to me!"

Quickly realizing there was no exit, Ashley said, "Shit! This is a dead end!" She looked back, just to make sure the ape-creature hadn't already caught up with them. Not yet, but she knew it was on its way. To McCready, who was still staring down at his wristcom, she said, "There's no exit back here, McCready!"

180

"Then we'll have to make one!" He pulled a device from his belt and aimed it at the wall. "Cover your eyes!"

Ashley shielded her face and looked down at the ground. An extremely bright light filled the darkened area, flashing and pulsing in various degrees of intensity, causing her eyes to squint tightly. Hearing a searing, crackling sound, she said, "What is that?"

"Plasma torch," he said. "I'm cutting us an exit. And I'm just... about...finished. Alright," he said as the burning sound ceased, "you can look up now." He walked over to the molten-lined, makeshift exit, forcefully kicked it out, then reached for another device and cooled the top of the opening. "C'mon, let's go," he said, allowing Ashley to exit first. "Just watch the sides–they're hot."

Ashley carefully stepped through the hole, out into the wide alley behind the club. The rain was falling down from the sky as a fine mist. A few cigarette-smoking onlookers stood nearby, their mouths agape with surprise.

McCready threw down a pellet which exploded into a thick cloud of smoke, then joined her outside just as the Polaris™ started to descend from the skies. "Open doors," he said to the wristcom.

The Chevy® landed right in front of them, passenger-side facing Ashley, its doors opened. She hopped into the car.

McCready swiftly slid across the hood, landed on his feet, and joined her inside the vehicle. He exhaled a sigh of relief as his door shut closed. "That was close."

Then Rex slammed into Ashley's window like a rabid dog, his bullet-torn face leaving a reddish smear across the plexiglass.

Ashley let out a startled scream. Rex's fists started to hammer at the window, causing the plastic to fissure and crack.

"Lift off, N.J.!" McCready said.

The Polaris™ shot into the air, rising high above the alley-way–with Rex on its hood.

The simian creature stared in through the windshield with its one eye, futilely shouting something as it gripped its long arms around the vehicle's sides.

"Seatbelts," McCready said. Shoulder harnesses and belts automatically strapped into place.

Rex's lone eye glowed red, then he creepily looked at Ashley–the ripped flesh hanging from his forehead, his eye socket bleeding pale biomatter–and fired a laser directly at her.

"Oh my goddess!" she said, trying to lean away from his line of fire as the window began to melt.

"Hold on to your stomach," McCready said to her, then shouted, "N.J.–roll!"

The car flipped over, and they were now looking at the world upside down, their bodies held securely in place by the seatbelts.

Unfortunately, Rex was still on the car, his fingers and toes sticking to the hood like he was Spider-Man®, his single laser still burning its way through the dense windshield.

"No way," she said with disbelief, just as Rex reached his hand through the hot plastic.

"Jesus fuckin' Christ!" McCready said. "Pulse him, N.J.!"

As Rex's seared hand was about to grab her, there was a sudden look of surprise on his mangled face, as an electromagnetic pulse coursed out from the car. Rex instantly lost his magnetic grip, and rapidly plummeted to the alleyway below.

Ashley tilted her head upwards–or downwards, in this case–and through the Polaris'™ clear roof, she watched Rex brutally smash down onto the unyielding concrete. "I think you just killed him," she said, feeling more than slightly sick to her stomach as McCready rolled the car back into position.

"Nope." He pointed his finger to the lower-right quadrant of the rear-view screen, which showed Rex staggering up to his feet.

"What *is* that thing?" she asked, glancing her eyes from the screen to the windshield to the blood-smeared window.

"A Rex," he replied, manually flying the car away from the club. "Reconnaissance Escort–Xi series. Tough little fuckers."

"Shyeah," she agreed, touching her fingers around the windshield's melted hole, which had been sufficiently cooled by the rain that was now coming down in much thicker droplets. "I'll say."

"Watch your fingers." He waited for her to pull her hand back, then pressed a button on the dash, causing the damaged windshield to drop down into the hood. A new, undamaged pane emerged from the same place to fill the empty void.

"So what the hell is going on, McCready? Was that really the government, or was that the Presence posing as the government?"

"The Presence? What are you talking about? God?"

"No," Ashley said, realizing McCready had no clue about the Presence's existence, "I'm talking about the thing that's attacking my family. Was that just part of its plan or was that really the government?"

"I don't know," McCready said. "But I'm gonna find out. N.J., connect me to–"

"Marc," the cartoon Marilyn interrupted, holding up a bright yellow caution sign. "I detect a rapidly approaching vehicle from behind. Would you-"

"Fuck," he said, slamming his foot down on the accelerator. "Here we go again. How about some theme music, N.J.?"

"Any requests?" she asked.

"Rock 'n' roll, baby."

"737 comin' outta da sky!" growled a gravelly voice through the speakers.

McCready quickly dropped the car's altitude, barely squeezing it through a narrow passage between two buildings.

Ashley looked back to catch a glimpse of the pursuing vehicle, but all she could see were its two HID lamps, blindingly shining out at the Chevy®–that is, until the red and blue sirens started to flash atop its hood. "It's the government again," she said loudly over the blaring music.

"Or the terrorists," he countered, deftly maneuvering the Polaris™ through the airborne traffic. "We still don't know which."

"So how are we gonna find out?"

Streaking into a tunnel meant for only gravity-bound vehicles, he said, "I'm still workin' on that one."

The governmental vehicle–which she could now see was some type of sleek, navy blue Ford®–followed them into the tunnel, both cars dangerously skimming over the traffic below.

"Marc," Marilyn said, connecting some cables on an old-fashioned switchboard, "the driver of the vehicle is attempting to open a line of communication. Should I answer?"

"No, it's too risky–that might be their way of infecting our systems." He increased the speed, causing an annoyingly big knot to form in Ashley's stomach. "We're just gonna have to ditch 'em for now."

"McCready..." Ashley said uneasily, bracing herself against the back of the seat.

"N.J., ready the afterburners."

"Afterburners?" she quietly said to herself. "...shit."

They reached the end of the tube and entered an open-spaced area which separated them from the next tunnel. "Hold on," McCready said. He then released his foot from the accelerator, pulled back hard on the gravity-lever, quickly spun the car around 180 degrees, and shouted, "Fire, N.J.!"

Just as their backward momentum was about to send them

careening into the gigantic glass sculpture atop the next tunnel, the rear jets kicked in, and immediately propelled them up into the opposite direction, straight towards a glimmering skyscraper.

"Kill the jets!" he shouted, spinning the wheel all the way to his left, somehow managing to barely miss the wide high-rise.

They emerged from the side of the building unscathed, only to find themselves in the middle of oncoming airborne traffic. "Oh, Goddess," Ashley said, closing her eyes as a GS Winnebago® headed directly towards them. Feeling no impact, she reopened her eyes, but was not all relieved to see more vehicles coming at them.

Darting in and out, above and below, McCready finally maneuvered the decelerating Polaris™ to a safe, street-level altitude. "Motherfucker," he said, touching the car's tires down onto the road with a loud screech. He wiped his brow with his sleeve. "I need to think for a minute... N.J., activate cloaking field."

Marilyn clicked open a Star Trek® communicator, transporting herself into the cockpit of a spaceship. "Cloaking field activated," she said, as the spacecraft turned invisible.

Running her fingers through the top of her hair, Ashley said, "I think you just melted the world's largest Chihuly sculpture."

"That's not what I fuckin' need to hear right now," McCready said in an agitated tone. Shaking his head, he added, "Man, those better have been terrorists, or I am in *deep* shit."

As they pulled into a near-empty parking lot on the outskirts of downtown, the falling rain became a downpour. "Don't worry, McCready. If you get into any kind of trouble, my dad'll find a way to get you out of it. Believe me—I know from experience."

"Yeah, we'll see," he said, bringing the car to a rest. "N.J., kill the music please."

Marilyn, now playing lead guitar inside of a crowded arena, raised her instrument over her head, then smashed it down onto the stage. "Music deactivated," she said.

McCready gave Ashley a look of concern, and said, "Release seatbelts."

"Seatbelts released," the car confirmed, retracting its straps.

"Oh, no." McCready quickly reached over to Ashley's side of the car, manually opening her door. "Get out!"

"What?"

"Now!!" He pushed her out onto the wet concrete, immediately scrambling out the same door after her.

As they stood to their feet in the pouring rain, Ashley brushed herself off and said, "What did you do that for?"

"Her system's been corrupted." He took a careful hold of Ashley's hand and backed away from the car. "I turned off the vocal confirmation yester-" The car suddenly rose into the air. "I think the terrorists just made their next move."

Through the heavy rain, she watched the Polaris™ rise higher and higher into the sky. "Wow, I don't think it's gonna stop. It looks like–oh, wait–I think it's coming back down. Fast." She and McCready turned and ran, and didn't stop until they heard the deafening impact of the Chevy® crashing to the ground and exploding behind them.

McCready turned to face the flaming wreckage, a look of dejected gloom across his rainsoaked face. "N.J...." He touched his wristcom, and asked, "N.J.?"

But there was no answer on the other line.

McCready said nothing further. He simply stared ahead, the bright orange flames flickering across the wet, black lenses of his Obsidians™.

Seconds later, the Ford® came flying into the parking lot, accompanied by another Polaris™ and four SPD squad cars. The vehicles surrounded Ashley and McCready, their occupants swiftly emptying out, weapons drawn.

"Stay where you are, Agent McCready," said the driver of the Ford®–the same older man who had been leading the sextet inside the club. "You too, Ms. Huxton."

The Asian woman, whom Ashley also recognized from the club, said, "McCready, I hope you have a good explanation for all this."

McCready let out a deadened laugh. Under his breath, he said, "Yeah, Jung. Me, too."

Approaching them, the older man, whose hair was graying at the temples, clicked open a one-handed umbrella, pulled out his badge and said, "I'm Agent Carter Stone of the DCC. I'm gonna need you both to come down to the station with us."

Her entire body soaking wet, Ashley wrapped her arms around herself and looked at McCready. Shivering slightly from the cold, she offered an unsure smile, and said, "I think it's safe to say these aren't the terrorists."

∞

185

# Chapter 11
# ((Anamnesis))

*Others were like black holes, allowing no light to escape their pull,*
*choosing to forever exist in a perpetual, vacuous void of darkness.*
*Or did they?*
*When encountering a black hole, one could not say for sure, for one*
*knew not the mysteries contained within.*

The six of them entered the loud, hologram-filled auditorium of the Tiger's Lair, which was packed nearly as tight as Essence in her body suit. Ignacio looked down at his wristcom, and said, "Ey, I'm not seein' a Ray Davis on this anymore. You sure he's still in here?"

The older REX glanced back at Ignacio, and in a voice that could only be produced with inhuman vocal chords, replied, "He's not. Ray Davis is gone." Returning his gaze forward, he added, "But the man we seek is still here."

"Come again?" Essence said.

"He's changed identities," said Carter Stone, his eyes surveying the area like a famished hawk. "It's still the same perp, but he's fooling the biochip system."

"If he's able to do that," Jung said, "it's no wonder you've had so much trouble catching up with him. He might as well be invisible."

"Invisible or not," said the younger, fiercer-looking REX, forcefully exhaling a spray of moisture from his nostrils, "he still has a scent."

Pointing his wet snout up towards the ceiling, the older REX swayed his head back and forth, sniffed the air a few times, and said, "I think I have something, Agent Stone."

"Yes?" eagerly asked the DCC agent.

"I detect a smell which matches the olfactory information you downloaded into me," said the REX. "It must be him."

A smile appeared across Carter's clean-shaven face. "Good."

"I smell him, too," said the younger REX, his nostrils flaring in timed pulses. "This way."

As they followed the REX to the left-hand side of the crowded auditorium, Ignacio was approached by a couple of twenty-something frat boys, their eyes watery and bloodshot, their bodies rapidly shaking, both obviously as amped as a transistor.

"Hey, man," one of them said, tugging on the sleeve of Ignacio's leather jacket. "Are you a freeker? Hunh?" He laughed maniacally, his frees sporadically oscillating from gamma to alpha. "You freekin' too?"

Ignacio glanced down at his sleeve, saw an oily, viscous residue which had been left behind, and angrily looked up at the wannabe freeker. Quicker than the eye could see, he backhanded the rich punk with a closed fist, then slammed the same hand into the other side of his drugged-out head.

A stunned look of incomprehensibility passed across the frat boy's face. His knees buckled, he started to stagger around like a crippled drunk, the amp being the only thing keeping him up on his feet.

Wiping his sleeve on his pants, Ignacio rejoined the others.

"Wildlife troubles?" Jung asked.

Ignacio rubbed his knuckles. "Not anymore."

"I've found him," announced the lead REX, as they reached a less-crowded area of the club near the northern wall. "There," he said, pointing ahead to an Asian man garbed in a simple robe, who was speaking with an attractive white girl. "Cheng-tao Bankei is Ray Davis."

"Wasn't Ray supposed to be black?" Essence asked.

"Ray is," Carter said, "but Cheng isn't. His appearance changes with his identity."

Essence stared at Bankei. "Holograms? Then why aren't I sensing any?"

"Because that's the level of technology we're dealing with." Still looking ahead, Carter said, "Damn. He just noticed us. Freemon Ignacio, T-REX—you two are the quickest—cover Bankei when he tries to make his break."

"I'll make sure he doesn't get far," said the younger REX.

"Freemon Sommers," Carter continued, as they all began to move forward, "take the lead–attack on my cue. A-REX–you're on the woman he's talking to–make sure she doesn't escape. We need to find out if she's really Ashley Huxton."

Bankei's image started to flicker, Essence raised her hand, and Carter said, "Freemon Kwon, stay with me. We're probably gonna have to deal with the Ordocops™ to our right–they've already spotted us and they're moving in." He reached towards his laser. "Sommers, get read–"

Before Carter could give the word, Bankei suddenly bent the light around himself and turned invisible.

"Follow me!" T-REX shouted, taking off in a flash of hyperspeed.

Ignacio immediately followed,
the
world
    slowed
        down,
and he began to snake his way through the mannequin-like crowd. "Activate aural IR," he said into his wristcom. Without disrupting his normal vision, a colorful aura appeared around every person or object which transmitted infrared radiation. He could now see Bankei as an animated, reddish-orange, humanoid outline, which was just shooting through one of the auditorium's emergency exits.

T-REX jammed through the opened door after the invisible quarry, Ignacio right behind him. They spilled out into a wide alleyway, rapidly ran its length, then the three of them started to zip their way through the busy city streets.

The cars, while moving noticeably faster than the people, were still fairly slow in comparison to their hyperspeed, and it didn't take much effort to avoid contact with them–just a whole helluva lot of concentration. Because all it took was one slip-up, one lapse out of hyperspeed, and the world would instantly be returned to normal. And Ignacio would instantly be turned into roadkill.

Erratically dodging back and forth between same-way and oncoming traffic, Bankei was making the chase as tough as possible. Whenever it seemed like Ignacio or T-REX were about to catch him, Bankei would throw some wild juke worthy of an ESPN® highlight, and quickly regain his lead. But, as they turned on to the freeway-like Madison Avenue, Bankei started to run out of gas–which was a godsend for Ignacio, since he was already running on empty himself.

The REX on the other hand, showed no signs of hydrocarbon shortage, and was swiftly gaining on the see-through silhouette.

Bankei overtook a monstrous semi, made a sharp turn in front of it, and T-REX followed.

Pushing himself to his limit, Ignacio also rounded the semi, and as he did, he was surprised to see the REX being crushed underneath the truck's massive frame–evidently the victim of some type of speed-slowing attack.

Moving off the busy thoroughfare onto a sidestreet, Bankei reached his limit and slowed down to a near-normal speed.

Ignacio felt like he was about to hyperventilate, and desperately wanted to slow up also. But he realized if he did that, he'd lose Bankei for good–so he kept his concentration as focused as a laser's beam and zeroed in on his target like a living smart bomb.

The next instant, he exploded into Bankei, sending them both crashing down to the sidewalk. They tumbled along its unyielding surface until they reached the entrance to an alley, slamming into the side of a building with a painful thud. Luckily for Ignacio, Bankei took the brunt of the impact.

Gasping for air as a misty rain began to fall, Ignacio rolled over on top of the transparent outline, pinned him down by his throat, and reached for his disruptor.

The red-orange aura suddenly filled in again. But it wasn't Bankei this time. It was Ignacio–albeit about twenty years younger with a bright red, holographic symbol painted onto his forehead.

$$\delta$$

"Lo siento," his younger self said, his eyes full of sadness.

A feeling of déja vu passed over Ignacio. He released his grip on his likeness, unable to look away from the crimson symbol.

$$\delta$$

"If you're hearing me right now," his younger self continued in

189

Spanish, "then it means you're about to capture one of us, and we've been left no other choice but to awaken you."

"No..." Ignacio whispered, his mind trying its best to avoid the veracity of his own words. "No."

"Please try to relax," he soothingly said to himself, gentle waves of energy emitting forth from the symbol, "and take a deep breath. You're about to learn the truth."

δ

His self uttered the wordsounds,

"  "

The symbol became brighter, losing its color, becoming all colors.

Then a flash of white light, and
there                       was
                                con
           fu

                    si
on.

                              Dis

or

der.

T

h

e

w                                    o                        r

l

d

sud                              d

en

ly

no        l                                o

n        g        e

r            m                        ad

esensel

o                        g

i

cc                        e a

s

e            dddddddd

ddddd

dddddddddddddddddd

ddddddddddd

ddddddddddddddddddddddd    dddd    dddddd

ddddddddddddddddddti

mefol

dedinu

pon                    i

tsel

fandmemoryslowlyreturned,

andtheloss

of forgetfullness

commenced.

191

And Ignacio began to remember...

In a darkened room–a basement, maybe–with rubble, dust, and cob-
webs all about–somewhere in Seattle.

Too large for a basement, actually.

In a darkened room–crushed brick and mortar strewn about,
an antiquated smell of mustiness and dust in the air, archaic spi-
derwebs and aged patches of moss hanging from every corner and
crevice–somewhere underneath downtown Seattle.

The old underground, amongst the earthquaked ruins.

A chiselled, fortyish African-American man sits across from
him at a dilapidated wooden table. The man's face, while handsome,
reveals much wear.

Wellor.

Adrian Wellor is his name. He asks a twenty-two year old
Ignacio, "You do realize what you'll be sacrificing by doing this,
don't you?"

"Sí," Ignacio replies with a nod. "Myself."

"Yourself," Wellor says. "Yes." Elbows resting on the dusty
table, he leans forward. "You will *completely* lose the essence of who
you are now. The person inside you who wants to see change, who
wants to see revolution–will be gone forever. And he will be replaced
by a man who wants nothing more than to uphold the system and
maintain the status quo." Wellor wets his lips, and continues, "You
will become someone you despise. Someone you loathe. Possibly even
hate–because you will take advantage of the weak and you will
protect the strong. Laws will mean more to you than morals. Order
will be more important than freedom. You will arrest people because
of their thoughts, and you will be violent. And most assuredly–you
will be responsible for the deaths of innocents."

Wellor looks deeply into Ignacio's eyes. "You will *become* the
Gestapo." His jaws clench, his nostrils flare, he breathes in. "Now,
Morris Ignacio, I ask you again–is this what you want? Is this move-
ment so important to you that you would sacrifice your own self?"

Ignacio's stomach feels queasy. Nervous. Uneasy. Then he
thinks of his cousin, Ernesto, and his friend, Andre. In workcamps for
their thoughts. It shouldn't be like this, he knows. But it will take
great sacrifices to change it.

"Well?" Wellor asks.

# ((FREQUENCIES))

Becoming the beast to fight the beast. Nobility through ignobility. The one sacrificing for the many.

"Does it mean that much to you?"

Self sacrifice. He thinks of Jesus on the cross. The rest of his life, for a better, more just future. He sees children laughing. People living free. The light of God shining down on all. The fear and loathing pass through him, hope and strength enter in. His stomach settles, he nods his head, and answers, "It does."

God's light shines down upon him.

A flash of white light again.

Ignacio found himself on his hands and knees in an alleyway, staring down at his reflection in a small pool of water created by the falling rain. Why was he here? Why did he look so old? Was that rain running down his face? Or tears?

Water everywhere. And white light.

A walkway on the water, cedar chips underfoot. Leaning against a wooden railing, trees behind him, Lake Washington in front. The University of Washington. The arboretum's waterfront trail. Dawn.

Someone standing next to him, a fellow U-dub student. The one who introduced him to Wellor. He's talking to Ignacio right now.

"Un momentito, Griffin," Ignacio interrupts, watching a few kayakers in the distance. "Hold on. If I'm never gonna be in contact with any of you *ever* again..." He looks at Griffin. "Then how am I supposed to get you the surveillance information you need? What good is a sleeper if he doesn't report back?"

Griffin smiles. "That's what's so fucking brilliant about this, Ignacio," he says in his native English accent. "You don't have to." He waits for a jogger to pass, double-checks his white-noise generator, and says, "We'll be able to remote-view the information via your signature pattern, while you're sleeping. Without you ever knowing that we're doing it."

Ignacio gives him a look of disbelief. "You're sayin' that you're gonna be inside my head?"

"Yes. But only while you're dreaming."

"Why not when I'm awake?"

"Because your frequential state of consciousness is too jumbled then. There's too much interference–too much stimuli. The signature pattern becomes nearly impossible to lock onto, let alone decipher." The floating walkway gently bobs up and down as a large boat passes by. "We have to wait until you've achieved dreamstate, when your frequencies become relaxed and focused, and your SP emerges clearly. Then we can lock on to the pattern, enter your consciousness, and obtain the data from that day."

Ignacio laughs. "Privacy isn't one of the pluses of this assignment, ey?"

"Unfortunately, no," Griffin says. "Each time that we tap into your SP, we'll see what you saw, feel what you felt, and think what you thought. Your life will become like an open book."

There is nothing but the sounds of lapping waves, distant boats, and waterfowl. The word "sacrifice" won't leave Ignacio's mind. The sun beginning to grow brighter, he asks, "So when does all this begin?"

"As soon as we finish the frequential testing."

"How long's that gonna be, Griffin? It feels like this is takin' forever."

"I'm sure it must, Ignacio, and I apologize. But it'll take a few more weeks of testing in order to precisely get your signature pattern down. It's a lengthy and complicated process."

"I know it is," Ignacio says, "but...when you make a decision like this, you just want it to begin. You don't want to have to keep thinkin' about it. You'll start second guessing yourself, and I don't want to do that. I want to be sure of this." He stares off into the morning sky and exhales a deep breath. Shaking his head, he says, "This better not be for nothing, Griffin. That's all I'm saying."

"It won't be, my friend." Griffin places his hand on Ignacio's shoulder. "You have my word."

Ignacio briefly looks into the bright, rising sun and squints his eyes.


White light.

A car drove by. It was raining. Ignacio was in an alley, huddled near a dumpster, violently vomiting onto the wet pavement. The alley seemed familiar, as if he'd been there before in a dream.

A flash of lightning.

A flash of white light.

# ((FREQUENCIES))

In the basement again.

The city's basement, weeks later. He and Wellor are not alone this time. Other people–fellow revolutionaries–are in the room also. A few are focusing their attention on him, most are engaged in other activities.

As Wellor removes a neural-netted device from off of his head, Ignacio blinks his eyes hard, sits up in the recliner, and asks, "Is that it? I didn't feel anything."

Wellor smiles, places the device onto a monitor. "Good." The monitor's screen is filled with colorful frequential animation–pulses, waves, spikes, vibrations, oscillations. "You're not supposed to."

"I-" Ignacio looks around. Different faces than when he was placed under hypnosis. Jesse still there, but not Griffin. Or Jason. "How long have I been out?"

Jesse runs a scanner over him and glances at its display. "About twenty hours."

"Say what?"

She sets down the scanner. "Twenty hours," she says, touching his cool forehead with her warm hand.

"But I don't feel like any time passed..." She places her fingers on the underside of his wrist, closes her eyes, and gently applies some pressure. "I remember closing my eyes, you saying some things...and that's it. I don't remember anything else. No dreams, no images, no waking... Nada."

Her eyes still closed, her fingers moving back and forth along various pressure points on his head and forearm, Jesse nods and says, "That's normal for this kind of frequential hypnotism. It acts like a spiritual anesthetic."

"Your true essence was temporarily submerged," Wellor says, "so that the new essence could enter into you. Thus, you–the *true* you, the one I'm speaking to now–has no memory whatsoever of the consciousness transfer. You could say that you were away while it happened..." He traces his finger along a purplish energy pulse on the monitor's screen. "Deep within the realm of your subconscious."

Jesse continues to rub Ignacio's pressure points. He feels waves of energy rush over him. "Qué bueno," he whispers, closing his eyes. "So where is the new me?"

"He has retreated to your subconscious, just as your true self has emerged forth," Wellor says. "And there he will stay, until next you sleep."

"Then?" Ignacio asks, seeing bluish-purple colors in his mind's

195

eye, harmoniously corresponding with Jesse's fingertips.

"Tomorrow you will wake," Wellor says, "and you will be a new man. You will have absolutely no interest in subversive activities, and you will find yourself with an undeniable calling to pursue a career with the FBI. You will have no recollection of ever encountering any of us, and this chapter of your life shall fade from your mind completely." He paused. "Like a dream that never existed."

A flash of white light.

A flash of lightning.

Leaning against a wall, Ignacio slid himself up to his feet. There was soggy vomit near his shoes, and his stomach muscles were sore. His throat burned, his mouth felt acidic.

He was crying, it was raining, and he wanted to go home.

But he couldn't remember where home was, and there was this overwhelmingly bright light suddenly emanating from within his mind.

The basement. Hours later.

Jesse stands in front of him, a thin paintbrush in her hand. She leans forward, her sandy-blonde tresses swaying softly with her motion, and adds a few, final strokes onto his forehead. The holographic paint feels cool. Soothing.

"There," she says, removing the brush from his forehead. She stares at him. Her eyes squint. "Perfect." She sets down the brush and hands him a mirror. "Have a look."

Ignacio looks into the mirror. A bright, red, 3-D symbol painted on to his forehead.

$$\delta$$

"Arabic?" he asks, shifting in his chair.

"No, Greek. It's a delta."

He smiles. "Delta. Sleeper. I get it." Still examining the symbol in the mirror, he says, "Isn't this supposed to be shaped like a triangle?"

"Only if it were an uppercase delta," she says, setting up

some kind of camera-like device in front of him. "That's lowercase."

"Why not the triangle?"

"It's too linear and shallow. The dimensions aren't right."
She adjusts a knob around the camera's lens. "Memetic triggers work
best when they're housed within curves and circles," she says, peering into a viewfinder. "Which is exactly what the lowercase design
provides."

Ignacio watches her tinker some more with the camera-
device, then says, "So, Jesse–if we end up needing to use this..." He
glances at himself and the symbol in the mirror again.

$$\delta$$

"What's gonna happen to me?"

Jesse stares at him for a second, saying nothing. Then she
replies, "First of all, Morris, the possibility that you'll actually
capture another one of our agents is-"

"Jesse," he says, setting the mirror down. "Just tell me."

Her bottom lip wraps around her lower teeth, she bites down
lightly and nods her head. "Okay." She walks over, kneels down
beside him, warmly places her hand on his, and says, "If awakened,
your true essence is going to emerge forth from within your subconscious, and then it'll begin to merge together with the implanted
essence. They'll continue to combine until both essences' memories are
fully integrated, then..." She pauses. "Then the old essence reasserts
itself. You'll once again remember the entirety of your life, know
all of your implanted essence's memories–but now you'll feel like
your true self again. You'll be who you are now–with additional
memories."

Ignacio thumbs his mustache. "Then I won't be who I am now.
Memories make you who you are. I'm gonna be different."

"Well, yes," she says, "of course. But your essence will be the
same as it is now."

He looks away from her, uneasily saying to himself, "It's
gonna be a miracle if I manage to stay sane through all this."

She rubs the top of his hand with her thumb. "You will,
Morris. You'll make it through. I promise." She firmly grasps his
hand and hugs him. "Trust me. You will." She slowly releases her
embrace, then walks back to the camera. "Don't forget–in all likelihood, this is never going to happen. This is just a precaution. The

whole point of our sleeper system is to allow you to experience a normal life. And needless to say..." She smiles compassionately. "Awakening you would really mess that up."

Ignacio smiles as he looks at the sincerity in his compatriot's face. "I'm gonna miss you, Jess." He looks over various parts of the gigantic room, at all of the others, realizing that these are some of his last moments being around them. "I'm gonna miss all of you."

Jesse laughs awkwardly. "C'mon, Morris," she says, her voice slightly strained, "I'm trying to get through this without crying."

He laughs, touching the corner of his eye. "Yo se. Pero...I just wanted to let you know."

She swallows hard. "I'm going to miss you, too, Morris. We all are." Clearing her throat, she says, "Alright. Now...look at the lens, and imagine you've come face to face with your awakened self. You're confused, disoriented, and you're looking for answers." Jesse looks into the viewfinder. "What do you tell yourself?"

Ignacio stares into the lens, imagining the situation. "Lo siento," he says, tears still present in his eyes. "If you're hearing me right now..."


A flash of white lightning.

White light. Still there. Not flashing, but a subtle ebb and flow of informational luminescence.

Back in the ((chase.bankei)) alley. Back? Was he here ((yes)) before?

Head up at the ((wednesday)) night sky, droplets of rain ((seeing.himself.delta)) splashing off his ((remembering)) face. Slapping at his face. Someone slapping at his face.

"Mo!" she shouted, one ((morris)) of her hands holding him up by the collar, the other ((FBI)) grasping his face at the cheekbones. Shaking him, she made ((freereads)) eye contact and asked, "What the hell's wrong with you?"

It looked like the woman ((she.didn't)) had no pupils. He focused his eyes. He knew ((freemon)) her. From where?

"Ignacio!" she shouted ((essence)) louder, shaking him ((morris.ignacio)) harder. "What happened?"

Too much information, his brain awash in a sea of frequential data.

"What happened?" he repeated ((memetic.trigger)) after her. Home. He knew he had ((irena.children)) to get home.

Information overload.

"Carter," she said into ((dcc.terrorists)) her wristcom. "Ignacio's alive but incoherent. His frees look ((wellor.training)) funny and his eyes are starting to roll up into his..."

Systems crash.

Fade to black.


<<irena.children>>
        <start>
<<irena.children>>
        <received>
<<irena.children>>
        <today>
        <breakfast.

carter stone?irena asks.is he new?

no,ignacio says,placing some beans,chorizo,and eggs into a warm flour tortilla.he's one of the dcc guys i was telling you about yesterday.one of the bureau's big boys.he sprinkles some fresh cilantro onto the filling.he'll be heading the riot investigation.

so they're sure it's terrorism?she asks.

looks that way,he says.

terrorism,she says.i hope it's not that.my mother told me some horrible stories about the terror years.

he wraps the tortilla into a burrito,saying,it's never gonna get that bad again,irena.we've got too much control now,he says.we can nip any insurrection while it's still a bud.he bites into the burrito.all this'll blow over before you know it.

irena picks at her food.she asks,when was the last time the bureau sent a dcc agent to work with you?

he thinks for a moment.never,he replies.>


"Never," he said ((ignacio)) groggily.

"Ignacio?" she ((essence)) asked. "You up now?"

It took a considerable amount ((memetic.effects)) of effort for him to open his eyes. He was in the backseat ((freemon.polaris)) of a car. She was looking ((beautiful)) back at him from ((beautiful?)) the driver's seat.

"We're heading back to HQ to meet ((beacon.hill)) up with Carter and((dcc.terrorists)) Kwon," she said. "We're gonna ((jung-ran)) run some tests on you to see ((frequential)) what happened. Are you getting this?"

The sea of information, rolling over him.

"Sea," he ((memory.integration)) muttered.

"Good," she said. "'Cause they also ((dcc.terrorists)) nabbed your boy McCready while ((marc.trustworthy.friend)) they were chas-" She stopped.

Drowning in information.

"Aw, shit, Mo," she said. "C'mon!"

Submerged. Sinking.

Dark.


<<dcc.terrorists>>
        <start>
<<dcc.terrorists>>
        <received>
<<dcc.terrorists>>
        <today>
        <headquarters.

how reliable is this informant?ignacio asks the female dcc agent.

very,janet vegas responds.if he says davis is going to be at the tiger's lair tonight,then that's where he's going to be.

and you really think wellor is behind all this?he asks.after all these years?

carter solemnly looks at ignacio and says,we don't think he's behind it,freemon ignacio.we know.

ignacio moves over to the room's window,gazes at the busy city outside.i still think we're jumping to conclusions here, carter.even with all the evidence you say you have.

neither of the dcc agents say a word.

watching the vehicular traffic fly by,ignacio says,we're ignoring possibilities.how are we supposed to even fully understand this case if we're not looking into all the possibilities?he turns from the window and faces them.

vegas asks,you're still bothered by the policemen issue?

of course,ignacio says.don't you find it strange that your superiors have extradited all three of them back to dc?and denied us access to their frequential records?he laughs.c'mon, these are the cops who set the riots off in the first place–they're the first ones we should be talking to.

     ignacio,carter says,cutting the air with his hand.relax.we've got everything under control.>


His arm ((ignacio)) was placed around her ((essence)) shoulder, and he was being dragged through ((freemon.hq)) a well-lit hallway.

     "We're almost there," she said ((frequential.testing)) to him.

     "Terrorism," he ((dcc.riots.propaganda)) mumbled. "Control."

     "What?" Continuing to ((dcc.lies)) move him forward, she said, "Damn, Mo, they fucked ((himself.underground)) you up good."

     His head dropped ((wellor.training)) forward and down.

     Consciousness retreated.


<<wellor.training>>
     <start>
<<wellor.training>>
     <received>
     <an image in his mind's eye.
     a bright green electromagnetic pulse.
     pulsing.soothing.speaking.
     wellor's voice.
     think before you speak,
it sa((wordswithinwordscompresseddata))ys.be calm.control your frequencies.allow memories to integrate.will help asap.sleep.make peace with old life.prepare for new.remove biochip/freeread.find safe haven.wait for contact.>


Ignacio realized ((memory.integration)) that his eyes were open. They felt dry. He felt tired. He ((sleep)) blinked. Slowly.

     Very slowly. He was lying on his ((headquarters)) back, and there were others ((medical.ward)) in the room with him.

     "Everything seems normal," the man in ((freemon.doctor)) the white coat said, lowering a scanner. "I think he's okay now."

     "So what happened to him?" she ((essence)) asked.

     "My ((dr.richardson)) guess is that he got hit with some kind of synaptic disruptor. One that ((memetic.trigger)) wasn't very powerful either, because his frees have already attained normality."

     "You don't think it might have been something worse?" she

asked. "Like ((compressed.information)) an infobomb? His frees were buggin' ((delta)) about twenty minutes ago."

Richardson looked at a large ((frequential.images)) monitor. "I noticed that, but..." He shook his head, still staring at the screen. "It's just not the right pattern for ((rapid.oscillations)) an infobomb. And I'm not seeing any residual traces. I think that was just his mind's response to being ((true.self.emergence)) synaptically disrupted."

"He must'a been having some fucked up dreams then."

Richardson laughed. "Probably." Turning his gaze to Ignacio, he asked, "Were you?"

Ignacio said ((yes)) nothing, but smiled slightly.

Essence looked at Ignacio. "Is he up?"

"He can hear us now," Richardson said. "But he's going to need a lot more sleep before he's fully ((almost.integrated)) cognizant."

"How long's this gonna keep him out of action?"

"At least until ((next.awakening)) the end of the week. We'll have someone notify his wife that ((irena)) we'll be keeping him here overnight. That way, we can run some more tests ((frequential)) on him in the morning, after he's had some ((sleep)) rest." Richardson moved across the room towards Ignacio, a small metallic device in his ((sleepscan)) hand. "For now, though," he said, setting the device onto Ignacio's forehead, "he needs ((final.integration)) to sleep."

The sleepscan stuck to Ignacio's ((magnetic.adhesion)) skin, emitting soothing ((frequential.sleep.induction)) undulations of ((electromagnetic)) energy.

His eyes started to feel heavy. He closed them. Slowly. Ignacio fell asleep.


<<final.integration>>
     <start>
<<final.integration>>
     <received>
<<final.integration>>
     <in.progress>

$$\Delta/\delta$$

# α
## Chapter 12
## ((Checkmate))

*Other celestial bodies, however, were less of an enigma. Like stars*
*or suns, they shined for all to see, their intentions as clear as day.*
*They announced their presence to the world unabashedly, and showed*
*all who gazed upon them their power and glory. These radiant*
*displays allowed them extraordinary pull, and other masses*
*gravitated toward them in great numbers.*
*And while this sometimes had the effect of drawing unwanted objects*
*and bodies into their orbit, it rarely, if ever, posed a threat to their*
*existence. For the starlights were a force to be reckoned with, and*
*only a select, few cosmic entities could challenge their strength."*

Inside Xanadeux's subterranean nerve center, Mason sat comfortably in
the contoured chair, looking up at the gargantuan uniview screen
before him.

On it was a beautiful Tibetan woman, dressed in a long, thin,
orange cloth which had been carefully and delicately wrapped
around her body. She was sitting in a lush tropical garden filled with
flora and fauna from around the world. Visible in the distance behind
her were the jagged, snow-capped peaks of the southern Himalayas.
Stroking an ocelot lying next to her, she asked, "Are you sure you don't
want to leave a message for him?"

"Yes, Lhasa," he said. "I'm just checking–*again*–to make sure
he hasn't been attacked."

She smiled. "No attacks, Mason. Gonpo is just busy. But he'll
appreciate the concern."

"I doubt it," Mason said.

"You know how your father gets when a project comes to fruition," Lhasa said, as a toucan flew onto the branch of an African mahogany tree behind her. "He can't think of anything else."

"Yes, but it would be rather nice–not to mention courteous–if he at least took the time to check in with his family when they're experiencing a crisis."

"He thinks you can handle it on your own, or else he-"

"Yes, yes," Mason said. "I saw the message. But a call? A simple call? Is that too much to ask?"

Lhasa smiled. "Well..."

Mason shook his head. "I know. Don't answer. I'll see you Friday, Lhasa."

"Friday," she said. "Take care." The screen transformed into the Ordosoft™ logo.

Mason swiveled in his chair to face Xanadeux, who was standing directly behind him. "That man absolutely confounds me sometimes, Xanadeux," he said.

"Your father *is* a difficult man to get hold of, sir," the android agreed. "But judging from the message, this project's results will be well worth the lack of correspondence."

"Yes, but one would think..." His voice trailed off. "Bah. What one would think rarely applies to my father."

"Rarely," said Xanadeux.

"Well," he said, swiveling back around to face the giant screen, "enough time on that matter. There's work to be done. Xanadeux, please connect me with Mr. Webber."

"Certainly."

The Ordosoft™ logo morphed into the image of Mr. Webber, standing in a brightly lit laboratory. A few doctors and scientists were in the room with him. All were dressed in black. "Good evening, sir," he said, smiling his ferocious smile. "Good news."

"You've made a breakthrough?" Mason asked.

"More," he said. "Nature of attack has been determined." Behind him, a bruised male body was lying on an operating table. It was completely nude, save for a thin black veil which covered its face. The top of its head was being attended to by two of the masked scientists. "Carrier identified."

Mason leaned forward. "I'm impressed, Mr. Webber. Please continue."

Mr. Webber nodded, and began to walk toward the body.

# ((FREQUENCIES))

The camera's POV switched perspectives. Rather than seeing from behind Webber, Mason was now seeing directly through the head of security's cybernetic eyes.

"Extensive interrogation revealed Benjamin knew nothing," Webber said, looking over the entire length of the badly mutilated body. Missing toes, contused skin, numerous bite marks, damaged genitalia, broken fingers–it was a horrible sight.

Mason cringed in his chair.

Webber's gaze passed over the body's veiled face, then stopped at the top of its head. Its brain was exposed, glistening brightly under the lab's abundant lighting. Scores of needlelike, fiber optic tubes had been inserted into it. "Technocyte deployment and subsequent brain examination revealed him to be the carrier."

"Then he...he didn't know he had been infected?"

"Correct," Webber said, as a scientist pulled one of the long, flexible glass fibers from out of the wet organ. "Infobomb uploaded itself without subject's knowledge."

"I see," he said, momentarily turning his eyes from the screen. "Were you able to gather any evidence from his augmentations?"

"Negative. Infobomb wasn't carried within subject's augmentations."

A look of puzzlement crossed Mason's face. "Pardon?"

"Infobomb was housed within subject's brain cells."

"What?" Mason said.

"Interesting," Xanadeux commented.

The body's head twitched slightly as another glass tube was pulled from its brain. Webber's gaze averted from the body. He began to walk toward a scientist who was inserting one of the tubes into a cylindrical device. "Report for Mr. Huxton," he said.

The goggled, masked scientist looked at Webber, and said, "Hello, Mr. Huxton. At this point, we've determined that the informational infection found within the subject's brain is one of a previously unknown nature–a biological infobomb that requires no implants or memory augmentation to carry it." He turned to a monitor near the device which housed the tubes, and touched his gloved finger upon the image of a magnified cellular object. The cell image grew larger in size, past its membrane, past its cytoplasm, until it reached the nuclei. Pointing to one of the bluish growths attached to the cell's nucleotides, he said, "This is it."

"A virus?" asked Mason, whose voice was projecting through a microspeaker attached to Webber's lapel.

"Yes," he said. "A genetically-specific viral infection which somehow allows an informational attack to be stored within the host's RNA. We've found traces of the virus in the subject's brain cells, spinal fluid, blood, lungs... It's penetrated his entire body."

"Odd," Mason said, rubbing his chin. "Is it transmitted like an ordinary virus?"

"That's very probable, sir, though at this point, we're not quite sure. We're going to need some more time before we can give you a definite answer."

Mason nodded. "I understand. Thank you for the report."

"You're welcome, sir."

The camera switched perspectives. Mason was now looking at Mr. Webber again.

"Would like to make a suggestion, sir," Webber said.

"Of course, Mr. Webber. Proceed."

"Since infobomb is a biological virus, recommend quarantining Mrs. Huxton until tests can be done on her. Possibility that she may have contracted virus, and that virus may be programmed to attack you also."

"Isn't it a bit late for that?" Mason said. "I've already come into contact with her numerous times."

"Nature of virus is still unknown. Possible that it requires lengthy gestation period in host before it can attack. Recommend that you remain in nerve center until Mrs. Huxton is isolated and Xanadeux can check for virus' presence within your home."

Mason turned to Xanadeux. "What do you think?"

"Mr. Webber has a good point," Xanadeux said. "It's better to be safe than sorry."

"Very well," Mason said. "Thank you for the suggestion, Mr. Webber. Keep me updated on any new developments."

"Of course, sir." His image morphed into the logo.

"This doesn't make any sense, Xanadeux," Mason said. "If these terrorists are wielding weapons such as these, then why haven't they simply tried to kill me?"

"It would seem that they're playing a game of cat and mouse, sir," Xanadeux said.

"But why? For what end?"

"Why does one climb a mountain?"

"Hm," he said. "Just to do it. That's a possibility...but I'm sure it's something more. It has to be something more." He faced the screen once again. "Where is Dominique, Xanadeux?"

"In her studio, sir," the android said, as the image of Dominique appeared on the screen. Her back was facing the camera, and she was painting thick, harsh strokes onto a large canvas. "I'm currently on my way there."

Mason nodded as he watched his surrogate wife continue to paint her bleak picture. It was all blacks and blues, randomly scattered across the painting's fabric. Nothing like the bright, effervescent work which Dominique *used* to produce. "You poor creature," he said to himself.

Two Xandys entered the room. "Mrs. Huxton?" one of them asked.

Startled, she turned and said, "Yes?"

"I apologize for the inconvenience, but I need you to come with me right now."

She set her paintbrush down. "What-what for?"

"There's some tests that need to be done."

"Now?" She looked at a nearby clock. "Can't they wait until the morning?"

"Unfortunately, no," it replied, taking a few methodical steps toward her.

She stood up, obviously afraid, and backed away from it. "Where's Mason?"

"Patch my voice through," Mason said to Xanadeux.

"Go ahead," the android's voice said from behind him.

"Dominique?" asked Mason's voice through Xanadeux's vocal speaker.

"Mason?" she said.

"Yes, it's me, dear. I'm busy in the nerve center right now, or else I'd come up personally."

"What's going on?" she asked, her face full of fright.

"We just need to run some tests, Dom," he said. "That's all. Please go with Xanadeux. I'll join up with you shortly."

She started to cry, as she dispiritedly walked to the Xandys. "What's going on?" she whispered through her tears. "Nothing makes sense."

"Don't worry, dear," Mason said. "Everything will be fine."

She said nothing, and exited the room with the androids, leaving the dreary painting the centerpiece of the camera's cold gaze.

"This has all gone so wrong, Xanadeux." Mason wiped his face with both hands. "All I wanted was to be with my wife again..."

Xanadeux comfortingly placed its hand on Mason's shoulder.

"...but this has all gone so horribly wrong..."

"Sir?" Xanadeux asked.

Mason sighed. "Yes?"

"I realize that the timing of this is unfortunate, but there's something you should see." Upon the screen appeared an image of a darkened, crowded nightclub. Obnoxiously loud music began to blast through the nerve center's speakers. Two Ordocops™ were in front of the camera's view, their weapons drawn and aimed toward a motley group of four individuals.

"Freeze!" shouted one of the Ordocops™.

"What is this?" Mason asked.

"The club where Ashley is at," Xanadeux said.

Mason felt his heart sink. "Oh, no."

The next instant, a volley of lasers flew through the air, the shouting increased, and the club turned into a vortex of chaos.

Mason shot up from his seat. "No!" he shouted. As it became increasingly harder to see what was happening, he turned back to Xanadeux and asked, "What's going on?"

"Apparently our security forces have been forced to fire upon a group of government agents."

"What?" He looked back at the screen, but all he could see were people running every which way. Sounds of panic and fear joined the blaring music. "But why?"

"It seems they were threatening Ashley's safety. She was talk-" Xanadeux suddenly stopped.

Mason's face drooped. "What now?"

"I've just been contacted by something calling itself the 'Presence.' It claims responsibility for the attacks, and would like to speak with you."

"That bastard," he said. "This is all his fault."

On the screen, the battle continued. An Asian woman pulled out a nunchaku-like device whose chain greatly extended as she flung it forward. One of its ends wrapped around the legs of an Ordocop™, she pulled back on it, and swept the cop clean off of his feet.

"Can you put it through without compromising your security?" Mason asked.

"Yes," Xanadeux said.

"Then do it–but disable the outgoing cameras."

The shivering black creature from the MUD morphed onscreen. "Hello, Mason," it said in its buzzing voice, its face flashing a streetcam image of Adam being hit by the truck. "Remember me?"

Mason clenched his fists together. "You obviously want something, you bastard. What is it?"

Flash: the Ordosoft™ logo in flames, the American flag in flames, the UN's symbol a pyre. "Isn't it obvious? I want to play a game."

Mason turned to Xanadeux and mouthed, "Is Ashley all right?"

Xanadeux nodded.

"What kind of a game?" Mason asked loudly.

"A game of chance," it said, as a DISORDER pulse of ENTROPY words shot across its ANARCHY face at a DESTRUCTION subliminal pace.

Mason couldn't catch the rest. "The stakes?" he asked.

"You know," the creature replied, half of its face a living human fetus, the other half a close-up of a suction abortion.

"I want specifics," Mason said.

Flash: A SWAT team kicking in someone's back door. "Stalling?" it asked.

"Hardly. I simply want to know what I have to gain."

"What you're trying won't work." Flash: A man stabbing another man in his spine, graphically severing through vertebra.

"The odds, beast. What are they?"

Its face showed a satellite, a wristcom, a shackle, then a police car. "You can't trace my physical location."

"I'm waiting," Mason said impatiently.

It laughed, a swarm of insects in a psychotic frenzy. "Your attempts to distract me are amusing, Mason." A flash of a woman laughing, then suddenly coughing up blood and choking. "But much like your attempts to find me, they're futile."

"We'll see about that."

"Don't believe me?" Flash: A priest, slipping his head into a noose. "Just ask your android slave."

Mason looked back at Xanadeux.

"Go ahead," the creature said.

"Well?" Mason asked.

Xanadeux shook its head. "I'm sorry, sir. I can't seem to pinpoint where it's transmitting from."

"Damn," Mason said gloomily.

The creature laughed again.

Mason turned to the screen. "Just tell me the stakes, damn it!"

"All right, old man," it said, showing an image of a gray-haired man sprawled on a tile floor, clutching his chest in pain.

209

"Don't have a heart attack. Here's the odds: You win, and I leave your family alone." Flash: A photograph of Mason's family, posed for a publicity shot. "You lose..." The same photo, but now they were all desiccated corpses, still posing for the camera.

"And the game?" Mason asked.

"Since you're so fond of medievalism," it said, showing an image of a man being stretched upon the rack, his skin just beginning to split and tear. "I propose a quest. An immersible cyberquest for the king." Flash: A man wearing a crown being violently drowned underwater. "You *do* have an immersible, don't you?"

"Of course," Mason said, looking over at the giant, fluid-filled sphere which occupied the eastern section of the nerve center.

Flash: A man submerged in an immersible, the intelligent fluid around him solidifying into a blade and slicing open his gut. "And it's capable of inflicting realtime damage?"

"It is."

The image of a woman being burned at the stake. "Good. Then you accept my challenge?"

"No details?"

"Details come when you get to the domain." An image of a man being guillotined. "Take the offer..." The man's severed head, rolling away from its body. "Or leave it."

"Very well," Mason said. "I accept."

"Of course you do," it said. "I'll send the domain's location to your slave." Flash: A handcuffed man being raped with a soiled plunger. "See you there." The creature's vibrating body scattered into thousands of tiny particles which blackened the entire screen.

"It's gone," Xanadeux said, turning off the uniview.

Mason stood from his seat, still fixedly staring at the blank screen, the game's monumental stakes weighing heavily upon his mind. Were he to sustain enough damage while inside of the domain, it could mean permanent—or worse—mortal injury. Were he to fail, it could mean the death of his family. But were he to succeed...

Mason started to undo his tie.

"Would you like me to prepare the immersible?"

"Yes, Xanadeux," he said, slipping off his tie as he began to walk toward the large sphere. "Let's put an end to this madness."

The lights at the bottom of the sphere turned on, causing the clear, intelligent fluid inside to glow with a greenish hue. It did a few multi-directional rotations upon its magnetic axes, then came to a rest with its entrance facing the ground.

# ((FREQUENCIES))

As Mason reached the immersible, another Xandy emerged from behind it, and said, "All systems are go, sir."

"Good." Mason tossed his jacket aside. "We can't afford any mistakes." He removed the rest of his clothes, save for his briefs.

The android extended its upturned palm toward Mason. A small black disc rested atop it.

Mason picked up the disc between his thumb and forefinger, pressed in the two tiny buttons at its sides, and placed it on his chest. Releasing his fingers, the disc magnetically adhered to his skin.

"Shall I activate the suit?" Xanadeux asked.

"Go ahead," Mason said.

The android placed its index finger in the center of the disc. The device glowed for a brief moment, then hundreds of thin black tendrils sprouted out from it in every direction. They quickly grew themselves along Mason's trunk, arms, legs, and head, forming a complex, interconnected web of neurological stimulators and receptors. Within a manner of seconds, his entire body was covered with a technorganic neural net.

"Does everything feel all right, sir?"

Mason flexed his electrode-covered fists, wiggled his neural-netted toes, tilted his wired head from side to side, and said, "Superb."

"Excellent." Xanadeux handed him the immersible suit's headpiece. "Here you are."

Grasping the black plastic/magnetite mask with his right hand, Mason held it up before his face. His eyes passed over the large obsidian lenses, whose sideways-teardrop shape caused them to resemble the eyes of a graylien; the silvery, metal material that covered the mouth and nose, shaped like an oval and looking like it was comprised of near-microscopic links of chain mail; the speaker components on each side, custom-molded to precisely fit the shape of his ears. "'Twas armor he donned..." Mason said, bringing the mask to his face, "...a king or a pawn?" After it had magnetically adhered itself in place, he asked, "Can you hear me?"

"Perfectly, sir," Xanadeux answered through the headpiece's speakers.

"Then I'm ready to be immersed." Mason walked under the sphere, which was raised about eight feet off the ground, and placed himself directly beneath its entrance. The transparent door slid open, and the intelligent fluid inside began to gently ooze out and around him. As it seeped over his head and shoulders, down past his hips, he could feel it smoothly, logically molding itself around him. When he was completely engulfed by the viscous liquid, he said to himself, "Here we go." It then sucked itself back into the sphere, with him now inside it. The entrance closed below, and it brought him to the center of the immersible. "Activate all systems," he said. The mask started to pull the air from the surrounding fluid, while the visor began to project images directly onto Mason's retinas, so that his entire field of vision was now taking place within cyberspace.

He saw before him the east garden of Xanadeux. Tulips, roses, carnations, and a plethora of other flowers encircled him. The sounds of wind, birds, and insects came through the mask's speakers, sweet, familiar smells emitted themselves via the olfactory processors, while a soft breeze blew lightly at his face, courtesy of the IS's neural net. Mason bent down, picked a single yellow buttercup, and as he did, he could feel the stimulators within the suit and the surrounding liquid perfectly mimic the sensation of grasping and plucking a flower's stem. And as he moved in cyberspace, so did he move in realtime, suspended by the intelligent fluid such that he could maneuver any way he wanted, but always remain centered in the middle of the sphere. Mason stood up, the transmutable fluid solid beneath his feet, and brought the flower to his nose, the fluid around his arms as light as air.

From behind him, he heard Xanadeux ask, "Stopping to smell the roses, sir?"

Mason turned to face the android, the retinal projectors scrolling along with his motions perfectly. "Actually, the buttercups. You've already received the domain location?"

"Yes, along with the Presence's instructions."

"Which are?"

"That you may enter the domain as the avatar of your choice, but you may not change once there, nor access anything from the outside." Xanadeux held out its palm. Various avatars that Mason had used in the past began to holographically rotate over its hand. "And, you must remain within the domain until the challenge's end. Otherwise, the deal is off."

"That's it?"

"That's all."

"Hmm," Mason said, examining the avatars. "Walking blindly into battle..." He raised a single finger above the choices. "Arthur would be best prepared." He touched the miniature figure, and was instantly transformed into the King Arthur avatar.

"A good choice," Xanadeux said. "Especially considering the Excalibur program's previous performance against the Presence."

"Yes," he agreed, touching the hilt of the regal sword which rested at his hip. "Not to mention its new additions." Placing the single buttercup into a leather pouch attached to his belt, Mason said, "Shall we begin?"

"At once." Xanadeux waved its hand, and a swirling portal opened up in the fabric of virtual reality before them. Motioning to the opening, it said, "After you, sir."

Mason nodded, then stepped into the portal. Xanadeux followed, and together they began their journey toward the Presence's realm.

It was an odd sensation, traversing the virtual tunnel, much like walking through thick, soft, ankle-deep mud–but with the hallucinogenic addition of bright, kinetic colors all around, and a foundation that simply would *not* stop moving. Mason imagined the experience to be what LSD or psilocybin would feel like, but had no idea if this was the case, since he had never dabbled in the province of illegal narcotics. Nearly tripping on the spinning floor, he said, "Of course it couldn't be a *simple* portal."

"Of course," Xanadeux said, its arms resting comfortably at its sides as it floated its way across the tunnel's shifting surface. "The Presence seems to enjoy making things as complicated as-" Xanadeux paused, as a large shape suddenly began to morph up from the ground below. "-possible," it finished.

Mason immediately drew Excalibur, and readied himself for battle with the unknown entity.

The multicolored, liquidous shape quickly congealed into a gigantic, human head... One which he recognized...as the head of...

"George Washington?" Mason asked.

"You're free, Mason," boomed the voice of the president, as the portal abruptly stopped swirling around them.

"What?" Mason said, doing his best to maintain his balance on the now-stable ground.

"Free, Mason," the head repeated, its voice slowed down to the point that its words became incredibly distorted. "Free to leave now." It smiled, its mouth full of rotten, wooden teeth. "Leave now, and I'll even spare one of your children–your choice which."

"Are you reneging on your challenge?"

"No." Within its pupils, Mason could see the image of a young George Washington chopping down a cherry tree with a large axe.

213

"I *never* go back on my word." It blinked, then its eyes showed an older George Washington ruthlessly chopping into a Native-American woman and her baby. "I'm merely offering you a deal."

"To hell with your deal!" Mason said, slicing his sword through the presidential mockery.

Its pupils showed the image of Mason's blade splitting George Washington's skull into a bloody mess. "Your choice," it said, then liquified back into the colorful ground.

The tunnel started to swirl once again.

"Madness, Xanadeux," Mason said, sheathing Excalibur as he trudged toward the portal's exit. "Sheer madness."

"Indubitably, sir."

They soon reached the end of the phantasmic passage, emerging onto a grassy hilltop which overlooked an enormous forest. "Here we are," Xanadeux said, as the tunnel closed behind them.

"But where is here?" Mason asked, his breaths exiting into the cold air like fog as he scanned his eyes around the area.

"Good question."

An ominous, three-pronged castle rose up directly before them, beyond the forest's clearing. Its architecture was strange, very gothic and mysterious, with elements of both the medieval and the modern. A small dirt path led down the hill toward it. Behind them was more forest, but much denser, and an aquamarine ocean could be seen far, far in the distance yonder. Another dirt path led down the hill to their right, into a thinner strip of the all-surrounding forest, and continued out toward an impressive mountain range, in which Mason could see several gigantic caves. To their left were dark gray clouds and monstrous patches of fog. From this direction, it was possible to see a small portion of the forest, and not much else.

Turning to Xanadeux, Mason said, "The creature's allowing you to stay?"

"It hasn't informed me otherwise."

"Good," he said, watching an unusually large bird fly through the skies overhead. "Now, the question remains, what is our challenge?"

The galloping of hooves could suddenly be heard in the distance. Two horses—one white, one black—appeared on the hill's horizon, from the direction of the fog. An armored man was riding upon the black one, holding a tether connected to the other horse's muzzle. "Arthur!" he wearily shouted, barely able to remain seated upon his ebony steed. His armor was badly damaged, his face beaten and battered, his entire body splattered with blood. "Arthur!"

With a bewildered look, Mason glanced over at Xanadeux, and was even more surprised to see that the android now appeared as a gallant, black-haired knight dressed in splendid white armor, a long shining sword at his side.

"I'm not sure what the challenge *is*, sir," Xanadeux said, curiously looking over its appearance, "but I believe it has begun."

"Indeed." Mason reached down to draw Excalibur, but found in its place an ordinary sword. "What?" he asked.

"What is it?" Xanadeux said.

"Excalibur..." Mason checked the other side of his belt, but found only the leather pouch, the flower still safely tucked inside. "It's...it's gone."

Realizing that they could not retrieve the Excalibur file without breaking the rules of the game, Xanadeux said, in a low, hushed tone, "Oh, dear."

"Arthur," the knight said as he neared them, blood and saliva trickling from his mouth. Mason could now see that the knight's damaged armor had been ripped and torn, as if by the claws of some great beast. Reaching them, the knight slumped off of his horse, hitting the ground with a loud clang. He clutched within his hand a weathered scroll.

Moving over to the fallen knight, Mason drew his sword and asked, "What's happened?"

"Perceval and I," he stammered. "We-we were ambushed by hellhounds in the Forest of Fog. I managed to escape, but he-" He pounded his armored fist onto the frozen ground. "I'm sorry, my liege, I tried but I..." He looked at Xanadeux. "I failed, father. Our mission succeeded...yet I failed to save Perceval."

"Father?" Xanadeux asked.

Mason turned to Xanadeux, eyed his white armor, and said, "You're Lancelot."

"Of course," Xanadeux said. "Arthurian legend."

To the knight, Mason said, "Galahad?"

He grimaced with pain. "Sire?"

Mason planted the blade of his sword into the ground, kneeling beside the wounded knight. "The mission—you've found the Holy Grail?"

Galahad laughed. "The Grail?" He laughed harder, coughing up blood. A few crimson droplets splashed off of the frosted ground, onto Mason's boots. "Surely you jest, sire."

"Why would I?" Mason asked.

"Because-" His face grew deathly serious. "Because you removed the Siege Perilous..." He hacked up more blood. "...and abandoned the quest for the Grail."

"That doesn't make any sense," Mason said. "Why would I do such a thing?"

Galahad wiped his mouth. "You said that God no longer exists."

Mason quizzically looked at Xanadeux.

"It appears the legend has been twisted," Xanadeux said.

"To put it mildly," Mason said. "Sir Galahad, what of this mission?"

"The mission," he said, extending the scroll toward Mason with an unsteady hand. "We were told by the witch, Kundrie, that upon this parchment..." He coughed, spraying red mist everywhere.

Mason took the scroll, and stepped back from Galahad.

"...is written the answer..." More coughing from the knight, yielding more blood. "...to where Excalibur is." He rolled over on his back, his head dropping onto the cold, hardened ground.

"Galahad?" Mason asked, peering over him.

His eyelids barely open, Galahad stared into the sky above. "The Grail..." he whispered. "Do you see it?"

Mason looked up at the sky. "I see nothing."

Galahad continued to stare at his vision. "Then I pray for you, my liege." He then closed his eyes, placed his hands together, and said, "I'm ready." The youthful knight's body went limp, and he discontinued breathing.

Xanadeux asked, "Is he...?"

Mason nudged Galahad with his bloodstained boot, but there was no response. He nodded. "He's gone."

Xanadeux walked over to the body to examine it for itself. "What does the scroll say?"

"We'll see." One of its spools in each hand, Mason unrolled the scroll, briefly inspected it, and said, "Hmm. The message reads:

> Though a king of rhyme and reason
> shall know the nature of what is betwixt
> Exceptional swords of the finest calibre
> lie within the stronghold of the demon son
> A king must know his given name
> should he wish to receive the lady's gift

"Demon son..." Mason looked up from the scroll. "Merlin."

"And that would have to be his stronghold," Xanadeux said, pointing its sword toward the techno-medieval structure.

Mason nodded. "Where we can find 'exceptional swords of the finest calibre.'"

"Excalibur."

"Yes," Mason said. He stared at the castle, then looked down at the scroll again. "But that's far too simple. And there's still the other verses." He read over the lines once more. "'A king of rhyme and reason, shall know the nature of what is betwixt.' The nature of what is between..."

Xanadeux moved over to Mason, quickly glanced at the scroll, placed a finger onto the middle two lines of verse and said, "Looking at the number of syllables per line as a numerical code, these don't belong here. It reads: 8, 10, 12, 11, 8, 10." It lifted its finger off the parchment. "The 12 and 11 are out place."

"Meaning there's no rhyme to them," Mason said.

"Or reason," it added.

"Therefore, the nature of the 'betwixt' verses is illogical. False. Look," he said, pointing to the fourth line, "the word 'lie' is even embedded within this verse. Thus, if we eliminate the nonsensical lines, the stanzas now rhyme:

> Though a king of rhyme and reason
> shall know the nature of what is betwixt
> A king must know his given name
> should he wish to receive the lady's gift

"And we have a poem which makes sense," Mason said, utterly immersed within the riddle. "Now, the giv-"

"Sir?" Xanadeux said.

He looked up from the parchment. "Yes?"

Xanadeux pointed down at Sir Galahad, whose body was shaking in jerky, spastic motions. His flesh had turned gruesomely pallid and purpled.

"He's alive?" Mason asked.

Galahad's movements became more spasmodic, then thick, mucosal blood began to flow profusely from his mouth and nostrils, spilling down his face and neck as a river of gore.

Xanadeux raised its sword. "Not exactly."

Mason pulled his sword from the ground, the opened scroll

217

still hanging in his other hand, and prepared himself for battle.

A low, infernal rumbling sounded from somewhere within Galahad's throat. His body then shot up into the air, hovering about two meters off of the ground, a weightless, reanimated corpse. "The kingdom is dead!" he shouted in a demonic voice, vomiting up something which could only be a portion of his viscera. "Your world is dead and you don't even know it!"

Mason clenched his jaw and tightened his grip on his sword.

Galahad's digestive juices began to eat their way through his stomach, dumping food and bile all over himself and the ground. "You're all walking dead men, dressed in shrouds of lies!" he hellishly moaned. "Infecting everything you touch with your lifeless ways, your need to conquer, your need to capitalize, your nee-"

Mason's blade cut a clean swath through the possessed knight's neck, sending Galahad's severed head rolling along the grassy knoll. The headless body instantly dropped to the ground, splashing malodorous fluid in all directions.

After shielding himself from the miasmic spray, Mason surveyed the scene. The body was no longer animated, and the head was sitting a few feet away, its blank, expressionless features facing toward them. "Well," he said to Xanadeux, "that's that."

"Dead!" shouted the head. "Dead!"

The decapitated body suddenly grabbed hold of Mason's leg with its left hand, as its right hand grasped the bottom spool of the opened scroll, tearing off the majority of the parchment.

Mason let out a startled yell, swung his sword, and chopped into the arm gripping his leg, leaving only a severed forearm behind.

A forearm that wasn't releasing its grip.

The head screamed, "Your world is dead!" as its body stuffed the ripped scroll into its opened stomach. It moved to its knees and attempted to stand, but Xanadeux swiftly sliced through one of its knees, sending it back down to the frozen turf.

The forearm tightened its grasp on Mason's leg, crushing his enchanted armor.

Outside the domain, the liquid turned solid as steel, tightly squeezing itself around Mason's shin. Before it could break his bones, he let fly a few well-aimed swings. The body's forearm was soon reduced to nothing more than segments of twitching fingers and flesh, which Mason then ferociously trounced upon with his armored boots.

"You've killed everything!" continued the head.

The body, with only one good arm and one whole leg,

attempted to upright itself, but Xanadeux once again slashed it to the ground, this time dismembering it at the thigh.

Mason severed its other arm, chopped it into smaller pieces, then he and Xanadeux began to work away at the torso.

"Genocide!" shouted the head. "Genocide! You always have to resort to genocide to achieve your goals!" It laughed maniacally.

Mason, his sword and armor splattered with blood, angrily looked over at the head, then he started to march toward it.

"You were given Eden!" it screamed.

Passing one of the horses, Mason pulled a flanged silver mace from its saddle, tossing his sanguine sword aside.

"And you turned it into Hell!"

Mason stood before the shouting head, grasped the mace's shaft with both hands, and calmly settled himself into his customary golfing stance.

"You butchered every living thing you could!"

He sized up the shot, swung the mace back...

"Raped and pillaged and violated and desecrated–"

And teed off. The smashed head went flying into the distance, down the hill toward Merlin's castle. Mason held his follow-through for a moment, then flipped the mace onto his shoulder like a club. A satisfied expression upon his face, he walked back to Xanadeux.

There were now quivering pieces of Galahad scattered everywhere, and the scroll was lying in a heap of coagulated blood and spilled bile. "I take it you have the verses memorized?" Mason asked, eyeing the revolting substance.

His white armor now not so splendid, Xanadeux said, "I do. 'A king must know his given name.'"

"Arthur," Mason said. He thought for a moment, then added, "Arthur Pendragon. Both of his names are essentially given names."

" But Pendragon is a surname," Xanadeux said.

"Yes, it became that. But Pendragon was originally a title given to military chiefs wielding kingly powers."

"That's right."

"Next verse," Mason said.

"'Should he wish to receive the lady's gift.'"

"The Lady of the Lake gave Excalibur to Arthur..." Mason slowly surveyed the area. "I see no lakes though, only ocean." His eyes stopped at the giant caves. One of the large winged creatures he had seen earlier was circling the area around the caverns.

"Pendragon... Dragons live in caves." He placed the mace back into the saddle holster, mounted the black horse, and pulled its reins toward the caves. "That's where we'll find Excalibur. Let's go."

Xanadeux riding the white steed, they started down the path into the forest, spurring the horses to move as fast they possibly could.

Reaching the end of the forest, Mason and Xanadeux entered a rocky terrain covered with shrubs, brush, and a few small trees. Three gigantic caves rose up from the earth a few hundred yards in front of them, dark and foreboding. The dirt path led straight into the largest cave, located in the center of the mountain range.

Nearing the cave's entrance, they came upon a shallow pond. The horses stopped and began to drink. "I suppose we'll leave the horses here," Mason said, dismounting his steed, "and continue into the cave on foot."

Xanadeux hopped off its horse. "Are you sure this is the dragon's cave?"

Mason knelt down, picked up one of the large, platelike scales scattered about the area, and showed the shedded piece of reptilian skin to the android. "Positive." He tossed the scale aside, and drew the mace from the horse's saddle. "Do we have any torches?"

Xanadeux searched its horse's saddlebag, pulled out two sticks of resinous wood, and replied, "We do." It grabbed a handful of small rocks from the same pouch. "And also some flints."

"Good." As Xanadeux struck the flints against the hilt of its sword, Mason walked over to a glistening pool of water which had formed in a hollowed tree stump. Peering into it, he saw a perfectly still, crystal-clear surface which reflected his kingly image like an aqueous mirror. The water then began to ripple, his reflection shimmered, and the image of Ashley dashing into a car appeared. "Xanadeux, come here!" Mason shouted.

Xanadeux ran over to him, two lit torches in its hands. "What is it?"

"This pool..." Mason said, as he watched some type of simian crossbreed jump onto the hood of the car, which he now recognized to be McCready's Polaris™. "Ashley's still in danger. The creature's breaking the deal."

"Actually, sir, it's not," Xanadeux said. "The Presence only said it would leave your family alone *if* you won the challenge." On

220

the water, the image of McCready's car, falling to the ground below and exploding. "And we've yet to do that."

"True," he said, relieved to see Ashley and McCready running away from the car's flaming wreckage. He looked up from the realtime window. "Let's get to it then."

Xanadeux handed him a torch, and they marched into the daunting, darkened cave. It was damp and musty, the earth soft and muddy beneath their feet. The temperature was cool, though an occasional warm, sulfuric breeze blew from somewhere up ahead. The rustling of bats, rats, and other cave-dwelling creatures could be heard all about, in addition to other, unidentifiable sounds. The torches provided enough light for them to see the path ahead, a bit of their periphery, but none of the roof above. How high the cavern rose, they could only imagine.

Deeper and deeper they moved into the cave, passing skeletons, ragged remains of clothing and armor, and the occasional piece of treasure. They often saw smaller, divergent paths, but since none of them were really "dragon-sized," they chose to remain upon the larger, main path.

As the cave grew warmer, and the sulfur smell became stronger, Xanadeux came to a halt. "Do you hear that noise?"

Mason stopped and listened. "Yes," he said. "It sounds like...like smacking."

Moving in the direction of the wet, noisy sounds, the light from their torches revealed a thin, greenish, wart-covered creature who was dining on the fresh remains of a human being, its long tongue repeatedly dipping into the person's cracked skull.

"A troll," Mason said, keeping his distance.

Lifting its mouth from the body's brain, the troll looked up at them with its beady, black eyes. "Them pyre...never diet," it growled, sputtering saliva-drenched gray matter down its pointy chin. "Roam and...I wander...fit dice..." It pointed a long, bony finger at Mason. "Wilt chew?" It licked the specks of tissue from its jaw.

"Let's leave it to its meal," Mason said, seeing that the deranged creature was speaking nothing but nonsense.

"Let's," Xanadeux agreed.

They continued on their way, soon reaching a slope which ascended to an area glowing with a gorgeous, golden light. Climbing the rocky incline, they came to a colossal, treasure-filled lair which reeked of sulfur, and was somehow, magically generating its own luminosity. The sweltering heat, which also had no visible source,

221

caused the jewels, coins, weapons, and other valuables to appear like a mirage. Mason stepped in, coins clinking underfoot. "I believe we've found the dragon's lair." At the far end of the den, embedded halfway into a large stone which rested atop the treasure pile, was Excalibur. "And our prize."

"And our dragon," Xanadeux added, pointing up to a monstrous red dragon perched on a ledge above.

"Congratulations," it said in a thunderous voice. "You've found the sword." It spread its leathery wings, swooped down on top of the treasure, and blocked the way to Excalibur. Blowing smoke through its nostrils, it said, "Now all you have to do is get it."

Mason cast aside his torch and quickly picked up a nearby shield, just as the dragon released a torrent of fire from its mouth. He ducked behind the large triangular shield, but could still feel the blistering, burning heat building up all around him. In realtime, the immersible increased its temperature to a near scalding level, and had it not been for the enchanted armor he was wearing within the domain, the heat would have kept increasing, and Mason would have been boiled to death right then and there.

When the dragon had ceased its fiery attack, Mason peered his head around the partially melted shield, and saw that Xanadeux was already off and running toward the sword. "Dragon!" he shouted, hoping to draw its attention away from the android. Discarding the useless shield, he again yelled, "Dragon!"

The dragon paid him no mind, its eyes fixed upon Xanadeux.

Mason hurled his mace at the reptilian creature, but the weapon harmlessly bounced off of its thick, scaly hide.

"Yes?" the dragon asked, calmly watching Xanadeux reach the sword. "Something on your mind?"

Xanadeux grasped Excalibur's handle, pulled it with all of its might...but the sword would not budge.

"Only Arthur can draw the sword, Lancelot." The dragon whipped its muscular tail into Xanadeux, rocketing the android clear across the room. "Or hadn't you heard?"

"Damn," Mason said, picking up a long, sharp spear as he watched Xanadeux crash headfirst into the treasure pile.

The dragon turned toward Mason. Nostrils flaring, it bared its vicious teeth, and said, "Your turn." It then rushed forward, its gargantuan claws digging into the golden ground, its huge wings flapping in the hot, humid air, and roared with prehistoric fury.

Mason's eyes widened, his heart raced. He quickly backpedaled toward the cave's entrance, hoping to lure the dragon outside of its lair. But when he turned to face the opening, he found that there was now a huge pile of boulders blocking the way. "Oh, no," Mason said, looking back to see the wide-open jaws of the dragon coming right at him. Realizing he had nowhere to run, Mason jumped straight into the creature's mouth, just as its swordlike teeth snapped down on the space where he had previously been. As everything went dark around him, he landed on top of a slick, wet surface, nearly slipped, but stabbed his spear into the soft, fleshy floor in time to regain his balance.

A combustive, booming sound reverberated from somewhere behind him, the smell of sulfur became terribly pungent, and it suddenly felt like he was standing inside of a broiling oven. Bright, yellowish-orange light started to illuminate from the back of the dragon's throat, then an enormous fireball exploded forth from its gullet. As the dragon's jaws began to open once again, Mason firmly gripped the spear with both hands, planted it deeper into the living floor, pole-vaulted himself high into the air, and rode the explosive wave of fire out of the creature's mouth.

Landing without injury on a cushioning mound of gold pieces, Mason swiftly scrambled towards a nearby battle axe. He grabbed hold of it, stood up, turned to face the dragon, and was rudely slammed to the ground by one of the creature's enormous feet.

Mason's head barely sticking out from the webbing between two of its toes, the dragon lowered its gaze, dripped some blood from its maw, and said, "That hurt." It increased its pressure upon him, squeezing its scaly toes around his neck.

Mason felt the immersible's fluid strangling him as his armor crushed beneath the monster's weight. He started to feel dizzy, was about to lose consciousness, when Xanadeux suddenly rushed forward and drove a long lance deep into the dragon's ear canal.

The beast howled in agony, wildly flapping its head and wings in an attempt to dislodge the implanted weapon.

The dragon's frantic motions caused it to raise off of the ground a few inches–just enough for Mason to roll out from beneath its crushing grip. Dazed, he looked up and saw that Xanadeux was still hanging on to the lance, even though the dragon was thrashing its head about in a frenzy. As the blood began pumping back into his brain, Mason took a deep breath, sprang to his feet, clenched his battle axe, and dashed toward Excalibur. He was within twenty feet of the sword in the stone, when suddenly the treasure before him rose up, magically transforming into four, armed soldiers. Gold pieces as their flesh, jewels and gems for their eyes and mouth, equipped with armor, shields, and weapons, they charged forth at Mason.

The lead soldier, armed with a cutlass and buckler, was quite sloppy, and Mason was easily able to slice his axe through its ruby eyes, reverting the animated creature into treasure. The next one, brandishing a thin rapier, wasn't much better, and he disposed of it just as quickly. The other two, unfortunately for Mason, were *much* more skilled in battle.

The soldier dressed in plate mail, wielding a morning star and shield, smashed its heavy, spiked weapon into Mason's chest, rending open his already-damaged armor. As Mason reeled back from the blow, the other soldier fired a quarrel from its crossbow at his exposed chest, hitting him in the shoulder, just below his collarbone.

The bolt's impact knocked Mason off his feet. He crashed hard into a sizeable treasure box behind him, sending splinters of aged wood flying in every direction. In realtime, the fluid had brutally forced itself through his flesh, piercing him exactly like the arrow in the domain. Mason grit his teeth, then swiftly hurled his axe at the soldier with the crossbow, just as it started to take aim once again. End over end, the battle axe raced through the air, hitting the soldier dead between its amethyst eyes before it could fire another shot. It instantly fell apart, its bodily coins jangling to the ground like a slot machine's jackpot.

The final soldier ran forward, raising its enormous spiked mace high above its head.

Wounded and weaponless, Mason had no other choice but to run. Grimacing with pain, he attempted to head in the direction of Excalibur, but before he could fully get on his feet, the armored soldier smashed its morning star into him once again. Mason tumbled into the treasure, his ribs cracked and bruised. He scanned around for a weapon, but saw only gold pieces and jewelry. He looked back at the soldier.

The armored creature stood directly over him, its morning star aimed at his head.

Mason raised his forearms in front of his face.

It swung the weapon forward.

And then an unconscious Xanadeux came flying into the soldier, shattering it into a thousand gold pieces. The spiked mace immediately fell from its grip, landing roughly one inch from Mason's head.

# ((FREQUENCIES))

As armor and gold rained down all around him, Mason painfully clambered toward Excalibur. Within seconds, he had reached the stone, but when he stretched his hand for the sword, he was smacked clear across the lair by one of the dragon's immense wings. He rapidly arced up through the air, and slammed into the pile of boulders with a dull thud. Barely conscious, Mason rolled down the rocky incline and slumped to the treasured ground, his face falling into a pile of of smooth, cut diamonds.

He heard the dragon approach him, could feel its hot, sulfuric breath as it said, "We've reached the end of the game, Arthur. Any last words?"

"Y-yes..." Mason said, his face contorting with pain as he pushed himself up with his good arm. "I..." He shakily knelt down on one knee, reached into his leather pouch, and pulled out the single buttercup. "...I humbly ask for your mercy." He gently set the flower onto the heap of treasure in front of him.

"A flower?" The dragon laughed like rolling thunder, as wisps of smoke puffed out of its mouth and nose. "All this treasure, and you expect to bribe me with a *flower*?"

"It's...it's a buttercup," Mason said, grasping his bleeding shoulder. "A...a special kind...inspired by *Alice in Wonderland*."

Unimpressed, the dragon growled, "And...?"

"And, well..." he said, as the pink flower began to sparkle, "...it's special."

A cheshire grin appeared in the air above the flower. "How are you getting along, dear dragon?" it asked, as Mason crawled behind one of the large boulders.

"Trickery!" shouted the dragon, exhaling a gust of flames toward Mason and the grin.

The heat passed deathly close to Mason, reducing the protective boulder to mere ashes.

"Are you blind?" asked the grin, which was now to the dragon's left. "I'm over here!"

The dragon whipped its head in that direction, blowing fire as it did.

"No," it said, as another grin appeared to the dragon's right. "Over here."

"I'm over here, stupid!" said the one directly in front of the dragon's face.

The dragon angrily snapped its mighty jaws at the grin.

"Over here!" another said from behind it.

As multiple grins popped up everywhere, all of them taunting and teasing, the full, black-and-white cheshire cat formed in front of Mason. "Grab hold of my tail," it said, its pencil-drawn lines starkly contrasting with the vivid, colorful detail of the Presence's domain.

The dragon took notice of the cat.

Mason grasped its soft, furry tail.

The red beast drew in a titanic breath.

Mason and the cat turned incorporeal, just as the dragon exhaled a mountainous gust of fire. The blaze harmlessly passed through their fading forms, but utterly destroyed everything else around them, turning treasure into slag and boulders to dust. The next instant, Mason and the cat reformed–right beside Excalibur.

Realizing they had teleported to the stone, the dragon quickly turned around, but it was already too late.

Mason had drawn the sword.

"No!" shouted the dragon, retreating a few steps back.

"Yes," said the cheshire cat with its enormous grin.

Mason pointed Excalibur at the dragon. "You lose." Bright, blue energy burst forth from the enchanted blade like lightning, immediately spreading itself over the dragon's frame.

The creature screamed, thunder and lightning everywhere, as its entire body became corrupted by the Excalibur virus. It began to transform into pure blue energy, trying in vain to flap its wings and fly away. It grew brighter and brighter...brighter still...and then it let out a final, earth-shaking scream.

And its light died out completely.

Mason dropped to his knees, still holding Excalibur.

"We did it," said the cat.

"We...we did," Mason said, letting out an exhausted sigh.

"And if Xanadeux and I updated the virus properly," the cat said, slinking its tail back and forth, "the Presence...well, to put it nicely..." It smiled at Mason. "Should no longer exist."

Mason slowly nodded, then looked over to the area where Xanadeux had landed earlier.

The android was shaking its head, lifting itself up from the treasure.

"Are you all right, Xanadeux?" Mason asked, clutching his wounded shoulder.

"Fine, sir." It brushed off its damaged armor as it walked toward them. "Just a tad shaken."

"But not too stirred, I see," said the cat. To Mason, it said,

"Mr. Huxton, I do believe we can call it a day."

"Indeed, Agent Takura," Mason replied, wincing as he stood to his feet. "Indeed."

When Xanadeux had reached them, the cat sat on its hind legs, extended a fore paw to each of them, and said, "Take a paw. But watch the claws–they're sharp."

Mason and Xanadeux each took hold of a paw.

"And away we go," said the cat.

The three of them began to fade from the domain, their legs first, then their torsos, then their heads, until all that remained were their mouths.

"I thought we were going," Mason said.

"We are," the cheshire grin said. "I just like the effect."

The mouths then rippled, vanished entirely, and they triumphantly exited the arena.

Game over.

$$\alpha$$

# Ω

# Chapter 13
## ((Everything Changes))

*"It is said that the only constant in life is change.*
*I understand this now, better than I ever have before."*

••

"Ms. Huxton, Agent McCready," Carter Stone said, seated across from them at the black table, an opened laptop sitting in front of him. "Please keep in mind as you answer our questions that you *are* being frequentially monitored, and we *will* be able to tell if you're lying to us."

An extremely annoyed look upon his face, McCready stared straight at the DCC agent, unblinking. Like I didn't already know that, you fuckin' cretin. Get on with it already.

"And needless to say," Stone said anyway, "lying will only make things worse."

McCready and Ashley were being detained inside one of the claustrophobic interrogation rooms located within Freemon headquarters, sitting in rigid metal chairs which were making his ass sore and his patience thinner. Behind them, a large uniview screen projected their frees so the interrogators could see a more detailed image of their thoughts.

"We just want the truth," added Janet Vegas, the butch DCC agent leaning against the table, next to Stone. "That's all."

"Alright, already," McCready said with an irritated laugh. "Get on with the fuckin' show, or the truth's gonna get hella bored and leave."

Ashley laughed.

Vegas sucked her teeth at McCready. He smiled.

Stone tried to throw a hard stare at him. "Okay, Agent McCready," he said, slowly nodding his head, "let's begin then." Stone looked down at his laptop. "Are you aware that you attacked and damaged a federal agent tonight?"

"Tonight?" McCready checked his wristcom. "It's past midnight. Don't you mean last night?"

"Fine, McCready," Stone said. "*Last* night, were you aware that you attacked a federal agent?"

"Yup."

"And are you aware that's a punishable offense?"

McCready stared up at the dull white ceiling. "Yup."

"Then why did you do it?"

"Why the fuck do you think I did it?"

"That's what I'm asking you, smartass. Answer the question."

"Because I was hired to protect Ms. Huxton," McCready said, placing a toothpick between his lips, "and your little ape-boy attacked her. That's why."

Vegas said, "But if you knew it was a federal agent who was attempting to detain her, then you also must have known that Ms. Huxton was in no real danger."

"Bzzt. Wrong answer, lady. First off," McCready said, leaning back in his chair, "since I *am* a federal agent, I know that Ms. Huxton *was* in danger at that moment. Maybe you hadn't noticed, or maybe you don't want to notice, but we 'accidentally' fuck people up all the time when we're 'detaining' them."

Both of the DCC agents had shocked and surprised looks upon their faces.

"Secondly," McCready continued, his tone doused with acid, "the terrorists who've been attacking Ms. Huxton's family have already proven that they can do so from a remote location. So it didn't seem that far-fetched to me that they may have overtaken the REX's OS and used it to attack Ms. Huxton."

"Okay," Stone said. "At least that makes some sense."

"Um," Ashley said, lifting her hand, "I'm wondering...can we just call me Ashley? I know you want to be formal an' all, but this Ms. Huxton thing...it feels like you're talking about someone else."

"The interrogation records will list you as Ms. Huxton," Vegas said. "So that's what we're going to call you."

"Okay," Ashley said. "Just thought I'd check."

"I'll call you Ashley," McCready said.

She smiled. "Thank you."

"Now, Agent McCready," Stone said, "once you had escaped from the REX, why did you ignore my attempts to contact you, and why–*why*–did you pull that stupid, reckless car-chase stunt?"

"Same reasons," McCready said. "I wasn't sure if fielding your call would infect my car's systems, and I wasn't even sure if your car was really being controlled by you. I was just trying to get Ashley to safety so I could figure out what the hell was going on. But you fuckers never gave me the chance. And besides, why the fuck were you chasing me?"

"We knew your car had cloaking capabilities," Stone said. "We didn't want to lose you."

McCready laughed. "It's not like you couldn't have asked me later. You know where I live."

"But we had no way of knowing whether or not you two were planning on disappearing," Stone said.

"Disappearing?" McCready asked, rubbing his eyes. "What the fuck would we do that for?"

Vegas stood up, her arms crossed. "Maybe Ms. Huxton could better answer that question, Agent McCready."

"Me?" Ashley said. "Why me?"

"Let us ask the questions, Ms. Huxton," Vegas said.

"Okay," she laughed. "Go ahead."

"Prior to all hell breaking loose," Stone said, "who was the man you were talking to inside the Tiger's Lair?"

"The Asian guy?"

"Yes."

"I don't know his name," she said. "He's just a guy who I've seen around at different gatherings."

McCready wanted to turn around and see her frees for himself, but since that could have made her–and him–look suspicious, he resisted the urge.

"You have no idea who he is?" Stone asked.

"Not really."

Stone studied the screen in front of him, and said, "What were you talking to him about?"

"Um, let's see..." Ashley said, her eyebrows raising slightly. "Life, death, love, frequencies...the past, the future...Zen, the present..." She smiled. "Y'know...the usual."

"You're saying you *always* have conversations like this with people you barely know?"

"Umm..." She thought for a moment, looking out of the upper corners of her eyes. "Yeah. Pretty much. Yeah."

"Interesting," Stone said, tapping out a few notes on his laptop. "Now, you say you were talking about frequencies and the past. Could you be more specific?"

"Like...?"

"Did you talk about any particular events or people...mention any names–that sort of thing?"

"Let me think." Ashley closed her eyes, breathing in slowly through her nose. She shook her head, and said, "Hm-mm. We didn't get into any specifics. It was more of a general kind of conversation...real holistic, y'know? It was neat."

Stone stared past her at the large screen, carefully scrutinizing the detailed images of her frequencies, then looked at Vegas. He lifted his eyebrows in a questioning manner.

Vegas nodded, lightly tapping her thumb against her chin as she examined the frees.

Ashley circled her index finger round and round on the table, gazing directly at both DCC agents with a look that McCready could only describe as defiant.

Stone exhaled loudly, obviously frustrated. "Okay, Ms. Huxton. Let's get straight to the point."

"Sure," she said. "Which point?"

"I think you know," Stone said.

She smiled. "You think?"

Stone squinted his eyes, and said, "During the course of the quote 'holistic' conversation you had tonight–" He paused. "Did the name 'Adrian Wellor' ever come up?"

McCready looked at Ashley.

"No," she assuredly responded.

"Have you ever *heard* of the name 'Adrian Wellor'?" Vegas asked.

"Hm-mm," she said, shaking her head. "Should I have?"

McCready turned his eyes from Ashley, his mind trying to figure out what the hell was going on. Why wasn't she telling the truth? What did she have to hide? He looked at Stone and Vegas, who were carefully studying her frees. And what were they going to do, now that they knew she was lying?

Stone closed the laptop. "Well, Ms. Huxton," he said, "it appears you're telling us the truth. I apologize for the inconvenience. You're free to go."

Confused as hell, McCready stared at Carter. Ashley knew about Wellor–so why weren't they busting her on her lie?

"Thanks," Ashley said, standing up from her chair and stretching her lower back. To McCready, she said, "You coming?"

"Actually," Stone said, "we'd like a few words alone with Agent McCready."

"Oh," she said. "Okay." She looked back at McCready. "I'll wait for you outside?"

"Nah, it's fine," McCready said, still puzzled as a jigsaw. "Xanadeux's already here, it's already hella late... You should get home and get some sleep."

"I'm a night owl, Agent McCready. I won't be asleep for a while. And besides, you're gonna need a ride," she said, painfully reminding him of N.J. "I'll be outside, 'kay?" She smiled warmly.

"Alright," he said, his mind wondering, who the hell are you? as Ashley walked past him, lightly brushing her hand along his shoulder.

As Vegas closed the door behind Ashley, she asked, "You two have a little thing going, don't you?"

"Whatever, chick," McCready said. "Just get to the point, alright? I'm fuckin' tired."

Vegas smiled, shaking her head. "You must be a bitter man, Agent McCready."

"Yup. So fuck off."

"Enough of this childish bullshit," Stone said, standing up from his seat. He placed his palms on the table, stared at McCready, slowly leaned forward, and asked, "Agent McCready, are you working for Adrian Wellor?"

"No," McCready said indignantly. "What kind of a fuckin' question is that?"

"A logical one," said Stone, quickly glancing up at the screen. "Now let me ask you something else. How long have you known Ms. Huxton?"

"Not very. Maybe forty...forty-eight hours."

"And has she done anything suspicious while you've been with her?"

"No, not really," McCready said. "I mean, the girl's a trip, for sure. She's definitely a freeker, but...whatever, right? She's got money, she's got clearance... She's free to do that."

"Is she lying to us?" Stone asked.

McCready stood up, stretching his arms. "I don't know, man.

You got the freereads, what are you asking me for?"

"You're avoiding the question, Agent McCready," Vegas said.

"Does she know about Adrian Wellor?" asked Stone.

"I-" McCready laughed. "I have no fuckin' idea, alright?"

They both stared at the screen behind him.

McCready turned around and looked at the screen. Yellow with patches of bright orange, erratic pattern changes, some occasional, tiny spiking–it was frequentially obvious he was lying.

"That's what I thought," Stone said. "You're in deep shit, Agent McCready."

He turned from the screen. "Yeah, well, I guess that makes two of us, hunh? 'Cause your ass is on the line, too," he said, pointing his finger at Stone. "You attacked Mason Huxton's *daughter*, genius. In the midst of a family crisis, no less. And then, you had the fuckin' audacity to bring her down here, badger her... And now what the fuck do you got? Jackshit, Stone. Jack. Shit." McCready snickered. "You fucked up, man, and now all you got to look forward to is a big, fat-ass, Ordosoft™-sized lawsuit."

Stone stared him down, unfazed by the verbal barrage. "We'll see about that, Agent McCready," he said. "You're forgetting this is a matter of national security. Different rules apply."

"I guess we'll see, won't we?" McCready put on his shades. "So, are you two wanting to sit around here and shoot the shit all night? Or can I go now?"

"You can go," Stone said. "For now."

"Alright then," McCready said, adjusting the collar of his trench as he walked towards the door.

Stone placed his arm in front of him. "But let me remind you of something, Agent McCready."

"What's that?"

"The *only* reason you're not sitting in a cell right now is because you pulled this stunt while you were under the employ of Ordosoft™. But that doesn't mean you're getting off scot-free. We're going to press civil charges against you for the damage you caused to federal and city property." He moved his arm out of the way. "And pending further investigation, you're being placed on suspension."

McCready moved to the door. "Whatever, man. I'm already on leave."

"Not anymore," Vegas said. "Now it's going on record as a suspension." She smiled. "Meaning your income has come to a stop."

"Well, guess what?" McCready pulled out his badge and

dropped it on the floor. It opened on impact, his picture facing up. "I quit."

"You can't just quit the Freemon like it's an ordinary job, Agent McCready," Stone said, raising his voice as McCready left the room. "There's procedure to be followed!"

"Fuck your procedure," McCready said, walking down the hallway towards Essence and Jung.

The door shut loudly behind him.

"Looks like that went well," Jung said.

"Peachy," said McCready. "How's Ignacio doing?"

"He's alright," Essence said. "They're gonna keep him here overnight, then run some tests on him in the morning."

"Did anyone call Irena yet?"

"Richardson did," Essence said. "After he diagnosed him."

"Alright, good," McCready said. "So what did the doc say happened to him?"

"He thinks he got hit with some type of disruptor," Essence said. "A mild one."

"What'd the contact records show?"

"Nothin' but static once Mo caught up to the attacker. No audio, no video–nothin'."

"Fuck," McCready said. "Well do you at least know who attacked him?"

"In a way," Jung said. "We know it's the guy who the rich girl was talking to."

"Great," he said, wondering how this day could possibly get any worse.

"But we don't know *who* he is," Jung added.

"What, he had some kind of biochip scrambler?"

"If only," Jung said. "This guy can change identities, McCready. Instantly. Holographically *and* on his biochip. He's good."

What have you gotten yourself into, Ashley? he asked himself. Hell, what have *you* gotten yourself into, Marc? "Alright," he said, "I'm outta here. I gotta go fuckin' sleep. Tell Ignacio I'll call him tomorrow, alright?"

"Sure," Jung said. "Take care of yourself, McCready."

"I'll try," he said, walking off in a pissed-off hurry. Reaching the exit, he scanned his thumb and entered the parking lot. A white stretch limo was waiting for him, Xanadeux standing beside it. "This is fuckin' surreal," he muttered as he approached the Rolls®.

"Good evening, Agent McCready," Xanadeux said, opening the rear doors without touching them.

"Yeah, right," he said with a laugh.

Ashley was seated inside of the opulent and spacious interior, a bottled water in her hand. "Hey," she said. "Everything go okay?"

"Are you serious?" he asked, slumping into the cushy seats across from Ashley.

Xanadeux shut the door behind him.

She sipped her Evian®. "That bad, huh?"

"Worse." Between them was a small table with a mini liquor cabinet. McCready opened it up and browsed its contents.

The car rocked slightly as Xanadeux seated itself in the driver's seat and shut the front door.

McCready looked behind him. There were three Xandys in the front seat, all staring directly ahead. The tinted partition began to raise. "Take me home, Jeeves," he said, just before it closed.

Ashley asked, "Wanna talk about it?"

Going back to the rummaging, McCready pulled out a tiny bottle of Jack Daniels®. "Nope." He opened the bottle and took a sip.

As the limo's engines started up, she said, "You sure?"

"Yup." He downed the rest of the bottle, set it on the seat, reached for another.

The Rolls® lifted into the air.

Twisting open a bottle of Absolut®, McCready looked out the window and watched the Beacon Hill headquarters become smaller as they ascended. He toasted the tiny bottle towards the window, touched it against the glass, and downed it all in a single swig.

"My dad said the attacks are over," she said.

He placed the empty bottle next to the other and reached for a regular-sized bottle of wine. "They caught the terrorists?"

"Apparently so."

Digging at the wine's foil wrap, he asked, "How?"

"I'm not sure. He didn't go into details."

McCready tossed the shredded foil aside. "At least that's one less thing to worry about. You got a corkscrew?"

"You don't need one."

He looked down at the bottle's top. A pull cork. He popped it off and examined the front of the bottle. "Port? This shit any good?"

"Not to me, but I don't really like alcohol."

McCready took a sip. "It's alright." Then another. "It's hella sweet, though."

235

"It's a dessert wine," Ashley said. "You really don't want to talk?"

McCready leaned back in his seat, kicking his boots up on the table. "I really, really don't want to talk." He rested the bottle on his stomach, holding it with both hands.

"Okay," Ashley said. She looked at him for a few moments, just to make sure he wasn't going to talk.

He wasn't.

She turned on some soft music, leaned back, and closed her eyes.

McCready gazed out the window at the bright city lights below, and took a long, slow sip of the port.

When the car had settled onto the ground, McCready sat forward and said, "Well, I guess this is it."

Ashley sat up. "I guess so, huh?"

The doors opened up.

"It's been fun," he said, scooting towards the exit. "I think I can honestly say..." He laughed. "I'll never be forgetting these last two days." He laughed harder as he stumbled out of the limo.

She moved to the doors. "Agent McCready?"

"Agent who?" He took another drink. "I'm just Marc now. Call me Marc."

"Okay. Marc..." She took a way-too caring hold of his hand and smiled that fuckin' gorgeous, pure smile. "Thank you."

Her touch felt amazing. And comforting. So he pulled his hand away from her. "Don't mention it," he said. He started to turn away, then turned back towards her.

Ashley's eyebrows lifted.

He was tempted to spill his guts. Open up to her, he thought. Let her in. "Ah..."

"Yeah?"

Then he remembered what happened the last time he decided to do that. Fuckin' bitch ripped his heart out. Holding up the bottle, he said, "Care if I take ol' porto with me?"

She laughed. "What do you think?"

Shrugging his shoulders, he replied, "Fuck if I know." He staggered backwards towards his house, bottle in hand.

"Are you sure you're gonna be okay?" she asked.

"Ask me tomorrow," McCready said. He turned from her, took

236

a few unsteady steps along the path, and heard the door shut behind him. As the car flew by overhead, rising up and over his house, McCready placed his fingers onto his lips, blew a kiss towards the vanishing taillights, and watched his best chance at happiness fly away into the night.

Then he went inside, got as shitty drunk as he possibly could, and passed out on his living room couch.


McCready woke to the sound of ringing.

"Wha..." he said, struggling to open his eyes. His head was throbbing.

Ringing.

He dizzily looked around the area.

It was the fucking uniview.

"Fuckin' shit."

It was early morning, he was on the couch, he had a massive fucking hangover, and there was an incoming call on the uniview. Turn the motherfucking ringer off when poisoning self with alcohol, he reminded himself as he grasped the remote control. Putting the display right in front of his blurry eyes, he touched a button.

The ringer turned off.

He put the remote down.

He went back to sleep.


McCready didn't wake up again until late afternoon, this time of his own volition. He was still groggy, but at least the throbbing in his brain wasn't so severe. And he wasn't covered in puke. That was good.

He sat up slowly, thumb and middle finger rubbing his temples, and grumbled something incomprehensible. Resting his head against the couch's cushioned back, he sat there for a few minutes, simply staring at the walls of his living room in an attempt to get a hold of his bearings.

The black-and-white, framed glossies of James Dean, Audrey Hepburn, Clint Eastwood, Brigitte Bardot, Marlon Brando–and Marilyn. Norma Jeane. Fuck. He loved that car.

A Salvador Dali print of melting clocks. Time out of joint. Him out of job.

A poster of the album cover to Earth Wind and Fire's *That's the Way of the World*. Ain't that the truth? McCready thought. He stood up from the couch, walked to the bathroom, and took a much-needed piss. It was relieving, but his head still hurt. He zipped up, and opened the cabinet above the sink without looking in the mirror. He grabbed a bottle of Tylenol®. Extra Strength. He popped a few in his mouth, drank from the sink's faucet, walked back out to the living room, plopped onto the couch. "Voice-rec on," he said.

The thin wallscreen immediately lit up. A message in its upper corner noted that the ringer was off.

"Ringer on," he said. "Who called today?"

The screen listed seven calls. Five messages. Two of them he erased without viewing–the one from a telemarketer and the one from an ex-girlfriend. The ones from Harold Moore he put on save. When he reached the one from Mason Huxton, he said, "View message."

The head of Ordosoft™ appeared on the screen, attired in a velvety robe, sitting in his breakfast nook. His face looked like it had been scratched or something. "Hello, Agent McCready," he said. "I hope your morning is going well."

McCready let out a short, audible, "Ha."

"As I'm sure you've already heard from Ashley, the terrorist attacks against my family have been remedied, and life has begun to return to normal. This was due in large part to the efforts of Agent Takura, and I wanted to personally thank you for the recommendation." He took a sip of orange juice. "I also wanted to thank you–sincerely thank you–for protecting my daughter during this whole wretched affair. You went above and beyond the call of duty, and I mean to compensate you accordingly for these sacrifices."

McCready sat up a bit.

"Your director has informed me that you've been placed on suspension, and that there are several lawsuits which are going to be brought against you." Huxton smiled. "You needn't worry, Agent McCready. You will have the full and complete backing of Ordosoft™, its lawyers, and most importantly, its finances–meaning that everything will be settled out of court in a quick and timely manner. *Without* anything going on your records."

"Alright," McCready said, "I like the sound of this. Keep going."

"Mind you, this is simply restitution, Agent McCready–not rewards. *Those* are something that I would like to discuss with you in person." He set down the juice. "Therefore, I am offering you an invitation to spend the weekend with me and Ashley in Tibet."

McCready's brow scrunched up. "What?"

"There, we can go over some of these things in detail, and you can have the opportunity to learn a bit more about Ordosoft™. It should be a...rewarding experience. For both of us." Huxton picked up a white cloth napkin and dabbed it at the corners of his mouth. "I'll be preparing for the trip most of today, but you can reach me at any time with your decision. I look forward to hearing back from you, Agent McCready. Good day."

Huxton morphed into the message display.

Somewhat stunned, McCready walked over to the fridge and pulled out a canned latté. He felt like his headache was receding, but maybe it was just that all these thoughts were suddenly displacing it. Rewards. Tibet. Ashley. Tibet? Unreal. Was he still going to quit the Freemon? Fuckin' DCC bastards. Is she really involved with Wellor? Have to call Ignacio. Wonder how Irena's doing? But Tibet? *Tibet?*

McCready walked back to the living room and sat on the couch. "Call Ignacio," he said.

Seconds later, Irena answered, looking naturally beautiful as usual. "Marc?" she said. Her face appeared concerned. "You okay?"

"Yeah," he said, a bit surprised by the question. "Why?"

"You don't look so good."

"Oh, right," he said, realizing that he must look like shit. "Long night. How are you doing?"

"Better, now that Morris is back," she said. Aurora and Esperanza ran by behind her, chasing each other. "But I'm still a little worried about him. He came home about an hour ago, and he just..." She paused. "He just didn't seem himself."

"What do you mean?"

"I-I can't really explain it, Marc. He just felt distant."

"I'm sure it's only the aftereffects of the disruptor, Irena. It takes a couple of days to get over 'em. I'm sure he'll be fine."

"Yeah," she said uneasily. "You're probably right. He'll probably feel a lot better once he's done resting."

"He will, sweetheart. I promise. But just remember it takes a while."

Irena nodded, her expression revealing that she was obviously more troubled than she was saying.

"You gonna be okay, Irena?" he asked. "You need me to come over or anything?"

She smiled. "No, it's alright, Marc. I'll be fine. My sister's gonna come by in a little, so I'll have some company. I'll be fine. But thanks."

"Alright then," he said, not entirely convinced. "But you call me if you need anything, okay?"

"I will, Marc. Thank you."

"You're welcome, Irena. And tell Ignacio to call me when he wakes up, alright?"

"Sure."

"I'll talk to you later, then. Bye-bye."

Irena disconnected, the message screen reappeared.

McCready sipped the latté, then looked to his right, through one of the living room windows. The sky was a light gray color. Overcast, but not overbearing. A contemplative cloud cover, full of possibilities.

And of course, decisions.

He looked back at the screen, at the saved messages from Director Moore. He knew he couldn't go back to the Freemon. Regardless of whether or not Huxton could fix everything. Not after her. Not after Ashley. She'd shown him things. Things new, and things he once knew, but had let himself forget. And now he felt different. About everything. He felt...felt...he *felt*. That was what it all boiled down to–feeling. Whether she had blessed him or cursed him, he still hadn't decided–but she'd changed him. That much was undeniable. She was the catalyst, she-

The uniview started to ring.

She...

The words "Ashley Huxton" blinked upon the screen.

She was calling.

McCready rubbed his fingers through his tangled hair. Was he ready to talk to her yet?

The uniview continued to ring.

Maybe he should wait and call her back–after he'd had a shower and some time to think.

Her name continued to blink.

That way he could figure out what the hell it was that he wanted to say to her. Give him a chance to put things in perspective.

Still ringing.

Let alone the chance not to look hungover. Plus, he could...

Still blinking.

He could watch the taillights fly away again. "Aw, fuck it," he said, setting down the latté. "Answer call."

The ringing stopped.

Ashley morphed into view wearing a sports bra and green

240

tights, her hands on her hips. "You're there," she said. "I was just about to hang up."

"Yeah, I was just, ah," he said, smoothing out his hair, "doing some–sorting some things out. Basically." He covered his mouth with his fist and cleared his throat. "How are you?"

"I'm good," she said. "You?"

He grabbed a lighter and a pack of Kamels® from the coffee table. "Not bad."

"Long night, huh?"

McCready smirked as he lit up a cigarette.

Ashley smiled. "Me, too." She looked down briefly, placing her hands behind her back. "I think we should talk, McCready."

He blew out some smoke while nodding his head. "Yeah. Probably should," he said. "Where were you thinking?"

"Here, I guess. Unless you wanted to go somewhere else."

"Nah, your place is cool." He tapped off some ash. "What time?"

"Whenever. I'm just gonna be here dancing, so...whatever's good for you."

"Alright. Let me take care of a few things here–shower up, get something to eat–then I'll head over."

"You don't need a ride?"

He laughed. "Actually, yeah."

"Mm-kay," she said. "I'll send my car over now. That way you can come whenever you want."

"Cool. You want me to call first?"

"Hm-mm. Just come on over."

"Alright then. I'll see you in a bit."

Walking towards the screen, Ashley smiled. "You will. Peace."

The message screen appeared again. "Uniview off," he said.

The screen went black.

With a relaxed expression on his face, McCready turned from the uniview, gazed out at the overcast skies, and enjoyed the rest of his smoke.

Light, gray puffs, full of possibility.


McCready stood at the front door of Ashley's house, staring at the swirling spiral.

The intercom turned on, but the whorl remained. Ashley's

voice said, "McCready?" The sound of water was all around her.

"Yeah," he said. "It's me."

"I just got in the shower," she said. "Come on in." The door-knob turned, the deadbolt unlocked, and the oval door opened. "I'll be out in a few minutes."

"Alright," he said, stepping into the ivy-covered hallway.

"Just make yourself at home," he heard her say, as the door shut behind him.

When he reached the row of shoes sitting next to the cylindrical wall, the second door hissed open. He took his boots off, placed them neatly beside her footwear, and entered her place, his least-raggedy pair of socks adorning his feet. The lighting inside the sphere was subtle and soft–candles, the overcast sky, and a few dimmed, full-spectrum lamps. There was background music playing, not very loud, but very present, since the music was coming from numerous microspeakers placed around the sphere. The sounds of light drumming, with a cello and a sax. From a nearby room, he could hear the flowing water from Ashley's shower.

McCready stopped at the bedroom staircase and slowly looked around the room, deciding how he was going to make himself at home. When his eyes reached the tall bookcase, he had his answer. He walked over to the curved wooden shelves and browsed some of the library's titles. He ran his finger along the spines of a row of books, past one titled *Valis*, another called *The Man in the High Castle*, and pulled out a tattered hardcover volume whose spine read: *Pools–Collected Reflections*. He opened its yellowed pages and scanned its table of contents.

"Still Waters." Page 5. "Nothing Can't Happen." Page 41. "Silent Majority." Page 88. "Behind the Sphere." Page 113. "Reality, Inc." Page 139.

McCready turned to page 88, and began to read the first page of the story.

An unshaven, but neatly dressed man is pacing around a room. His face shows signs of distress and conflict, his movements emulating these same conditions, fists clenching and unclenching repeatedly. The room also mirrors his state, books and clothes strewn about chaotically. He looks at the desk sitting in the far corner of the room. A wire-bound journal sits upon it, open and ready to be filled with the thoughts from his mind. He walks over to the desk and seats himself at the chair in front of it. He picks up a pencil. The writing begins...

My name is Phil Martin. I'm a writer. I'm thirty-two years old, single, and living in Atlanta, Georgia.

And oh yeah, I'm in deep shit.

Like deep enough to suffocate me.

I write science fiction. Alternate realities, possible futures, that kind of thing. Visions of what may come or what might never be.

McCready turned the page and skipped ahead.

After two years of writing, I finished it, and many rejection letters later, the novel was picked up and eventually published. It didn't do as well as I had hoped, but some people did pick it up.

The wrong people.

Now I'm forced to make a huge decision, one that will affect my life forever. But I'm getting ahead of myself here. Let me tell you about how it all began, or rather, me being a writer, why don't I tell you a story about how it all began? It's the story of this guy, Marty Phillips we'll call him, who sets out to write a novel to open people's minds...

Feeling the dryness in his throat, Marty Phillips reached into his backpack and pulled out his water bottle. He drank for a few seconds, wiped his mouth, then returned the bottle to the pack. It was Tuesday and business was fairly slow at Disc Haven.

Sensing a long intro, McCready jumped ahead a few more pages.

243

The ride went by quickly. Marty was removed from the car and taken up what felt like a neverending flight of stairs.

Finally, they came to a door. One of the men opened it. They entered.

An old, gruff voice stated, "I hope your trip was as pleasant as possible. Please have a seat, Mr. Phillips and we will begin."

They sat Marty down, removing his blindfold.

Seated directly in front of him at a table was an older man. Slightly fat and slightly balding. He wore a black and white suit like the other men, but his was of a different style. The blonde man was standing behind Marty, and the mustached man was standing to his right.

He looked around the room. It appeared he was in a hotel suite. All the windows were shut, but judging from the stairs, Marty knew they were fairly high up.

The old man's left hand was moving back and forth across a hardcover book, caressing its cover. With his other hand, the old man picked up a glass filled with an amber-colored liquid, most likely alcohol, and took a sip. He then said to Marty, "Mr. Phillips, I'm sure you're wondering why you are here."

Marty nodded. "To say the least."

"Yes." The old man tapped the novel. "Your book. We found it very interesting. You have some very innovative ideas in it."

Marty said nothing.

"We especially enjoyed the chapter in which the 'villainous' government creates that new form of population control...what was it that you called it?"

Marty rubbed his eyes. "Silent Majority."

"Yes, 'Silent Majority.' An enlightening concept."

McCready flipped the page, skimming to its bottom half.

"But that's the whole reason I wrote the novel," Marty said. "To get people prepared in case you tried to do something like that. Don't you remember in the last chapter, when the protagonist explains to his friend how to defeat the strategy?"

"Yes, I remember," he said. "But there are two things you didn't take into account, Mr. Phillips. Number one, most people don't read fiction to understand their society and reality. They read fiction to *escape* from their reality." He sipped his drink. "Number two, as I said before, we are modifying the ideas to suit our purposes. When we finally implement your 'Silent Majority,' you may not even know that we are doing it. We will have modified it *that* much."

McCready heard the sound of water being turned off. He skipped to the last two pages of the story and continued reading.

"There is no such thing as a sure thing, Mr. Phillips. Only a fool believes that." The old man leafed through the pages of the book. "We always have a need for people like you."

"But if my intention was to help people, why would I start writing propaganda for you? Why would I do that?"

The old man took another sip. "You know the answer. Because of Karen. Because of your mother and father. Because you don't want anything to happen to them. You wrote about that in the first chapter."

Marty put his face in his hands and sighed a breath of frustration.

"You don't really have a choice, Mr. Phillips. But we'll let you sleep on it tonight. Give us a call in the morning and let us know your answer. I'm sure you'll make the right decision." He looked at the other two men. "Gentlemen, please escort Mr. Phillips back to his house and give him the phone number where he can reach us." He looked back at

Marty. "I needn't remind you to stay silent, Mr. Phillips. Good day."

That was last night. End of story.

Now what do I do? The only definite thing is that my life as it was before is now over. Even if their job allowed me to keep the same relationships, I'm still going to have to lie to everyone around me. My whole life will be a lie. I'd probably end up killing myself, I'd be so ashamed. I can't believe this has happened. I mean, I can, since this is the stuff I write about, but at the same time it's unbelievable. By setting out to reveal oppression and control, I inadvertently created it. And now they want me to do it intentionally.

But maybe I can salvage something out of this. Maybe I can give them ideas that I know will ultimately fail. Craft the ideas in a way to make them seem like they would work. Conceptual Trojan horses.

Yeah, right. They'd probably catch anything like that *long* before they'd ever implement it. I'm sure of that. But... What was it that the old man said again? That's right. "There's no such thing as a sure thing."

The man puts down the pencil and closes the journal. He walks over to the nightstand next to his bed. He opens the drawer and pulls out a lighter.

Walking towards the phone, he picks up the journal. He puts it and the lighter in one hand, and with the other picks up the telephone receiver. He lets it rest between his ear and shoulder, then grasps the lighter. He flicks it on. The dial tone hums. He raises the flame to the journal's pages.

They begin to burn. He puts the lighter on the desk, right next to the number given to him by the two men in black. As he dials the number, he throws the ignited journal into the metal wastebasket, watching the ideas within it burn away.

THE END

# ((FREQUENCIES))

McCready stared at the empty space at the bottom of the page. That's it? Not much resolution. And the prose wasn't anything to rave about, that's for sure.

As he closed the book, Ashley emerged from the bathroom dressed in nothing but a brown bathrobe. "What'cha readin'?" she said.

"Short story collection from some twentieth century hack," he replied, wedging the book back into place. "Never heard of him."

"*Pools*?" she asked, walking directly to the bedroom staircase.

"Yeah," he said, as he watched her wind her way up the spiral. "How'd you know?"

"It's the only short story collection in that section." Nearing the top of the stairs, she said, "I'll be right down, 'kay?"

"Yeah, sure." He walked over to the sunken center of the room and sat down in one of the large beanbag chairs. Through the half-dome skyview above, he saw that the clouds had turned a darker shade of gray. The color of rain. He molded himself into the chair, relaxed his eyes on the cloud gestalt, and waited for Ashley.

When he heard her coming down the stairs, he said, without moving from his seat to face her, "This chair's bomb."

"You look comfortable," she said.

"I am. I don't want to get up."

"Then don't." Ashley moved in front of him, seating herself on a nearby futon. She was now dressed in baggy sweatpants and an oversized T-shirt, both a similar shade of dark green. "It's good to relax." She set down a wooden cigar box on the cushion next to her, then stretched out her arms. "I know I'm ready to."

"Yeah," he said, sitting up slightly in the chair. "'Bout to fall asleep though, if I relax any more."

She smiled, placing the box on her lap. "How much did you drink last night?"

He laughed. "No comment."

She looked up from the box. "Did you get sick?"

"Nah," he said, catching a whiff of the box's herbal contents. "But I still got a fuckin' headache."

Ashley pulled out a hemp Zig-Zag®, crumbled some weed onto the paper. "You're welcome to have some herb with me. It's good for hangovers."

"Cool," he said. "Thanks."

As she rolled her joint, she said, "So... Did you talk to my dad today?"

"About Tibet?"

"Mm-hm."

"I got his message, but I haven't called him back yet. I'm still deciding."

She acknowledged his words with a nod, smoothly rolled up the joint, then delicately licked the paper. Putting on the final twist, she said, "You have any plans for the weekend?"

"Nothin' special."

She blew lightly on the joint. "You should come then."

McCready scratched his chin. "Yeah, maybe." He glanced up at the skyview. Tiny sprinkles of rain, pitter-pattering against its surface.

"Decisions..." she said, pulling a flameless lighter from the box. "Always decisions." She closed her eyes and took in a deep breath...then placed the joint between her lips, ignited the tip, and flared the embers up in slow, sensuous pulls.

McCready watched the wisps of white smoke dance and whirl as they released from the burning end, rising into the air until they were freed of their form.

Exhaling the minty vapors as if she was blowing a gentle kiss, she passed the joint to McCready.

Cigarette-sized, the smoke felt natural between his fingers. He watched it burn for a moment, then placed the moist end on his lips. He breathed it in.

Ten seconds later, the boundaries at the edge of his mind began to ebb. And flow. The flow of the music more evident now, the flow of his heartbeat too. Sensorium expanding. Senses extra marked. Sensorium, he wondered, is that a word? Fuck it. He took another pull, smoky herbal air passing over his tongue, down his throat, into his lungs. He extended the joint to Ashley. "Thanks," he said, their fingertips pressing together as the joint changed hands.

She smiled. "You're welcome." She drew in a small puff and asked, "You want anymore?"

"Nah," he said, watching the smoke curve and flow around her lips. "I'm good."

"Me, too." Reaching underneath the futon's edge, she pulled out a round ceramic ashtray. She placed the joint's cindery end into its center, then gradually put it out by tracing a spiral out to the ceramic's edge.

As she set the ashtray back under the futon, he asked, "What is it with you and spirals?"

"Me and spirals?" she asked with a laugh. "What is it with you and Marilyn?"

"Nah, c'mon," he smiled, "I asked you first. They're everywhere. What's the deal?"

"Well, let's see," she said. "To put that into words..." She licked her lips. "The spiral, to me, is like...the best visual representation of whatever infinity, life...Goddess and forever is, y'know?" She concentrated, her eyes squinting slightly. "Like a two- or three-dimensional representation of everything." She touched one of her silvery earrings, two spirals shaped into an "s," then glanced at him with a smile. "That's about as good as I can do with words."

Tripping off her response, he said, "Good enough. Shit."

"So what about you?"

"What about what?"

"Marilyn," she reminded him.

"Oh, right," McCready remembered. He tried to concentrate, but his thoughts were becoming more tangential. "I'm not sure, really..." He latched onto the closest tangent, saying, "She *looks* cool. That's one thing I can definitely say. She's visually appealing." Suspending from the first tangent, he reached for another. "But, ah, beyond that...I don't know. It's just that whole era or something. It's like beautiful and tragic at the same time. And I guess she represents that." He shrugged his shoulders and laughed. "Whatever that means."

"It means what it means, y'know? It is what it is."

McCready nodded and smiled, no verbal reply necessary.

The raindrops' sound as poetry. Horns and strings conversing. Stories written upon each other's faces.

No words needing to be said, and yet...

"Damn," he said, leaning forward. "I wish there wasn't so much shit going on right now." He stared down at the patterns of movement shaded into the thick carpeting. "I want to be able to relax and just kick back, but I got all these fuckin' questions runnin' around my head. About the attacks, last night at the club..."

"Me?" she intuitively asked.

"Yeah," he said. "And about you."

"I understand. I'd be curious, too."

He nodded. "So where do we begin?"

"I don't know...just ask the first question that comes to mind."

"Alright." Different things he wanted to know, but out came the initial doubt, "Did you have anything to do with the attacks on your family?"

Emphatically, she answered, "No," her face revealing her repulsion to the notion. "Have you *really* been worried about that?"

"Not really. But the thought had crossed my mind," he said, neglecting to mention Mason's influence on the query.

"Wow," she said with a small laugh. "Attacking my own family...that would be pretty crazy. I'm almost afraid to ask, McCready, but..." She looked at him carefully. "What else have you been wondering about me?"

He thought for a moment, and said, "Last night, with the DCC, why di-"

"Okay," Ashley said. "Hold up. Before we talk about last night... I need to know if I can trust you, McCready." She stared him right in his eyes, and said, "Straight up–tell me now, and look at me when you do. Can I honestly, truly, trust you?"

Without wavering, McCready met her gaze, and said, "Yeah. You can trust me."

Ashley continued staring into him, then nodded her head. "Okay then," she said, her eyes no longer checking his. "Ask away."

McCready gathered his thoughts, and said, "Last night, why did you lie about Adrian Wellor?"

"What makes you think I lied?"

"You said you'd never heard of him, but I saw his name in that sketchbook over there," McCready said, pointing to the same one he'd looked through yesterday. "So that means either you've never seen the pages inside that book...or you're lying. Why?"

"Why?" she said. "Maybe because I think my thoughts should be my own. Because I think the 'authorities' don't need to know *everything*." She paused. "Because *I'm* still trying to figure out what's happening right now..."

"Alright," he said. "Fair enough. But can you at least try to give me *some* sense of what's goin' on with you? 'Cause this shit is confusing the hell out of me, Ashley. I mean, you're talking to people who the DCC is after–the *same* ones who happened to have attacked my best friend–you obviously know something about Wellor, you're fooling the fuckin' freereads..." A short laugh, and he said, "What's the deal, sweetheart? What are you involved in?"

"I don't know. It's like I'm telling you...I'm still not sure." She stood up, running her hands through her long brown hair. Gazing down at the floor, she said, "It's...it's like I've always been on the fringes of this...this *something*. This feeling, this movement. It's like an undercurrent of change that I've always sensed, but I've only been getting my feet wet in it, y'know? I've only been playing around its edge." She paused. "But now the current's rising, McCready..." She looked up at him. "And I think I just started swimming in it."

"Swimming?" he asked. "Or are you being swept away?"

"No, I'm swimming. There's no doubt about that." Sitting down on the futon, she smiled. "I'm just not sure where the current leads."

Precipitation falling harder now, rivulets of rain running along the skyview above them.

"Alright, so let me try to get this straight." He paused, the webbing of his left hand on his brow, attempting to piece the puzzle Ashley together. Fragments of evidence, waiting to be joined...

The sketchbook. "Something has made you want to look into Adrian Wellor," he said, "or else you wouldn't have been asking yourself where he is. The fact that you *don't* know where he is, means you aren't that involved with anything he's doing." He looked at her. "Am I close?"

"Yeah," she said.

"Good."

Two more fragments: the rapper and Jung's update about the identity changer. "So you go to the Tiger's Lair, looking for information. You talk to the guy in the robe because you know he has some connection to Wellor."

"Actually, I didn't know for sure. I just knew he was someone who knows things."

"That's pretty lucky," he said, somewhat skeptical.

"Yeah, I know. But that's been the theme of my week, McCready. Synchronicity after synchronicity...things just keep on falling into place. It's bizarre."

"I guess so." His tongue moved around his cottony mouth. "You care if I get some water?"

"I'll get it. I need some, too."

As she moved over to the kitchen cove, he said, "So now, the rapper–he's the same person as the guy in the robe, right?"

"Right," she said. "And you think he attacked your friend."

"That's what the evidence says."

Pouring two glasses full of water, she said, "I don't think he did it, McCready. It's not his way." Glasses in hand, she walked back over. "Seer's not a violent person."

"Anybody can get violent when they're cornered."

"Maybe." She handed him a glass. "But I doubt it."

McCready took a big sip of the ice-cold water. "Oh, man, that's good. I had some serious fuckin' cottonmouth. Thanks."

"Mm-hm," she said, taking a drink. "So is your friend gonna be okay?"

"Looks like it, yeah. Fortunately. He's just gonna need some rest."

"That's good, at least." She paused momentarily, then said, "McCready...do you know why they want Wellor so bad?"

He shrugged his shoulders. "They probably think he has something to do with the riots. That's what they were flying in from D.C. to investigate."

"Hmm... So what are you guys taught about Wellor, anyways? What do the Freemon records say?"

"Not a whole helluva lot," he said. "Just that he was one of the scientists involved in the creation of the freereads...and that at some point, he turned seditious and went underground."

"That's all they say?"

"Basically. I mean, they also talk about how they pulled his files from the public database and what not, but that's just general stuff. That applies to anyone who's been labeled an enemy of the state."

"Wow..." she said, shaking her head. "So you guys don't even know."

"Know what? What are you talking about?"

"A conspiracy, McCready." She laughed. "A really, big, huge fucking conspiracy."

"Which is...?"

"Wellor wasn't just involved with the the frequency emission technology–he created it."

"History says it was Michael Brennan."

"Yeah," she said. "But history's bunk."

"Well, yeah, I'm not gonna argue with you on that one," he said. "But, ah, in Brennan's case...that's sort of like saying Einstein didn't come up with the theory of relativity."

"Maybe he didn't."

McCready laughed, then finished off his water with one large gulp. "So where did you hear about this conspiracy?"

Completely serious, she said, "From Michael Brennan."

His brow wrinkled. "*What*?"

"Yeah," she said. "I met with him the day before yesterday,

and he..." Her voice trailed off, her body language revealing that she was still trying to comprehend the situation. "He spilled it all to me."

"Are you sure it was actually him?"

"What do you mean?"

"It could have been one of Wellor's group in holographic disguise."

Ashley put her finger on her lip, much like her father would. "I guess anything's possible, but...it had to have been Brennan. I'm positive. It was him."

"And you think he was telling you the truth?"

"Yeah. I don't see any reason why he'd lie to me. There'd be nothing for him to gain," she said. "Not to mention the fact he's been a friend of the family for as long as I can remember. It just wouldn't make any sense for him to lie."

"Trippy," McCready said, the implications of her words mingling with the herb to make him feel extra budded. "But why did he decide to leak the truth now? After all these years?"

"I think it was just time. He's getting old, and I think he's scared of dying with all that guilt. Telling me was like...like a way to purge himself, I guess."

"That is fuckin' trippy." He rubbed his eyes and laughed. "This world is *so* fuckin' nuts, Ashley. It never stops."

"I feel you," she said, picking up the lighter and the joint. "Fully."

"Oh well," he surrendered. "Whatever. Fuck all the nonsense and all the bullshit. Fuck jobs, fuck terrorists, fuck the DCC–you're here, I'm here, the vibe is cool..."

Ashley handed him the joint, holding in the smoke with a smile on her face.

"So let's just have a good fuckin' night," he said, then took a strong fuckin' hit. Holding it in, he smiled, and added, "Alright?"

Ashley laughed as she exhaled. "Alright."


Minutes flowed into hours, moments into montage...

"What if," Ashley said, breathing out the joint's final hit. "Do you ask yourself 'what if' questions a lot?"

"Like 'what if your life is just a dream' kind of shit?"

"Mm-hm."

"Oh yeah," McCready said. "For sure. You, too?"

Ashley laughed. "Constantly."

"Were you just thinking of one?"

She nodded. "A second ago, when I was talking to you, I started thinking, 'what if I'm saying something *completely* different than what I think I'm saying? What if the words coming out of my mouth aren't the same ones I'm hearing in my head?"

"I know what you're saying," he laughed. "I've tripped on that before." He paused, then laughed again. "I remember one time, when I was about...fourteen, I think...no, fifteen–it was fifteen. Anyway, I had this one 'what if' that just kept trippin' me out for days."

"What was it?"

"Well, it was one day in class, when we were learning about the EM spectrum and gravity-shielding, and I just started trippin' on 'what if somebody built this big fuckin' GS device around the Earth?' One that totally shielded the planet from gravity's effects. Like utterly and completely shielded it."

"Sounds like you were a little freeker," she said.

He smiled. "Yeah, so like for days, I had these nightmares about people and animals, and oceans and cars, and just fuckin' *everything* floating up into the sky, and then into space, and..." He laughed. "Now it's just fuckin' funny to me, but, back then...man, that shit freeked me out."

"Yeah, they freak me out, too," Ashley said.

"I hate 'em," he added, as they stepped out into the forested backyard of Ashley's estate. "They're fucked up. I had to use one a few years back with this one girl I was dating 'cause she was so paranoid about germs. Every single time we had sex, I had to put one on. It was fuckin' brutal."

"I take it you two didn't last long?"

"Nah, not at all. It ruined the whole experience." He chuckled, kicking a pine cone out of his path. "This one guy I knew when I was on the force, he had the absolute best fuckin' line I have ever heard about condoms. He said that wearing a condom is like eating your favorite food with a balloon on your tongue."

She laughed. "That's good."

"Yup, that pretty much sums it up." He looked up at the darkening sky. "I can't even imagine what sex was like before the AIDS vaccine."

"AIDS," she said, shaking her head. "Don't even get me

started on that one."

"Why not?" he asked, pulling out a pack of smokes.

"It just pisses me off," she said. "It was such an obvious example of genocide and no one even talks about it. They always try to pretend like it was Mother Nature's way of controlling the population. Bullshit, y'know? If nature wanted to halt human growth, she would have started AIDS in Europe or America, *not* Africa. And she would have started it in the cities, not the forests."

"So you think it was gengineered?"

"Oh, no doubt," she said. "They've been using viruses to control human and animal populations for like hundreds of years now. I mean, doesn't it seem a little shady to you the way the vaccination suddenly appeared *after* the AIDS virus had decimated the African population, after the malls were set up, after the gates...?"

He ashed his cigarette. "Shady as venetian blinds."

"The whole thing's shady. It's just a big fuckin' con," McCready said, seating himself on one of the bar stools. "There's no such thing as security and convenience." He popped an orange slice into his mouth. "But they'll keep selling 'em to us anyway."

"That's 'cause we buy them up," Ashley said.

"Exactly. That's the problem. We're too gullible or lazy not to see through it, and then these world controllers, these con artists, they're always finding new ways to make the scam seem more appealing. 'Buy this device to make your life easier,' they're telling us. 'Pass this law and you'll be more safe,' or 'move in behind the gates and you'll be more secure.' But it's all bullshit. They know no matter how many gates they put up or how many laws they pass, we're still not gonna be any more safe or secure, 'cause *they're* the ones who are making the poverty and creating the fuckin' crimes in the first place."

"True," she said, biting into a kiwi.

"It's ridiculous. I'm tellin' you, Ashley, without security and convenience, society as we know it..." He peeled off another orange segment. "Falls apart."

"I don't mind," Ashley said, sketching something onto the tablet. "Go ahead and ask me."

McCready looked at her inquisitively. "How'd you fool the freereads?"

She smiled. "You won't believe me."

"Try me."

"Okay." Her pencil moving in smooth, wavy lines, she said, "It's a technique someone taught me."

"Seriously?"

"Yeah. It's kinda like meditating."

"Well," he said with a laugh, "you were right–I don't believe you."

She shrugged her shoulders. "Told ya."

"She told him," Ashley said. "She gave him fair warning, but he didn't listen." She smiled, shaking her head. "And so the second he reached his hand around her thigh and touched that sensor she installed...the alarm went off." Ashley laughed. "*Really* loud. It was hilarious."

"I bet," McCready laughed. "Right in the middle of the fuckin' movie. Damn, he must've felt stupid."

"Yeah, he did. He just sat there for a minute, not sure what to do. Then he got up and left."

"Did they talk again?"

Ashley smiled. "Nope. In fact, after that, he couldn't even face her in the hallways any more." She sifted through the contents of the cigar box. "Which was just fine with Dawn. 'Cause even then–even at sixteen–she demanded respect. And she was always smart enough and strong enough to know how to get it. Which is probably why she's done so well in Hollywood..." Ashley paused, then said, "Hey–I just thought of a freeky 'what if.'"

"Yeah?"

"Mm-hm."

"Alright then. Let's hear it."

"What if..." She looked him in the eyes with a playful grin. "...we were just characters in a movie? Or a book?"

"Well," McCready said, "then whoever wrote my life story had a lotta angst or something."

Ashley laughed. "Okay, so," she continued, still smiling at his comment, "if we were just characters in a movie, then that would mean an audience was watching us *right* now, talking about them and how they're watching *us* talking about them." She placed a joint between her lips. "It'd be a weird infinity effect, wouldn't it?"

"Now, watch this," Ashley said as the lights dimmed down. She touched a few more buttons on the holographic remote, and the skyview above started to glow with thousands of psychedelic hues. The pouring rain reacted with the colors, forming infinite droplet patterns across the sensitive surface, as the sound of every single raindrop was transmitted through the room's speakers.

"Whoa," he said, easing back into the beanbag and taking a toke. "That's fuckin' sweet."

Ashley laid back on the beanbag next to him, their shoulders touching together, and said, "Yeah. Chaos is beautiful, isn't it?"

"It is," he said, the misty rain sprinkling lightly upon his face.

They stood on the balcony of her Kremlin-like tower, staring out into the night sky at the city lights, the adsats, and the air traffic laid out before them.

"Even though it's all crazy," he said, "there's still something beautiful about it. There's no denying that." His eyes passed over the full moon, which currently had the red Coca-Cola® wave projected across its surface, the slogan "Always Coca-Cola®" written around its lower rim, then he looked over at Ashley and said, "I'm having a good time tonight."

She smiled, moved in closer to him. Leaning her head against his shoulder, she said, "Me, too."

He placed his arm around her, and they continued to watch the night unfold.

Unfolding the blanket beneath her down pillows, Ashley shifted, causing the water beneath McCready to roll from one end of the bed to the other, gently rocking him back and forth. As she wrapped the crocheted blanket around herself, she looked down and said, "I still miss her so much."

"Yeah," he said, petting one of the cats sharing the spacious waterbed with them, "it's hard to lose a parent." He thought about being nine years old. "Real hard."

She studied his face for a moment, and said, "You sound like you're speaking from experience."

He nodded slowly, surprised he was doing so.

"Recently?" she asked.

"Nah," he said, rubbing the edge of his sleeve. "It happened when I was nine."

"Your mom or your dad?"

"My dad, he, ah...he..." His lip quivered slightly. "He got taken away. Right in front of me an' my mom. They fuckin' smashed the door in..." He cleared his throat. "And they fuckin' took him."

"Oh my Goddess," she said, covering her mouth with one hand, holding his hand with the other.

"They killed him, Ashley. Those fuckers killed him."

She placed her other hand on top of his, and said nothing.

"And you know what's so fuckin' sick about it all? What makes me so fuckin' sick I just wanna die sometimes? I..." McCready struggled to let out the words. "I fuckin' became one of 'em, Ashley. I became the thing I hated most." He breathed out hard through his nostrils. "I became a Freemon."

She gently placed her hand under his chin. "But then you quit, McCready. You changed. You're *not* that anymore."

McCready looked away from her, shook his head, stared at the pyramidal walls through bleary, tired eyes.

"You took the first step," she said. "And now all you need to do is forgive yourself...and accept. Life doesn't always make sense, believe me, I know..." Her voice cracked a little. "'Cause I'm still trying to understand why my mom was taken away... But life happens the way it does for a reason. It really, truly does." She grasped his hand. Comfortingly.

He looked back at her.

Bittersweetly, she smiled, saying, "And when someone dies... It just means it was time for their energy to change form...and time for their life vibrations to change their frequency." She closed her eyes, breathed in deeply. "But they're still part of the life spectrum, y'know? Forever." Her eyes opened, sparkling, shining with life. "That's what's so beautiful." A tear trickled down her face, around the corner of her smile, and she said, "Nothing ever really dies...it just changes."

And much to his amazement, McCready started to cry. The most genuine, heartfelt cry to come out of him in a long while. Years of cynicism and apathy melting away in the hopeful glow of her eyes. A timeworn veneer of indifference dissolved by inspiration.

He felt exhilarated. But also exposed.

Unmasked. Bared.

And she could tell. So she smiled back reassuringly.

Soothingly. Lovingly.

Instinctively, driven by the desire to comfort her as much as the want to be comforted himself, he slowly leaned forward, closed his tearing eyes, and touched his lips to hers.

Passionately, they kissed.

# ((FREQUENCIES))

Both looked into the other's eyes for the briefest of moments, and then like polar opposites coming together, they embraced each other tightly for what felt like a magnetic eternity.

Human electricity combining, positive and negative currents flowing as one. Polarity reversing within him.

Nothing dying.

Everything changing.


An eternity later, they lay next to each other, a light silk sheet draped over their naked bodies.

Her inner thigh resting comfortingly on top of him, Ashley kissed him softly on the cheek, and said, "So...are you gonna be okay?"

"What?" he asked.

"I asked you that last night, and you told me to ask you tomorrow." She smiled. "Tomorrow's here. Are you gonna be okay?"

McCready smiled, laughed a little, and nestled the back of his head into the soft down pillow. "Yeah," he replied. "I'm gonna be fine."

# Ω

# Chapter 14
# ((The Wizard of Is))

*"It is time.*
*I must go away, far away, on a journey which shall lead me to my*
*salvation.*

The front door slid open, revealing a nicely decorated, though not too tidy, living room. Rumpled blankets strewn across the black leather couch, beer and latté cans on the glass coffee table, and a gorgeous hardwood floor in need of a good vacuum.

McCready looked at Ashley, scratched the back of his neck, and said, "Excuse the mess. I, ah..." He laughed as he walked into the house. "Wasn't really expecting to have company."

It was Friday morning, and the sun was shining.

"Don't worry about it," she said, following him inside. "I wasn't expecting you to expect me."

"Yeah, even so, it's still a little embarrassing." He moved over to the coffee table and scooped up the empty cans with both hands. "Place looks like a pig sty."

"C'mon," she said, nudging him as he walked towards the kitchen. "It's not that bad."

Arms full, he reached the recycler, dropped the cans in, and gave her a halfcocked smile. "It is. But thanks for trying." Rounding up some stray dishes, he asked, "You want anything to drink?"

She shook her head as her eyes passed over the room's 20th century-themed decorations. "Hm-mm. I'm fine."

"Alright then," he said, moving back into the living room.

"I'll just go ahead and throw my shit together real quick and we can bounce out of here." He passed by her and began to walk down the hallway. Stopping suddenly, he turned around and said, "I still can't believe I'm going to fuckin' Tibet."

"Yeah," she smiled. "You're going to fuckin' Tibet."

McCready shook his head and laughed. "Crazy." Turning back around, he continued down the hallway, still laughing.


The SST's door slid open, just as they reached the top of the stairs leading up to it.

"Good morning," Xanadeux said. "Welcome aboard."

"Thanks," Ashley said, stepping into the plane's spacious interior.

"Yeah, thanks," McCready said.

"My pleasure," the Xandy replied. To Ashley, it said, "Your father is in the rear of the aircraft."

"As usual," she said as they entered the lobby, which was beautifully decorated with rugs, couches, chairs, paintings, chandeliers and more, all specially designed for air travel.

"And he'd like you to join him before takeoff," it added.

"Okay," she said.

"This is a fuckin' baaadass plane," McCready said, pushing his fingers into the soft, cushioned material of one of the couches. "You guys fly in style, I gotta say that."

Walking to the bar, she said, "Yeah, it definitely beats coach."

"Can I get you something to drink?" asked the Xandy bartender.

"Just cranberry juice," she said. "On ice."

It turned to McCready. "And you?"

"How about..." He looked around at his surroundings. "How about a martini?"

"This early?" Ashley said.

McCready smiled. "Seems fitting."

As the Xandy at the bar prepared the drinks, the one who greeted them motioned towards a set table and said, "Breakfast will be served at the dining table once we've reached our cruising altitude. In the meantime..." It bowed its head towards them.

"Enjoy," said the Xandy at the bar, setting their drinks down on the counter.

"I plan on it," McCready said, grasping his martini glass by its thin glass stem.

Ashley picked up her juice and moved past a spiral staircase, towards the door at the far end of the room.

"What's up there?" McCready asked, pointing upstairs.

"Stargazer lounge," she said. "We'll go up there after we say hi to my dad."

"Sounds good to me."

The door slid open as they approached, revealing the aircraft's conference room. Fittingly, it had a very businesslike atmosphere–sparsely decorated, with thin uniview screens on its walls and a round meeting table in its center. The table, which prominently displayed the Ordosoft™ logo across its sleek, shiny surface, was surrounded by twelve executive chairs.

Passing through the room without stopping, they reached the tail of the aircraft. It was just as palatially decorated as the lobby, though a bit different in shape and design. A giant, transparent window formed the entire back end of the tail, providing a perfect view of the airstrip and mountains behind the SST.

Her father sat in an emerald, king-size armchair, his back turned towards them, facing the view. "You're here," he said. The throne-like seat began to rotate in their direction. When it faced them, the chair's motion stopped, and he stood up from it with a pleased expression on his face. "It's good to see you both." Walking towards her with a slight limp, he said, "Ashley." He placed his cheek next to hers, kissing towards her, his lips not touching her skin. "It's so good to see you safe."

"You, too," she said. "How are you feeling today?"

"Much better. Thanks to the nanotech therapy, I'm nearly one hundred percent." He looked at her for a moment and smiled. "Thank you for asking." He extended his hand to McCready. "And Agent–rather, I should say, *Mr.* McCready..." They shook hands. "I'm pleased you could make it. You're in for a quite a treat this weekend."

"I'm looking forward to it," he said.

"Splendid." Her father looked at them both. "Will you be joining me back here for takeoff?"

"Actually, I'm gonna show him the stargazer," Ashley said.

"Very well. Then I'll see you both at breakfast."

"You will." Ashley turned to McCready. "C'mon. Let's go upstairs."

"Alrighty," he said, munching on the martini's olive. "Lead

the way."

As the SST's engines hummed louder, they walked through the conference room, then climbed the stairs leading to the top floor. "Here we are," she said upon entering the stargazer lounge, which contained, among other things, recliners that allowed its occupants to stare up at the transparent ceiling. "Where do you wanna sit?"

"The middle," he replied.

Ashley moved to one of the comfy chairs in the center, set her drink into in the armrest's cupholder, and said, "Good choice."

McCready finished off the remains of his drink and sat down next to her. "Do these recline all the way?"

Leaning back all the way in her chair, she smiled. "Of course."

"Epic," he said, joining her in her reclined position as the aircraft began to move.

The sky above was blue, with lots of puffy white clouds scattered about. "I love this kind of sky for takeoff," she said, watching the cumulus shapes pass by.

"I can see why."

"Please prepare for takeoff," Xanadeux announced over the loudspeaker.

"You gonna wear your seatbelt?" McCready asked.

"No," Ashley said. "You?"

"Nope."

The plane started to move faster, as did the clouds above.

"Here we go," she said.

"Alright," McCready said, as the SST rose up from the ground and her stomach dropped slightly. "We're off to see the wizard."


The aircraft reduced its altitude and speed as they reached the Himalayas of southeast Tibet, skimming over the snowy, jagged peaks which topped the spectacular mountain range.

Standing in the lobby before one of the large lookout windows, Ashley, McCready, and her father gazed out at the breathtaking view below.

"Goddess," Ashley said, watching a herd of yaks move across the wintry landscape. "Nature is amazing."

"Indeed," her father said.

McCready was simply speechless.

They passed over summits and lowlands, villages and

towns, bridges and monasteries, surveying the sacred land from their heavenly viewpoint. When they reached the valley where her grandfather's retreat was located, Ashley pointed down to it, and said to McCready, "There it is."

A magnificent, gleaming city nestled into the snowy terrain, encapsulated within a gigantic iridescent dome. Completely protected from the harsh elements, it contained within its barriers small jungles, forests, and deserts, all aesthetically interwoven into the fabric of the city, all sustained by the magical technology wielded by her grandfather.

"Spectacular, isn't it?" Mason said.

McCready nodded. "Fuck yeah, it is."

The plane further reduced its speed as they neared the winter wonderland. Ashley said, "It always reminds me of one of those little Christmas-scene bubble-toys you get when you're a kid...the ones that you shake up and watch the snow fall." She smiled. "Except all the snow is on the outside of this one."

A portal in the dome swirled open, allowing entry.

"And you can go inside it," McCready added, as they entered the city's airspace.

Joined by two security-escort vehicles, the SST switched to its GS mode, circled around the area, and, utilizing its VTOL capabilities, descended onto a wide landing pad near the outskirts of the desert domain.

When the aircraft came to a complete rest, her father let go of the gold, overhead handrail, and said, "Here we are."


Outside the SST, the desert air was warm and dry, and the artificial sun was shining brightly. They were greeted by four crossbred security guards, each attired in a distinctive uniform reflective of the region from whence their animal traits came.

"Tashidelek," the humanoid cobra said, slithering to the fore, his skin-hood flaring out. He bowed his head, one arm across his underbelly, the other behind his back. "Tibet welcome to."

"Thank you, Dorje," her father said, as the Xandys loaded their luggage onto the open-aired SEVs. "It's good to be here."

To Ashley, Dorje smiled and said, "Long time has it been."

"Two years," she said.

"Time flies how. Welcome back."

She smiled. "Thanks."

He turned his reptilian eyes to McCready. "I've before met you not. I Dorje am."

"McCready," he said with a sup. "Good to meet you."

Dorje nodded. "You well as." He motioned back to the other guards. "Allow me my guard to introduce." His scaly hand pointing towards the antelope-like crossbreed, he said, "Kudu."

"Greetings," Kudu said, reverently bowing his head, his corkscrewed horns dipping down. "And salutations."

Dorje pointed to the next guard. "Gila."

The black and orange-skinned, lizardlike woman flicked her tongue and said, "Pleasure to meet you."

"And Canis."

The jackal, clothed in regal Egyptian dress which made him look like a living hieroglyphic, merely nodded, and uttered no words.

"We will to the palace your escort be." Dorje looked over at the two SEVs, which were now loaded with their luggage. To her father, he asked, "We shall go?"

"Let's," Mason replied, and they all began to walk towards the circular vehicles.

"We will four to a ship ride," Dorje said. "Two Canis and I with, two others Gila and Kudu with. Preferences any?"

"Why don't you take Ashley and Mr. McCready," her father said. "Xanadeux and I will ride with the others."

Reaching the vehicles, Dorje said, "It so be," and the two groups branched off.

Canis walked up the vehicle's ramp, onto its flat, circular platform, and moved directly to its center.

Dorje followed after. He slid up the ramp, turned back towards Ashley, and extended his arm. "Aboard welcome."

"Thanks." Ashley grasped his smooth, scaly hand. Always an interesting sensation–cool reptile skin with human bones beneath.

As he walked up the ramp after Ashley, McCready held up a pack of Kamels® and asked, "Can you smoke here?"

"You can," Dorje replied with a charming smile.

"Alright," McCready said, tapping out a cigarette with satisfaction. "This place just keeps getting better and better." He moved over to the four-foot railing that surrounded the circular vehicle and leaned his butt against it. Lighting up the cigarette, he looked around at the SEV's dimensions and said to Ashley, "You feel like you're on a giant coaster?"

As her father's SEV lifted off the desert sand, Ashley

laughed and said, "It does kinda look like that."

Canis gestured his hands in a sorcerous manner, causing a plantlike stalk to grow up from the SEV's center, straight out of the metal floor. It stopped growing when it reached the height of Canis' chest, then its top formed into a gelatinous, amber-colored substance the shape of a sphere.

"What?" McCready said.

Canis placed both of his fur-covered hands atop the sphere. It morphed around them, then quickly reshaped itself.

Dorje turned to McCready. "Interface organic."

Moving his fingers around the inside of the jellylike interface, Canis lifted the ship off the ground.

Though the platform barely lurched as it rose into the sky, Ashley still leaned back a little past its railing, just to test the invisible barrier surrounding the vehicle. It was soft, like a cushioning rather than a wall, gently preventing her from going back too far, while at the same time keeping the wind off of her face.

Noticing the effect, McCready pushed against it. "Cool."

As they cruised over the golden sand, Ashley could see all kinds of desert plants and animals below them. Saguaros, camels, creosote bush, saigas, tortoises... The range of species was so diverse, she imagined that a sample from every major desert of the world must have been represented there. Far off in the distance to her right, where desert became jungle, she could just barely make out rainclouds. To McCready, she said, "It's raining in the tropics right now." She pointed in the gray clouds' direction.

He took a puff from his Kamel® and moved forward. "So over there, there's all these jungle animals and plants?"

"Mm-hm."

"Underneath the same dome..." McCready blew out some smoke, the lack of air resistance causing the wisps to drift in front of him as if they were in an enclosed room. "That's fuckin' incredible." Seeing the way the smoke cleared–not a smooth dissipation, but more of an abrupt disappearance–he looked at Ashley, and said, "You're seeing that, too, right?"

She smiled. "Oh yeah. Get used to it. There's always more to come."

The city's royal palace was now visible up ahead, its domed architecture curving along the horizon. "Kinda looks like the Taj Mahal," McCready said.

"Yes," Dorje said . "Lama by that influenced was."

"Lama?" McCready asked.

"My grandfather," Ashley said.

"Your grandfather's a *camel*?"

She laughed. "Buddhist."

"Oh, right," McCready said. He laughed, then glanced at the two crossbreeds. "It wouldn't have surprised me."

"Me neither," she said, watching a coyote chase after a jack-rabbit.

"So, Dorje," McCready said, walking towards him. "Is it just you guys out here, patrolling this whole place?" He scanned the horizon. "Where are the other security ships?"

Canis looked at Dorje. They both gave each other a knowing smile.

"Everywhere security is," Dorje said. "Rest assured."


When they reached the palace, the SEV's hovered a few feet above the ground and extended their ramps.

Ashley waited for McCready to disembark, then walked down the SEV's ramp, onto the palace's marbled steps. "Thanks for the lift," she said to Dorje and Canis, who remained behind on the vehicle.

"Our pleasure," Dorje said, as the two SEV's began to ascend. "Your stay enjoy."

After Ashley joined the rest of the group–consisting of her father, Xanadeux, McCready, and Kudu–a beautiful Tibetan woman, adorned in the ochre outfit of a Buddhist lama, emerged from the palace's entrance, balancing a wide silver tray in one of her hands. Four long white scarves were draped across the tray.

"Nga-to delek," she said as she reached them. Removing her hand from beneath the tray (which continued to hover in the air without her support), she picked up one of the scarves, draped it across both of her hands, and walked over to Mason. She smiled, then delicately placed the fabric around his neck.

"Thank you, Lhasa," he said.

"You're welcome." Lhasa performed the same welcoming ritual to Xanadeux and McCready. Reaching Ashley, she said, "It's so good to finally meet you."

"Thanks." Ashley bowed her head to allow the kata to be placed around her neck. "It's nice to meet you, too."

Lhasa smiled. "I've heard a lot about you."

"Really," Ashley said, wondering to herself exactly who this woman was, since she had never seen her before on any previous visit.

Lhasa nodded. "Yes." She walked over to the silver tray and brushed her hand along its underside. The tray dissipated into the air. "Please follow me," she said. "Gonpo is being inside."

As the group started to follow, McCready drifted back to the rear with Ashley. "Gonpo is your grandfather?" he asked.

"Mm-hm," she said. "It's his honorific name."

"What's it mean?" he asked, slowing down to examine a marbled pillar which had leaves and branches growing out of it.

"Sorcerer," she said. "Or protector. He likes both translations."

Touching the palace's floral growth, McCready said, "This building...it's growing things." He looked at her. "It's alive."

"Yep," she said, beginning to move. "It has roots, too."

"Unreal," he said with disbelief, as the two of them caught up with the others.

Inside the palace's courtyard, which contained streams, waterfalls, fountains, and other types of flowing decor, in addition to a fascinating menagerie of small, uncaged animals, Lhasa led them over to a large pond filled with orange and white carp.

Across the pond, Ashley's grandfather was kneeling at the water's edge, clothed in a robe which synthesized the designs of those worn by Buddhist and Christian monks. His eyes were closed, his hands were folded together before him. He looked younger than the last time she had seen him.

"Gonpo la," Lhasa said respectfully.

Ashley's grandfather nodded his head, eyes still shut, then cupped his hands, reached into the water, and washed his face. Standing upright, he motioned his hands in a manner similar to Canis, opened his eyes, and smiled. Then he stepped out onto the water's surface, and began to walk across it.

"Jesus," McCready said, startled by the display.

The water rippling slightly with each step he took, her grandfather said, "I'm so pleased you all could make it." As he neared the water's edge, he allowed a sparrow to land in the palm of his hand. "Welcome."

"Hello, father," Mason said.

Gonpo handed the sparrow to Lhasa. "Hello, my son." He grasped both of his hands with Mason's. "How are you?"

Touching his forehead to his father's, Mason said, "Good. Thank you."

"Excellent." Gonpo looked at Xanadeux, bowed his head, did the same with Kudu, then moved over to Ashley. She held out her hands for him as he said, "Granddaughter." He grasped her hands, they touched foreheads.

"Gonpo," she said.

He asked, "How are you?"

"I am."

Gonpo smiled as he pulled his forehead from hers, nodded, and said, "Yes, you are."

"You look younger," she said.

"Do I?" he asked rhetorically. Turning to McCready, he bowed his head and said, "Welcome back for the first time."

"Thanks," McCready said, a somewhat bemused look upon his face as he lowered his head. "It's quite a place you got here."

"It is what it is," Gonpo said. He then walked to Lhasa, turned around, and said to them all, "Let us show you the rest of the phodâng. Then we will have some cha. Come."

Gonpo began to walk. All began to follow.


After the grand tour of the palace, and after the tea and lunch in the garden, Ashley was inside of her room, unpacking her suitcase's contents into the curvy wooden dresser which sat near the open window. A warm nighttime breeze blew through it, very calm and relaxing, a perfect blend of temperature and humidity. She placed the last item of clothing into the top drawer, walked over to her canopied bed, sat down, and looked around the room.

The accommodations were exactly what she wanted. Simple yet elegant, candlelit, with a minimum of objects–just a bed, a dresser, a wicker chair, a Persian rug, a jade spiral sculpture, and a colorful oil painting of a Lorenz attractor. No clocks, no univiews, no cellphones, no nonsense...perfect. A true vacation from Metropolis.

She laid back on the soft downy bed, stretched her arms and legs to their fullest, then relaxed and closed her eyes. Just about to fall asleep, she heard a knock outside her doorway.

"Ashley?" McCready said.

"Yeah?" she said, sitting up and yawning.

"Is it cool if I come in?"

"Yeah. Go ahead."

McCready stepped through the rows of green hanging beads which served as her door. Ashley's eyebrows raised. He was dressed in a silken, hunter green shirt, pressed khaki slacks, and his usual pair of tims, the leather all polished and shiny. His wet, black hair was combed back, and for the first time since she'd known him, his face was clean-shaven.

Scooting to the end of the bed, Ashley smiled and said, "Look at you."

He laughed, picked up the wicker chair, and brought it next to the bed. "Figured I'd dress nice for dinner."

"You look great."

"Thanks," he said, pulling out a pack of Old Skools™ from his shirt's front pocket. "So do you."

Ashley looked down at her casual summer dress. "I'm not even dressed up yet."

"Yeah," he said, flicking open his silver lighter, "but you still look beautiful."

She smiled as he lit the cigarette. "Thanks."

"It's the truth." He looked around the place as he took a puff. "Your room's a lot different than mine."

"I'm sure it is," she said. "What's yours like?"

He smiled. "It's fuckin' bad-ass, Ashley. I got a Wurlitzer® in there, Marilyn photos, neons, an old TV that plays nothing but old movies–it's fuckin' incredible. Is your granddad an antique collector or something?"

"Not really."

"What's up with my room then? It's so perfect."

"Yeah," she said, lightly rocking back and forth, her legs hanging over the edge of the bed, "they usually are. He creates the rooms specifically for each person."

"But how? I didn't even decide I was coming until this morning. He couldn't have had time to fly all those antiques in here."

"He didn't," Ashley said. "He created it all today."

He gave her a funny look. "What do you mean 'create?'"

"Just that. Create."

Watching the smoke at the end of his cigarette magically disappear, he asked, with a deadpan delivery, "What is this place, Ashley?"

"That's hard to say..."

"Well, what's the first word that comes to your mind?"

She thought for a brief second, then said, "Alive?"

He leaned back in the chair, breathed the tobacco in deeply. "Alright." He blew it out. "Please explain."

"Okay." Ashley tried to figure out the proper words... "This entire place, is...it's kinda like the ultimate nanotech heaven. Everything's alive and interconnected, and Gonpo can shape and mold it in any way he wants to. He's like God here." She laughed. "Or Satan, depending on your perspective."

"Holy shit," McCready said. "That's nuts. Seriously?"

She smiled. "Yep."

"Holy shit." He looked away from her momentarily. "So that's why my cigarette is burning like this? The air *knows* to turn the smoke into more air?"

Ashley nodded.

"Jesus," he said, taking another puff. "And that's why the security seems so lax–it really *is* everywhere. They weren't joking."

"Huh-unh," she said. "The moment you enter into Is, it enters into you. You become a part of it."

"Meaning that Gumpa can play God with your fuckin' molecules."

"Basically," she said. "And it's 'Gonpo.'"

"Gonpo," he quickly corrected himself. "Right." He sat forward and cautiously looked around the room. "He couldn't hear that, could he?"

She laughed. "Don't worry, McCready. Gonpo's not petty."

"You sure?"

"Yeah."

"Alright." He leaned back, taking another comfort puff. "I think it's gonna take me a sec to get used to this."

"Well, you've got plenty of time before dinner. So relax, McCready..." she said, rubbing her toes along the inside of his thigh. "You're on vacation, after all."

He smiled, nonchalantly flicked his cigarette aside, and gently placed his hand around her calf. "Thanks for the reminder," he said, softly running his hand along her taut muscle.

Watching the cigarette fade from existence before it reached the ground, she said, "You learn fast."

He moved his mouth to her bare leg. "I've got a good teacher."


McCready plunged his fork into the chop and took a large bite of the juicy, white meat.

"How is it?" Ashley asked.

Still chewing, McCready said, "Luscious."

271

Dinner had just been served in the palace's regal dining room. Ashley, her father, McCready, Gonpo, Lhasa, and Xanadeux were seated around a circular table which had been beautifully crafted into a yin-yang symbol. Each of them had their particular dinner in front of them, while the table was filled with all kinds of fruit and appetizers for them to share. Above them, dozens of GS chandeliers hung magically in the air, each one comprised of a different kind of precious gem. Around them, streams flowed, plants were, and birds sang, as Kudu played the flute, lying in a lace hammock that was attached to nothing but air.

McCready swallowed and said, "Man, this is the best fuc-" He cleared his throat. "This is the best pork chop I've ever had. No lie." Beginning to cut off another piece, he looked at her grandfather and said, "This meal is beyond words, Mr. Huxton."

Gonpo smiled. "There could be no better compliment." He bowed his head. "Tujay-chay."

"Everything is fabulous, father," Mason said, carving into his bloody-rare filet mignon.

"I'm pleased to hear that." Gonpo scooped up some baba ghannouj with a piece of pita. "Now, back to what we were discussing before we were served..."

"Okay," Ashley smiled. "I'm into that." She crunched down on a broccoli crown.

"Two sides of the same coin, you two," Mason laughed. "You both could debate up until your final breath, I swear."

"But not you?" Lhasa asked.

"I don't enjoy debate," Mason said.

"He doesn't like people to question him," Ashley added.

"This is true," Mason said.

Lhasa laughed. "I see."

"So where were we?" Ashley asked.

Gonpo said, "You had just said that you didn't see the point of immortality since there was no such thing as time."

"No," Ashley said, "we were past that."

"Autoevolution and transhumanism," Xanadeux said.

"That's right," she said, the train of her previous thought returning. "Thanks, Xanadeux."

"My pleasure," it said.

"Okay," Ashley began, "so you were essentially saying that humans have to evolve out of their bodies, right?"

"I said that intelligent life should not be *limited* to human form," Gonpo replied. "That doesn't mean we *have* to evolve out of our current form, it just means that we should not be limited by it. We should be willing to explore the possibilities that technology presents to us."

"Like uploading our consciousness into a CPU?" Ashley asked.

"Among other things," he said. "Yes."

"Aren't you worried that something's gonna get lost in the translation?"

"Not if we're using the proper technology," Gonpo said. "Everything is pure information–including ourselves–and it's simply a matter of deciphering that data and transferring it to a new host."

"That's not a simple matter," she said.

"Simpler than you would think," he said, taking a sip of tea.

"Alright, I got a question," McCready said. "Say you transfer our consciousness into a computer... What then? Would we just live inside the uniview forever, or would we live in cybernetic bodies? What would we do?"

"Anything we wanted," Gonpo said. "When immortality becomes possible, then the possibilities become endless. We'll be limited only by our imagination. We could do any of the things that you just mentioned, we could transfer our intelligence into a completely new, gengineered lifeform... Anything."

"And what would you do with the technology, father?" Mason said. "What would be your personal choice?"

Gonpo took a sip of tea, and answered, "I would upload our intelligence into von Neumann probes."

"A noble endeavor," Mason said. "Not the first thing I would choose, but noble nonetheless."

"Von Neumann probes?" McCready asked. "What are those?"

"A way to spread our infection into space," Ashley said.

"Or a way to spread intelligence throughout the universe," Gonpo countered.

"So what do they do?" McCready said.

"They build intelligent life wherever they land," Gonpo said, filling his teacup with a wave of his hand.

"That's putting it euphemistically." Ashley looked at McCready. "They're galaxy colonizers."

"Interesting," McCready said, dabbing some Tabasco® onto his fried catfish. " So how do they work?"

Gonpo motioned his hands. "I'll show you." A hologram of the Earth and its solar system appeared over the dinner table. "The idea is that these probes will be able to travel to other solar systems and land on a planet or a moon." The hologram showed multiple probes being ejected from Earth in all directions. It then followed a single probe as it hurtled its way through space. When the probe reached another solar system, it landed on a red planet, and Gonpo said, "Each probe would contain within it the most advanced molecular assemblers available, and its stored records would contain consciousness uploads from a comprehensive sample of Earthlings and their technology."

The probe opened up, released a few clouds of foglets, and created a biosphere which resembled her grandfather's. "Utilizing the planet's indigenous materials," he continued, "the assemblers would create an environment hospitable to human life..." The foglets began to create a multiracial mix of cybernetic humans. "And then they would actually begin to *build* human life. After this bio/technosphere is completed, and intelligent life is established, the foglets would then build replicas of the original probe and launch those off into the next solar system, where they proceed to do the exact same thing."

The POV pulled way back, showing the probes spreading, viruslike, throughout the cosmos. "And since the probes will be programmed with a metahuman level of AI, they will constantly evolve and update themselves and their creations as they travel further and further across the universe." As the hologram continued to mirror his words, Gonpo said, "Life will evolve into posthuman forms which we can barely fathom with our current level of intelligence. Plasmoidal humanoids, intelligent stars, suns, and planets, cognizant wavelengths, sentient cosmic rays..."

"So you wanna become the universe," McCready said.

"I want the universe to become intelligent," Gonpo said, as the POV pulled back again.

"It already is," Ashley said. "You just don't recognize it."

"I do, granddaughter. But I want to increase its intelligence." The massive stars within the holographic universe started to burn out, transforming themselves into black holes and neutron stars as its overall shape began to shrink. "Because currently, at some point in time, this universe *will* come to an end. Regardless of whether it is expanding or collapsing, its present lifespan is finite."

"And you think an 'intelligent' universe will decide to live forever?" Ashley said.

"Yes. Intelligent life preserves itself."

"That's a good point," Mason said.

"But what if the intelligent universe comes to accept the cycle of birth and death?" she asked. "What if it understands that everything exists always? Once was, will be...you taught me that, Gonpo."

"And it will understand that, Ashley," he said, as the cosmos continued to shrink. "But it won't have to accept it. It can choose to break out of that cyclical loop of forgetfulness and remember everything." The hologram became smaller and smaller. "This is a crucial step in evolution, because every time a universe reaches its omega point, it loses all of the information that was previously contained within it." The hologram turned into a single, small point, then disappeared. "All of its data is completely obliterated, and intelligent life can only *hope* that it will be recreated after the next alpha point."

The universe appeared again, as it was before the stars burned out. "But, if we avert this end," Gonpo said, "all of that infinite data is preserved. Intelligent life can evolve forever, learn forever, and the universe can become omniscient. Omnipotent. Life can become immortal within itself, and the ultimate aims of both science and religion are achieved." Gonpo waved the hologram away. "We truly become one with the universe."

"Sounds like we become God," McCready said.

Gonpo smiled. "Call it what you will." He scooped up some more of his roasted eggplant and took a bite. "Mmm..." He slowly chewed. "Food is wonderful, isn't it?"

Her father dug his fork into his baked potato. "Indeed."

"Better enjoy it while you can, daddy," Ashley smiled, moving some peas around on her plate. "'Cause God don't eat dinner."


The next morning, Ashley awoke to the sounds of singing birds.

She rubbed the sleep from her eyes, yawned, and stretched her arms into the air. Pushing the light, silky sheets from off of her, she crawled to the edge of the queen-sized bed, parted the canopy, and looked towards the opened window.

Three little birds were perched upon the sill, paying no attention at all to her movement. As they continued to sing their pure, cheerful melody, Ashley walked over to the dresser. Surprisingly, there was an old book sitting atop it. She stared at it for a moment, wondering how it got into her room. Silly question, she realized. At Gonpo's, things just happen. She picked it up.

It was a blue book with a black tape binding, much like the

ones people used to use in lab classes. There was no writing on its stained, weathered cover, so Ashley began to skim through the lined pages within. The words were handwritten in various colors of ink, sometimes cursive, other times printed–obviously a journal of some sort. She turned to the first page and looked at the inside of the front cover. In the lower right-hand corner, was scrawled the initials: "A.W."

She started to read the first page.

*Life is never quite what it seems, is it?*

*One thinks they know everything, and in the blink of an eye, the turn of a phrase...they realize they knew nothing. Their paradigms are shifted in ways which they never would have imagined, even in their wildest dreams...*

*Or their most terrible nightmares.*

*Unfortunately, circumstances surrounding the Brennan Commission have caused in this life just that–a paradigm shift of nightmarish proportions.*

*Those who claimed to be mentors revealed themselves to be Judases. Academic institutions which purported to exist for the good of humankind, showed themselves to be tools of the devil. A government claiming to pursue life, liberty, and happiness, in truth only seeks death, oppression, and misery.*

Ashley looked back at the initials.
"A.W."
Her eyes widened.
It was the journal of Adrian Wellor.
The book still in her hand, Ashley rushed through the hanging beads, out of her room.
And crashed right into Lhasa, spilling the silver breakfast tray she was carrying–and its contents–all over the floor.
"Oh my Goddess!" Ashley said, bending down and attempting to pick up some of the mess. "Lhasa, I'm so sorry!"
"Don't worry," she said reassuringly. "It's nothing."
Ashley continued to pick up the spill. "Yeah, but-"
Lhasa touched Ashley's arm. "Really." The spilled food began to disappear. "It's nothing."

Ashley looked up at her. "I guess not, huh?"

She smiled. "Are you all right?"

"Yeah," she said, standing up. "I'm fine. Do you know where Gonpo is?"

"He's in the courtyard, meditating."

"Is it okay if I go talk with him?"

"Of course," Lhasa said. "He's expecting you."

"Of course," Ashley said. "Thanks." She turned from Lhasa, and jogged through the winding hallways until she reached the palace's courtyard. Finding her grandfather at the pond's edge, meditating in the lotus position with his eyes closed, she said, "Gonpo?"

"Ashley," he said without opening his eyes. "You found the gift."

"Is this for real?" she asked, tapping on the journal. "Or is this just one of your creations?"

"It's as real as you or I."

Ashley stared at him for a moment, then asked, "How did you get this?"

Remaining within his meditative state, Gonpo replied, "How I obtained it is unimportant. What *is* important, is that you now have it."

"Okay..." she said. "Why?"

"Why what?"

"Why are you giving this to me?"

"So that you may do with it what you will."

"I don't get it," she said.

"You do," he said, only his lips moving. "You just haven't realized it yet."

"Wanna give me a clue then?"

Gonpo smiled. "No."

Ashley laughed, slightly frustrated. "Why not?"

"Because."

"Because why?"

He let a few, long seconds draw out, then said, "Because you have those rare and special qualities, Ashley."

A rush passed through her body.

Her mind flashed back to her meeting with Brennan.

"Ashley," Brennan said, as he stood up from the bench, "you have those rare and special qualities that are required to make a positive difference in this world, and I encourage you wholeheartedly to do just that–make your presence felt and let your voice be heard." He straightened out his coat and picked up his cane. "Your privilege and status, combined with your intelligence and intuitiveness, allows you a very unique position within this society, and I hope that you do fully and truly realize that." He paused, looking into her eyes. "And then act upon that realization when it's time."

Ashley stared at him, unsure of what to say. Why was he telling her all this? For what purpose? Curiouser and curiouser...

Brennan looked at his watch. "I must be going now, my dear. I have a conference to attend in Los Angeles, and my flight leaves in a few hours." He patted her gently on the shoulder. "Take care of yourself. We'll speak again soon." Then he walked away from her without saying another word.

She watched him climb the steps leading towards Red Square, and... Did he just flicker?


"It was you..." Ashley said. "But how? He...you touched me."

"Hard-light hologram," Gonpo said.

Ashley was silent then, trying to take everything in. She heard a fish break the surface of the water, and asked, "So was any of it the truth?"

"All of it," he said, his eyes still closed. "Minus the part about the wife and the regret. Brennan regrets nothing. And he's still married."

She laughed, shaking her head. "What...?"

"His motivations for telling you wouldn't have been believable without a logical catharsis. Divorce seemed sufficient."

"That's crazy," she said. "Why didn't you just tell me yourself?"

"I enjoy games," he said. "Don't you?"

"Uh...yeah, but I kinda like to know when I'm playing one."

"You've known."

"No, I haven't."

"Yes, you have."

"*No*," she said, "I haven't."

He smiled. "You have."

Ashley didn't bother to respond again, realizing that Gonpo wasn't just talking about the Brennan situation.

He let a few seconds pass, and said, "You've known the game

since an early age, granddaughter. It's a very, very old game, and it's been played many, many times throughout history." He paused, as an owl flew onto a nearby branch. "And now you must decide what part you're going to play in it."

"And you're showing me what that part is," she said.

"Maybe. Or maybe I'm leading you astray. Time will tell." He smiled. "If you can tell time. Now go. I must meditate. And so must you."

Ashley didn't move. She just stood there, her mind contemplating, her eyes moving back and forth from the book to him to her surroundings.

"Yes?" he asked.

"You know," she replied.

Gonpo nodded. "Yes."

Ashley left his presence, and in the distance behind her, she could faintly hear him saying, "You're welcome."

# δ

# Chapter 15
# ((The Lowdown))

*I will leave everything behind, undertaking this odyssey with myself as my only companion. Alone, I will walk away from yesterday's failures and yesterday's regrets, strengthened by the knowledge that I have learned the lessons that my past was meant to teach me.*
*I will not make the same mistakes again.*
*I will not be blind or ignorant to what is happening around me.*
*I will not place my trust in those who are not worthy.*
*I will not forsake my dreams.*
*I will die without regret.*
*The eternal present now awaits me.*

At 2:17 a.m. on Saturday morning, Ignacio finally awoke.

Not just a partial awakening, like the ones he'd been doing for the past few days, stirring just enough to sip some fluids or go to the bathroom—but a full and complete cognizance of where and who he was.

And what he needed to do.

He looked over at the woman lying next to him in bed. Irena Alma Ignacio was her name, and she had been his wife for eleven years. Yet despite all that time, he didn't really know who she was. He'd only had the opportunity to experience her through someone else's eyes. Though memory resonances from his previous self allowed him to know the details of their life together, he had no feelings with which to associate those memories. It was like trying to hear

laughter with no ears, or trying to love with no heart. The consciousness mergence had left him with no emotions from his former life,
just hollow and empty reminders of what was, and what could now
never be.

Only the facts remained. Cold, raw data, callously streamed
to him from another self.

As he laid there watching Irena sleep, he was filled with
a profound sense of sorrow. These were the last moments he would be
spending with her, and he couldn't help but feel mournful, even for a
life he hadn't ever really known. Endings were never easy, and the
fact that this one had no real beginning didn't make it any easier.
In many ways, it only made it worse. But the worst part of it all, by
far, was the guilt. He was about to violate her and her family. Take
from them a husband, a lover, a father, and a friend. *His* family,
he reminded himself, as hard as it was to do. It was still his family.
Her...and the children. God, the children. He knew their names,
ages, what they looked like...but he didn't know *them*. Their essences. His body had experienced time with them, but *he* hadn't. Yet
somehow, he had, because he saw their beautiful little faces in his
mind. *His* girls.

Ignacio felt queasy. He had to leave. Now. Before they woke.
"Esposa," he whispered to Irena, softly removing her arm from his
chest. "Lo siento."

She smiled dreamily, letting out a small nonverbal sound as
he carefully sat up and got out of bed.

Wearing only his boxers, he crept in the darkness over to his
dresser, quietly pulled out a change of clothes, moved to the closet
and grabbed a large backpack. Without looking at her again, he left
the bedroom, walked straight past his daughters' room, down the
stairs, then into the bathroom.

After dressing himself, he opened the medicine cabinet and
reached for a pack of razor blades and a bottle of rubbing alcohol. He
placed them into his backpack, walked into the kitchen, looked inside the fridge, and pulled out some cold leftovers. Without heating
them up, he ate as much as he possibly could, as fast as he possibly
could. He put the near-empty container of rice and beans back into the
refrigerator, then walked to the cupboard and filled his pack with
two cases of Power Bars®.

Food necessities taken care of, he exited the kitchen and entered into the adjoining garage where his Harley® was parked. He
flipped open one of the hoverbike's side compartments, grabbed his

spare utility belt, and put it around his waist. Hoisting the backpack onto his shoulder, he was about to leave...but couldn't bring himself to do it. Not without seeing his little girls with his own eyes.

He set the pack onto the Harley's® seat and went back into the house. He walked to the stairs and climbed them slowly, his palms sweaty with trepidation. As he approached their room, he felt a shortness of breath. He paused just before the door, swallowed hard, and entered.

There they were, sleeping in their beds. Two beautiful souls which his body had brought into this world. Which *he* had brought into this world. Him.

Ignacio approached them. Standing right in between both of their beds, he watched them sleep. So peaceful, the expressions on their faces... But so different it would be when they found out their father was missing. This was all so fucked up and crazy. It should never have happened. He cursed himself for ever becoming a sleeper. Now he would never rest easy again.

And neither would his loved ones.

"Aurora," he said, dropping to his knees. "Esperanza..." He placed a hand on each of their shoulders, bowed his head, and began to weep. "Please forgive me for what I've done... Te quiero mucho. Siempre." His sobbing increased, and he could say no more words.

Nor could he stay any longer.

Ignacio stood up, took a long, last look at his babies, and turned to leave.

But in the doorway was Irena. "Morris?" she said with concern. "What's going on? Why are you dressed?"

Unable to hold back his tears, he said, "I'm sorry, Irena. I'm so sorry."

Confused, she asked, "What? What's wrong? I don't understand."

He walked to her and embraced her tightly.

"Tell me what's going on, Morris," she said, rubbing the back of his neck with her soft hand. "Let me know."

He wanted to, but he couldn't. It would only make things worse than they already were. Still holding her with one arm, Ignacio reached down to his belt with the other and snapped off a sleepshot. He pressed his face against hers, placed the hypospray against her neck, and fired it.

Irena instantly fell asleep in his arms.

He picked her up, carried her to the room, and placed her

back into bed. Kissing her on the forehead, he tucked her in and whispered, "Cuídate, Irena." He turned off the nightstand alarm so only the girls or herself could wake her up mañana. She deserved a final night of restful sleep. God, she deserved a lot more than that, but he couldn't give it to her. Pulling his hand away from the alarm, he noticed the framed 3X5 portrait of his family that sat atop the nightstand. He picked up the photo, stared at it momentarily, then placed it in his leather jacket's pocket and walked back down to the garage.

Ignacio strapped his backpack on, mounted the Skyhog™, and activated its computer. "Voice-rec on," he said. "Open garage."

The large doors parted, unveiling the open road before him.

Placing his thumb on the scanner, he fired up the Harley's® engine and slowly looked around his garage, fully aware that this was the last time he would be seeing it. He then revved the throttle a few times, and cruised out of the garage.

And left his home for good.


At 3:09 a.m., Ignacio set his Skyhog™ down in a Denny's® parking lot near Seattle Center. He removed everything of value from the vehicle's compartments, placed them into his backpack, and walked into the 24-hour restaurant. He sat down at a booth, ordered a black coffee, and paid for it right away. He drank it quickly and kept to himself. There was nothing he had to say to anyone. Nothing to say, only things to do.

When he finished the coffee, he picked up his backpack and went to the bathroom. He entered a stall and locked the door behind him. He put the backpack onto a hook, reached into it, and pulled out the razor blade and rubbing alcohol. Kicking the toilet seat down, he placed the blade between his teeth, opened the alcohol bottle, and poured it over his right thumb. The liquid trickled off his digit, splashing onto the bathroom's sticky floor. He set the bottle on top of the toilet lid, pulled the blade from his teeth, snapped off his microtorch, and sanitized the razor's steel. As Ignacio clicked the torch back onto his belt, he heard the bathroom door swing open. He looked through the stall's thin slit.

Just an employee, walking over to one of the urinals to take a piss. Ignacio waited until the man had washed his hands and left, then he turned his biochipped thumb towards himself, and readied the blade in his other hand. Carefully examining the fingerprint, he followed the epidermal spiral to its center, placed the razor's edge upon it, and pressed it into his flesh. A rush of pain and adrenaline shot through him as he started to move the blade around inside his thumb. He clenched his teeth and growled. Blood dripped down his palm, joining the spilled alcohol and urine on the tiled floor.

When the razor touched the tiny embedded microchip, he cut a small circle around it, then scooped it and the surrounding flesh from out of his thumb. He picked up the alcohol bottle, kicked open the toilet's lid, and dropped the blade, biochip, and excess tissue into the bowl. He poured the alcohol over his bloodied, gored thumb, grimacing as the liquid fire began to burn intensely.

Tossing the bottle aside, Ignacio reached into his backpack and grabbed a mini canister of Band-Aid®. He sprayed the liquid onto the wound, and it quickly congealed into a skinlike bandage. Ignacio replaced the can, rummaged through the pack, and pulled out a headfield. He put the device—which resembled a banded necklace with a small, dialed pendant—around his neck and activated it. His head was now protected with an emfield, and most importantly, his freeread's capabilities had now been disrupted. He put his backpack on, made sure the toilet flushed, and exited the bathroom.

Walking back into the dining area, his stomach dropped. Two police officers were now talking to his waitress. The biochip must have already notified them of its removal, and since Ignacio was databased as a Freemon, they were probably there to make sure that nothing had happened to him. But they might as well have been there to capture him. Once Freemon HQ was contacted, either motive would lead to the same result.

The cops were holding a handheld uniview, showing the waitress a picture of something, more than likely a photo of him. She glanced down at it, nodded, then pointed her finger towards the bathroom. At Ignacio.

The officers looked in his direction.

But they only caught a glimpse of him, because Ignacio had already rushed forward and rendered them both unconscious with a sleepshot. Without slowing his hyperspeed, he jammed through the door and distanced himself from the establishment. He now had a few minutes to get to where he was going, before more cops were called and the redeyes started to sweep the streets for him.

Alternating back and forth between hyper and normal speed, Ignacio reached his Capitol Hill destination in less than a minute. It was an old two-story house which had been recently renovated and refurbished. Its windows were tinted and surveillance cameras were located at various positions around the front lawn. A black gate separated the property from the sidewalk. There was a sign posted on it that warned: "Trespassers will be obliterated."

Ignacio walked up to the gate. He paused to catch his breath, then pressed the intercom button and said, "Jack. It's Ignacio."

A few moments passed. A groggy voice said, "Ignacio. It's three in the morning, man."

"I know," he said, cautiously looking around his surroundings for any rollers. "I need that favor, Jack."

"*Now*?"

"Now."

"Can't this w-"

"No," he interrupted. "It can't."

Ignacio could hear a male voice in the background, Jack whispering something back to him.

"Tell him to fuck off," he heard the whiny voice say.

"Jack," Ignacio said firmly.

The whispering more intense now, Jack telling his boyfriend to be quiet.

"You owe me," Ignacio said. "Remember?"

Silence at the other end of the line, as Jack was undoubtedly remembering the time Ignacio had saved his ass from going to the workcamps.

The locks on the gate clicked.

"I remember," Jack said.

The gate swung open.

"I'll meet you at the door."

"Bueno." Ignacio walked through the gate, up the short concrete path which led to the porch. He waited at the front door, his fidgeting causing the wooden floorboards to creak underfoot. Police sirens wailed away in the distance. A cold wind kicked up, swaying the porch bench so that its chains grated noisily. He walked over to it and stopped its motion.

The front door opened.

"Ignacio?" Jack said. He stretched his violet-haired self around the corner. "There you are." He motioned with his head. "Come on."

Ignacio entered the house.

Jack closed the door behind him. He touched Ignacio's backpack and said, "What's with this? Your old lady kick you out?"

"I wish," he said, moving into Jack's comfortable living room.

He set his pack down and seated himself in the middle of a large, neon blue couch.

"Have a seat," Jack sarcastically said, sitting down across from him in a matching loveseat.

Ignacio reached into his backpack and pulled out a couple of Power Bars®. "Thanks," he said in the same tone as Jack, tearing open the wrapper on a guava-flavored bar.

Jack adjusted the sash on his silk robe. "You know I'm not in the business anymore, don't you?"

"That's what I heard," he said. "But I know you still got connections." He voraciously devoured the rest of the energy bar. "Jack Jax *always* has connections—whether he's still a fence or not."

Scratching the violet hairs on his forearm, Jack looked down pensively. "What is it you need?"

Ignacio unwrapped another Power Bar®. "I need to get rid of my freeread." He took a bite. "Immediately."

With a bewildered look, Jack said, "What the fuck did you do, man?"

"It's a long story, Jack. And I don't have time to get into it. I need it out. Now."

"Are you a fugitive right now?" His lip curled up. "Motherfucker! You're gonna bring the heat to my house!"

"Jack—calm down. They can't trace me." Ignacio raised his right hand, showing him his wounded thumb. "My biochip's already gone." He lifted the necklace. "And this is a Freemon-issue headfield. You're safe. Everything's chill. ¿Comprende?"

Calming down a little, Jack said, "Yeah. Okay. But you're still putting me at risk here, man. Aiding and abetting a felon's no small offense."

"I know. And I wouldn't be doing this if I didn't have to. But I do." Ignacio leaned forward. "Now—can you help me?"

"I don't know, man. Freereads take time," he said, one leg anxiously bobbing up and down. "Not a lotta people have an extractor, and even if they do they usually re-"

"Can you?" Ignacio said. "Or can't you?"

Jack stared at him. His leg stopped bobbing and he said, "This is it, man. If I do this for you, I don't owe you shit anymore. Is that straight?"

Ignacio nodded. "Straight as a razor."

"Okay then." Jack stood up, walked over to a coffee table, and picked up a remote. He sat back down and clicked it on. A holographic, 2-D uniview screen projected into the air between them, both of its sides showing the exact same image. He widened the screen's size to about forty inches. "Call Otto," he said. He peered his head around the screen and said to Ignacio, "If anyone can do it at this hour, it's Otto."

When Jack moved back behind the screen, the image of a man in a black fedora appeared upon it. His face was very pasty and angular, his cheekbones prominent. A pair of thin, round, wire-rimmed glasses rested at the edge of his nose. The lenses were tinted a dull gray. "Jack," he said without emotion. "Since when did you become a vampire?"

"Since never," Jack replied, almost defensively. "That's your bag, Otto. I'm just not sleeping well tonight."

"Surely," Otto said, scratching the corner of his mouth with his pinky finger's long, black-painted nail. "What's the problem?"

"I've got a headache," Jack said. "A bad one."

"And you want me to come over and kiss it." Otto lowered his gaze. "And make it all better."

"Yeah."

"You naughty boy, you," Otto said. "I'll be there within the hour. Be still."

His face disappeared from the screen. Jack clicked the hologram off.

"Strange character," Ignacio said.

"He's beyond strange," Jack replied. "But he gets the job done." He stood up. "I'm gonna go back upstairs, man. Someone's waiting for me. I'll listen out for the door, and we'll deal with Otto then. Meantime..." He tossed Ignacio the remote. "Mi casa es su casa."

"Thanks," Ignacio said, as Jack walked out of the room. He waited a moment, then clicked the screen back on. "Directory assistance," he said, setting the remote aside.

The screen displayed the Qwest® logo. "For what city?"

Reaching into the front of his pack, he pulled out a silver pen and said, "Seattle."

"For what listing?"

"Rosario. Raquel Rosario."

"Thank you," the feminine voice said, displaying Raquel's address and phone number in bold, black letters. "Would you like to download this information for later use?"

"No," he said. "Leave onscreen. Voice-rec off." He touched the 'record' button on the pen, then spoke Raquel's address and phone number into its microphone. He pressed the button again, and replaced the pen into his backpack. He picked up the remote, slouched down in the couch, and began to flip through the thousands of brain-numbing channels as he waited for Otto's arrival.

At 4:31 a.m., Otto showed up.

Dressed in all black. Black tweed coat. Black slacks. Black Doc Martens®. Black everything. Except for his pallid skin, which practically glowed in contrast to the darkness of his attire. As he walked into the living room, he removed his fedora, placed it under his arm, and said, "Good even. You must be my client."

Ignacio turned off the uniview. "Sí."

Jack said, "Ignacio, this is Otto. Otto, Ignacio."

Ignacio started to stand up, but Otto said, "No need to get up." He extended his hand, his long, painted fingernails pointing at Ignacio like little black daggers. "I prefer my clients to be seated."

"Fine with me." He shook the pale man's hand, which was much warmer than he had expected. Almost hot. Nothing like the icy, corpselike hand he thought he'd be grabbing. "I just want it out."

"Surely," Otto said, releasing his strong grip. "Now, the details..." He clicked his fingernails together. "What do you have to offer in collateral for my services?"

Ignacio handed him his utility belt.

Otto held it up by one end, looking over the devices. "This is not police issue."

"Freemon," Ignacio said. "Everything's there but the laser."

"No matter," he said, running a finger along the napper. "Lasers are easy to come by." He draped the belt over his arm. "What else?"

"This." Ignacio touched his necklace. "It's a headfield."

Otto crouched over, bringing his face right up to the apparatus. "*Very* intriguing..." He pulled back slightly, moving his hands in the space around Ignacio's head. "Yes, very nice..." he whispered, his breath smelling like a combination of dust and ginseng. He stood back up and said, "You have a deal."

"Bueno."

Otto set the belt and his hat onto the couch. "Are you ready to begin?"

Ignacio checked him up and down with a curious expression. "Where's your extractor?" he asked.

288

# ((FREQUENCIES))

Otto smiled. He parted his light, pink lips, and slowly let out his long, grayish tongue. It undulated like a centipede, then its tip unfurled, revealing within it something which resembled the mouth of a leech.

Disgusted, Ignacio said, "What the fuck?" He scowled at Jack. "What kind of maricón shit is this, Jack? Hunh? What the fuck?"

"It's what'll get that fuckin' freeread out of your head, man, that's what."

Ignacio pointed his finger at him. "If this is some kind of bullshit, Jack, I'm gonna fuck you up. You hear me?"

"Yeah, man, I hear you. It's not. He's legit, okay? Fuck."

Ignacio looked back at Otto, whose tongue-thing had now retreated. "Well?" Otto asked. "Do we still have a deal?"

Ignacio shook his head and reluctantly said, "Sí. Let's just get this shit over with."

Otto walked behind him. "Please lean your head back."

"This shit's not gonna turn you on, is it?" Ignacio said.

"Truthfully?" Otto asked, his hot hands touching Ignacio's temples.

"Forget it," Ignacio said. "Just get it out."

"Surely." He lowered his lips towards Ignacio's head. "Now just relax," he said, "this won't hurt a bit." Otto's open mouth pressed against his skin. He softly began to suck, spreading his warm saliva all around Ignacio's forehead.

As calm as he possibly could, Ignacio said, "What the hell are you doing?"

"Sterilizing the area," he said between kisses. "My saliva's a disinfectant...and an anesthetic. Now...don't move." Otto's opened mouth pressed down harder. The tongue-thing started to ripple around the lip-enclosed area. It quickly centered itself, stopped its motion, then opened up at the tip. Ignacio felt a slight tingling sensation. Otto quietly moaned as his hands continued to massage Ignacio's temples.

Ignacio had the urge to pull away. Not because it hurt, but because he was actually finding the experience tolerable. He wanted to hate it, but he couldn't. The reality was, Otto was somehow making him feel comfortable. It didn't make sense. But that was seeming to be the theme of his life.

There was a subtle pull on the center of his forehead, then the tip of Otto's tongue began to rapidly vibrate. Ten seconds later, Otto retracted his tongue, sucked up the excess saliva, and released his hands from Ignacio's head.

"It's gone," Otto said, standing upright.

Somewhat in a daze, Ignacio leaned his head forward. He touched his forehead. There was no mark whatsoever. He checked his fingers. No blood either.

Circling around in front of him, Otto said, "A mechanical extractor would have left a scar." He picked up his hat and the utility belt from the couch. "I don't." He placed the fedora on top of his head. "The rest of my fee, please."

"Right." Ignacio deactivated the headfield, slipped it off, and handed it to Otto.

"Thank you," Otto said. "It was a pleasure doing business with you." He smiled fiendishly. "I'm sure we'll talk again."

"I doubt it," Ignacio said, rubbing his numbed forehead.

"You never know. Stranger things have happened." Otto turned to Jack and said, "Good morrow, Jack. I'll let myself out."

"Yeah. Go ahead," Jack said.

Otto exited the living room, then the house.

As the door shut closed, Ignacio said, "You should've warned me it was gonna be like that, Jack. That shit was fuckin' extraño."

"Hey, beggars can't be choosers, man. I got you what you needed, didn't I?"

"Yeah, you did," Ignacio said. "I'll give you that."

"And maybe a 'thanks?'"

"Sí. Gracias, amigo."

"You're welcome, man," he said, rubbing one of his violet eyebrows. "I owed it to you. Are we even now?"

"Almost."

Jack frowned. "What do you mean, 'almost?'"

Ignacio stood up. "Let me use your shower first. I got another man's spit all over my head."

"That's it?" He let out a relieved laugh as he walked out of the living room. "You had me worried there for a minute, man. I thought you were gonna go back on our deal."

Ignacio picked up his backpack. "That's not mi estilo, Jack. I follow through." He trailed after him. "Believe me, boy–I follow through."


At 5:49 a.m., Ignacio was standing in the shadows, across the street from the brownstone building that matched Raquel's listed address.

He looked towards the eastern sky. A birdie was shining its

redeye on the streets below, searching for any signs of wanted criminals or biochipless citizens. It was the eighth one he'd seen during his trek to her Central District residence–way more than the routine. They were obviously looking for someone in particular.

Unfortunately, he was probably that someone.

Ignacio checked for any signs of rollers, then zipped across the street at hyperspeed. He stood before the complex's callscreen, smoothed his hand over the top of his bald head. The air felt cool against his newly exposed scalp. Same with his upper lip. Remembering the information from his recorder pen, he touched the onscreen icon for apartment #11. He waited, but there was no answer. He pressed it again. And waited. And pressed again.

"Go away," Raquel suddenly said through the dented metal speaker.

"Raquel," he said. "It's me." He looked into the camera's eye.

There was a long pause. "Iggy?" she asked.

"Sí. I need to talk to you."

"I can't believe you're actually here," she said.

"Me neither. Can I come up?"

"Yeah," she said. "Of course. I'm on the third floor." The glass entry door buzzed open.

Ignacio walked into the rundown lobby, headed straight for the stairwell, and climbed up to the third level. When he reached her apartment, the door immediately opened.

"Iggy," she said, giving him a strong hug. "You came."

He hugged her back. "I did."

"You're cold," she said. "Come inside, sweetie. You need to get warm."

He entered Raquel's heated apartment. It was a small place, with not a lot of amenities, but it was clean and well-kept. There was a living room with a kitchen built into it, a bathroom, and apparently, two bedrooms. "You live with someone?" he asked.

"Pam," she said, walking over to an old, reddish-brown couch. "My roommate. But she's in Tacoma for the weekend." Raquel sat down, patting the seat next to her.

Ignacio set his pack aside and seated himself.

She rubbed her sleepy eyes and tried to smooth out her crinkled hair. "Sorry if I look crappy right now."

"You look fine. Don't apologize."

She smiled. "Thanks." Crossing her legs, she said, "So what made you decide to come and see me?"

Ignacio thought about various things he could say. Stories that would make things easier. But the last twenty-two years of his life had been a lie, and he was *more* than ready for the truth–so he gave her the lowdown, straight, no chaser. "I'm in trouble, Raquel. I need a place to stay for a day or two."

"You can stay here as long as you need, Iggy." She took his cold fingers into her tiny hands and warmed them up. "What happened?"

"It's a long story," he said. "But what it all amounts to is that I know too much."

She blew her warm breath onto his hands. "But how? You're a Freemon."

"Not anymore."

Her eyes widened. *"Really?"*

"Sí."

"Jeez, Iggy," she said. "I can't believe it. You're in trouble with the *law*?"

Ignacio nodded slowly.

"Jeez, I can't believe this..." She looked up at his bald head and touched his bare upper lip. "So that's why you have the new look, huh?"

He nodded again.

She let out a small laugh.

"What?" he said.

"It's funny..."

"What is?"

"I was always thinking you were gonna come and rescue *me*." She smiled. "And now here I am..." She embraced him lovingly. "Rescuing you. Funny, huh?"

Allowing his exhausted self to fully collapse into her arms, Ignacio said, "Hilarious."

Raquel began to rub the back of his neck. "It's nice to have you here, Iggy," she said.

"It's nice to be here," he replied, and fell asleep shortly thereafter.

$$\delta$$

# α

# Chapter 16
# ((Futurosity))

*I eagerly embrace today, with a careful, hopeful eye on the future.
Everything will be as it should."*

As McCready joined Mason and Dorje aboard the SEV, he asked,
"Where's Ashley?"

"She's still inside the palace," Mason said, shining a golden
delicious with the bottom of his tan, lightweight safari shirt.

"She didn't want to go?"

"She said she had to catch up on some reading," he replied,
as Dorje formed the organic steering column. "She'll join us for dinner
when we return."

"Alright," McCready said. "Just the guys, hunh?"

"So it seems." Mason motioned his hand toward the grand
cornucopia hovering in the air beside him. "Fruit?"

"Nah," he said, leaning back against the vehicle's railing,
"I'm good. But thanks."

Mason took a bite of the gilded apple. "Suit yourself." He
looked at Dorje. "We're ready to go now, Dorje."

The humanoid cobra nodded as he placed his hands inside
the globular steering device. "It so be."

The SEV smoothly lifted off. It cruised forth in an easterly
direction, hovering about twenty feet above the ground as they
headed into the savannah. Their destination, the tropical rainforest,
was visible far ahead. Light rainclouds floated over parts of it, but
all in all, the weather in that area of the dome looked perfect for a

Saturday afternoon safari.

"So what do you think of the duds?" McCready said, tugging on his beige nylon jacket. "Lhasa whipped 'em up for me this morning."

Mason nodded approvingly as he looked over McCready's nanotech wardrobe. It consisted of a white tanktop beneath the jacket, multi-pocketed cargo shorts, thin wool socks, and a pair of dark brown Timberlands®. "Very nice," he said. "You look well prepared for a jungle excursion."

"Yeah, seems like it." He reached into one of the shorts' compartments and pulled out a Swiss Army® device. "There's even a bunch of gadgets in the pockets."

Mason smiled as he took a final bite of the apple. "What will they think of next?" He tossed the partially eaten fruit aside, allowing the ambient intelligence to disassemble its molecular structure.

McCready smirked as he watched the apple disappear. "I'm not sure I wanna know." Averting his gaze to the forested horizon, he said, "So there really are tigers and pumas out there?"

"And jaguars," Mason said, adjusting his lightweight Seattle Sombrero™. "And leopards and boars, monkeys and macaws..."

"Boas," added Dorje. "Anaconda, python..." He smiled, his fangs showing slightly.

"All types of jungle creatures," Mason said. "It's miraculous."

"Hunh," McCready said, still staring out at the rainforest as they passed a herd of elephants. "This is gonna be a trip."

"Indeed," Mason said.

They continued toward their destination at a relaxed pace, exchanging few words between them, both men content with the language of the scenery. It said so much more than mere words. For the totality of his father's domed creation could not be faithfully described, only beheld. It was truly a miraculous gift to the world, a wonder which could rival even the great pyramids of Giza...and it was his father who had created it.

When they reached the halfway point of their journey, McCready asked, "What are those?"

"What?" Mason said, turning and walking in McCready's direction.

"Those," he replied, pointing two fingers toward an out-cropping of white geodesic domes which could barely be glimpsed upon the southern horizon. "The Disney World® things."

"The geodesic domes, you mean?"

"Right. What are they for?"

"Laboratories," Mason replied.

"Gonpo's?"

"Yes. Though visiting scientists often work there as well."

"Hm..." He took a draw from his cigarette. "They don't fit with the rest of the place."

"That's the idea," Mason said. "They're the only part of Is which is not affected by my father's thoughts."

"Why's that?"

"It would alter the results of the experiments performed there."

"Interesting."

"Isn't it all?" Mason asked, watching zebra and impala bound across the grasslands.

McCready nodded. "No doubt."

As they passed a pride of lions on the prowl, Mason said, "I suppose, Mr. McCready, this is as good a time as any for us to discuss your compensation."

"Uh...yeah," he said, a bit surprised by the suggestion. "Sure. Sounds good."

Mason rested his hand atop the railing's edge. "I have two offers to make you," he said. "The first is a short term one, which consists of a single, lump sum payment of 750,000 DC's, credited to the account of your choice."

"Seriously?" McCready said, his cigarette dangling from the edge of his lip.

Mason looked at him. "What do you think?"

"Whoa..." McCready removed the cigarette from his mouth. "Thanks, Huxton, I, ah..." He laughed. "Thanks."

Mason nodded. "The second option is a long term offer, one which I will straightforwardly tell you I prefer." He paused, eyes fixed on the acacia-covered horizon. "You see, Mr. McCready, you've proven yourself–on many levels–to be quite a...valuable asset, shall we say. So much so, that I would be very, *very* interested in retaining your services."

McCready raised the cigarette back to his lips. "What did you have in mind?"

"A job offer," he said. "I'd like you to work for Ordosoft™."

"Doing what?"

"Various security-related duties, depending on the needs of the company and myself."

"What, like an Ordocop™?"

"No, not at all. The job would be much more prestigious than that, and you would wield *far* more power than they do–and much more freedom. You would be my...utility man, so to speak, doing various jobs as the need arises. And barring any emergency situations, you would be able to set your own schedule as you wish."

"Alright," McCready said, flicking his cigarette aside. "I'm listening. What's it pay?"

"Annually..." Mason said. "Four million."

McCready's eyebrows raised. "Four million DC's? A *year*?"

"Yes."

"Holy shit."

"Indeed," Mason said. "And in addition to the salary, all living and food expenses will be covered, and a vehicle will be provided for you." He paused, a confident look upon his face. "When I told you I was prepared to reward you generously for services rendered..." He smiled. "I wasn't joking."

McCready laughed a little, and said, "I guess not."

As they reached the outskirts of the jungle, the air became more hot and humid. "Well, Mr. McCready," Mason said, "which would you prefer? Option one? Or option two?"

McCready thought for a moment. "I'm, ah...I'm not even sure." He rubbed the sides of his clean-shaven face. "Four million DC's... Damn."

"You needn't give me an answer now," Mason said, seeing the astonishment in McCready's face. "Don't worry, there's no rush."

"No, actually, I, ah..." He nodded, his expression becoming more focused. "I think I already know."

"Oh. Very well then. Which will it be?"

"Two," McCready said. "Definitely two."

The SEV started its descent, passing through a small clearing in the forest's thick canopy.

"I'm pleased to hear that." Mason extended his hand to McCready. "Shall we shake on the deal?"

"Yeah, sure," McCready said, firmly grasping his hand.

Mason smiled. "Welcome to the company, Mr. McCready."

The vehicle dropped further into the forested shroud, stopping about five feet above the ground. The wails of howler monkeys could be heard all around, as well as the individual sounds of countless other birds and insects. Rainforest smells wafted through the humid air, moist and sweet.

# ((FREQUENCIES))

"We'll iron out the details back in Seattle," Mason said. "But for now..." He motioned to the surrounding jungle. "We have better things to do." He looked at McCready. "Wouldn't you agree?"

McCready, whose wide-eyed gaze was fixed upon the tropical paradise in amazement, simply replied, "Word."


Mason and McCready returned from their day trip about six hours later, arriving just in time to shower up before supper.

As expected, the results from the jungle trek were very positive. Both he and McCready had thoroughly enjoyed themselves, sharing many miles and stories with one another. For the first time since he'd hired him, Mason could honestly say that they both had developed a full level of mutual respect for one another. It wasn't strictly business anymore, but an actual friendship.

Which was just fine with Mason. After all, not only was McCready trustworthy, brave, and very good at what he did, but his influence on Ashley had already been considerably noticeable. Mason expected that, in time, McCready's influence over her would only increase...as would *his* influence over McCready, and thus, ultimately, Ashley.

Despite the week's chaos, the future was falling into place nicely. Structures were reasserting, and matrices were reappearing. Mason was seeing, quite clearly, the ways in which he could better organize his family and his corporation. He felt all at once inspired, invigorated, and hopeful for the future.

Order had returned.

After they had showered and dressed, Mason and McCready joined Ashley and the others for dinner. As was fitting for their final night there, the dining experience was spectacular, a royal feast in which they were joined by all of the dome's humanoid inhabitants.

It was an open-aired celebration, filled with things and events which would best be described as magical. Luminescent faeries dancing in the night sky, avian crossbreeds singing songs older than humankind, photonic guitars playing alongside cowhide drums, holographic tone poems materializing in the air around them... It was a magnificent display of innovation and control; a celebratory exhibit of informational dominance, the likes of which only his father could have dreamed up and actualized.

Many hours later, when the bonfires ceased burning and the music stopped playing, after the indigenous creatures went home and the four moons hung high overhead; after McCready and Ashley had left for their midnight stroll, and Xanadeux and Lhasa had returned to their rooms, Mason was descending the onyx stairs leading down to the palace's cellar. A goblet of ruby port in his hand, humming a cheery tune he knew not the name of, he entered the treasure room-like substructure at the base of the stairs. He walked amongst the eclectic collection of objects, some of which were ancient, others which were novel, and a few which were impossible to tell. He stopped occasionally to examine a particular item or thing, but never stayed so long as to delay his meeting with his father.

He was much too excited to linger.

"We will speak tonight of the events of the past week, my son," his father had told him earlier at dinner. "What has happened and what it means. And we will also speak of the future...of what is to come."

Reaching the far end of the room, he approached a wide, ten-foot-high brass mirror which sat against the black chalcedony wall. He looked at his reflection, placed his knuckles against the glass, and knocked a particular pattern of sounds. He waited a few seconds, then stepped into the mirrored surface, causing it to ripple and wave like water.

Through the looking glass, he emerged into his father's study, which was a room that wasn't a room...a polychromatic space which seemingly had no beginning or no end; an everchanging, colorful dimension which made Mason feel as if he was in the heart of another galaxy with different natural laws than those of his own. There were no visible floors or walls, yet he could feel the ground beneath his feet and see the various objects suspended upon its nonexistent walls. He could look down, see forever into infinity, and do the same when he looked above or to the side.

Endless, varicolored space all around.

And though he was used to these types of sensations in virtuality, it was an entirely different experience when it happened in actuality, and it always took Mason a few moments to fully adjust.

"Watch your step," his father said, seated low to the ground in front of a short table which was completely transparent, save for its thin, glowing red outline. The items on top of it appeared to be hovering in the air, perfectly still.

"Believe me," Mason said, carefully maneuvering around the outlined, see-through furniture, "I am."

"So you are," he said.

Reaching the luxuriously soft chair in front of the table, Mason took a sip of his port, and said, "Made it."

His father smiled. "You did. And now we can begin." As an iridescent meteor shower occurred in the distance behind him, he cupped his hands around his ceramic teacup, and said, "Ask me whatever you would like to know, and I will try my best to answer."

Mason placed his finger on his lip, tapped it a few times, and asked, "Why didn't you answer my calls this week?"

"I thought it best not to."

"Why? I could have used your advice on how to handle the terrorist situation."

"It was better for you to handle it alone."

"But I've always consulted with you on major issues that affected the family or company. Why, when something was affecting them both so severely, would you decide to change that?"

"It was time." He sipped from his teacup. "Did you not handle the situation by yourself?"

"Yes, I did, but-"

"No buts then," he said. "If you did, you did, and if you did, then you didn't need. Correct?"

"I suppose," Mason said grudgingly. "Though I would have at least liked to have spoken with you about it in *some* manner, even if it wasn't in regards to how to deal with it."

"You can do that now. The opportunity hasn't passed."

"Yes, but sometimes people like to speak to loved ones *while* the crisis is occurring, father. Comfort, support...those kinds of things are nice sometimes, you know."

He smiled. "Yes. But so is change."

"It can be..." Mason drank from his silver goblet, staring off into the mesmerizing colors. "Depending on the situation." He wiped his lips, and said, "On to the next...I take it Xanadeux has informed you of the details surrounding the attacks?"

He nodded.

"What do you make of it?"

"Which aspect?"

"All of it," Mason replied.

"It is what it is," his father said.

He gave him a semi-mock look of annoyance. "Could you be a *bit* more specific, father?"

"Yes, if your questions were a bit more specific."

Mason sighed. "Very well," he said. "What do you think it

was that attacked the family?"

"Tell me your theories first, and then I will tell you mine."

"You're impossible, you know that?"

"So I hear." He picked up a kettle from the table and refilled his cup. "Well?" he said. "No theories?"

Mason chuckled. "You know, father, sometimes I think it's amazing that I turned out as well as I did, considering that I've had to deal with..." He playfully stammered as he motioned to their otherworldly surroundings. "...with *this* all my life."

"Miraculous, I'd say." He sipped the tea. "Theories, please?"

"All right. I'll indulge you." He drank from his cup, and said, "When the attacks first occurred, I thought they were being committed by a group of crackers–possibly underground, possibly hired by a rival corporation...possibly former temps or other disgruntled employees..." His words trailed off as a particularly bright color pattern caught his attention. "Whatever the case," he continued, "I assumed it was something of a conspiratorial nature, conceived and carried out by a group of individuals. But, as this 'Presence' further revealed itself, it felt less and less like it was a group creation, and more and more like it was just one single person...or thing."

His father waited for him to continue.

"You see," Mason said, "neither Agent Takura, nor Xanadeux, could find a single realtime port which the Presence might have used to carry out the attacks. There was not even the faintest trace of a connection to the real world. Everything had been carried out from *within* the uninet, not from without...meaning that no human was giving the orders." He finished the port, and set his cup onto the table. "The three of us came to the conclusion that by the time it ·
attacked our family, the Presence–regardless of where it originated from–existed only within cyberspace. It was a creation which had no corporeal, realtime form... A true ghost within the machine."

His father nodded a few times. "I agree with your theory."

"You do?"

"Absolutely."

"Well," Mason said, surprised that his father didn't have his own spin on the situation, "I'm pleased to hear that. My question for you then wou-" He stopped mid-sentence, noticing for the first time a small, clear cube which sat atop the table. Inside of the cube was a swirling collection of energy resembling the shape of a black hole, but with much more color. He reached forward, touched the top of it, and asked, "What is this?"

"A wormhole," his father replied.

Mason picked it up, staring into the kinetic whorl. "Fascinating."

"That one leads to some sort of microscopic pocket universe," he said. "I only recently sent a probe into it, so I haven't fully had a chance to understand what's on the other side."

He looked up from the cube. "You mean you have others?"

"Yes, but they're much larger than that. Now, back to what you were saying..."

"Of course," Mason said, still staring at the miniature wormhole as he set it down on the tabletop. "The Presence..." He collected his thoughts and said, "The thing about it that was terribly confusing, and which none of us can quite figure out, is why this ghost chose to haunt *our* family in particular. And why it did so in the way that it did. It had numerous opportunities to kill us, yet it only sought to terrorize, and...the only word to describe it is 'play.' It was as if this creature was playing a game with us the whole time, not really interested in destroying us, but in...I don't know. I can't fathom its reasoning, father. There's no logic to it."

"Maybe that's the answer."

"That it's illogical?"

"Yes."

"If it is, then that's a very unsatisfying answer," Mason said. "It doesn't explain anything."

"But it does," he said. "Who or whatever created this entity, whether they realized it or not, brought into this world a living chaos equation. An extremely powerful entity whose sole purpose appears to be the disruption of order." He sipped his tea. "And what represents order in this world more than the corporation?"

Mason thought for a moment, then nodded. "That *would* explain why it chose Ordosoft™. After all, we've been as instrumental as any force in achieving world order...and I suppose even our name would tempt it, not to mention the control we have in our market. But still... That doesn't quite explain its behavior. It wasn't chaotic *enough*. The Presence was too calculated, its actions too deliberate for it to have been a being of pure chaos."

"Is there not order within chaos?"

"There is," Mason agreed.

"And were a being to act only in random and haphazard ways, wouldn't it then be somewhat predictable? If it never calculated or planned, could it still be called a creature of chaos? Or would its adherence to randomness now make it predictable and ordered?"

"I see your point," he said. "Considering the infinite targets available to it, were it only to attack at random, it would achieve nothing."

"Precisely. Some order is needed to disrupt order."

Mason mulled over the possibilities. "Say that Xanadeux and Takura's attack didn't really destroy the Presence, and it's still alive somewhere in the net... Am I to believe that it will keep its word about not attacking our family?"

"Maybe, maybe not. That's chaos."

"That's unnerving, is what it is. How can I deal with something that doesn't make any sense?"

"You just do."

"That sense of unknowing doesn't bother you?"

"No. I accept it as a part of life."

"Then you're not at all worried that this creature might come for you as well?"

"I consider the possibility," he said. "And then I let it go. It weighs naught upon my mind. Whatever will be, will be, and the future...will unfold as it will."

"The future," Mason said. "You mentioned that earlier at dinner. You said we'd be speaking about...how did you put it... 'What is to come.'"

"Yes," he said. "And now we've reached that time." He set his teacup down, and the room instantly transformed into its actual state. Mason could now see the walls, the ground, the furniture, other doors...everything as it truly was.

A sense of reality returned to the moment.

"I have two things with which to discuss with you, my son. One is a forewarning, the other a gift. Which would you like first?"

His eyes still adjusting to the candlelit lighting, Mason said, "Work before play. The warning first."

"Certainly." He paused momentarily, then said, "I believe the appearance of the Presence is a sign...an omen of things to come. Order has ruled supreme for nearly this entire century–for the last *few* centuries, even–and I believe it is now come time for its rule to be challenged. In the coming months, you must prepare yourself for events which will shake the very foundations of your world."

"I've already had that happen," Mason said, thinking of Dominique in particular.

"I'm not referring to your personal world," he said. "These

events will affect the entire Earth."

Mason looked at his father intently, studying his face for any sign of humor. There was none. "How do you mean?" he asked.

"Let me explain," he said. "When chaos fully descends upon this plane, innovation and confrontation will increase exponentially, leading to a period in humankind's history which will be as volatile and unstable as any that has been experienced before. In fact, I would dare say it may even be *the* most volatile period in human history, especially when taking into account the realities of a global government. On one side," he said, extending his hand out like he was checking for rain, "we have the power of worldwide security and scientific cooperation." He raised his other hand, palm also facing upward. "On the other, we have an interconnected system of nations that is vulnerable to attack from any place on Earth. And if one should fall...will the others follow?" He moved them up and down, as if he was balancing the air. "We shall see."

Resting his hands on his lap, he continued, "As an agent of order, your role will become more important than ever. You must be as a rock in a storm, steadfast and unyielding, for others will look to you for guidance. You must become stronger than ever, my son, and learn not to be reliant upon anyone else but yourself. Ultimately, no man, woman, or construct can help you through this coming time. Only *you* can help yourself. While certain individuals may aid you at certain times, it is essential that you remember where the true power lies... Within you. Always." He stared at Mason without saying a word, then asked, "Do you understand what it is that I'm telling you?"

Still grappling with the weight of his father's words, he said, "I...I believe so, father. It seems...so unreal to think of this scenario, but...I understand what you're saying. About my role." As the thoughts sunk in, his voice became more confident. "And I'll fulfill that duty if it comes time. I'll be ready for the future."

He nodded encouragingly. "Then that is all I have to say on the subject," he said. "At least for the time being. And now, the gift." He stood up, and walked around the table to Mason. "A project which I have been cultivating for a *very* long time has finally borne its fruit, my son." He set his hand on Mason's shoulder and smiled. "Prepare to be astonished." His father snapped his fingers. One of the room's doors began to slowly open.

Mason stood up from his chair, his head tilted to one side in attempt to sneak a peek. "What is it?" he asked.

"My son..." his father said, as a familiar figure emerged from behind the door.

"Consciousness uploading has been achieved," his father's other body said, the door automatically closing shut behind him.

"What?" Mason said, taken aback by both the sight of two fathers and the words they were speaking.

"He is me," the emerging father said, seating himself where the original father had been.

"And I am him," said the father standing next to him. "Our consciousness is one and the same."

"I don't believe it," Mason said with awe.

"Believe it," they both said.

He looked back and forth between the two of them. "You're *exactly* the same?"

"Identical," the father next to him said.

Mason felt a rush of adrenalin pass through him as he thought of its applications to Dominique. "You're completely sure, father? Without a doubt?"

"Yes," the seated father said. "Otherwise..." He pulled out a small device and aimed it at the other father. "Would I let myself do this?" The next instant, he fired a laser beam at the original father, cleanly splitting him in half from head to toe.

Horrified, Mason stepped back.

The original father's bodily halves fell to the ground, jerked a few times, and ceased their motion.

"I'm still me," the seated father said. "Don't worry."

Mason looked at his father, adrenalin borne of excitement *and* fear now passing through his being.

"I apologize for the grotesque theatrics, but it seemed the simplest way to convince you." He peered over the table at his other body. "May I clean up the mess now?"

Without looking at the body again, a nauseous Mason replied, "Please do."

His father motioned his hands, and the ambient nanotech cleaned up his remains. "There," he said. "Much better."

Mason stood there, motionless, attempting to quell his sickness.

"Son?"

He looked at his father. "I feel sick."

"No..." his father said with a subtle laugh, drawing out the word as if Mason was a boy again. "There's no reason to."

"No reason?" Mason said. "Father, I just watched you *die*."

He laughed. "No, you didn't," he said, still speaking to him like a child. "You saw one of my bodies die. There's a world of difference between the two." He poured himself some more tea. "You must stop thinking of this breakthrough in yesterday's terms. It won't do you any good. This is the future, son." He raised the tea to his lips. "Get used to it."

Mason slowly seated himself back in the chair. "All right," he said. "Just give me a moment." He picked up his goblet to take a drink, but quickly remembered there was nothing left in it. "Damn," he muttered.

"Allow me," his father said, motioning his hands.

Mason's cup filled up with fresh port. He took a sip, then said, "Could I have something a bit stronger?"

"Of course." He twinkled his fingers.

The ruby liquid turned amber. Mason drank a large gulp. "Much better," he said, the old fashioned's aftertaste soothingly lingering on his palate.

"I took the liberty to mix in a little Diazecalm™, too," his father said.

"Many thanks."

His father nodded with a smile.

When Mason's mind was completely settled, he once again thought of the implications of his father's technology, and why it would be such a gift. "This really is happening, father?" he said. "This isn't a hologram or a test of some sort?"

"Not at all," he replied. "This is my gift to you."

"Then..." Mason's heart filled with excitement. "Then that means you can bring back Dominique."

"I can."

"Thank you, father," he said, bowing his head and closing his eyes. "Thank you." He breathed in, then looked back up at the miracle-maker seated in front of him. "You don't know what this means to me."

"I do," he said.

Mason smiled. "Yes. You do, don't you?" He shook his head with blissful disbelief. "Dominique..." His mind filled with images of his beloved wife, their time spent together, the times to come...

And that was when reality rudely reasserted itself.

"Dominique..." Mason repeated, this time more gravely, as he thought of his reborn wife back in Seattle.

"You're thinking of the clone." his father said.

"Yes. The..." He couldn't believe he was saying it. "...the clone. That *is* all she is, isn't it?" Mason asked unassuredly. "All she ever was?"

"And nothing more," he said. "But now you can have the real thing."

He somberly stared at his father, and said, "You realize what this means, don't you?"

His father nodded slowly. "I do."

Mason sighed heavily. "God forgive me."

$$\alpha$$

# α

## Chapter 17
## ((Brief Lives))

*"There could be no other way than this one.*
*Old things must pass, in order that the new may come forth.*

They arrived back in Seattle on a cold, wet, and thoroughly miserable Monday morning.

After they had said their goodbyes at the airstrip and parted their separate ways, Mason immediately attended to his dreadful duties. There was no time to waste.

The future was now.

As he entered the quarantine area, Dominique's clone smiled at him from behind the thick plate glass. She enthusiastically walked toward the barrier, and said, "Mason."

"Hello," he said, as coldly as possible.

She was in a medium-sized room furnished with a few possessions from their house, but not nearly enough to make it feel homey. The walls were stark white, combining with the harsh fluorescents to make everything–including her–unrealistically bright. "I'm so glad to see you," she said, pressing her palms up against the glass. "It's been so lonely in here."

"Yes," he said.

Noticing his distance, her face frowned. "What's wrong?" she asked.

"Nothing," he said unconvincingly.

"Did they find something bad, Mason? Did they?"

He was unable to reply, as he was too caught up in his own

internal conflict, tempted to try to save her somehow, but knowing that simply was *not* a realistic option.

"Please tell me what they're saying about me," she said worriedly. "All they tell me is that they need to run more tests, but I know they have to know something by now. Tell me, Mason, please... What's happening? When can I go home? I don't want to be here anymore." She rested her forehead against the glass and began to cry.

Mason timidly reached his hand toward the clear barrier, and placed it next to her face. His hand was shaking as he told her, "You won't be here much longer, Dominique."

She looked up at him, a small trace of hope in her eyes. "Really?"

"Yes," he said truthfully.

"Then I can go home soon?"

He nodded, a low murmur building in his throat. "Yes," he managed to say. "You'll be...going home." He traced his finger along the glass outline of her smiling face. "Soon. I promise."

She closed her eyes as if he was actually touching her, a look of peace upon her face.

"I have to go now," he said, stepping back from the barrier.

She nodded, wiping her eyes. "I understand."

Mason stared at her for a moment, then said, "I'll see you soon, Dominique." He swallowed hard. "And I promise everything will be better."

"I believe you." Both palms still pressed against the glass, she said, "I love you, Mason Huxton."

"I..." He whimpered painfully. "I...I'm sorry, Dominique," he said, and without uttering another sound, he left the room.

Xanadeux was waiting outside. "Sir?"

"Don't speak to me," he said, covering his eyes. "Just walk."

They moved quickly through the quarantine wing, out of the private hospital, to the limo parked out front.

The rain was still falling.

"Sit in the front," Mason said to Xanadeux, as the back door opened for him. "I need to be alone."

"Of course," the android said.

Mason climbed into the backseat, and the door shut softly behind him. He leaned forward, reached his hands up to the top of his head, and tightly grasped at his hair.

"Where to, sir?" Burke asked.

"Just drive," Mason cried.

The car lifted off the ground.

Mason rocked himself back and forth at the edge of his seat, warm rain running down his face.

Webber had assured him that it would be painless. An injection in the day which wouldn't act until the night. She would pass quietly in her sleep, feeling nothing. "Cause of death," his head of security had told him, "aftereffects of the informational infection."

A flawless story. No one would dispute it.

But Mason would always know the truth.

He released his hands from his head, and reached toward the small mahogany cabinet in front of him. Opening it up, he pulled out the alpha-covered green cube and its accompanying headpiece. He placed the neural net onto his head, then twisted the cube at its fissure. The headpiece magnetized to his skin and the technorganic tendrils grew out of it, quickly forming their intricate network over his scalp.

Mason leaned back in the soft, cushioned seat, closed his eyes, and twisted the cube again.

Virtuality blossomed before him.

The day could not have been more perfect.

$$\alpha$$

# δ

# Chapter 18
## ((Life After Death))

*A seed must shed its shell so that it may grow once again.*
*I am but a seed.*
*Growing."*

Morris Ignacio was dead.

At least as far as he was concerned, that identity had been laid to rest. Put into the ground and covered with dirt.

"I've seen your face on some of the public unies, Iggy," Raquel said, setting a bag of groceries onto her countertop.

Unfortunately, the law was already attempting to dig it up. "They're really lookin' for you."

"I know," Ignacio said, turning off her uniview. "I'm all over the local news." He stood up from the couch, set down the remote, and walked towards her. "There's already been a few national mentions, too. I guess it's the first time in a while that a Freemon's disappeared."

She smiled. "Didn't you always want to be famous?"

"Famous, maybe," he said. "Infamous, never." He kissed her on the cheek. "Thanks for shopping, Raq."

"De nada," she said, as he picked up a blue banana. "It's actually kinda nice to be shopping for someone else. Me an' Pam always get our own stuff."

Peeling the azure fruit, he said, "She's supposed to come back today, ey?"

"That was the original plan, yeah." Raquel placed some of the groceries into her small refrigerator. "But she called me on my cell while I was shopping and said she wouldn't be coming back 'til Wednesday." She looked over her shoulder at him. "So you're clear to stay here for a few more days."

"Bueno." He walked behind her, placing his hand on her back. "Let me get this, Raquel. You've done enough already."

She laughed as she continued to pack the fridge. "All I've done is gone shopping, Iggy."

"You've done more than that," he said. "You saved my ass." He gently took an Odwalla® from her hand, set it onto the refrigerator's top shelf, then placed his hand beneath her chin.

She looked up at him, her beautiful brown eyes sparkling.

"Thank you, Raquel," he said. "From the bottom of my heart. Gracias."

"Thanks," she said. "It's, um...I'm not really used to people telling me things like that." She stared at him for a moment, then hugged him tightly. "I love you, Iggy," she said.

Ignacio held her in his arms, pressing his lips against the top of her head. "I love you, too, Raquel."

And that was the pure, unadulterated truth.

The previous memories he had of her were all positive ones, and now that his true self had gotten a chance to know her and to experience her compassion personally, the memories synergized with the feelings to make a complete whole. It was like knowing a lover for a long time then suddenly being able to experience their freshness and newness all over again.

"I really do," he said, softly releasing his embrace. "Let me put these away, okay?"

Raquel smiled. "Okay." She walked over to her couch and sat down. As Ignacio began to put away the remaining groceries, she said, "You know how you were telling me last night about this group you were a part of? The ones who sent you undercover?"

"Sí."

"Are you supposed to join up with them again?"

"That's the idea," he said, putting a box of Life® cereal into the cupboard.

"But if you don't have any chips, then how are they going to find you?"

"Through my thoughts," he said. "They can pinpoint individual frees like they were GPS transmitters."

"How do they do *that*?"

"I have no idea," Ignacio said, placing the final item away.

"But they can." He walked over to the couch, sat down next to her, and put her feet on top of his lap.

"So why haven't they contacted you then?"

"My frees are still stabilizing from the awakening," he said, massaging her tiny foot with one of his hands. "It's like there's a bunch of static in my head right now. Once the static's gone and my frees settle down, they'll be able to tune in and find me."

"And then what?"

"I don't know," he said. "I'll cross that bridge when I get there."

Raquel placed her hand on top of his. "I hope we'll still be able to see each other."

"Me too, Raquel..." He stared down at their interconnected hands. "Me, too." He looked over at her and smiled. "You're a beautiful soul, you know that?"

"No." She smiled. "But I'm learning."

"Bueno," he said, lying down next to her. "Por que eres." He wrapped his arm around her waist, her smile widened, and they began to kiss.

And despite the numerous issues his awakened mind still had to deal with, Ignacio felt content with the present. The future may have been uncertain, but one thing in this new life was for sure–he would know love.

And that was enough for now.

# Chapter 19
# ((Overstandings))

*"When the tale has been told and the lines have been drawn, what then remains? When all is said and done, and the facts and the truths and the lies and the dreams have been presented before us, what are we left with?*
*We are left, as always, with but one single thing.*
*In the end, it all boils down to choice.*
*We choose how to interpret the tale, and how the tale will affect us. We choose how to perceive the lines, and what they will mean to our being. We choose for ourselves what will be fact and what will be fiction; what will be lie and what will be truth; what will be reality and what will be dream.*
*We choose whom we will trust.*
*We choose whom we will love.*
*We choose with whom we will do battle.*
*We choose with whom we will build.*
*We choose how to live our lives.*
*Fate only acts after a choice has been made.*
*And though other forces, whether they be individuals or institutions, will try to persuade or dissuade us in the decisions we make along our life's journey, in truth, that is all they can ever really do: try.*
*Only we can do.*
*So do.*

*Do what must be done, and do it without fear. Do what you know is right, and do it without hesitation. Do what you must, and you shall set yourself free.*
*True freedom lies within you.*

*Awaken it.*

*Now.*

*For tomorrow may never come, and time waits for no one. Act before it is too late, while understanding the paradox that it is never too late to act. While there is still breath, there is still hope.*

*I know this for a fact. All seemed hopeless around me, my dreams turned to dust. Yet I still drew more breaths, and I dreamt new dreams.*

*And I have seen that dreams become reality for those who are willing to believe in them.*

*Do you believe in dreams?*

*I do.*

*And so should you, because in your hands you're holding one. Feel its weight? Feel its substance?*

*The dream is real.*

*The choice is yours.*

*Choose wisely.*

*—Adrian Malcolm Wellor*

Ashley stared at the journal's final entry.

"Choose wisely," she said to herself. She closed the book and looked up at the lush, green, Tiger Mountain scenery surrounding her. Ferns and spruce, moss and lichen, birds, streams, rocks and earth...

Gaia in her full splendor.

After the week's events, the forest was the perfect place for Ashley to come and think...and relax...and decompress. So much had happened in so little time. So many confirmations. So many revelations.

So many choices...

She looked down at the stream beside her, into the fresh mountain water. Everything was so clear. She could see things coming to the surface. Other things moving on. Others approaching nearer.

The current of change.

Ashley placed the journal into her backpack, then dipped her fingers into the cold water and swirled them around. She took off her hiking boots, her wool socks, and pulled her stretch pants up to her knees. She slowly lowered her bare feet into the stream...

# ((FREQUENCIES))

It was chilly, but refreshing. She wiggled her toes around, allowing the undercurrent to pass between them. It felt good getting her feet wet...she enjoyed the sensation. It was a way for her to feel alive. And free.

But somehow, it wasn't quite enough. Not anymore.

Ashley took off her fleece sweater, set it on top of her pack, and placed her hands beneath the water's surface. She leaned forward, cupped her hands, and brought the cool water to her face...

Wonderful.

She did this a few more times, then pulled her feet from the water. She put her knees beneath her, placing her hands at the edge of the stream. Ashley closed her eyes, and gave thanks to life.

For everything.

She slowly took in a breath, then immersed her head in the gentle current. The amplified sounds rushed around her. Beautiful, flowing, chaotic music. She delicately swayed her head to the melody, dancing until she was out of breath.

Ashley emerged from the water and breathed in again. She smiled. She opened her eyes.

A thrush was singing from a cedar's branch. A squirrel scampered into a blackberry bush. Life was all around.

A black and red butterfly flittered by, dreamlike.

But was it her dream? Or the butterfly's?

Ashley laughed.

It didn't matter. Either way, the dream was real.

*That* was what mattered.

She wrung the excess water from her hair, and put her fleece back on. Then the socks, and then the shoes. She fastened the laces, picked up her backpack, and stood to her feet. She faced the trail leading back down the mountain, and walked towards it.

There was work to be done.

People to network with. Things to be changed. Old structures to bring down, and new ones to build.

Ashley stepped onto the path without hesitation.

The choice was hers.

315

# Ω
# Chapter 20
# ((Ad Infinitum))

"No way," McCready said, as he eagerly stepped out of the limo. "No fucking way."

In his driveway was parked a gorgeous, cherry red, '57 Chevy®. Mint-condition. Freshly waxed. In *his* driveway.

He quickly walked up to it, and stood there before the machine in amazement.

Xanadeux followed behind him. "Mr. Huxton wanted you to have a surprise bonus, Mr. McCready," it said. "I hope that you approve of my suggestion."

He looked back at the android. "*You* suggested this?"

"Yes."

McCready laughed. "Xanny, if I did hugs, I'd hug you right now." He turned back around to the car and lightly rapped his knuckles against its sides. "Steel. This is so fuckin' bomb."

"I'm pleased to see that I made the right choice."

"Me, too," he said, running his fingers along one of the fins. "So does she actually run on gas?"'

"She does. And her tank is currently full." McCready heard a jingling noise, as Xanadeux said, "Here are your keys."

"Keys," he said, grasping the Chevrolet®-logo keyring. "Sweet." He closed his hand around them. "Alright, I gotta know–is this baby actually mine, or am I just borrowing her?"

"She's yours, Mr. McCready."

"Fuckin'-A." He walked over to the front door and opened it. He touched the red vinyl interior. "I am in the *sweetest* dream right now." He clicked on the antique radio's knob and dialed it up and down the different stations. "Does this only pick up FM/AM?"

"Yes, but we could have it modified if you would like."

"No way," he said, clicking off the tunes. "An old radio fits her just perfect." McCready climbed into the front seat, put the key into the ignition, turned it forward. The engine roared to life. He pushed his foot on the gas pedal and revved it a little. The sensation was awesome.

Xanadeux tapped on the window.

McCready rolled it down. "Yeah?"

It reached its hand towards him, palm facing up. "You'll need the proper permit to drive a leaded, gasoline-burning vehicle."

"Oh yeah, right," he said, placing his thumb on the small scanner in the center of the android's palm. "I got it?"

It nodded. "You now have it."

"Great." He pressed his foot on the brake and shifted the car into reverse.

"Mr. McCready," Xanadeux said.

He held his foot on the brake. "Yeah?"

"A few more things before you go."

"Sure."

"Your company car will be delivered shortly, after we make some final modifications on it."

"Alright."

"And Mr. Huxton has requested for you to meet with him tomorrow morning to discuss the details of your employment."

"But I'm free today, right?"

"Correct," Xanadeux said. "Also, with your permission, I can load your bags into your house."

"Fine with me. Is that it then?"

"That's all for now."

"Then I'm gonna go cruisin', Xanny," he said, releasing his foot from the brake.

"Enjoy yourself," it said.

"I will," McCready said. "Believe that."


For the next four hours, McCready cruised around various parts of the Eastside and Westside, listening to an oldies station that he found on AM. He would have stayed out cruising all day, but he only had so much gas, and didn't want to ask Xanadeux for a refill already.

He'd wait until tomorrow. That'd be enough time.

Entering his apartment, McCready still had a childlike grin stretched across his face. He couldn't help it. It was like he'd found a little piece of heaven on Earth.

He set his keys onto the counter, went to the bathroom, then walked over to the uniview. Time to tell Ignacio the good news.

"Voice-rec on," he said. "Call Ignacio."

He waited for about fifteen seconds, but there was no answer.

"Would you like to leave a message?" the unie asked.

Before he could answer, the doorbell sounded.

He said to the screen, "Yeah, leave message. Ignacio, this is McCready. I got some good news, amigo. Call me when you get this. Late." He touched the screen. "Show door camera," he said.

Ashley appeared upon the uniview.

McCready smiled. "Open door," he said, walking around the corner to greet her.

"Hey," she said with a bright smile. "How are you?"

"Awesome," he said as they hugged each other. "How 'bout you?"

"Same." She kissed him on the lips, and walked into his living room. "Today's been incredible."

"Yeah, it has." He sat down on the couch. "You see the car?"

Ashley sat next to him, placing the book she was holding on her lap. "Mm-hm. I like it."

"Did you know they were gonna give that to me?"

She shook her head. "No...but it doesn't surprise me."

"Surprised the hell outta me," he said. "I was like a kid on Christmas, Ashley. You would've cracked up. I hopped right in that baby, and just..." He flattened his palm, moved his hand forward like a plane, and made a whistling noise. "*Cruised*. It was bomb. It was like I was in a movie, or something."

"That's neat," she said.

"Yeah, it was. So what did you do after the airport?"

"I went over to Tiger Mountain and hiked for a few hours... Relaxed, thought about things..." She held up the book. "Went over this a little more."

"The journal?"

"Mm-hm." She opened it up and thumbed through its pages. "There's really some amazing stuff in here."

"I bet," McCready said. "You'll have to show me some of it."

"Definitely," she said, continuing to look through the journal. "There's actually this one part in here I wanted to read you... It really sums up a lot of what I feel right now. And the way he put it was just really neat."

"Cool. I'd love to hear it."

"Okay," she said, "let me find it."

As Ashley searched through the journal, McCready leaned against the side of the couch and peeked out the window. The rain had completely stopped, and the sun looked like it was about to come out.

"Here it is," Ashley said, resting her head onto his lap. She looked up at him and smiled. "You ready?"

He lightly touched her damp hair and smiled back. "Shoot."

"Okay." She propped the book in front her of face. "So he was talking about the way our lives go through cycles, and the way that one thing always leads to the next. How one door will close and then another will suddenly open."

"Like how you'll quit a job and then get offered one that's even better?" McCready laughed. "Like that?"

"Exactly," Ashley said. "That's basically what the theme of this entry was. But what I liked about it so much, was the *way* he said it. So here it goes, his words now: 'We each write our own individual stories as we move through the years of our lives, filling them with events both good and bad, things both right and wrong, and people both loved and loathed. But unlike fiction, our tales have no simple resolution. Though chapters of our life may have their particular conclusions, the overall story keeps on going, ad infinitum. For even when we reach our last heartbeat–even then–does the tale truly end? Do our frequencies truly stop vibrating? Or does our energy simply change form, loop back into the life spectrum, and commence its story all over again? Who is to say? Ultimately, we can only answer these questions for ourselves.'"

Ashley paused for a moment, noticing the room growing brighter.

McCready glanced out at the sky.

The sun had pierced the clouds, its energy now shining through the window, onto them. The warmth felt good.

They both smiled, and she continued, "'This then, is what *I* have come to know: There are no such things as endings. Only infinite beginnings.'"

Ashley closed the book.

$$\Omega$$

:

Ω

# OMEGAPPENDIX

Ω

# TABLE OF CONTENTS

ΩΩΩΩΩΩΩΩΩΩΩΩΩΩΩΩΩΩΩΩΩΩΩΩΩΩΩΩΩΩΩΩΩΩΩ

# Freekspeek:
## A glossary of frequential terms
ΩΩΩΩΩΩΩΩΩΩΩΩΩΩΩΩΩΩΩΩΩΩΩΩΩΩΩΩΩΩΩΩΩΩΩ

**AAS:** *abbr.* See **automatic anti-collision systems**.

**ADD:** *abbr.* See **attention-deficit disorder**.

**Adsat:** *n.* An orbiting or geostationary satellite used to display slogans and/or advertisements which can be viewed by the naked eye from the surface of a planet or moon.

**Aeonomics:** *n.* The study of how economics will be affected by a world populated with immortals.

**AI:** *abbr.* Artificial intelligence.

**Alpha-beta:** *n.* **Freemon** term for someone who thinks within the acceptable range of FE's for normal citizens.

**Alpha point:** *n.* The beginning of the universe; the **big bang**.

**Alpha wave:** *n.* A frequency transmitted by a source (a **uniview**, a radio tower, etc.) which induces a feeling of calm and complacency. Also, the **frees** emanated by someone when they are calm or "normal."

**American Empire: Headquartered** in the United States, this empire directly or indirectly controls the Earth's entire Western Hemisphere and also has influence or dominion over much of the Eastern Hemisphere. Has been compared by many to the **Roman Empire**.

**American Revolution:** Also known as the **Revolutionary War**, this conflict led to the creation of the **American Empire**, which was officially founded in 1776, and is still active to the present.

**Amp:** *n.* A powerful illegal stimulant which is a synthesis of epinephrine, ephedra, cocaine, and concentrated caffeine. *–v.* To be on amp or to act in a hyperactive manner.

**Anamnesis:** *n.* Latin term meaning "the loss of forgetfulness."

**Anasazi:** *n.* A term used for the Native American culture that once inhabited Colorado, Arizona, Utah, and New Mexico. Ancestors of the Pueblo, the Anasazi are often associated with basket-making, cliff dwellings, and petroglyphs.

**Androidal:** *adj.* Of, or relating to an android.

**Armas:** *n.* Spanish for "weapon" or "arm."

**Arthurian:** *adj.* Of, or relating to **King Arthur**.

**Ash:** *v.* To tap or flick the ashes from a cigarette, cigar, or **blunt**.

**Astral travel:** *v.* To leave the body and travel over physical or mystical distances in spirit form.

**Attention-deficit disorder:** *n.* The label branded upon children who exhibit signs of hyperactivity or restlessness, especially when in a scholastic setting. Treatment for the "disorder" usually involves a form of **neurochemical** therapy.

**Aural IR:** *n.* A device which displays infrared radiation as an outline surrounding the object being examined.

**Auto:** *adj.* Automatic. Also, *–n.* Automatic pilot or autopilot.

**Autobus:** *n.* Public transportation buses which are programmed along specific routes and are controlled remotely, usually by a computer.

**Autoevolution:** *n.* Evolution controlled by intelligent **lifeforms** rather than **natural selection**.

**Automatic anti-collision systems:** *n.* An intelligent technology that prevents **GS** vehicles from coming too close to one another during their operation. Required by law and standard-equipped in all **GS** vehicles and crafts.

**Avatar:** *n.* The icon which someone uses to represent themselves in a virtual domain or setting.

**Baba Ghannooj:** *n.* A Middle-Eastern dish consisting of smoky, fire-roasted eggplant, tahini, garlic, lemon juice, and spices.

**Babylon:** *n.* A place containing an abundance of luxury and conveniences which have been gained through the exploitation and oppression of human and animal beings. *–Babylonian: adj.* Utilizing the methods of, or having the traits associated with a Babylon.

**Back:** *n.* Back-up; reinforcements.

**Bad-ass:** *adj.* Awesome; amazing. Also, fierce or formidable. *–n.* One who possesses or exemplifies bad-ass qualities.

**Banistered:** *adj.* Containing a banister.

**Barre:** *n.* A rounded bar, usually wooden, used in ballet for stretching exercises.

**B-chip:** *n.* See **biochip**.

**Benzy:** *n.* A Mercedes-Benz®.

**B/free scanner:** *n.* A device which can simultaneously sense both **biochip** and **FE** information. The **Freemon** are equipped with B/free scanners (usually housed within contacts or implants) so that they can directly gauge a suspect's **frees** without having to rely on the **freeread**'s data. Since a **freeread** senses its owner's **frees** and then transmits the information via **satellink**, there is much more room for error with it than with a B/free scanner.

**Bi:** *adj.* Bisexual.

**Big bang:** *n.* See **big bang theory**.

**Big bang theory:** The theory that the entire universe originated from a singular, infinitely-dense state of being.

**Biochip:** *n.* A tiny microchip (less than half the size of a small grain of rice) which is encased inside of a **biocompatible** material and injected under the skin at birth. Once inside the body, it becomes surrounded by a thin sheath of protein which securely holds it in place for the duration of its owner's life. Usually located on either thumb, the **biochip** contains all of its owner's personal, financial, and medical records, their bank accounts, credit cards, and **digital cash**, their electronic keys and passwords, **live-feed** biological information, a **GPS** transmitter, and a **satellink** hookup which allows them to perform countless other functions and duties via the **uninet**. Also commonly referred to as a **B-chip**. Less commonly referred to as the **Mark of the Beast** (see **freeread**). *–v.* To inject, or to be injected with a biochip.

**Biocompatible:** *adj.* Having little or no adverse effects upon a biological organism. Usually used in reference to vertebrates.

**Bioinformatics:** *n.* The study of how **information theory** and technologies are applied to the fields of **biotechnology** and genetic analysis research.

**Biological fundamentalism:** The belief that death is a natural, essential part of the life equation which should not be removed. *–n.* Biological fundamentalist: One who adheres to the principles of biological fundamentalism.

**Biomatter:** *n.* Biological material.

**Bioreadings:** *n.* The data provided by a device or apparatus during or after the examination of a biological organism.

**Biostasis:** *n.* The complete suspension of an organism's biological functions and activity in order to perfectly preserve it until a later date. Also called **suspended animation**.

**Biotech:** *n.* See **biotechnology**.

**Biotechnology:** *n*. The synthesis of biology, medicine, engineering, and technology, and its applications (see **gengineer**). **Biotech** is the most profitable industry of the 21st century.

**Birdie:** *n*. A police or law enforcement helicopter.

**Black Panther Party:** An organization founded in 1966 by Huey Newton and Bobby Seale in the hopes of bettering the welfare of their community (i.e., free breakfast programs, protection against police brutality, etc.). One of the favorite targets of the **FBI**'s **COINTELPRO**s.

**Blud:** *n*. Man or fellow; dude.

**Blunt:** *n*. A hollowed-out cigar which has been filled with marijuana. Also, a large **joint** which has been rolled up in a tobacco leaf.

**Borg:** *n*. See **cyborg**.

**Bounce:** *v*. To leave or go somewhere.

**Brennan Commission:** A think-tank formed in 1999 by **Michael Brennan** to explore the implications, possibilities, and applications of the **FE** technology. The commission was comprised of **Brennan**, **Dr. Adrian Wellor**, **W.A. Huxton**, members of the **FBI**, **NSA**, and **CIA**, and certain, carefully selected biologists, physicists, sociologists, psychologists, anthropologists, political scientists, and **futurists**.

**Brennan, Michael Jude:** Born 1943. Founder of the **Brennan Commission**, and the official creator of the **FE** technology. One of the most respected men in all of science, Brennan still conducts research and occasionally teaches upper-division courses at the **UW**.

**Bubastis:** In Egyptian legend, Bubastis was a cat-headed sun goddess who was the daughter of **Isis** and the sister of **Sekhet**. Whereas her sister represented the fierce aspects of the sun, Bubastis symbolized the kindly, life-giving aspects.

**Bubble gum:** *adj*. Having no substance or depth; sugarcoated.

**Budded:** *adj*. Under the influence of marijuana. *–n*. **Budder**: one who partakes in the consumption of marijuana.

**Bugged:** *adj*. Strange, odd, or unusual; **trippy**.

**Bumbaklaat:** *n*. Jamaican slang which roughly translates to "bullshit." Also can be used as a verb or an interjection.

**Bueno:** *adj*. Spanish for "good." *–interj*. Spanish for "all right" or "okay."

**Bureau, the:** The Federal **Bureau of Investigation** (see **FBI**).

**Butch:** *adj*. Being a, or having the characteristics of a masculine lesbian. Can be derogatory or friendly, depending on context. *–n*. A short haircut; a buzz cut.

**Bzzt:** *interj*. Used to voice disapproval with someone's statement, opinion, or response.

**Cabróna:** *n*. Spanish for "bitch."

**Callate:** Spanish for forcefully saying "be quiet."

**Callscreen:** *n*. A closed-circuit **uniview** which is located at the entrance of a residence and is used primarily to screen visitors.

**Cancer stick:** *n*. A carcinogenic cigarette.

**Canny:** *n*. Cannabis; marijuana.

**Capoeira:** *n*. A Brazilian martial arts/dance with heavy African influences. Pronounced "Ka-pway-da."

**Carnivore:** Officially acknowledged in the year 2000, Carnivore is the **FBI**'s e-mail interception and surveillance tool. Essentially a wiretap for the Internet, Carnivore does for American e-mail what **Echelon** does for the world.

**Casa:** *n*. Spanish for "house."

**Cascadia:** *n*. The region consisting of Southern British Columbia, Washington, Oregon, and Northern California.

**Cauterizer:** *n*. A device that uses a combination of laser light and protein solder to weld a wound shut.

**CDC:** *abbr*. See **Centers for Disease Control**.

**Cell:** *n*. Cellphone; cellular phone.

**Centers for Disease Control:** Founded in 1946 and based in Atlanta, Georgia, the **CDC** is a major division of the United States Public Health Service, and is responsible for many programs, including disease control and prevention. The **CDC** research program is credited with developing the AIDS vaccine.

**Central Intelligence Agency:** Created by the National Security Act of 1947 in order to replace the **OSS**, the **CIA** oversees work done by America's other intelligence agencies, as well as having its own particular duties, including the conducting of research in various fields of study, providing counsel for the president and the **NSC** on international affairs, monitoring global electronic communications, and conducting **counterintelligence** operations in foreign countries. The **CIA** also owns the research company **In-Q-Tel®**.
**C'est la vie:** French for "that's life" or "so life goes."
**Cha:** *n.* Tibetan for "tea."
**Chaos theory:** Deals with the seemingly random, chaotic fluctuations found in the natural world. For a much more thorough explanation, read James Gleick's *Chaos*.
**Cheshire:** *adj.* Having the characteristics of the Cheshire Cat from *Alice's Adventures in Wonderland*, namely a wide, ear-to-ear grin.
**Chica:** *n.* Spanish for "girl."
**Chihuly:** *n.* A glass sculpture designed by artist Dale Chihuly.
**Chill:** *adj.* Very good; cool. *–v.* To relax or take it easy.
**Chocolatey:** *adj.* Of, or resembling chocolate.
**Chorizo:** *n.* A spicy, red, flavorful sausage used in many Hispanic and Latino cuisines.
**CIA:** *abbr.* See **Central Intelligence Agency**.
**Clearance:** *n.* A requirement for having vocal interaction with others while possessing frequencies which fall outside of the acceptable range of **FE**'s for normal citizens (see **FE Act**).
**Clobacco:** *n.* A **gengineered** synthesis of clove and tobacco.
**Clown:** *v.* To ridicule or make fun of. *–n.* A ridiculing statement.
**Coherent light:** *n.* A light source whose waves are in phase and of the exact, same wavelength.
**COINTELPRO:** The **FBI**'s acronym for its domestic **counterintelligence** program. Originally named COINTELPRO-CP, USA, the first official COINTELPROs were directed towards American communists in the 1950's, and later were focused on the various radical groups which emerged during the 1960's and '70's (see **Black Panther Party**). The methods used by the COINTELPROs ranged from the expected (surveillance, infiltration, etc.) to the bizarre (attempting to coax Martin Luther King, Jr. into committing suicide). Due to public scrutiny and criticism, the **FBI** officially ended its COINTELPROs in 1971. However, the programs still live on today in other guises, both official (see **DCC**) and unofficial. To find out more about the exciting exploits of this strange and fascinating program, read *The COINTELPRO Papers* by Ward Churchill and Jim Vander Wall.
**Comemos:** *v.* Spanish. A conjugation of the verb, "comer," meaning "to eat."
**Compañero:** *n.* Spanish for "companion" or "friend."
**¿Comprendes?:** Spanish for "Do you understand?"
**Concernedly:** *adv.* To be interested, troubled, or anxious.
**Consciousness uploading:** *n.* A process in which an organism's consciousness is uploaded into a new host.
**Coordinator of Information:** A governmental office which was replaced by the **OSS** in 1942. To be continued in *~VIBRATIONS~*...
**Corpo:** *n.* See **corporate police**.
**Corporate police:** *n.* As the corporation's power increased, so did their need for security, leading them to develop their own internally-operated police forces. **Corpos** are officially sanctioned by the U.S. government, wield many of the same powers as the local police, and in many cases (see **Ordocops™**), have extralegal capabilities which make them more similar to an intelligence agency (see **FBI**, **CIA**, **NSA**).
**Counterintelligence:** *n.* The division of an intelligence agency that is responsible for gathering and databasing information about potential political and military threats, preventing sabotage and subversion, engaging in sabotage and subversion, and deceiving the enemy (see **snakes**).
**CPU:** *abbr.* Central processing unit.

**Cracker:** *n.* One who is adept at breaking into computer systems and networks. Also, a derogatory term for a Caucasian.

**Crossbreed:** *n.* A **gengineered** synthesis of two or more distinct organisms.

**Cryo:** *n.* Cryogenic storage.

**Cuidado:** Spanish for "be careful."

**Cuídate:** Spanish for "take care."

**Curb:** *n.* An illegal narcotic which is a synthesis of long-acting barbiturates, antihistamines, and **meperidine.**

**Curbed:** *adj.* To be on **curb** or to be extremely intoxicated.

**Cybernetic:** *adj.* Of, or relating to **cybernetics.**

**Cybernetics:** *n.* 21st century bionics. Also, the science of control processes and communication, especially in regards to the similarities and differences found in biological and artificial systems. From the Greek word "kybernetes," meaning "steersman."

**Cyberspace:** *n.* **Virtual reality,** or the space in which all electronic and photonic communication occurs. Coined by William Gibson in *Neuromancer.*

**Cybertrail:** *n.* The trail of information left behind when travelling through **cyberspace.**

**Cyborg:** *n.* A **cybernetic** organism comprised of both biological and artificial systems.

**Dancehall:** *n.* A type of music originated in Jamaican dancehalls in the late 1970's when DJ's started to toast and chant over **dub** versions of popular recordings. Soon after, "dancehall" became something of an umbrella term for Jamaican music of the 1980's and 1990's. Classic dancehall artists include Shabba Ranks and Supercat.

**Darwinian theory:** A theory of evolution put forth by Charles Darwin which revolves around the concept of **natural selection.**

**Data mining:** *v.* To extract information about someone or something from computer records and data. –*n.* Data miner: One who is employed in, or adept at data mining.

**DC:** *abbr.* See **digital cash.** –*pl.* DC's.

**DCC:** *abbr.* See **Domestic Center for Counterterrorism.**

**Deevolution:** *n.* Gradually evolving towards something that is simpler and less complex, whether it be a lifestyle or a **lifeform.** Purposefully spelled with two "e's" rather than one (devolution), so the word is pronounced "Dee-evolution" instead of the negative sounding "Devil-lution."

**De nada:** Spanish for "it's nothing" or "no problem."

**Department of Defense:** Founded in 1949 (as a by-product of the National Security Act of 1947), the **DOD** controls the Army, Navy, Air Force, and Marines. The largest of all the federal departments, the DOD is **headquartered** in **The Pentagon** and is chaired by the secretary of defense. Usually receives at least 25% of the entire federal budget.

**Diazecalm™:** A trademark used for a powerful antianxiety drug which relaxes the user without making them drowsy.

**Digital cash:** *n.* Paper money's electronic replacement, **DC**'s are stored as encrypted digital code and accessed via **biochip.** Digital cash was initially met with much resistance, but was readily accepted after terrorists (see **Terror Years**) found a way to house highly infectious diseases within physical cash's cotton fibers.

**Dios:** *n.* Spanish for "god."

**Dis:** *v.* To disrespect or ridicule. –*n.* A statement of disrespect.

**Disinfection:** *n.* The removal of an infectious meme from an infected individual.

**DOD:** *abbr.* See **Department of Defense.**

**Domestic Center for Counterterrorism:** Quietly set up in the late 1990's, this secretive branch of the **FBI** specializes in domestic **counterintelligence** programs (see **COINTELPRO**). While very active during the first part of the 21st century (see **Terror Years**), DCC operations have greatly declined in the last few decades, in direct proportion to the instances of terrorism. The DCC is now called upon only to handle cases of the utmost importance to national/world security.

**Dominica:** Officially named the Commonwealth of Dominica, this small country is located in the Lesser Antilles, and is one of the Caribbean's least developed and most mountainous islands.

**Dope:** *adj.* Cool, very good; **fresh.**

**Doublespeak:** *n.* A euphemistic, linguistic code where what is said is altogether different from what is meant or actually occurring. Used especially by political, corporate, and military leaders. Examples would be: when armies are called "peacekeepers," when "friendly fire" kills, or when Western nations bring "democracy" to Latin America, Africa, or Southeast Asia. *-v.* To engage in doublespeak.

**Dreadlocks:** *n.* Long hair which has become so clumped or tangled together that it assumes the shape of rope or cord. Associated with **rastas.** *-adj.* Dreadlocked: To have or wear dreadlocks.

**Drop:** *v.* To start or begin playing a musical beat, usually from a record.

**Dub:** *n.* An instrumental remix of a single, often featuring an increased bassline, snippets and pieces of the original vocals, and/or the use of delay and echo effects on the instruments. Though a creation of reggae, dub is now also used by musicians in other genres as well. Classic dub reggae artists include Prince Far I and Augustus Pablo. *-v.* To make a dub.

**Dynamical system:** *n.* A system whose behavior changes through time.

**Eastside:** The east side of the greater Seattle area, separated from the west by Lake Washington. Includes **Redmond**, Bellevue, **Mercer Island**, Juanita, Kirkland, Medina, Factoria, Newport Hills, Eastgate, and Newcastle.

**Echelon:** The most powerful and far-reaching eavesdropping network in the history of the world. In operation since at least the 1990's, **headquartered** in Sugar Grove, West Virginia, overseen in large part by the **NSA**, Echelon can intercept and translate any kind of electronic communication, regardless of its point of origin. Utilizes **voice-rec**, **keyword**, and **language translation** technologies. Thus, if the word "terrorist" is input into its systems, all electronic communications–whether phone, fax, e-mail, or **uniview**–containing the word "terrorist" will be recorded and monitored in their entirety.

**Electrified baton:** *n.* A **handheld** weapon capable of inducing paralysis or unconsciousness through the use of **UV** laser light and/or an electric shock. Used by police and the **National Guard** during civil disturbances and riots.

**Electrochromic:** *adj.* Of, or relating to materials that change color or opaqueness in response to electrical input.

**Electromagnetic:** *adj.* Of, or relating to **electromagnetics.**

**Electromagnetic field:** *n.* The field of energy produced when an object or body emits **electromagnetic radiation.**

**Electromagnetic radiation:** *n.* Energy which is emitted as waves possessing both magnetic and electric components. X-rays, radio waves, **FE's**, **UV** rays, and visible light rays are but a few examples of **electromagnetic** radiation.

**Electromagnetic spectrum:** *n.* The distribution and range of **electromagnetic radiation** (see the table contained within this appendix for more detail).

**Electromagnetics:** *n.* The science of **electromagnetic radiation** and its related technologies and applications.

**EM:** *abbr.* See **electromagnetic.**

**EMF:** *abbr.* See **electromagnetic field.** Also, electromotive force.

**Emfield:** *n.* See **electromagnetic field.**

**Emvest:** *n.* A vestlike device which projects an **EMF** around its wearer to protect them from **electromagnetic** attacks.

**Epigem:** *n.* Gems or jewelry which are implanted into the skin for cosmetic purposes.

**Esposa:** *n.* Spanish for "wife."

**Esta bien:** Spanish for "it's good" or "it's fine."

**Estilo:** *n.* Spanish for "style."

**Excalibur:** In **Arthurian** legend, the sword which **King Arthur** drew from a stone was shattered after many years of use in battle. **Merlin** took Arthur to the **Lady of the Lake**, and she offered him an enchanted sword, Excalibur, which was held by an arm rising out of the lake. Arthur rowed to the sword, took it, and the blade became his sword for life.

**Existencia:** *n.* Spanish for "existence."

**Exoskeleton:** *n.* An intelligent device that replaced casts and splints, and greatly improved the recovery time for broken bones. Like casts, exoskeletons surround the injured bone and keep it in in place. But, as the injury heals, an exoskeleton can gauge how much pressure and mobility the bone can bear, and then adjust its mechanisms accordingly. This helps to prevent muscular atrophy and allows for a much more natural, gradual recovery to occur.

**Extractor:** *n.* A device or mechanism which can remove a **freeread**.

**Extraño:** *adj.* Spanish for "strange" or "odd."

**Eyemouse:** *n.* A device which allows its user to move an indicator or cursor around a **uniview** screen with only their eyes.

**Fat-ass:** *adj.* Big; enormous. *−n.* One who possesses fat-ass characteristics.

**FBI:** *abbr.* See **Federal Bureau of Investigation**.

**Federal Bureau of Investigation:** Founded in 1907 (as the Bureau of Investigation), the **FBI** handles cases involving the violation of federal criminal laws. Also has jurisdiction over domestic **counterintelligence** operations and plays a large role in maintaining national and international security. Both the DCC and the **Freemon** are special divisions of the **FBI**.

**FE:** *abbr.* See **frequency emissions, frees**.

**FE Act:** See **Frequency Emissions Act**.

**FE scanner:** *n.* See **frequency emissions scanner, B/free scanner**.

**Fellatio:** *n.* Oral sex administered to a penis.

**Finalmente:** *adv.* Spanish for "finally."

**Firewall:** *n.* A protective barrier of code and data which is erected to prevent unwanted users from gaining access to a private online network, or to control the outside access privileges a user has while inside of a private network.

**Flaky:** *adj.* Prone to breaking plans or arrangements; not reliable.

**Flashback:** *v.* To vividly remember a previous occurrence. Other tenses include flashbacks, flashbacked, flashbacking.

**Flatline:** *v.* To pass into a state of inactivity, dormancy, or death.

**Focus:** *n.* To elementary and **precollege** students what a major is to college students.

**Foglets:** *n.* A foglike cluster of **nanomachines** that have grouped together (usually in the air) to create an interconnected network which has total molecular control over its surroundings.

**Fractal:** *n.* A fragmented, irregular, geometric pattern that repeats itself into infinity and whose parts are exactly the same as its whole.

**Frat:** *n.* A fraternity.

**Freek:** *n.* See **Freeker**. *−v.* To do something that would cause or elicit a **freeky** response (i.e., "He's **freeking** him out."). Also, to approach a concept with a new or unusual twist (i.e., "I'm gonna **freek** this rhyme.").

**Freeker:** *n.* Originally **Freemon** slang for a **frequency emissions violator**, now also used by the general public to describe someone who has strange or unusual thoughts, especially those of a subversive, revolutionary, or reality-shattering nature.

**Freekspeek:** *n.* The words, terms, and sayings used by a **freeker**.

**Freek sweeps:** *n.* Nickname given to the mass arrests that occurred following the passage of the **FE Act** of 2012. Now also used when the **Freemon** conduct a raid on a **gathering**.

**Freeky:** *adj.* Exhibiting the unusual, **trippy**, and often dangerous characteristics associated with a **freeker**. *−adv.* freekily.

**Freemen:** *n.* The name given to freed slaves or those having citizen's rights. Also refers to the governing body of the early **Pilgrims** at **Plymouth Colony**, and the title adopted by some of the **militia** movements of the late 20th/early 21st century.

**Freemon:** Or FREquency Emissions MONitor(s). A special division of the **FBI**, officially founded in 2012 (see **Frequency Emissions Act**) in order to monitor, database, and investigate potential **frequency emissions violators**. The Freemon have no dress code or uniform, negotiable hours, and are considered by many to be the most independent and least restricted branch of the **FBI**. The Freemon recruit not only from within the **Bureau** itself, but also from the local police, corporate police (see **corpos**), other federal agencies, and on rare occasions, colleges and workcamps. Each Freemon is awarded a single, government-provided, **cybernetic** enhancement upon completion of their extensive training, and have the option to receive others as their career progresses. The acronym Freemon was said to be coined by **FBI** special agent Dale Hoover in homage to the **freemen** of **Plymouth Colony**, but others have argued that the abbreviated name is nothing more than a clever exercise in governmental **doublespeak**.

**Freeread:** *n.* See **frequency emissions reader**.

**Frees:** *n.* **Freemon** slang for **frequency emissions**, now also used by the general public. To frequencies what vibes is to vibrations (i.e., "She's got some **trippy** frees.").

**Frequency emissions:** *n.* The **electromagnetic radiation** produced and emitted by all living organisms which is capable of being measured with an **FE scanner**. The term **FE**, and its related concepts, were unofficially created by **Dr. Adrian Wellor**, and officially created by **Michael Brennan**.

**Frequency Emissions Act:** Passed in December of 2012 in the face of increased terrorist activity (see **Terror Years**), this act was a direct response to the nation's inability to effectively identify potential terrorists before they became an actual threat. Among other things, the **FE Act** officially created the **Freemon** and also established an acceptable range of **FE**'s for normal citizens as defined by the findings of the **Brennan Commission**. Though many arrests occurred in the years following the passage of this legislation (see **freek sweeps**), the **FE Act** succeeded in bringing a sense of order back to America. Interestingly, similar legislation was passed in the other **technologized** nations at nearly the exact same time.

**Frequency Emissions Monitor:** See **Freemon**.

**Frequency emissions reader:** *n.* A microchip about the size of a **biochip** which is encased inside of a **biocompatible** material, and injected at birth underneath the skin of its owner's forehead. Once inside the body, the **freeread** painlessly grafts itself onto the front of its owner's skull, and remains there for the duration of its owner's life. The **freeread**'s primary purpose is for the remote monitoring of its owner's **frequency emissions**, though it also has the capacity to receive certain kinds of information. Along with the **biochip**, sometimes referred to as the **Mark of the Beast** .

**Frequency emissions scanner:** *n.* A device which is capable of detecting, sensing, and transmitting an image of an organism's **frequency emissions** (see **B/free scanner, freeread**).

**Frequency emissions violator:** *n.* See **freeker**.

**Frequential:** *adj.* Of, involving, having the nature of, or relating to frequencies. *–adv.* frequentially.

**Fresh:** *adj.* Cool, very good; **phat**.

**Fucking-A:** *interj.* Used to express amazement or wonder. Also used to express anger or dissatisfaction.

**Fuck-up:** *v.* To mess up, interfere with, or harm something (a person, an object, a situation, etc.). *–n.* The act of fucking-up. Also, one who commits such an act.

**Funhouse:** *n.* A carnival attraction featuring warped mirrors, optical illusions, and other types of similar entertainment. *–adj.* Something which evokes the strange or entertaining qualities of a funhouse.

**Fusion reactor:** *n.* A device which creates a nuclear fusion reaction, and can contain and harness its energy. In essence, fusion reactors create, hold, and command the power of a small star. One of the most important scientific breakthroughs of the 21st century.

**Futurist:** *n.* An individual, usually noted in the fields of academia or literature, whose opinions on the future are held in high esteem.

**Futurosity:** *n.* The state or quality of being futuristic. Also, an interest in or an appreciation for the future.             ((...if somewhere, someone is reading this...))

**Galahad:** In Arthurian legend, **Galahad**, the son of **Lancelot**, was a **Round Table** knight so pure, he was able to see the vision of the divine **Holy Grail**.

**Gates, the:** *n.* See **gated community**.

**Gated community:** *n.* A community (including its grounds, services, property, and entertainment) that can be accessed only by its residents and their guests, and is surrounded by a partition which is patrolled by private security agencies. Living behind **the gates** usually requires a sizeable income and an adherence to certain uniform standards as determined by the community's corporate owner(s).

**Gathering:** *n.* An event which brings people together to be **freeky**.

**Gelaform™:** A trademark used for a soft, moldable, gelatinous substance used in a variety of applications, both commercial and personal. Other, similar forms of the substance are used in law enforcement equipment and as a shock absorber for structures built within earthquake-prone areas.

**Genetically accelerate:** A process by which living cells are made to develop and mature at an exponentially faster rate than normal. A common process in cloning and transplants.

**Gengineer:** *v.* To engage in genetic engineering or a related form of gene manipulation.

**Ghost:** *v.* To go or to leave. Used in the present tense, even when referring to something that is already gone.

**Glimmeringly:** *adv.* To have or possess glimmering qualities.

**Global positioning satellites:** *n.* A ring of orbiting satellites which can accurately pinpoint the location of any object carrying a **GPS** transmitter. Personal **GPS** technology became especially popular after a missing children scare which happened just prior to the **Terror Years**.

**Goggles:** *n.* Compact, lightweight eyewear that houses a **uniview** screen in its lenses.

**Gogs:** *n.* Goggles.

**Golden delicious:** *n.* A sweet, golden-skinned variety of apple.

**Gonna:** Going to.

**Gonpo:** *n.* Tibetan for "sorcerer" or "protector."

**Goth:** *adj.* Gothic.

**Gotta:** Got to; have to.

**GPS:** *abbr.* See **global positioning satellites**.

**Gravity-bound:** *adj.* Not equipped with **gravity-shielding**.

**Gravity-shielding:** *n.* A technology which allows an object to be freed from the constraints of gravity. Operates off of the principle that gravity is an **electromagnetic** wavelength with a higher frequency than that of even gamma and x-rays, thereby allowing it to penetrate and affect all known matter. Gravity-shielding is achieved through the use of a superconducting disc(s) which can resonate gravity's frequency to a lower level where it can no longer penetrate normal matter. Thus, an object can be "shielded" from gravity's effects. –*adj.* Gravity-shielded.

**Graylien:** *n.* The gray, black-eyed aliens whose images appear in many cultures around the world. Often said to be the perpetrators of alien abductions.

**Grill:** *n.* Mouth or face.

**Grippable:** *adj.* Capable of being gripped or grasped.

**GS:** *abbr.* See **gravity-shielding**.

**Handheld:** *adj.* A small, portable device which can be held in the hand.

**Hard-light hologram:** *n.* A **hologram** whose light is so coherent (see **coherent light**) that it becomes tangible.

**Headfield:** *n.* A device which projects a protective **emfield** around its wearer's head.

**Headquarter:** *v.* To establish, or to be a headquarters.

**Hella:** *adj.* Very; exceptionally. Also, a large quantity.

**Hellhounds:** *n.* Demon-possessed canines.

**Herb:** *n.* Marijuana.

**Herbal café:** *n.* A café-like establishment in which marijuana can be legally served and sold.

**Hermano:** *n.* Spanish for "brother."

**HID:** *abbr.* See **high-intensity discharge lamps**.

**High-intensity discharge lamps:** *n*. A type of lamp which keeps metal halide or mercury vapor under high pressure in order to produce visible light (usually of a bluish hue). Used for a variety of purposes, including vehicular headlights.

**Hija:** *n*. Spanish for "daughter."

**Hill, the:** *n*. Seattle **Freemon** term for their headquarters, located in Beacon Hill.

**Hologram:** *n*. An exact replica of a 3-D image which is created through the projection of **coherent light** (usually a laser).

**Holistic:** *adj*. Involving a broad scope of things or perspectives.

**Holographic:** *adj*. Of, or relating to a **hologram**.

**Holoview:** *n*. A **holographic**, three-dimensional **uniview**, or a **2-D** uniview screen which can be projected into the air via laser lens.

**Holy Grail:** Said to be the cup which was drank from during the **Last Supper**. Also used by Joseph to collect the blood from Jesus Christ's wounds.

**Hoverbike:** *n*. A **GS** motorcycle.

**Huedo:** *n*. Mexican slang for "white boy."

**Hui jian:** Chinese for "see you later."

**Hunny:** *adj*. Pleasing; good; sweet.

**Huxton, Mason William:** Born 1995. The only child of **Ordosoft™** founder **W.A. Huxton**, and current president of the company. Responsible for the rebuilding of **Mercer Island**.

**Huxton, William Alan:** Born 1952. Raised in a wealthy family, educated in the nation's finest private schools, Huxton was declared a genius by the age of eight. After receiving an honors degree from Harvard in computer programming, Huxton single-handedly created the revolutionary operating system which would become the founding enterprise for his history-making company, **Ordosoft™**. After building **Ordosoft™** into one of the world's most powerful corporations, **Huxton** relinquished control of the company to his son (see **Huxton, Mason**) in 2028, and now lives in a miraculous retreat deep within the mountains of southwest Tibet (see **Is**).

**Hyperbar:** *n*. A type of establishment and/or scene which emerged from Seattle in the **post-Quake** 2020's, centered around **neurochemical** drinks and genetic modification of the body (incandescent skin, **gengineered** hair color, etc.).

**Hypersteroid:** *n*. A steroid which bulks up and strengthens a person to nearly inhuman proportions.

**Hypocenter:** *n*. The subterranean focus point of an earthquake. The epicenter is at the surface, directly above it.

**Hypospray:** *n*. A device which painlessly pushes a substance through the skin, into the bloodstream and/or cells of an organism. Replaced the hypodermic needle in most medical procedures.

**I & D:** *abbr*. See **isolation and detention**.

**Ice:** *n*. An offensive or defensive barrier of code. For the best description of ice, read William Gibson's *Neuromancer*.

**Icewall:** *n*. Layers of **ice**.

**IM:** *abbr*. See **instant message**. –*v*. To send or receive an **instant message**.

**Immersible:** *n*. A tank which has been filled with a liquid or a substance (see **intelligent fluid**) in order to allow a **virtually** connected individual to be immersed within it, thus giving the individual a greater range of motion and options.

**Immersible suit:** *n*. A **neural-netted** suit which is specially designed to interact with, and allow its wearer to survive in an **immersible**.

**Immobilizing foam:** *n*. A sticky, viscous substance used by law enforcement agencies to immobilize a perceived threat. Usually ejected from an apparatus (a gun, a riot shield, etc.) as a liquid, the foam immediately solidifies upon contact with an object, and requires a special agent in order to dissolve it.

**Immortalist:** *n*. One who seeks to live forever.

**Infobomb:** *n*. An informational attack which is transmitted via **electromagnetic radiation** and is directed towards an **intelligent system**. –*v*. To attack with, or be attacked by an infobomb.

**Information theory:** Deals with the way information is encoded and emitted from a source onto a channel, and the means by which that information is received, decoded, and understood.

**In-Q-Tel®:** A research and development company owned by the **CIA**.

**Instant message:** *n.* A personal communication sent to another individual(s) while online or in a **virtual** group, domain, or setting.

**Intelligent fluid:** *n.* A **transmorphous** substance which is linked to a **CPU**, and can form itself into a solid, liquid, gas, or plasma upon command.

**Intelligent system:** *n.* A system which possesses intelligent qualities, such as a human, an android, or a computer.

**Interact:** *n.* An interactive movie.

**IR:** *abbr.* Infrared.

**IS:** *abbr.* See **immersible suit.**

**Is:** An unofficial nickname for **W.A. Huxton**'s Tibetan **nanotech** wonderland, coined by his son, **Mason Huxton.**

**Isis:** In Egyptian legend, the goddess of the earth and the moon.

**Isolation and detention:** *n.* **Freemon** term for the routine procedure of isolating a **freeker** from other individuals (in order to prevent **memetic** infection) and then detaining them.

**Jack:** *v.* To make a connection to a computer or network (usually followed by "into"). Often refers to an unauthorized connection. Also, to steal or to take with force. Also, to interfere or mess with; to cause harm or injury to.

**Jackshit:** *n.* Nothing; zero; zilch.

**Jam:** *v.* To go or leave, usually in a hurry; to move quickly. Also, to do something extremely well, as in the playing of an instrument. Also, to force an object into something else.

**Jesus freak:** *n.* A derogatory term for an individual who preaches about or disseminates information on a Biblical (*New Testament*) religion.

**JFK:** *abbr.* John Fitzgerald Kennedy, Jr., the 35th president of the United States.

**Johnny courier:** *n.* Someone outfitted with a cerebral augmentation which allows them to carry compressed information within their brains, and who is paid to carry and deliver that information to a destination. The term's origins are found in the William Gibson short story, "Johnny Mnemonic," which is collected in *Burning Chrome.*

**Joint:** *n.* A marijuana cigarette.

**Joint Chiefs of Staff:** Comprised of a sole, head chairman and the Navy's, Army's, and Air Force's chiefs of staff, this group is the foremost military authority in the **DOD.**

**Juke:** *v.* To make a sudden change of direction while being pursued, chased, or defended (as in a football or basketball game). *–n.* A sudden change of direction that throws off a pursuer or defender.

**Kata:** *n.* A long white scarf used in certain Tibetan ceremonies.

**Keyword:** *n.* A word, or a series of words which a computer system is programmed to take special notice of.

**Kickback:** *adj.* Relaxed; easygoing or mellow.

**Kinda:** *adv.* Somewhat.

**King Arthur:** In **Arthurian** legend, Arthur was elected king of Britain when he was but fifteen years old, after he drew a sword that had been set in stone. With the help of **Merlin, Excalibur,** and his **Round Table** knights, Arthur went on to become the greatest of all English kings.

**Kundrie:** In **Arthurian** legend, Kundrie was a witch who admonished Sir **Perceval** for abandoning his quest for the **Holy Grail,** thus prompting the **Round Table** knight to renew (and succeed in) his divine crusade.

**La:** In Tibetan, la can be added to the end of a name or a title to be polite and show respect. Also, *–def. art.* In Spanish, the singular, feminine form of "the."

**Lady of the Lake:** In **Arthurian** legend, the enchantress Vivien, a.k.a. the Lady of the Lake, gave **Excalibur** to **King Arthur,** raised Sir **Lancelot,** and also imprisoned **Merlin** forever in an oak tree, using a spell which he had taught her.

**Lancelot:** In **Arthurian** legend, Lancelot was raised by the **Lady of the Lake,** and later became one of the greatest **Round Table** knights.

**Language translation:** *n.* A technology which allows a word to be instantly translated into another language.

**Laser pistol:** *n.* A **handheld** weapon capable of firing amplified **coherent light**. Standard-issue for all law enforcement agencies.

**Laserproof:** *adj.* Incapable of being penetrated by lasers.

**Last Supper:** The night before his crucifixion, Jesus Christ and his disciples shared one final meal together, called the Last Supper.

**Late:** *interj.* Used the same as "goodbye" or "see you later."

**Latté:** *n.* A drink that combines shots of espresso with heated milk. The official beverage of the city of Seattle.

**LED:** *abbr.* See **light-emitting diode.**

**Legit:** *n.* Legitimate.

**Lex:** *n.* A Lexus®.

**Licoricey:** *adj.* Of, or resembling licorice.

**LIFE spectrum:** Or Living Incorporate **Frequency Emission** spectrum. The range of **electromagnetic radiation** in which the **frequential** emissions of all **lifeforms** are contained. The theory behind it looks at life as one single physical phenomena whose components differ only in the frequency and wavelength of their emissions. Unofficially created by **Dr. Adrian Wellor.** Officially created by no one.

**Lifeform:** *n.* A form of life; an organism.

**Light-emitting diode:** *n.* A semiconductor diode which produces visible light. Used in digital displays and electronic equipment (usually as an indicator).

**Liquidous:** *adj.* Of, possessing, or relating to the qualities of liquid.

**Live-feed:** *adj.* Possessing a live feed from a broadcasting source.

**Lorenz attractor:** *n.* A type of **strange attractor** named after the American meteorologist Edward Lorenz.

**Lo siento:** Spanish for "I'm sorry."

**Lynchian:** *adj.* Evoking the strange, surreal, and disturbing qualities which are often found within the works of filmmaker David Lynch (i.e., *Eraserhead*).

**Maglev:** *n.* Silent, high speed trains which glide over raised tracks, levitating inches above the track's surface via **electromagnetic fields.**

**Magnetic resonance imaging:** *n.* A technique which utilizes spectroscopic devices and magnetic fields to create detailed images of molecular structures.

**Makah:** A Native-American peoples of Western Washington.

**Mano:** *n.* Spanish for "hand."

**Maricón:** *n.* Derogatory Spanish term for "homosexual."

**Mark of the Beast:** For the oldest (and probably best) description, read the Book of Revelation in *The Bible* (*New Testament*). 14:9 is the number...

**Martinique:** An eastern-Caribbean island which is a department of France.

**Mazy:** *adj.* Like a maze; confusing or complex.

**McCready:** *n.* An alcoholic drink consisting of a Kahlúa® and cream with a double shot of espresso.

**Meme:** *n.* An infectious information pattern which resides in the brain and can be transmitted to others. Sayings, slogans, proverbs, icons, images, scientific and religious beliefs, fashions, school lessons, songs, and job training are but a few examples of memes and **memetic** infection.

**Memetic:** *adj.* Of, or relating to **memetics.**

**Memetics:** *n.* The application of **Darwinian theory** to the ways in which knowledge is transmitted and received, the ways in which the mind functions and learns, and the manner in which culture develops and progresses. Looks at the transmission of thoughts, ideas, and culture as a virus which infects a brain and can influence it to varying degrees, both in positive and negative ways. Memetic theory was one of the most important scientific breakthroughs of the late 20th century, playing a large role in the proceedings of the **Brennan Commission** and the development of the **FE** technology. The **Freemon** are required to take a comprehensive course in memetics as part of their training.

**Mento:** *v.* Spanish. A conjugation of the verb, "mentir," meaning "to lie (not be truthful)."

**Meperidine:** *n.* A synthetic analgesic drug whose effects are similar to those of morphine. Also known as Demerol®.

**Metahuman:** *adj.* More than human; superhuman.

**Mercer Island:** Located in the center of Lake Washington, this land mass sustained extreme damage during the earthquake of 2022 (see the **Quake**), forcing its wealthy inhabitants to permanently evacuate the island. Its foundation and infrastructure utterly destroyed, Mercer Island was declared a disaster area and made off-limits to the general public. It remained this way until 2039, when it was rebuilt by **Ordosoft**™ (see **Huxton, Mason William**) as the world's first **skyland**, and has since been repopulated by many of its original residents.

**Merlin:** In **Arthurian** legend, Merlin, the child of a demon and an unconscious nun, was a powerful prophet and wizard who befriended **King Arthur's** father, and later, Arthur himself.

**Mic:** *n.* Microphone.

**Micronize:** *v.* To cause to be, or to become disintegrated by a **micronizer**.

**Micronizer:** *n.* A device that uses continuous sound waves to disintegrate nonmetallic materials into a fine powder which can then be separated and recycled as raw industrial material.

**Micropore:** *n.* A material that contains thousands of minute openings which replicate the effects and properties of pores. Used in clothing, bandages, and various other applications.

**Microwave pistol:** *n.* A **handheld** weapon capable of firing a concentrated, high-frequency **electromagnetic** wave which can disrupt or destroy an organism's internal organs without causing any obvious external damage.

**Militia:** *n.* An army of citizens, such as those used during the **American Revolution**, or an emergency-reserve military force (see **National Guard**). Also, the name taken up by groups of armed, mostly rural Americans who banded together during the late 20th/early 21st century around the common belief that the United States government (see **American Empire**) had become corrupt and unconstitutional.

**Mobius strip:** *n.* A theoretical **2-D** surface which possesses just one side. To visualize it in **3-D**, cut a 1" wide strip across the length of a piece of regular-sized paper, grasp the strip by both of its ends, twist one of its ends halfway around, then glue or tape the strip together at its ends so that it forms a twisty loop (which should resemble an infinity (∞) symbol when it is squeezed together at its center). Now get a pen, pick any point on the loop, draw a continuous line along it, and...What goes around comes back around again.

**Molé:** *n.* A Mexican dish with a spicy, **chocolatey** flavor.

**Molecular assembler:** *n.* See **nanomachines**.

**Momentito:** *n.* Spanish for "moment (short or brief)."

**Monorail:** *n.* Elevated **Maglev** trains used primarily for public transportation.

**Morning star:** *n.* A mace with multiple protruding spikes.

**Morph:** *v.* To smoothly transform or metamorphosize into something else.

**MRI:** *abbr.* See **magnetic resonance imaging**.

**MUD:** *abbr.* See **multi-user domain**.

**Multi-user domain:** *n.* A **virtual** domain capable of being occupied by multiple users at a single time.

**Muy:** *adj.* Spanish for "very."

**Nanomachine:** *n.* Self-replicating nanoscale devices which are the cornerstone of **nanotechnology**. Can be programmed directly and/or controlled via remote.

**Nanotech:** *n.* See **nanotechnology**.

**Nanotechnology:** *n.* The use of self-replicating nanoscale machines to precisely rearrange atoms at the molecular level. Operates off of the principle that everything is made of the same atoms, and therefore water can be turned into a banana, air into sand, or people into plasma, simply by rearranging their atoms into the proper configurations (see **nanomachines**).

**Nap:** *v.* To attack with, or be attacked by a **synaptic disruptor**.

**Napper:** *n.* Synaptic disruptor.

**Nasty:** *adj.* Excellent; outstanding. *–idiom.* get nasty: to do something extremely well or with extra flair.

**National Guard:** Established in 1903 by the Dick Act, redefined by the National Defense Act of 1916, the National Guard can be mobilized by state governors or the president. Usually called on to handle natural disasters, riots, and rebellions. Used extensively during the **Terror Years**.

**National Security Agency:** Headquartered in Fort Meade, Maryland, the NSA is not only the most clandestine of all U.S. intelligence agencies, but it is also the largest. Responsible for spying on foreign communications (see **Echelon**) and for maintaining the security and integrity of U.S. governmental communications.

**National Security Council:** Created by the National Security Act of 1947, the NSC acts as the president's advisor on matters of national security. Its members include the secretaries of defense and state, the vice-president, and the president. The NSC also receives counsel from the CIA's director and the **Joint Chiefs of Staff**'s chairman.

**Natural selection:** The ability of a species to adapt to its environment and produce viable offspring which can themselves successfully reproduce, thus ensuring that the genetic traits which allowed the species to survive and propagate will be selected by nature to be passed on to future generations under the same or similar ecological conditions. ((whew!))

**Net:** *n* The uninet or Internet.

**Neural net:** *n.* A vast, interconnected system of neuron-like stimulators and receptors which transmit and receive informational impulses through their connecting fibers in a manner similar to the human nervous system. –neural-netted: *adj.* To be outfitted with or surrounded by a neural net.

**Neurochemical:** *adj.* Of, or relating to the chemicals produced by the nervous system and/or the brain.

**Nicaddiction:** *n.* An addiction to nicotine.

**Ní-hao:** *interj.* Chinese for "hello."

**Nose job:** *n.* Plastic surgery performed on the nose.

**NSA:** *abbr.* See **National Security Agency**.

**NSC:** *abbr.* See **National Security Council**.

**Office of Strategic Services:** In 1942, the office of **Coordinator of Information** was terminated and replaced by this agency. The **OSS** was responsible for collecting and analyzing information about wartime enemies and their occupied territories, as well as engaging in missions of subversion and sabotage. Was replaced in 1947 by the CIA.

**OFT:** *abbr.* See **organic fluorescence testing**.

**Omega point:** *n.* The end of the universe; the point at which all matter and energy collapses back, or stretches out, into infinity.

**Op:** *n.* An operation (i.e., a law enforcement operation).

**Optic microprocessor:** *n.* Uses light rays instead of electrical currents to carry its information, providing an exponentially faster processing speed.

**Ordocops™:** Ordosoft's™ private police force (see **corporate police**).

**Ordosoft™:** Founded in 1984 by **W.A. Huxton** in his hometown of **Redmond**, Washington, **Ordosoft™** quickly rose from a fledgling startup into one of the most powerful corporations in the history of the United States, fueled by the innovative operating system created by its genius founder. To this day, **Ordosoft™** still controls the majority of the world's operating systems, and is now firmly established in many other sectors of the economy as well.

**Organic fluorescence testing:** *n.* The use of special lights and filters to detect the fluorescent emissions given off by organic residues (fingerprints, hair, semen, etc.). Used especially by law enforcement at the scene of a crime.

**OS:** *abbr.* Operating system.

**OSS:** *abbr.* See **Office of Strategic Services**.

**Overstand:** *v.* To understand something completely and fully; to go beyond, to transcend something. – *n.* overstanding.

**Panoptic:** *adj.* Of, or relating to a **panopticon**.

**Panopticon:** *n.* A structure or system in which individuals are isolated into small areas or rooms where they can be watched and/or monitored at all times from a central location. Once established, this system has the effect of making the watched individual very obedient, submissive, and predictable, since they will usually monitor themselves regardless of whether or not they are still actually being watched or observed.

**Papasan:** *n.* A wide, rounded, concave piece of furniture which is mounted atop a circular base, covered with a large cushion, and whose frame is usually comprised of wood or bamboo tied with wicker.

**Park:** *v.* **Freemon** term for the current placement of an individual's **frees.**

**Patrón:** *n.* Spanish for "boss" or "captain."

**Peace:** *interj.* Used to say goodbye or farewell.

**Pentagon, The:** Built in Arlington, Virginia in 1943, this five-sided, five-story structure is where the **DOD** is **headquartered.**

**Perceval:** In **Arthurian** legend, Perceval was the **Round Table** knight who finally located the elusive **Holy Grail**, and afterwards became its guardian.

**Pero:** *conj.* Spanish for "but."

**Perp:** *n.* Perpetrator.

**Pharming:** *n.* A process in which farm animals are **gengineered** to produce pharmaceutical drugs within their bodily fluids, organs, and/or tissues, which can be extracted and transferred to another recipient. –*v.* pharm: to engage in pharming. –*adj.* Something which has been pharmed.

**Phase space:** *n.* The multi-dimensional expanse used to study the chaotic behavior of **dynamic systems.**

**Phat:** *adj.* Cool, very good; **dope.**

**Phodâng:** *n.* Tibetan for "palace."

**Photonic:** *n.* Of, or relating to photons. As the 21st century progressed, many forms of electronic technology were supplanted by ones of a photonic nature (i.e., **optic microprocessors,** fiber optics, etc.).

**Pilgrims:** *n.* English Separatist Puritans.

**Pito:** *n.* Spanish for "whistle" or "flute." Also, slang for "penis."

**Plasma torch:** *n.* A portable device that produces extreme heat by harnessing the energy of plasma.

**Plasmoidal:** *adj.* Having the form or characteristics of plasma.

**Plymouth Colony:** Established by the **Pilgrims** in 1620 on the shores of Cape Cod Bay.

**Porto:** *n.* Port wine.

**Posthuman:** *n.* An intelligent **lifeform** which has evolved beyond the human state.

**Potlikker:** *n.* A Jamaican dish of stewed greens in a flavorful broth. Also, the juices which are left over from this or a similar dish.

**POV:** *abbr.* Point of view.

**Precollege:** *n.* A school which contains grades 7-12. As college attendance became increasingly more common, high schools were renamed, reorganized, and required to have students declare a **focus** by grade 10.

**Prometo:** *v.* Spanish. A conjugation of the verb, "prometer," meaning "to promise (pledge)."

**Prozac®:** A trademark for an antidepressant drug which regulates the body's natural release of serotonin. Also known as fluoexetine.

**Psilobrew™:** A trademark for a beverage which synthetically replicates some of the effects of psilocybin.

**Quake, the:** On August 16, 2022, a magnitude 6.6 earthquake was **hypocentered** six kilometers beneath the Earth's surface, directly on the fault-slip area located beneath the city of **Mercer Island.** The tremor caused extreme damage to the island and its structures, and was also responsible for the deaths of hundreds of its residents. Because the quake was so shallow, the greater Seattle area was not nearly as affected, and suffered relatively minor damage.

**¿Qué pasa?:** Spanish for "what's up?" or "what's the matter?"

**Quiero:** *v.* Spanish. A conjugation of the verb, "querer," meaning "to want (desire)."

**Rasta:** *n.* See **rastafarian.**

**Ras Tafari:** King Haile Selassie I, the former emperor of Ethiopia.

**Rastafarian:** *n.* One who practices or adheres to the principles of **Rastafarianism.**

**Rastafarianism:** A movement which originated in Jamaica in the 1930's and is largely centered around Biblical scriptures and the belief that Ethiopia is actually Zion and **Ras Tafari** is God. **Rastas** often live a life away from regular society (in the hills, the woods, etc.) and frequently use marijuana in their ceremonies. To understand more, read Leonard E. Barret's *The Rastafarians*, or listen to the music of Bob Marley, Peter Tosh, and Bunny Wailer.

**RCC:** *abbr*. See **remote controlled camera**.

**Realtime:** *n*. The physical, as opposed to the **virtual**, world.

**Reanimate:** *v*. To bring back from the dead or from a state of utter inactivity.

**Rear-view screen:** *n*. A screen connected to **live-feed** cameras mounted on the rear, bottom, or sides of a vehicle in order to increase the driver's field of vision.

**Reconnaissance Escort Xi:** An android **crossbreed** created by the federal government to assist their agents in the gathering of information and the inspection of potentially hostile areas.

**Redeye:** *n*. A wide, reddish laser light used by police helicopters to scan the area below them for a specific **biochip**, or for those lacking a **biochip**. Also, a late-night trip on an airplane.

**Redmond:** A city of Western Washington which is home to many of the nation's top technology companies, including **Ordosoft™**.

**Remote controlled camera:** *n*. A maneuverable, usually airborne camera which can be controlled from a distance. Ranges in size from the visible (such as baseball-sized **GS** spheres) to the nearly-microscopic (such as small, insectlike devices).

**Remote-view:** *v*. To view something from a distance, as with an **RCC**, via **signature pattern**, or while **astral travelling**.

**Reprogram:** *v*. To alter or change the programming of an **intelligent system**. In humans, this is often achieved through the use of **neurochemical** therapy.

**REX:** *abbr*. See **Reconnaissance Escort Xi**.

**Rollers:** *n*. Police cars which are on patrol.

**Roman Empire:** Read *The Decline and Fall of the Roman Empire* by Edward Gibbon. Some say the empire never died.

**Revolutionary War:** See **American Revolution**.

**Roots:** *n*. A type of reggae music that is a synthesis of **ska** and rock n' roll. Developed in Jamaica in the late 1960's, classic roots reggae artists include The Wailers, Culture, and Dennis Brown.

**Round Table:** In **Arthurian** legend, **Merlin** created a table for **King Arthur's** father which seated 150 knights. Later, Arthur would receive this table as a wedding gift, leading to the formation of the famous knights of the Round Table.

**Sativa:** *n*. A powerful strain of cannabis.

**Satellink:** *n*. A wireless link to a satellite, primarily used for transmitting or receiving information. *–v*. To use a satellink.

**Scope:** *v*. To survey or examine.

**Screwface:** *n*. An expressive contortion of the face made when angered, disgusted, or confused. *–v*. To make a screwface.

**SeaTac:** Seattle-Tacoma airport.

**Seattle Center:** A section of Seattle which contains the Space Needle, the Pacific Science Center, the Experience Music Project, and many other tourist and local attractions.

**Seen:** *interj*. A Jamaican term which roughly translates to "understand?"

**Sekhet:** In Egyptian legend, Sekhet was a sun goddess who was the daughter of **Isis** and the sister of **Bubastis**. She had the head of a lioness, and represented the aspects of the sun's heat which could cause pain and discomfort.

**Selective memory inhibitors:** *n*. A substance or apparatus which can be programmed to block or inhibit a specific portion of an individual's memory.

**Sensorium:** *n*. The full range of one's senses.

**Sexsim:** *n* . A sexual simulation (see **sim**).

**SEV:** *abbr*. Security escort vehicle.

**Shag:** *v*. British slang for engaging in sexual intercourse.

**Shout out:** *n*. To mention or thank someone, either verbally or written, at or near the end of an artistic work. Here's an example: Thanks to the reader for reading this far into the text. One way or another, random or planned, you've read enough of the story to reach this point. Glad you could make it. Hope you're enjoying the show. Now back to the regularly scheduled program...

**Shuriken:** *n.* Small, sharp projectile weapons usually thrown by hand. Also known as throwing stars or ninja stars.

**Shyeah:** *interj.* Used to express disbelief or skepticism; also means "of course."

**Siege Perilous:** In **Arthurian** legend, the **Round Table** seat that was occupied by the knight who was questing for the **Holy Grail**.

**Siempre:** *adv.* Spanish for "always."

**Signature pattern:** *n.* The distinctive pattern of **frequency emissions** which can be used to identify a particular individual. An **SP** is essentially a **frequential** fingerprint.

**Sim:** *n.* A simulation, usually occurring in a **virtual** environment. *–v.* To engage in a simulation.

**Site:** *n.* A website.

**Ska:** *n.* A type of dance music which blends Jamaican rhythms with American R&B. Created in Jamaica in the early 1960's.

**Skully:** *n.* A beanie or stocking cap; a skullcap.

**Skyland:** *n.* An island in the sky, kept aloft through the use of **GS** technology. **Mercer Island** was the first, though Manhattan, Alcatraz, and Hiroshima have now also joined the ranks.

**Skyscape:** *n.* An expanse of aerial scenery which can be seen in one single view.

**Skyvan:** *n.* A GS van.

**Skyview:** *n.* A large skylight.

**Sleeper:** *n.* An intelligence term for an agent who is sent to enemy territory to assume an ordinary civilian identity, and who remains that way until they are activated into duty by the proper signal.

**Sleepscan:** *n.* A device which uses **electromagnetic** pulses to induce sleep.

**Sleepshot:** *n.* A **hypospray** filled with a sleep-inducing substance.

**Slides:** *n.* Backless, **slip-on** sandals.

**Slip-on:** *adj.* A garment or item which is easy to put on or get into.

**Smartass:** *n.* A smart aleck; an impudent or obnoxious person.

**Smartbar:** *n.* A concentrated food bar which contains mind-enhancing **neurochemicals** and/or herbs (such as gingko).

**Smartdrink:** *n.* A liquid which contains mind-enhancing **neurochemicals** and/or herbs.

**SMI:** *abbr.* See **selective memory inhibitors**.

**Snakes:** *n.* Individuals or organizations who knowingly engage in practices of treachery and deception. Some examples would be: when an undercover cop poses as a drug buyer to buy illegal narcotics, when a publication is set up for the purpose of databasing or entrapping its subscribers (i.e., magazines about possessing or growing marijuana, or catalogs that sell books on how to make bombs and poisons), or when an **FBI** informant infiltrates an organization, rises to a level of respectability within the group, and then suggests to the other members that they do something illegal or ill-advised, such as robbing banks or shooting cops (as strange as this seems, it was done to both the **Black Panther Party** in the 1960's and the Viper **militia** in the 1990's).

**Sopa:** *n.* Spanish for "soup."

**Sorta:** *adv.* Somewhat.

**Soundsystem:** *n.* A stereo system (receiver, amplifier, speakers, etc.).

**Soy:** *verb.* Spanish. A conjugation of the verb, "ser," meaning "to be" or "am."

**SP:** *abbr.* See **signature pattern**.

**SPD:** *abbr.* Seattle Police Department.

**Spliff:** *n.* A marijuana cigarette; a **joint**.

**SST:** *abbr.* See **supersonic transport**.

**Steel whip:** *n.* A flexible, retractable weapon made from a steel-like substance. Resembles a tensile whip when extended, a baton when contracted

**Sterilization:** *n.* A medical procedure which became increasingly common in the 21st century as a means of population control. Encouraged worldwide through the payment of credits or the granting of tax breaks, sterilization permanently takes away an individual's ability to make babies, both physically and legally.

**Strange attractors:** *n*. Nonlinear **fractals** existing in **phase space** which describe the path a **dynamical system** takes when it becomes chaotic (see **chaos theory**).

**Streetcam:** *n*. A street-mounted camera. Streetcams are found on nearly every street in the city, and most are publicly-accessible via the **uninet**.

**Stun gun:** *n*. A type of non-lethal weapon which renders its victim unconscious or incapacitated via electric shock.

**Subs:** *n*. Subliminal messages or information. Also, a punctuation mark (( double-parentheses )) used to indicate a subliminal message.

**Subtractively:** *adv*. To have or possess subtractive qualities.

**Subversity:** *n*. The condition, property, or quality of being subversive.

**Sup:** *n*. An upwards nod used to greet or check someone. –*v*. To raise the head slightly in order to greet or acknowledge someone.

**Supersonic transport:** *n*. An aircraft which can travel faster than the speed of sound.

**Suspended animation:** *n*. See **biostasis**.

**SWAT:** *abbr*. Special weapons and tactics. –*n*. A specialized unit of the police force used for a variety of situations, including raids and riot control.

**Synaptic disruptor:** *n*. A weapon that emits an **electromagnetic** pulse which affects the normal functioning of an organism's nervous system.

**Tambien:** *n*. Spanish for "also."

**Tashidelek:** *interj*. A Tibetan greeting which roughly translates to "good fortune."

**Tattoodecal:** *n*. An image or design which is permanently synthesized into the skin. Unlike a tattoo, a tattoodecal does not need to be comprised of ink, and can be made from a near-infinite selection of colors, materials, and substances. –*v*. To administer or receive a tattoodecal.

**Te amo:** Spanish for saying "I love you" to a lover.

**Technodevils:** *n*. Those who use technology to oppress, control, or suppress others.

**Technologize:** *v*. To develop technology in a society, country, or culture. –*adj*. technologized (used exactly in the same context as industrialized).

**Technophobic:** *adj*. A fear of recent or advanced technology.

**Technorganic:** *adj*. A technological construct which resembles a biological organism.

**Teleport:** *v*. To disappear from one point, span space and/or time, and reappear again at another point.                    ((...it means it got through...))

**Telepresent:** *adj*. Being in attendance in a **virtual** domain or setting.

**Tell:** *n*. A sign, expression, or gesture which reveals someone's intentions or true nature.

**Technocyte:** *n*. A **nanomachine** used to patrol, investigate, or take action within an organism's bloodstream.

**Temps:** *n*. Temporary workers.

**Tengo:** *v*. Spanish. A conjugation of the verb, "tenir," meaning "to have (possess)."

**Terror Years:** The period from roughly 2006 to 2013 in which an unprecedented amount of domestic terrorism occurred, both in America and the other **technologized** nations. These tumultuous times led to the passing of the **Frequency Emission Act**.

**Thought police:** *n*. Any organization which seeks to monitor or control people's thoughts. Used especially in regards to the **Freemon**, who literally fit the definition. To understand the term's historical origins, read George Orwell's *1984*. And while you're at it, check out Aldous Huxley's *Brave New World*.

**Threads:** *n*. Clothes; garments.

**3-D:** *adj*. Three-dimensional.

**Tims:** *n*. Timberland® boots.

**Tipsets:** *n*. A device which fits over the fingertips and aids in the navigation and control of a **virtual** environment.

**Toon:** *n*. A cartoon and/or a character in a cartoon.

**Tracers:** *n*. The visual resonance an object in motion leaves behind it. Intensified when the object emits light, or when its viewer is experiencing the effects of a hallucinogenic substance.

**Transhumanism:** The belief that intelligent life should not be limited to human form, and the pursuit of a **posthuman** existence through scientific and technological means. –*n*. transhumanist: one who subscribes to or pursues the principles of transhumanism.

**Transmorphous:** *adj*. Able to change shape or form. –*n*. transmorph: An object or body which has transmorphous properties.

**Trench:** *n*. A trenchcoat.

**Triballet:** *n*. A term for a style of music and dance that combines African drums (congas, bongos, etc.) and rhythms with classical ballet compositions and moves.

**Trippy:** *adj*. Having strange, unusual, or **freeky** characteristics.

**Turbofan:** *n*. Relatively noiseless, solar/electric-powered engines which propel most **GS** vehicles.

**Twisty-fit:** *n*. A ring made of a **transmorphous** material which can adjust itself to fit the finger of its wearer by twisting the control dial upon its band.

**2-D:** *adj*. Two-dimensional.

**U-dub:** See **University of Washington**.

**Un:** *indef. art*. Spanish for "a" or "an."

**Unform:** *v*. To **subtractively** alter form or to lose shape via subtraction.

**Unie:** *n*. **Uniview** or **uninet**.

**Uninet:** *n*. A single, gigantic network of people, organizations, places, and things through which nearly all non-face-to-face communication occurs. Accessed via **uniview**, the uninet contains a near-infinite amount of databases, resources, entertainment, and information. Music, videos, games, software, applications, etc. are now rarely purchased in hard copy/material form, but instead are bought online and downloaded into an individual's personal database, which can be accessed from any **uniview** with the proper password/**biochip**. The uninet is the Internet's successor.

**Uninhibitor:** *n*. A substance or apparatus which releases a portion of memory that is normally inhibited or irretrievable.

**University of Washington:** Founded in 1861 and located in Seattle, the **UW** is one of the nation's most respected medical and research institutes. The birthplace of the **FE** technology.

**Uniview:** *n*. A combination television/computer/telephone/radio/answering machine with access to the **uninet**. Created in the early 21st century, univiews come in multiple shapes and sizes, everything from rings to **wallscreens**.

**UV:** A **uniview**. Also, –*abbr*. Ultraviolet light.

**U-Village:** University Village, a **gated community** near the **University of Washington**.

**UW:** *abbr*. See **University of Washington**.

**Vámanos:** Spanish for "we go" or "let's go."

**Vato:** *n*. Mexican slang for "man," "guy," or "dude."

**Verdad:** *adj*. Spanish for "true (factual)."

**Virtual:** *n*. The informational computer world as opposed to the actual "real" world.

**Virtuality:** *n*. The quality or state of being **virtual**.

**Virtual reality:** *n*. Reality as expressed through a computer-controlled medium.

**Vocal confirmation:** *n*. A feature used in **voice recognition technology** to inform the user that their command was heard by the computer.

**Voice-rec:** *n*. See **voice recognition technology**.

**Voice recognition technology:** *n*. A technology which allows a computer to understand a human voice just as it would lines of code, the strokes of a keyboard, or the click of a mouse.

**Voicewave:** *n*. A vocal fingerprint used mostly for security purposes.

**Von Neumann probe:** *n*. A device capable of interstellar travel, which contains **nanomachines** that have the ability to replicate themselves through the manipulation of their surrounding environment. The concept is credited to mathematician John von Neumann, although author Philip K. Dick may have predated him on the concept in a short story entitled "Autofac." (Which can be found within *The Collected Short Stories of Philip K. Dick, vol. 4*)

**VTOL:** *abbr.* Vertical takeoff and landing.

**Vulturic:** *adj.* Having the qualities associated with a vulture, namely opportunism, greed, and/or a scavenging nature. *–adv.* vulturically.

**VR:** *abbr.* See **virtual reality**.

**Wallscreen:** *n.* A thin wall-mounted **uniview**.

**Wannabe:** *n.* One who desires to be something that they are not.

**Wellor, Dr. Adrian Malcolm:** A scientist involved in the **Brennan Commission** who mysteriously disappeared in 1999, and has not been heard from since. Some rumors say that he is alive, others that he is deceased, but nothing has been officially confirmed. Unofficially the creator of the **FE** technology (see **Brennan, Michael**).

**Westside:** The west side of the greater Seattle area, separated from the east by Lake Washington. Includes Downtown Seattle, Beacon Hill, Queen Anne, Central District, Capitol Hill, Rainier Valley, University District, Fremont, Wallingford, Montlake, West Seattle, Ballard, Greenwood, Northgate, Sand Point, Lake City, Mt. Baker, and Ravenna.

**Wetware:** *n.* Electronic computers have hardware, humans have wetware (i.e., the nervous system = microchips, processors, etc.), and both run on software (informational stimuli). Also, humans connected to a computer network or system. The term's origins are often credited to Rudy Rucker, author of *Wetware*, *Software*, and *Freeware*.

**What:** *n.* Something. Usually used with "or" (i.e., he must be **freeking**, or what!).

**White noise:** *n.* Electric or acoustic sounds whose intensity is uniform across all frequencies inside of a given range.

**White noise generator:** *n.* A device which can block out sound within or outside of a specific radius through the use of **white noise**.

**Wo dong le:** Chinese for "I understand."

**Word:** *interj.* Used to indicate emphatic approval or agreement. Also can be used as a question in place of "really?" or "is that right?"

**Word-rec:** *n.* Word recognition technology.

**Word recognition technology:** *n.* A technology which allows a computer to recognize and/or record conversations and electronic transmissions through the use of specific **keywords**.

**Workcamps:** *n.* The natural evolution of the prison system within a capitalistic society, wherein inmates are paid far below minimum-wage to perform various types of labor for businesses and corporations. By earning enough credit, inmates can "buy" themselves out of the workcamps.

**Wormhole:** *n.* A type of tunnel which connects one region of space and time to another.

**Wraparound:** *adj.* A display screen which encompasses not only frontal vision, but also the periphery.

**Wristcom:** *n.* A watch-sized **uniview**.

**Wurlitzer®:** The world's most famous brand of jukeboxes.

**Xanadeux:** The name given to **Mason Huxton**'s **Mercer Island** estate and the artificial intelligence that controls it.

**Xandy:** *n.* A **Xanadeux** android.

**Xiexie:** Chinese for "thank you."

**Yin-yang:** *adj.* Evoking balance and equilibrium, or having visual elements which are reminiscent of the yin-yang symbol.

**Yo:** *pron.* Spanish for "I."

**Zoomcam™:** A trademark used for a unique camera design which allows for extremely high-resolution photos to be taken from a great distance.

## PUNCTUATION

**(( ))  Subs:** Used to indicate a subliminal message ((formed with double parentheses)).

# THE FE SPECTRUM

$\Delta / \delta$

Delta (Purple)

$\Theta / \theta$

Theta (Blue)

$A / \alpha$

Alpha (Green)

$B / \beta$

Beta (Yellow)

$\Gamma / \gamma$

Gamma (Orange)

$\Omega / \omega$

Omega (Red)

Always read the fine print.

# THE ELECTROMAGNETIC SPECTRUM

| Name | Frequency, Hz* | Wavelength, m* |
|------|----------------|----------------|
| Direct current (DC) | 0 | ∞ |
| Power (machinery, power lines, etc.) | 10-100 | $3 \times 10(7) - 3 \times 10(6)$ |
| Induction heating | 10(4) | $3 \times 10(4)$ |
| Long-wave radio | 10(5) | 3000 |
| AM radio | 10(6) | 300 |
| Short-wave radio | 10(7) | 30 |
| Television, FM radio | 10(8) | 3 |
| Radar | 10(9) - 10(10) | $3 \times 10(-1) - 3 \times 10(-2)$ |
| Microwaves | 10(10) - 10(11) | $3 \times 10(-2) - 3 \times 10(-3)$ |
| Infrared (IR) | 10(12) - 10(14) | $3 \times 10(-4) - 3 \times 10(-6)$ |
| Visible light spectrum | 10(15) | $3 \times 10(-7)$ |
| Ultraviolet (UV) | 10(16) - 10(18) | $3 \times 10(-8) - 3 \times 10(-10)$ |
| X-rays | 10(18) - 10(21) | $3 \times 10(-10) - 3 \times 10(-13)$ |
| Gamma rays | 10(21) - 10(22) | $3 \times 10(-13) - 3 \times 10(-14)$ |
| Cosmic rays/photons | 10(23) | $3 \times 10(-15)$ |
| Gravity | <10(23) | ∞ |

-------------------------------------------------

* Exponents placed in parentheses ( )

# FREQUENCY CLASSIFICATION (300 GHz - 30 Hz)

| Frequency | Classification |
|---|---|
| Extremely High Frequencies (EHF) | 30 - 300 GHz |
| Super High Frequencies (SHF) | 3 - 30 GHz |
| Ultra High Frequencies (UHF) | 300 - 3000 MHz |
| Very High Frequencies (VHF) | 30 - 300 MHz |
| High Frequencies (HF) | 3 - 30 MHz |
| Medium Frequencies (MF) | 300 - 3000 KHz |
| Low Frequencies (LF) | 30 - 300 KHz |
| Very Low Frequencies (VLF) | 3 - 30 KHz |
| Voice Frequencies (VF) | 300 - 3000 Hz |
| Extremely Low Frequencies (ELF) | 30 - 300 Hz |

------------------------------------------------------------

Hz = Hertz
KHz = Kilohertz
MHz = Megahertz
GHz = Gigahertz

Freeky comic book plug: Anything written by Grant Morrison (*The Invisibles*, *Animal Man*) or Alan Moore (*Saga of the Swamp Thing*, *V for Vendetta*, *Watchmen*).

# LEGEND

1. McCready's House
2. Farmaceutical Solutions™
3. University of Washington
4. Freemon Headquarters (Seattle Division)
5. Riot Zone
6. Ordosoft™ Campus
7. Xanadeux
8. Ashley's Estate
9. Tosh's
10. Deep Heat Massage Parlor
11. Ignacio's Home
12. The Invisible Hand
13. The Tiger's Lair
14. Seattle-Tacoma International Airport
15. Space Needle/Seattle Center
16. Jack Jax's Pad
17. Raquel's Place
18. Tiger Mountain

.·

# SEATTLE

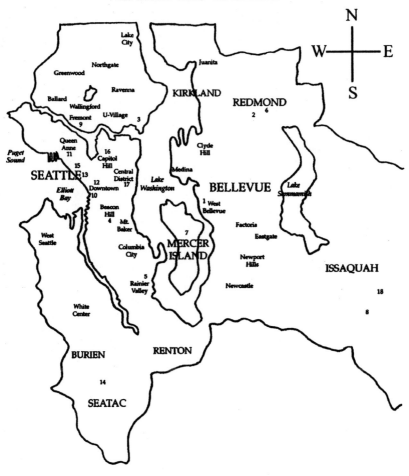

Puget Sound

Lake City

Northgate

Greenwood

Ravenna

Ballard

Wallingford

Fremont 9

U-Village 3

Queen Anne 11

Capitol Hill 16

Central District 17

Downtown 12 10

Elliott Bay

SEATTLE 13 15

Beacon Hill 4

Mt. Baker

Columbia City

Rainier Valley 5

West Seattle

White Center

Juanita

KIRKLAND

Clyde Hill

Medina

Lake Washington

MERCER ISLAND 7

REDMOND 2 6

BELLEVUE

1 West Bellevue

Factoria

Eastgate

Newport Hills

Newcastle

Lake Sammamish

ISSAQUAH

18

8

BURIEN

14

SEATAC

RENTON

N
W E
S

# 2051

# ABOUT THE AUTHOR

Joshua Ortega was born and raised in Sacramento, California, and now lives in Seattle, Washington. Along the way, he has worked at theatres and co-ops, managed apartment buildings, written for numerous magazines and newspapers, promoted musical acts, created his own publishing company, and has even received paychecks from the corporate giant known as Microsoft®.

He is simultaneously working on various stages of the ((FREQUENCIES)) project, including the screenplay, comic book adaptation, and its sequel, ~VIBRATIONS~. He has a few other things in the works as well, though if we told you about them it would ruin the surprise.

You can e-mail him from the omegapp.com website. We are not responsible for any freeky correspondence which might ensue.

A freeky shout-out 2 Prince 4 *Lovesexy* and Maxwell 4 *Embrya*.. see U at the Ω point...

# Ω  omegapp.com  Ω

To order ((FREQUENCIES)) t-shirts, posters, and/or
other merchandise, visit the Omega Point Productions™
website at:
http://www.omegapp.com

To order ((FREQUENCIES)) directly from the publisher (and
receive a signed copy of the book), please send a check or
money order for $17.76 to:

Omega Point Productions™
PO Box 85690
Seattle, WA
98145-1690

Please add $2.00 per book for postage and shipping.
WA state residents add 8.8% sales tax.
Make all checks payable to: Omega Point Productions™

To order ((FREQUENCIES)) via credit or debit card, visit
www.amazon.com or www.barnesandnoble.com.

# The future calls...

# ~VIBRATIONS~

## The evolution of
## ((FREQUENCIES))

# ομεγα ποιντ προδυχτιονσ

This is the end.

This is the beginning...

Visualize a void, the alpha point of this universe, then the big bang exploding forth from nothing, creating everything, time/eons passing in seconds of relativity, we zoom in on a lone comet/baby solar system shooting out through space, planet Earth is born, spins for a few moments in front of us and evolves, we pull back so our POV is of the totality of the universe, a long second passes, the universe begins to shrink to where only a void surrounds again, it gets smaller, faster, and shrinks into whence it came, the Omega Point

.

This is the end.

This is the beginning...

# ομεγα ποιντ προδυχτιονσ

∞